A 3rd Time

to Die

by

George A. Bernstein

Award Winning Amazon Top 100

Author

GnD Publishing LLC

A 3rd Time to Die
copyright © 2013 by George A. Bernstein.

G n D Publishing LLC

Palm Beach Gardens, Florida 33418
GnDpublic@aol.com
(561)762-5543
FAX: (561)625-1265

Publisher's Note: This is a work of fiction. Names, characters, and incidents are a product of the author's imagination. Locales and public names are sometimes used for atmospheric purposes and may have been altered to meet the demands of the story. Any resemblance to actual people, living or dead, or to businesses, companies, events, institutions, or locales is completely coincidental.

Ordering Information:

Quantity sales: Special discounts are available on quantity purchases by corporations, associations, and others. For details, contact the "Special Sales Department" at the address above.

A 3rd TIME to DIE/George A Bernstein - 2nd edition

ISBN 978-0-9894681-0-7

Other novels by

George A Bernstein

Trapped

A parapyscological Suspense
Winner in "The Next Great American Novel" contest
An Amazon Top 100 Novel
Available in e-book, audio book, and print at:
https://www.amazon.com/dp/0989468119

Death's Angel

The 1st Detective Al Warner Suspense
Available in e-book, audio book, and print at:
http://www.amazon.com/dp/B00P2V63X0

Born to Die

The 2nd Detective Al Warner Suspense
Available in e-book and print at:
http://www.amazon.com/dp/B016V6P7EK

The Prom Dress Killer

The 3rd Detective Al Warner Suspense
Available in print and as an e-book:
https://www.amazon.com/dp/B0743LCVCH

White Death

The 4th Detective Al Warner Suspense
Coming in early 2018
The 4th Detective Al Warner Suspense
Available in print and as an e-book:
https://www.amazon.com/dp/B07DGVDW6S

[3]

REVIEWS OF "A 3rd TIME TO DIE

Dianne O'Keefe 5 Stars A thrilling ride - don't miss it,

Bearing in mind that I like paranormal romance novels, I was pretty convinced that I would like this novel, especially since I also like horse riding. The big surprise was that I never expected it to be comparable to great writers of this genre such as Dean Koontz or Stephen King. "A Third Time to Die" really delivered, providing an intriguing storyline and very believable characters. As I reached midway in the book, I was turning pages almost as fast as I could read to find out what would happen next. I enjoyed it immensely and am glad I tried it out.

Fred - Another 5 Stars for the Author

George Bernstein has written another 5 star novel. In his prior book, "Trapped," the author takes you inside the brain of a coma victim. A unique idea that he pulls off quite admirably. In his new book, he creates a shocking tale of a women who is caught in a series of prior lives, who learns of her fate through hypnotic regression.... The exciting and refreshingly new plot will keep you engrossed to the very end. Definitely, a "do not miss!"

Gina 4 Stars paranormal & suspense combo

A bit of paranormal and a bit of suspense combine for one heck of a story. Past lives with visions of murder and a budding love story make for some sticky situations for Ashley and Craig, the two main characters. This was a very unique story with no angels, demons vamps or wolves involved. The suspense comes from something completely different. Quite refreshing for readers who are full up of those types of books. The plot is engrossing and will keep you up reading late into the night to find out what happens next.

DEDICATION

First, to my lovely wife, Dolores, whose passion for horses and Open Jumping provided the background and expertise for this novel. I learned a lot about the sport by watching her jump her horse, Redman, at competitions ... and filling our display cabinet with trophies. It's a beautiful and exciting sport, and we take every chance available to watch these great animals and their fearless riders challenges difficult courses. And she's become my toughest critic and an unrelenting first editor.

Secondly, I want to thank Dr. Brian Weiss, MD, for his great work in exploring Past Lives, and for Dr. John Cleveland (wherever you are) for guiding me through my own Regressions. I started them as research for this novel, finding nine previous "visits" to our world. Even if one does not embrace the concept, I found causes for personal skills of mine in this life that seemed to exist without reason ... until those regressions! I, at least, am now a believer.

And lastly, to the editors at GnD Publishing, who helped polish this work into something we all think is extraordinary and different. I hope you, the reader, will think so, too.

A 3rd Time to Die

George A Bernstein

A 3rd Time
to Die

A 3rd Time to Die

PROLOGUE

The year 1695 AD

"Sound the assembly. The Sun's up, and time's awasting."

Charles Wallace stood in his stirrups, long, equestrian-hardened legs raising his tall frame high above the restless conglomeration of horses and riders, milling about the glade in front of the gray granite mansion-house.

The Earl of Devonshire's nostrils flared, savoring the pungent odors of trampled, dew-laden grass and fresh droppings. He tugged at the cuffs of his taupe doeskin riding gloves, massaging palms together, as a shiver tiptoed across his spine. Anticipation, not the chilled morn air, was its author.

'Tis a glorious day, full of promise.

Puffs of cottony clouds spilled across a rich, aquamarine sky. Flexing broad shoulders, Wallace twisted in his saddle, scanning the melee.

What a bloody good turnout. Few local gentry dared miss the Earl's first spring foxhunt. Nobles and wealthy landowners converged from across southern England for this new, prestigious sporting event. Every guest room in his rambling country estate was filled, as were the stalls in his stables. Even George Villiers, the Duke of Buckingham, who recently popularized this sport, was hard pressed to compete.

Wallace's topaz eyes raked the crowd, all mounted and eager to be off. Sixty horse at least, edgily mincing and prancing in place, awaiting the blare of the hunting horn. Still, he scoured the sea of bobbing black and tan caps and flowered bonnets.

Ah. There—the copper-haired French seraph.

A 3rd Time to Die

He visualized her delectably curved long legs below full hips, cinched by a petite waist. Her heart-shaped face was illuminated by incandescent emerald eyes, hovering above a slender, tipped up nose. Arched cheeks bracketed Cupid's-bow-shaped lips. So deceptively feminine, slender and delicate she seemed upon her muscular white gelding.

Charles knew otherwise.

Victoria Chevalier was a passionate, willful maid, plainly disenchanted with her marriage to an effeminate dandy twenty years her senior.

When first he saw her, the young Countess du Beaujolais' sensuality swept over him, sucking away his breath and setting his heart thundering like the hooves of this very stallion he sat astride. Thick-limbed, masculine Clarice, his acidic, passionless wife, had never ignited lust in his heart ... or his loins.

But this nymph, Victoria, was God-sent. During the week as his guest, they were drawn together, as bees seek succulent clover. Sharp-witted and charged with life, she was full of sport. Quick dexterity with a 16-gauge brought three flushed grouse to hand ... just one less than he ... while her effete spouse was knocked ass over heels by his 12-gauge gun. Clarice had stayed abed.

And Victoria must have otter in her blood, out swimming him, crossing the river in swim garb much too brief for local customs. Long arms and strong legs sliced the water with astonishing ease.

He felt stirring, despite his tight britches, at the memory of his arms around her, teaching her to cast a fly for trout. Her soft chuckle hinted at greater expertise with the long rod than she admitted. 'Twas sport neither of which their partners showed interest.

Victoria Chevalier was truly akin in spirit, far different from either of their mates. This French beauty would be his that very day. His starving soul demanded it, boding a liaison far more intense than just a quick tumble in the grass.

How is it she was even wed to this foppish count? Arranged marriages. Bah. Neither Chevalier, nor the earl's icy wife will offer any real obstacle to their desires. Charles and Victoria had slyly courted for the entire week, and now was their chance to fulfill those promises silently made.

He smiled as she wound her horse through the mob. As she edged nearer, her devilish grin and sly wink snatched the breath from his lungs.

"We go," his strong tenor carrying to the page, standing atop a small stone wall. "Sound the horn, God blast it."

The brass trumpet echoed three times over the glade, and then thrice again.

Shouting riders urged their steeds ahead, each vying for a place directly behind the Earl, a sea of horses, sleekly muscled hunters, surging into the lightly wooded countryside. The drum of hooves and the echo of lusty shouts echoed through the trees like rolling thunder.

Immediately, a stone wall bordering a creek loomed as the first challenge, and two riders were quickly down. The hounds had drawn far ahead, hurdling through the underbrush, noses skimming the ground, seeking fresh scent. It won't be long. The Earl had spied several fox in the area just last week.

A movement at his right drew his glance, as the copper-tressed angel closed to his side. A few light strokes from her crop urged her steed ahead. She grinned, a playful challenge in her eyes, tossing her head, loosening burnished bronze locks from beneath her flowered hat.

They were swiftly upon a huge downed oak, vaulted by both animals with little trouble. Just as they landed, a hound let forth a melodious wail, and charged off to the south, head high, the call ringing from his throat, joined in full harmony by his brethren. A familiar wave of goose bumps skipped down his spine.

"Tallyho! Tallyho!" Wallace yelled, as he urged his dappled mount hard after the quickly disappearing dogs.

"Tallyho!" the two-legged vixen riding beside him howled gleefully, putting her crop to her snow-white steed. The cry echoed behind him again and again, as the others, strung out over a thousand yards, strove to follow. None could match the abandon of their host and his reckless female companion as they surged even farther ahead.

Ten minutes of hard riding, spiced by arduous jumps, had brought them within a few hundred yards of the hounds, their calls saying the fox was not yet bayed. Much of the party had fallen prey to the many obstacles they had crossed in their pell-mell charge after the dogs.

The countess' fearless attack of the hunt had kept her slightly to the front. Charles happily hung back, watching her with an ever-escalating appreciation. She was magnificent. Never had he known such a wild and exciting creature, so fully invested in all he held dear. He could barely wait to gather her in his arms.

The hounds were clearly visible ahead, just beyond a low, stone wall. The riders vaulted it, almost as one, and as they landed on the far side, Victoria began slowing her mount, pulling off to the side.

"What's amiss," he asked, slewing to a stop beside her.

"Fa. This foolish beast has come up lame. I'm unable to continue."

"Damn the luck. We were hot on the little bastard's trail." Turning to Count Armand, surging to a skidding halt with several other riders, Charles pointed south.

"Her horse has gone lame. Finish the hunt without us. I'll see the Countess safely back to the manor house." The mud-spattered Frenchman nodded, tapping his cap with his crop, and charged off in pursuit of the fast disappearing dogs.

He may be an effete dandy, who can't shoot oR fish, but the bugger can ride. Charles watched them vanish into the woods.

Dismounting, he took the lady's reins, starting back from whence they came. After a bit, they found themselves in a shaded meadow, a small brook tumbling cheerfully along one side. Cottonwoods lined its banks, their flowers in full bloom, perfuming the air with a heady scent.

"Come, m'lady. We'll take our ease here for a time before we continue. 'Tis been a hot, thirsty chase."

"Ah, truly said, m'lord. Your every wish is my command."

His lust-filled eyes caressed her every curve, lingering over each erotic swell. He licked parched lips, smiling up at her.

"An interesting proposition. You'll accede to anything I ask of you?"

She gave a throaty laugh, as he plucked her from her sidesaddle mount ... and into his arms. Once there, he had not the will to release her. The scent of lilies and musk sent him spinning.

She tilted her face, crimson lips slightly parted, eyes green pools of fire. The sweet smell of her hair laid waste to his senses. His manhood, trapped in the confinement of skin-tight jodhpurs, struggled to attention.

"You are but to ask, m'lord," she whispered, panting softly. "I am willing...nay, eager...to heed your every desire."

He crushed her to him, hungry lips entangling, tongues darting vipers, his breath snatched away by the heat of her response. The fire of her kiss consumed him in delicious flames. They grappled with sweaty garments, and luckily, riding habit was infinitely less complicated than the normal fashions of court.

Welded as one, they slid down upon the soft grass, moist

with dew. There was only sweetness in the salty taste of their skin. In a moment's time, they were lost in wonder, soaring high above even Heaven's Gate.

For uncounted hours they bared their souls as well as their bodies to each other. Charles, reluctantly struggling with his unwilling libido, glanced at the sky.

"Come." His voice still husky with ardor, he snatched up their garments and pulled her to her feet. "We must be off before we are found out."

"*Oui*," she said, but her flaming body, clinging closely to his, disagreed, rekindling the blaze within him. She raised liquid eyes to his, honeyed lips parted, wetted by the tip of her tongue.

They were quickly lost in a heated embrace, slipping again to the lush green carpet. He worshipped her skin with tender kisses and wet caresses of his tongue before entering her, her long legs trapping him urgently against her.

Their hearing filled by the thunder of unquenched passion as they lay entwined, they never heard the heavy tread of quickly approaching footsteps.

A sudden vicious blow to the back of his head slammed Charles against her, showering her with blood and gore, pinning her down.

"No!"

A fearsome beast hovered above her, swinging a weapon high above its beaked head.

"*Mon dieu*. No. Please, don't hurt—" The thud of heavy blows, the crunching of bones and rending of flesh, continued unabated for many minutes in the otherwise silent glade.

It wasn't until four hours after the last of the hunt had ridden in, two foxes in hand, before it was admitted that something was amiss. A hastily organized search party gave up, finally, three hours into the night.

The entire village was out again at dawn, searching ahorse and afoot for the missing couple. Two hours after sun-up, a hunting horn was sounded from a thick forest glade. The dogs had found their master. Searchers gathered in silent wonder in the small meadow that, sixteen hours before had hosted an idyll of love and passion. The ground was torn; blood and bits of flesh splattered everywhere. Two broken bodies lay heaped together, limbs twisted askew, heads crushed, faces gone, barely recognizable as having once been human.

The huntsmen agreed it was the work of some great beast ... mayhaps an angry bear. Had an enraged sow destroyed them while protecting her cubs? Surely a plausible answer. They would hunt down and kill her, if they could.

So two lovers, newly discovered unto each other, died with love and life unfulfilled.

It was a passion that might have lasted an eternity, were it not cut short.

So brutally short.

The year 1845 AD

Morgana Quincy's hazel eyes, shaded by arched, inky eyebrows, squinted against the sun, watching the one-horse coach clatter around a corner before she started down the cobblestone path. Her white parasol, protection against the mid-day sun, draped casually over a slender shoulder. She shook her head, glistening onyx curls swirling and bobbing about her gentle, round-cheeked face. She needed time to clear her mind.

Her father, Jonathan Denton, had immigrated to the Americas only fifty years before, and had distinguished himself as a blockade-runner in this new country's second war with England. Now, thirty years later, he owned a successful shipping business, with six sloops carrying goods to all the major cities of the World.

But a life that should be a cornucopia was not going well. She was a fortunate woman, raised in a warm and loving environment by her father, widowed now these past twelve years. She married eight years past to a handsome young pillar of Philadelphia society, something that should fill her life with joy. William came from one of the oldest families in the city.

At twenty-seven, the major thing missing from paradise was a child, but not for a lack of trying ... at least during their first five years together. Sex with her husband ... something she shamefully enjoyed ... was far less frequent now.

Just last month she discovered the cause: his affair with a sultry, voluptuous singer from a "high class" saloon near the harbor.

How could that bastard do this to her? What to do now? Take revenge? Something not in her nature, but the lure was strong.

They could try to work things out, but did she even care to make the effort? For what? If he pledged penance, would she let him back into her bed? She imagined he would try. She'd begun to suspect William was more enamored with her father's fortune than her. And despite promises, would he really forsake that sensuous trollop? Nay, nothing good could come of this.

Now she was plagued by greater worries. Father, her stout oak providing shelter throughout her life, was ill. Seriously ill. Some foreign thing grew tenaciously in his chest, consuming him, sucking the meat off his bones, casting him into a mere shadow of himself. He'd become somnolent from heavy doses of morphine. She could only hold his hand, weeping incessantly during her daily afternoon visits. Conversation, while lucid, was brief and strained.

Head lowered, lost in thought, she was sent spinning upon

colliding with someone on the walk. Strong hand caught her slender shoulders, steadying her until she regained her balance.

"Oh, I'm so sorry." She snatched a breath, her cheeks flushed, hazel eyes wide, as she glanced into a pair of fathomless, amber wide-set orbs. A long face, dominated by a strongly arched nose, smiled down at her. A mop of curly mahogany hair sprouted around the edges of his cap.

"'Tis I who owe an apology, Mrs. Quincy. I wasn't looking where I was about."

"Nor was I, sir. But how is it you know my name?" Her heart fluttered, her skin infused with a tingling heat. Who was this strangely exciting man? His was not a presence she would soon forget.

"I am your father's barrister. Robert Isaac, at your service."

"Oh, yes. Father mentioned you just today." Tears blossomed in the corners of her eyes. "T'was the most we have talked this whole week."

"'Tis a sad thing to see one so strong grow frail. It must be very hard on you." His long, smooth, tapered fingers magically encircled her hand, and honest compassion filled his eyes.

"Your father has been very kind to me. Few of this city's gentry show much interest in a Jewish lawyer."

"Father spoke of that as well, mocking their ignorance. You are the brightest of them all, he said...his gain and their loss. He also said you were the only compassionate barrister he'd ever met." *Can he hear the cacophony he has stirred in my breast?*

"He is too kind. Thousands of years of oppression have taught my people that virtue well. 'Tis a major tenant of our upbringing." Her hand still nestled in his, her knees trembled. A strange heat permeated her.

"He also instructed me to help you with any matter in which you might have need. He referred, rather obliquely, to something about your husband?"

[17]

A 3rd Time to Die

"He knows, does he?" She sighed. "Well, I shouldn't be surprised. He always fathoms when something is amiss. I dare say, he's a lot less innocent than I."

"Is it something you wish to discuss, ma'am? I am available, and anything told me is strictly confidential. It won't be repeated, even to your father, if you wish."

She looked at her pale fingers, still ensconced safely in his tanned hand. She was flooded with the strange sensation she had known this man all her life. Her heart fluttered with the wings of a small, frightened bird, but there was no fear in her. Finally, all that had been wrong would be set right.

She was awash with an inexorable sense Robert Isaac came from God to protect her, now that her father was unable. Her eyes turned to his. A delicate, bow-shaped mouth and aristocratic cheeks conspired to transform her smile ... the first in many weeks ... into a brilliant sunrise.

"I suppose I must confide in someone, although there's little enough to be done. Just talking to a person of trust would be a large load off my back. And I do sense you are someone to rely on, Mr. Isaac."

"There's a small cafe nearby," he said. "Quite secluded, and tables in the back allow for complete privacy. Shall we go there?"

Settled beside a scarred oak slab, perched on slick, dark leather benches in a dim corner of the sparsely occupied pub, she found herself pouring out her heart about things she had never before discussed with a single soul. His compassionate understanding of her grief over her father's illness and the illicit behavior of her husband were a strange catharsis. This was a connection she never felt with another person, especially a man.

Robert escorted her to her door as darkness began its approach, saying he had some ideas that might help in dealing with her husband, should things eventually come to an end in their marriage. She made an appointment to visit his office the very next day.

~~*~~*~~*~~

Almost a year to the day after she first met Robert Isaac, they rode his black lacquered surrey into the countryside for a picnic. Jonathan Denton had succumbed ten months past, leaving his fortune in trust to his only daughter.

William Quincy made many determined forays after a share of that wealth, but a phalanx of attorneys could not dent the ironclad instruments forged by Robert for his client. Denton had consigned Morgana's care and fate to the hands of this capable young man. It was duty he would have taken seriously ... even if he hadn't fallen hopelessly in love with her.

He had struggled to remain aloof and proper with his lovely client ... until the beating. William, in a fit of rage, peaked by his family's failing finances and his inability to touch his wife's vast wealth, had taken a riding crop to her.

Robert summoned all his self-control to keep from thrashing the man. Instead, he charged Quincy with assault and battery, a rare challenge to a husband's right to strike his wife. Eventually, charges were dropped with the court ordering William to keep his hands to himself.

It was the impetus Morgana needed to begin pursuing a divorce.

"I've found love with another man," she had told Robert, a merry twinkle in her golden eyes.

"Who is the lucky fellow?" his throat suddenly constricted, he could barely draw breath.

"Oh, he's a strong, handsome, gentle man of the utmost integrity. Completely unlike that lout I married."

"If you'll only give me his name," his eyes cast down to hide his despair, "I'll make inquiries to be sure he's as upright as you fancy him. 'Tis for your protection." He was resigned to step aside. Anything for the happiness of this angel he had grown to treasure so deeply.

"Oh, you ninny." She laughed, eyes alight, her face a picture permanently etched into the fabric of his brain.

"His name is Robert Isaac. 'Tis you I love, my sweet fool."

What? T'was he? How could this be? His wildest dreams fulfilled? Thunder hammered his breast as he took her hands, his eyebrow arched. Her smile dazzling his senses, she nodded, nestling in his arms, her face tilted, begging to be kissed.

They became lovers, enthralled by a familiarity and passion more profound than either ever expected. With her divorce to Quincy soon to be finalized, they were about to celebrate. The picnic basket was filled with delicacies and two cold bottles of wine ... a fine meal, capped off with tender lovemaking under the shade of great oaks bordering this idyllic meadow.

They nestled, naked, upon a light blanket, spread over the dew-dampened meadow, shaded from the warm sun by mighty oaks, full with spring bloom. Robert rolled to his side, propping his head against a hand, gazing down at her, snuggled in the crook of his other arm. Her velvety fair skinned, slender body was still flushed and moist from their recent ardor.

"'Tis a miracle I still cannot fathom that I am here with you. That such an angel professes to love me as deeply as I love her."

"The miracle 'tis mine, my love." She stroked his face with elegant, crimson-nailed fingers, "that I could be shed of that cruel bastard, William, and find myself in the arms of one such as you. I adore you more than I can say. 'Tis as if I've loved you forever, in my dreams."

"Aye. So 'tis with me." He handed her one of their partly filled glasses of wine.

"To our love, eternal. Nothing can ever destroy it." They clinked their glasses together, sipping the warming brew.

[20]

"We are already one, Morgana. Marry me, to make it official."

Her smile stirred him almost beyond bearing.

"Yes, my darling. As quickly as I'm shed of William. Our child will need a proper name, and I love you beyond my ability to say."

"Our child? Are you ...?"

"Yes. I missed my time, nigh three months past."

"But how? Eight years with William, and you never ..."

"Aye, but apparently t'was his lacking, not mine." Her smile ignited him. Their hands, their mouths, wended on amorous explorations, and soon he was entering her.

Nearing a wondrous finale, the earth seemingly trembled at their exquisite ardor. Her ears twitched, and the flames of passion were suddenly chilled by an ominous sense of danger.

A vague image of a horned beast and blood-soaked beak bloomed in her head. Eyes flared wide, she struggled to glimpse the wood beyond her lover's shoulder.

"Morgana? What's amiss, my love?" He snatched a breath, struggling from the depths of ardor.

An approaching heavy tread was clearly audible, as the air hummed with a strange whirring beat.

"*Non! Mon dieu, non.*" *French?* Terrified, she wondered, *I don't speak French.*

Locked in the steel band of her panicked arms, Robert tried to turn but before he could move he was slammed against her, his full weight pinning her to the ground. Reeling from the impact, her face drenched by blood and splattered with small spongy gray particles, Morgana's eyes flew wide.

Paralyzed by terror and the weight of her lover, she cringed at the large shadow above her, then the suddenly familiar fierce beaked head, the sun glinting off its silvery body, flailing the air with a spinning weapon.

"No, don't." A terrifying flash of memory bloomed ... a vision of being here before.

"*Arrête!* Not again. *Mon dieu. Non. Non.*"

The search party, led by Robert's brother, Aaron, found them the next afternoon. The small glade was a gruesome slaughterhouse ... ochre stains and shredded bits of flesh scattered across the verdant lea. Two naked bodies, tangled together, were rent beyond recognition. Not a single man there held down his gorge.

It must be the work of some wild creature, probably a bear. Destruction of the two and the grounds around them were too vicious to be dealt by human hand.

Still, the Sheriff made a thorough investigation. William Quincy had been in his office the entire day. No other possible perpetrator could be identified.

No, it had to be an animal. A hunt was organized to search for the beast, but none was ever found. It remained the mysterious end of a new and wonderful love, cut short.

So brutally short.

ONE

The current time

God, they're so beautiful.

Ashley Easton watched the big horses attack the course. Thoroughbreds, mostly. Few amateurs owned the more exotic breeds, like Warmbloods. Perched on the edge of cold metal bleachers overlooking the white-fenced jumping arena, gray eyes wistfully traced the action. She pressed forward, her knees squeezing imagined sweaty flanks as powerful brutes hurtled oxers and walls, and maneuvered through triple-bar in-and-outs.

She was breathless, filled with jealous nostalgia. So many years tiptoeing quietly by since she'd seen an Open Jumper class, much less ridden in one. Gently curled, shoulder-length locks swirled in a coppery cloud as she shook her head and sighed.

Training jumpers wasn't in the books while raising a family—and trying to make a life with a husband who seemed more and more distant and self-involved. She leaned back, hugging herself. Things were different now. The kids were no longer babies.

How did we drift so far apart? We were so in love ... so powerfully drawn to each other ... despite all that went wrong. We don't even have anything to talk about anymore.

She stood, slender and casually elegant in tapered tan chinos and a flowered cotton blouse. Stretching her five-foot-eight-inches frame, stiff from balancing on the hard metal seat, she ambled down from the bleachers, not really interested in the lower fence Novice Hunter class just beginning. She wandered aimlessly, musing, surprised to find herself at the entrance of the barn. A comfortable place, filled with happy vibes.

She turned, slouching against the railing, arms folded across a bosom surprisingly full for one so slim, idly watching a teenage girl work her bay mare over the low fences.

Moisture welled in her slate eyes at the memory of her parents cheering as she took Lady over the higher Open fences. Thirteen years had trundled by since she last showed a horse. Mama was always there and Papa usually came, despite his busy schedule at the mill. She missed them terribly.

But bad stuff happens. They were gone, wiped away in that one terrible instant. Now she and Keith seemed to have so little in common. Did they ever enjoy the same things ... besides each

[23]

other? She was into horses, and then home life, raising a family of happy children.

He was into ... what? Keith, mostly. The world revolving around the Big Jock. He expected her to be the Moon, spinning around his planet. But his sphere of egocentric gravity was repelling...not attracting...her.

Couples divorced for less, but Ashley was no quitter, eschewing the search for other solar systems. She'd keep her marriage together, if only for the children...make every effort...go more than halfway. The rest was up to Keith.

Of course, if he's rarely home, whatever she does makes little difference. She refused to give up her individuality, if it came to that. Pushing away from the railing, she shook herself like a dog out of a pond, casting off morose thoughts like droplets.

Ashley Easton functioned best happy rather than depressed. She glanced at the ring, the corner of her lips twitching up as an Appaloosa mare nimbly maneuvered through the Hunter course. How fulfilled and contented she was when riding and jumping.

Might as well visit the horses. Scratch a few ears. Enjoy the smells.

She entered the barn, kicking at straw strewn across the floor. Funny how the aroma of fresh hay and manure ignited a sense of happier times.

She strolled from stall to stall, stroking velvety muzzles and caressing behind ears. The animals rubbed her with their snouts and nibbled at her sleeve, recognizing her as a friend.

She paused at the stall where she'd boarded Lady as a teenager. A dappled gray leaned over the wood-rail gate, tossing its head, nickering. She sighed.

She came to Onwentsia Stables on a whim to watch the first Amateur Open Jumper competition of the spring, and the banked embers of the old fire burned brightly in her again.

Seeing those big muscular athletes bounding over rails and walls had her heart tumbling giddily.

Maybe it's time to get a horse ... even start jumping again. Thirty-one's not too old, and it's such great therapy. One thing's sure ... a four-legged buddy will always be there for me.

Riding created a sense of peace and a bond with the animal that no one but an equestrian would understand. The pressures of rearing a family were minimal now, with Maria living in for the last year, there to care for the children if she were away.

Time to get out and do my own thing. It'll be daytimes, while Keith's at work, so it won't interfere with our being together. Besides, when was the last time he spent any real time with me, doing something fun? Something I love. She couldn't remember, but it'd been years.

Ashley ventured deeper into the gloomy barn, absorbing the ambiance.

I can even get back into show jumping, if I get a good horse. Wonder what was wrong with that huge chestnut? A redhead, just like me. He seemed listless, even refusing fences. Hard to believe that big thoroughbred was unwilling to jump. You never know until you ....

A horse squealing in apparent pain, somewhere deeper inside the barn, brought her to an abrupt stop. She spun around, looking for a groom, but all stable hands were near the show ring.

"Better take a look. May be an animal in trouble." She hurried back, checking stalls as she went.

There it was again. She circled into a wing for visiting horses, slowly approaching the end stall. Peering over the gate, she staggered back, a hand clasped over her mouth.

"OhmyGod." Her eyes flooded. "You poor baby. What's *happened* to you?" It looked like the big roan gelding that had jumped so poorly in the Open Class, its flanks lathered and striped with bloody furrows. The horse nickered softly, ears up, sensing compassion in her voice.

"Jesus. You've been beaten." Salty streams spilled down her cheeks, her heart pummeling her chest, a soft moan slipping between her lips. A horse should be your friend and companion, not an outlet for anger and abuse. She held out her hand to him.

"Who *did* this to you?" The tall horse edged tentatively forward, ears flicking back and forth. She gently rubbed his satiny snout. He nuzzled her shoulder, nickering softly.

"Sweet boy." Her arms circled his neck and he brushed his face affectionately against her body. Why would anybody hurt such a lovely animal? Tears continued to gush, as she fished for a tissue to blow her nose and blot her eyes.

Damn, my mascara's running. I must look a mess.

"I'm gonna find some help, pretty boy. Somebody's gonna pay for this, I promise you." She hurried off. He neighed plaintively after her.

Ashley was turning into the main part of the stable when the horse trumpeted again. She skidded to a stop, searching again for help, but everybody was still out at the show ring. Another shrill whinny. Was some bastard beating that poor guy again?

"Looks like it's up to me." Gritting her teeth, Ashley hurried toward the stall, snatching up a nearby pitchfork. Who knew how crazy this guy might be?

She cautiously approached the stall on suddenly rubbery legs. The chestnut gelding was struggling to get away from a tall, lanky man in riding habit, brandishing a whip. A very *big* whip. He had looped a lead chain over the animal's snout for control.

"I got a real weapon now, you bastard. You'll never embarrass me like that again. I'll kill ya first." He hit the horse hard across the withers. The big gelding bucked and pawed, but without any real energy.

"Hey, quit that." Her shout raspy, she banged the gate with

the side of the pitchfork.

"Huh?"

"Stop beating that poor, defenseless animal." Energized, adrenaline flowing at flood tide, she danced from foot to foot, a redheaded Valkyrie, brandishing her weapon over the gate, beating the air. Angry tears flowed unabated.

"Hey, put that thing down before your hurt somebody." Lowering his whip, he backed away in the face of this very agitated woman, her cheeks streaked with black mascara war paint.

"Then leave that horse alone, godammit." She jabbed the pitchfork in his direction.

"What the hell business is it of yours, lady?" His eyes never left the sharp metal tines.

"No animal deserves abuse like that. What's he done that was so terrible?" She sniffled, rubbing her nose with the back of her hand, tears drying up from flood mode.

"You see him jump today?"

"Yeah, so what." She caught her breath, lowering her weapon, having deflected him from his attack. "Any athlete can have an off day."

"Been more like an off year. Supposed to be a great jumper, but he's got no heart. I've had it." No longer threatened, the horse stood quietly, head hanging, breathing hard. Blood dripped in red rivulets off his flanks.

Maybe someone *did* sell this guy a clinker, as far as jumping went, but the animal didn't look at all well. So thin.

Shit. When I get back into jumping, I'll want a good Open horse. She almost smiled, despite her fury, realizing the decision had just been made. She studied the horse.

This poor guy may never qualify, but I can't leave him in the hands of this cretin. The reek of booze on him was overpowering. She skewered him with two gray lasers, burning out from below arched scarlet eyebrows.

"Well, you'd better leave him alone. You can get in trouble for this kind of abuse." Sighing softly, giving a small shake of her head, she leaned her weapon against the wall and entered the stall.

"What's his name?"

"Injun, but he sure ain't no warrior." He edged away, keeping a wary eye on this crazy woman.

She studied the big red horse, watching her with soft brown eyes. He nickered, and she could almost hear, *Please help me,* in the forlorn sound.

Oh, damn. Trapped. She glanced at the man, still holding his whip.

"Want to sell him?"

"Huh?"

"Do you want to sell him? You clearly don't like him. Beat him again, I'll report you."

"Yeah?" He studied her for a moment. "What'll you pay?"

"Look, I wanted an open jumper, and you said yourself he's not cutting it. I could probably low-ball you, as angry as you are, but I'll make you a fair offer. I'll pay you whatever you paid. Just show me the invoice. Deal?"

"You bet. I got it right here in my locker."

A half-hour later, check written, she called the vet most highly recommended by the stable's manager. Luckily, he was nearby and would be there in an hour or so.

Good. This poor baby needs his wounds cared for and a good general check-up.

TWO

She was back in the bleachers, awaiting the vet and watching the Novice Open Jumper Class, struggling with growing apprehension.

How impulsive. Keith'll be furious. Have to deal with it. Couldn't let that guy maim that lovely animal. She sighed, giving a tiny shrug.

The Hell with him. At least the horse will give unquestioned love, which is more than I'm getting from my husband lately. She leaned back, arms akimbo, reflecting on the state of her marriage to Keith Easton. Her eyes pooled.

Where did our passion go? She blinked away moisture, thinking of their youth. Those were the times ... sometimes exciting and sometimes painful.

Passion was the problem. She never imagined how, at the exhilarating age of seventeen, her life would change when they moved from Chicago to the suburban North Shore. A new house, new school, new friends ... and the hopes of finally finding a boyfriend.

But things became unexpectedly complicated, especially after making the cheerleading squad. She smiled, remembering her new friend, Sue Malloy, talking her into to trying out ....

"Cheerleading? Jeez, I don't think so," she'd responded to Sue's urging.

"Why not? You're a natural, with your, coppery-colored hair. And you're so tall. I wish I were tall."

"Oh, c'mon. You look great."

"Yeah, but my hair color's phony, and blue eyes are a dime a dozen. You got that hot-looking hair and those neat gray eyes, and you're really stacked. Who can compete with that?"

Ashley chuckled. Sue had made her sound like a movie star. But cheerleading was how she met Keith, as if Fate forced them together, and her usually blissful life suddenly became a lot more confused. Not so uncommon for teens, but even at its most tumultuous, she never expected this.

It was cheerleading, Keith, and of course, horses that filled her life. She had taken jumping and dressage instruction since she was a little girl.

"You're the most instinctive rider I've ever seen," her instructor had said. "As if you were born on a horse. For a usually reserved girl, you attack jumps with an almost wild delight."

Taking Lady over fences released a hidden recklessness in her. She imagined being on a foxhunt, hurtling hedgerows and stone walls with ease. Somewhere in her head, a woman's voice (was it hers?) exalting in gleeful French. But she barely knew the language.

She blinked and sat up, casting away the web of memories, chuckling mirthlessly.

With a final wistful glance at the horses still performing, she strode toward the barn to check on Injun before heading home. Delaying a confrontation with Keith won't change anything. He was sure to go on a tirade over the horse.

Too bad. It's my money, and it's about time I do what I want for a change.

She thought of that fateful time in her youth. Cheerleading never proved a disappointment, but the complications stemming from it were unexpected. She had no inkling as an innocent, trusting girl, what joy ... and misery ... would follow.

No time to dwell on that now.

THREE

[30]

"Well, doc, what's the verdict?" She craved some happy news to shore her up against Keith's coming harangue about responsibility to the family. What a joke.

"Unbelievable." the vet said. "That animal's got the worst case of worms I've ever seen. Musta been going on for a year. No wonder he has no energy. He's lost a lot of weight, too. Who the Hell's been caring for him?"

"I bought him from Sean McNulty," glancing at the receipt.

"No wonder. That drunken Mic doesn't know squat about horses. Bought a nice little ranch out by Wheaton. Keeps half dozen Thoroughbreds but won't spring for a vet or a farrier. Does it all himself...badly at that. Stupid sots shouldn't own horses."

"I *did* I smell liquor on the guy. Injun's gonna be all right? Those whip marks will heal?"

"O'course. I already treated him and salved the welts. See they stay clean."

"Okay, I'll tell the groom, but I'll still probably check him every day or two."

"Good idea. I'm gonna collar him so he can't bite the scabs, and he should be pretty well healed in ten days or so. I'll check back in three or four days. I may have to worm him again in a week or two, maybe even twice. See he gets extra oats for a while to help fatten him up. No strenuous work for at least two or three weeks, until he regains his strength. Should be as good as new in a month or two. Looks like he also needs to be reshod. Typical McNulty."

"So he'll be okay?"

"Yep. Should be."

"Great. Maybe he'll turn out to be the horse he looks like, after all."

"I shouldn't be at all surprised."

FOUR

"You bought a ... *horse?*" Keith loomed over her, cobalt eyes narrowed, hands on his hips, lips screwed into a scowl. He shoved his face a foot from hers, using his five-inch height advantage to intimidate.

"What in Hell possessed you to do a foolish, expensive thing like that?" He ran a hand through his long, blonde mane, pressing even closer.

She stared back, trembling. They stood on the Travertine floor of the sprawling ranch house's vestibule.

Why am I surprised? If it's not about Keith, it's ....

"Here." He shoved the portable phone at her. "Call the guy and tell him you changed your mind. Buyer's remorse, or something. You're not keeping that stupid animal."

Gray eyes flared, stunned by his vehemence. Clenching her jaw, she straightened her back, thrusting her chin forward, closing the gap between them to inches.

"I will not. It's my decision, and by the way, it's my money to spend as I see fit."

"Yeah, I know. 'Daddy's' money, but I'm still the head of this house, and you're not ...."

"Stop it. D'ya hear? *Stop it.*" Her arms clenched at her sides, long fingers balled into fists. "You're not in charge of *my* money. What's *wrong* with you, Keith? What's wrong with *us?*"

"Nothing." He fidgeted, stepping back, looking away. "There's nothing wrong. Only I love you too much to see you blow your inheritance on a dumb animal, when ...."

Ashley shook her head, sighing, tension morphed into a

familiar numbness. She took his large, tanned hands, in hers, struggling to forge some sort of connection.

"Look, I appreciate your concern, but my folks left us more money than we'll ever spend. I need some time doing things I love. Everyone needs that. You play golf and racquetball with your pals. The horse will be my buddy. It's great exercise, and when the kids are older, it'll give them a chance to care for another being that will absolutely love them."

"So, get 'em a dog. A golden retriever or something. They're supposed to be very affectionate."

She sucked in her lower lip, catching it with her teeth.

"A golden would be great. I've been thinking about that, too. But the horse is for *me*, and in the process, riding will provide them an interest in something other than who's the best dressed in school or belongs to the elite clubs."

"Who'll want 'em in their club if they stink of horse shit?"

She chuckled, the last tension slipping away. "Actually, that's the smell of upper class, darling. I know that's important to you. Horseback riding and jumping fences or doing dressage is a money thing. Middle-class Joe Blow can hardly afford it anymore, even if he does all the grunt work himself."

"What about the kids, while you're out prancing around?" This said with little conviction, realizing he was losing this scrap.

"Maria's here. Now that she's living in, it'll be easy. She's like an aunt, and they can practice their Spanish and her English." She dropped his hands, turning toward the bathroom and a much-needed shower.

"Yeah, but what if you fall off the damned horse and get hurt? Riding is a dangerous ..."

"Not really." She paused, looking over her shoulder, her auburn hair falling over one smoky eye. "I'm pretty experienced, even though I've not ridden in years. I'll begin with some basic training to see what he knows. His previous owner was a cretin and may not have trained him. I'll start with cavellettis and very low fences. See how he works ... what kind of jump and heart he's got. Nothing very threatening."

"But, I still don't think ...."

"No 'buts,' Keith. I'm keeping the horse. It's not open for discussion." She strode off.

You'll do your thing, as usual. Finally, I'll start doing some of mine. It's about time.

FIVE

Ashley tossed the currycomb into the oak supply box and began braiding Injun's dark mane, weaving in black ribbons and tying off each strand with a tight little double-knotted bow. The chestnut thoroughbred rubbed her cheek with his velvety snout, nipping at one of the gold buttons on her riding jacket.

"Hey, quit that. I've got to look good when we go into that ring." She laughed, hugging the horse around his muscular neck. He nickered softly, as she went back to braiding his long mane.

"We'll look great out there, won't we, buddy? A pair of redheads having fun."

She grimaced, shaking her head. Was she really ready for this? She loved riding, and especially jumping this big horse she had bought on a whim, little more than a year ago. Once healthy, he turned out to be the enthusiastic jumper that guy had been promised, and then some. Her vow to Keith to take it slowly evaporated when she realized he was so eager to attack fences.

Now, after ten months of hard training, they were entered in her first tournament, the first major amateur show of the Northern Illinois season. Nothing like starting big.

Elation at getting back to the love of her teens with a wonderful animal under her was sadly dampened by Keith, that very morning.

"No way. You're not going," he had said.

"What are you talking about? Of course I'm going. This is what we prepared for."

"No. You could get hurt ... or worse. I forbid it. You've gotta take some respons...."

"You *what?*" She spun on him, smoky eyes sparking fire. They glared at each other for a moment. Then she gathered her riding jacket, black helmet and crop and exploded from the room, the front door reverberating as it crashed closed behind her.

She sighed, shaking her head at the memory.

What nerve. Who does he think he is, forbidding me to ride?

Being almost in her third month won't interfere with her ability to jump the course, nor will it endanger the fetus. She held a pregnancy with utter tenacity, playing tennis into her eighth month with her first two children with no ill effects.

She doubted he really worried about losing a baby he didn't even want. How had this even happened, as rarely as they managed sex anymore? That's all it was for Keith.

Sex.

They stopped making *love* years ago.

Partly my fault, I suppose. Not easy being romantic when I'm scouring the shadows for monsters, just when he's getting it on.

This strange, uncontrollable panic ... *The Terror* she called it ... blossomed early in their marriage. All was wonderful at first, as they kissed and touched, trembling with delicious passion. She'd close her eyes, descending into her special imaginary place, that tranquil little meadow, surrounded by massive oaks and firs. She'd even imagine the tinkling of a brook, tumbling over small rocks.

Mon amour. Mon amour.

That lusty French voice, whispering to her, spilling goose bumps down her spine. Where did it come from? Exciting, but kind of spooky.

Then something would change. Ardor and joy were quickly squelched by the specter of a fierce horned apparition, wickedly hooked beak and raking claws, charging from the woods, screaming death. She *knew* it was imagination, but The Terror clutched her heart, drying up her juices, stiffening her limbs with panic.

She'd fight through it, trying to relax, steadying her breathing, wanting to please her husband. She never discussed it with anyone, feeling foolish, but The Terror had no real bearing on what was going on between them now.

Keith's real concern seemed less about her being hurt, and more over not wanting to be saddled with caring for their children if she were laid up from a bad fall ... a fear without basis.

Maria loved her kids and was always there whenever Ashley needed her. Ricky and Beth were crazy about "Aunt Maria," and they were getting quite good at speaking Spanish with her.

Well, she'd deal with Keith later. Time to get Injun tacked up and out to the ring. Their ride was in less than thirty minutes.

SIX

She sat astride Injun just outside the fenced show ring, watching a massive dappled gelding attack the course. The young rider apparently had little control over the brute, crashing into crossbars and flattening walls, continually getting in too close to each jump before taking off.

Ashley again dried her hands on her fawn jodhpurs and adjusted her black riding vest. She tugged at the white collar of her blouse, as rivulets of perspiration trickled down her spine, despite a temperature in the low 60's.

Okay, I'm nervous. The practice fences didn't seem nearly this size. I've never jumped anything like this before. I aughta be better prepared.

Reflexively, she glanced at the well-filled bleachers, fruitlessly searching for her parents, and moral support they could never again deliver. Six years they'd been gone, perishing in that horrendous, flaming collision one icy night on Lake Shore Drive.

She blinked away tears, smiling ruefully. Still she sought their faces in the stands or at family occasions. But there were no more calls from Mama, full of gossip, or Papa, with clever stories. They were the bulwark that enriched her life with love and humor by their very presence ... things Keith ceased doing many years ago.

It wasn't only that she mourned them. That pain had finally been compartmented away, a place she rarely visited. But she missed their companionship terribly, exacerbated by the reality Keith no longer provided much of that either.

Should their joy, that magical connection, have perished so quickly just because of her restrained panic during sex? She never denied him anything and had struggled to enjoy that expression of love, despite her irrational fears.

Injun tossed his head and took several quick, mincing steps in place, sensing the time was near for jumping. She again scoured the stadium but noticed no familiar faces. Then she saw *him,* lounging by the arena's railing, his obsidian eyes riveted on her.

Who was this intriguing guy, lean and fit-looking, whom she observed several times in the last few days, watching her work Injun over the practice course? Again the beat of hummingbird wings fluttered in her breast, just as it had every time she felt his magnetic gaze on her. It was more a sense of anticipation than arousal, despite his rugged, somehow handsome face.

He effused a powerful, magnetic aura ... and something else. Something more compelling. As if she knew him, but she had no idea from where. He ran a hand through dark, curly hair, his wide mouth and narrow lips twitching into a small grin as she returned his gaze.

She shook her head imperceptibly, returning her attention to the stadium.

Brazen hussy. A tiny smile tugged up the corners of her pale, pink lips. She shifted her seat in the saddle, changing her focus, visualizing the challenging course before her.

All of the knocked down rails reset, the judges signaled her to begin her round. She was illogically filled with confidence, knowing *he* was there. Why should *he* matter? She didn't even know him. As she entered the ring, circling Injun, preparing to attack the course, she passed close to the railing where he stood.

"Stand off a bit," he called. "He'll jump anything out there, if you give him enough room." Surprised, she glanced at him, russet eyebrows arched.

"Show 'em how it's done, Red," he shouted, as she turned her attention to the course and began her run. The first jump was a brush and single-pole. Despite the man's encouragement, a wave of chills spilled across her back. She crouched low in the saddle, driving the roan forward with her knees.

Jeez, that's a big fence. But Injun cantered in, head high and ears forward, and as if understanding the man's words, stood off in full stride, soaring over it with ease.

Wow! Beautiful. Maybe we can handle this after all. She leaned left, sudden confidence surging through her. Her grip on the reins changed subtly, unfamiliar but somehow stronger. Her sometimes tenuous seat strangely firm, she eagerly drove toward the next obstacle, guiding with knee pressure as much as with the reins.

Ashley squinted, measuring the size and breadth of the jump, a wooden "wall." The world around her momentarily slowed to a crawl.

Allez.

Her head popped up, stunned at hearing that long forgotten sultry French voice, chortling in her head. Why suddenly now, after a fifteen year silence? A quick head shake as she fastened on the approaching barrier.

Eyes watering, momentarily blurring, the course shimmered and flickered like a movie film that had jumped the sprocket. Blinking, she lurched dangerously upright as they charged the fence.

What the ...? Where did the wooden barrier go? A boulder-studded four-foot wall, covered with moss and ivy, loomed in front of them.

Jesus. How did that ...? It's so big. We'll be killed if he doesn't....

Ignoring Ashley's now dubious seat and one stirrup lost, the horse gathered himself to jump, not awaiting a signal she was too stunned to send. She snatched a handful of mane, crouching low in the saddle, eyes closed and knees gripping tightly, hoping not to be "left" ... thrown from the saddle. No question Injun was going. He never refused a fence.

The jarring shock of landing clear of the jump brought her head up, as she fought to regain her stirrup.

A 3rd Time to Die

Oh God, oh God. We made it. When did they set that up? So realistic.

Fumbling to gain control of reins and stirrup, they pivoted right, Injun knowing the course as well as she. Instead of the expected oxer, they confronted a huge downed oak, tangled roots, like dancing snakes, grasping for the sky.

Allez! Allez! Ricocheted through her mind.

That voice again, joyous and eager, not reflecting her panic. She gritted her teeth.

Shit. This isn't the course. How the Hell ... did we get lost in the woods?

The big sorrel thundered on, oblivious of his master's confusion. He hurdled the rough trunk with Ashley clinging to his neck and mane, trying to regain command of the sweat-slick reins. She managed to thrust her foot into the flapping stirrup and gain tension on the bridle just as they burst upon an unruly tall brush line, bordering a bubbling stream.

Clenching her jaw, she signaled with her knees, leaning low, her head to one side of his neck, as they went airborne, sailing easily over both hedge and water. Before she could catch her breath, they were on to a wood rail fence followed closely by another wide, lichen-clad stone wall. Her brain was frozen, lost to her whereabouts.

Tally-ho, tally-ho! She grunted, shaking her head.

Damn. This is no fox hunt.

Clearly, whatever *this* was, there was no stopping the gelding until they ran free of whatever forest they had mysteriously stumbled upon, so she'd better take control. Despite her heart's jackhammer effort to burst through her breast, she grew strangely confident, leaning lower, urging the gelding on. They had to get out of here and Injun seemed to know the way.

Mon dieu, cette forêt est si belle.

[40]

She's blinked. *Damned French, again? This is too much.*

That language hadn't popped in her head since she last jumped an Open course, fifteen years ago. That same sultry voice.

Forget it. Gotta concentrate on finishing this alive. What's got into this crazy horse?

Somewhat in charge now, they raced on, weaving through sparse woods, thick with the smell of fir, hurtling rock and stone walls, trees and wooden fences, hedges and streams, until there were none left.

Where did they come from and how had she gotten there? She'd seek those answers later. Had to finish this first. Broken sunlight, like celestial spears, pierced the woods ahead. A meadow? Once clear, they could find their way home.

As they cantered into a grassy clearing, thunder echoed across the sky.

La Fin.

She shivered, glancing up, blinking again, surprised at the cloudless blue above. Sitting up in the saddle, shaking her head, squinting at the sudden brightness, they sped past the finish line ....

Back at Onwentsia.

Back on the course.

Back home ... thank God.

Applause rumbled across the ring, reverberating like an approaching cloudburst. Ashley trembled, struggling to stand in the stirrups on shaky legs, looking back, as electric goose bumps lanced her spine.

What the Hell was that?

There were the stands, full of strangers; there was the show-ring, filled with jumps, every pole and wall still in place; and there *he* was, standing by the railing, grinning as he executed a small salute.

A 3rd Time to Die

Riding pell-mell through a forest? French in my head? Am I crazy? That velvet voice, like when I was a teenager jumping Lady, hearing French then, too. But nothing like this.

In her youth it was that same elegant Gaelic voice, urging her over the Junior Open courses. But those fences were just fences ... unchanged. This was some other world, charging through a primeval forest, soaring over natural obstacles, not a man-made course. She shook her head, trying to regain her full sense of place and time.

Am I going psychotic?

She was dragged back to the present by the booming loudspeaker, announcing the results of her mystical and very terrifying ride.

"Injun, ridden by Ms. Ashley Easton. A clean round, in an incredible time of 52 seconds."

My God, 52 seconds. That's fast. So while I seemed to be tearing through that beautiful old forest, I was really here, riding the course? How can that be? I saw that other world so clearly.

Whatever had happened, she was in first place, with two horses yet to go.

Ashley cleared the ring, dismounting on shaky, new fawn's legs, hugging the tall red horse around his lathered neck for balance.

"You took care of me out there, Injun. You understood what was going on better than me. Thanks." He nickered, tossing his head, lifting her off the ground. Her giggle was mostly nervous release.

The next contestant, mounted on a huge brown and white Warmblood, trotted past and nodded at her.

"Hell of a ride," he said. "That time won't be topped today."

Her heart still pounding her ribs, she smiled weakly. Nice compliment, coming from a guy she's heard was a Grand Prix rider, mounted on a $200,000 horse. He had no idea what kind of "ride" that really was. Through the lingering terror and confusion, a sense of elation peeked through.

If I hadn't been scared out of my pants, that would've been the most exciting thing I've ever done. Can't figure it out. There's no history of schizophrenia in my family ... that I know of. Belting out "Allez" and "Tally-ho." Just like a fox hunt, I guess.

Injun nickered, tugging at her pocket with his teeth, searching for a carrot or apple.

"Well, buddy," she said, her voice cracking, as she stroked his nose, feeding him his well-deserved treat, "somehow we got our first leg toward winning that big trophy. Not doing too badly for a couple of psychotic amateurs."

She sucked in several deep breaths, trying to slow her still racing pulse. Two more rounds, one Saturday and one Sunday. Win those and she was champion of the show. Would they be jumping fences in the ring, or charging through some magical woods filled with stone walls, streams and hedgerows?

She shuddered, filled with angst, but also strangely eager to find out. Squinting against the afternoon sun, her gaze swept the show ring, pausing to examine each obstacle. They were typical Open Jumper fences. How were they so transformed in her head? And that evocative French contralto, chortling gleefully with ever jump?

Sighing again, she shrugged, gathered Injun's reins, ambling toward the stables. Crimson eyebrows pinched together, the corners of a usually smiling mouth turning down. There was little eagerness to get home to parade her trophies. The kids were at their grandparents, and Keith would be the antithesis of happy or supportive.

She sighed, her hair swirling in an auburn cascade.

Pausing, she idly scrutinized the slowly dispersing crowd.

Tiny mouse-feet tiptoed down her spine, evoking delicious goose-bumps when her gaze fell upon *him*, dressed in cocoa Chinos and a chocolate long-sleeve flannel shirt, leaning his six-foot frame against a fence pole, arms folded. He tossed off a casual salute, grinning.

"Great ride, Red," he called. "I'll be cheering for you every round. Do it like that again tomorrow, but maybe a little less recklessly, and you can't miss." He waved, turned and sauntered off.

Who *is* this striking Italian-looking guy, with curly inky hair and a lean, equestrian physique?

He seems so familiar. Is it a coincidence he pops out of nowhere, and suddenly her world seems transformed, her head bubbling with French while she blazes around the course, flying over walls and trees in some mysterious forest she doesn't even recognize?

Reckless indeed. He should only know how easy it was ... once I swallowed my heart and took some kind of control.

I should meet him. Maybe Sunday, after my last competition. He said he would be there. Wonder what the world gonna look like when I entered the ring then? Scary, again?

Despite the afternoon's mild temperatures, she wrapped her arms around herself, shivering.

SEVEN

"Ladies and gentlemen, I give you the Champion of the show, Open Jumper Division, finishing first in all three events: Injun, owned and ridden by Ms. Ashley Easton. I hope we're going to see a lot more of this exciting duo. Ms. Easton?"

Ashley strode into the ring leading Injun, prancing behind, urged on by considerable applause and cheering. Mama and Papa were there only in her heart, sharing her triumph, but not Keith or the children, conveniently off on a "promised visit" with his parents. There wasn't another person in the stands important to her.

Except maybe *him*. He said he'd be there.

She scoured the crowd, searching for that sun-darkened, charismatic face. And there he stood, elbows hooked over the white railing, grinning and shaking a fist in salute to her three incredible rides.

She smiled shyly, looking quickly away, a warm flush swooping through her. Who was this guy? This self-appointed mentor, whose brief advice *had* helped in three successful romps through very challenging courses.

No one can guess how very strange those rides were. Each time, after the first jump, the world tilted, spilling into fields and woods, filled with real fences, downed trees and walls.

She had no idea how the ring morphed into that old forest, then reappeared after the final fence. She would helplessly release herself to these visions, terrified, yet charging ahead with abandon, more in control than she'd ever been.

Injun, mindless of the change ... if he even saw it ... flew over one obstacle after another, following the directions she instinctively gave with her hands and knees. Despite panic, her seat was rock-solid, the reins held with casual confidence, her timing into each jump flawless, while her head bubbled gleefully in French, exalting each new obstruction.

Tallyho! Tallyho! Always as if on a foxhunt.

She needed time and iron will to collect herself after each round, shaken, her legs trembling so badly she nearly collapsed after dismounting. Despite her panic, she bubbled with exuberance from the adrenaline rush fired by those wild rides. Once tentatively back on her feet, still clinging to her saddle for support, she'd look for *him*, wondering if he somehow shared this strange adventure, yet knowing that was impossible.

Ashley struggled from her musing, accepting the large silver platter, already inscribed with her name, struggling to hold it high for all to see, glinting in fading sunlight. Injun nickered, nudging her toward the gate with his nose. He was getting bored, it seemed. Laughter rippled through the crowd.

Back in this world, she grinned, scratching behind his ears, and then led him toward the stables, her trophy wedged under one arm. This was his home, so their day was finished.

Then she saw *him* again, sauntering into the parking lot. Quickly, she found a groom who would hold her silver prize and see Injun was properly cared for. Hurrying through the crowd, she was stopped by acquaintances and strangers alike, showering her with praise.

"Great Show."

"What a gorgeous horse."

"You two are some great team."

"How much do you want for that horse?"

Thank you; thank you; thank you; *No* thank you. She couldn't be rude to so many well-wishers, but they were stalling her attempts to catch up to him.

Where *was* he? Shaking free, finally, from the small crowd surrounding her, she paused at the curb of the parking lot, one hand shielding her eyes from the glare of the western sun.

Damn. He came out here. How could he be gone so quickly? There. Just entering that maroon Jag convertible.

"Oh Hell." He was already backing out. No chance to catch him without looking the fool, dashing through the lot. Riding boots were never intended for running.

Well, she only wanted to thank him for his advice and to

discover if they'd met before. He certainly understood jumpers, so maybe she would see him at another show. Her thanks would have to wait until then.

She returned to the stables to check on Injun and collect her trophy before settling back in the stands to watch other competitions.

The memory of that guy's intense dark eyes and quirky smile, shouting encouragement, set her heart fluttering with a strange sense of anticipation.

Who *was* he, anyhow?

EIGHT

Craig Thornton turned into the Shell gas station, stopping his Jag convertible at the self-serve Super Unleaded pump. The only thing he regretted about his sleek sports car was the need for hi-test fuel, but, luckily, he could afford it.

Swiping his Amex card and beginning fueling, his mind drifted to the Open Jumping competition that just concluded. The image of that magnificent red-haired duo going Champion of the show, blowing away some very good competition, reeled across his mind with crystal clarity.

He'd been in the area on Thursday, stopping to watch the practices for the first important contest of the season, and saw her working the fences. Such beauty and grace, both rider and horse. He had been happily mesmerized, strangely filled with a sense of familiarity.

He'd been compelled to make the hour drive each of the next three days to observe them compete. Brazenly, he shouted advice to her as she had entered the course on Friday, and was rewarded with a smile that would bury a Key West sunrise, not the sneer such presumption was due. The sight of them recklessly flying over the course set his heart rumbaing, goose bumps trilling down his neck and back. He'd learned her name from a groom: Ashley Easton.

Ashley Easton.

It had a sweet, liquid feel about it, but it didn't ring any bells. A magnetic-like field drew him toward her as he feasted on that wild ride. His heart hammering its way into his throat, he watched in excited awe for all three events, as horse and rider flowed over one fence after another, never pausing, never even slowing ... each round a continuous, one-piece fabric of athletic grace and speed, despite her seeming a bit out of control.

What a team, working together as a unit. He'd love a chance to mold such abundant raw talent.

Was that all? He wasn't sure, but he knew he would certainly see her again.

As the pump automatically clicked off, he sighed, a single thought lingering in his head.

Ashley Easton.

Craig lingered in the folds of the soft leather bucket seat, mind drifting. A brief head shake brought him to the present, and the near-hour drive home. At least week-end traffic should be light. Home in time for dinner. Would Toni be there? Or was his wife plying her amorous wiles elsewhere again?

Why did he tolerate her callous infidelities? And why, after so many years of her catting around, did that suddenly seem important to him? Well, a guy can only take so much.

Unbidden, the redheaded Ashley, astride her sorrel gelding, flew over fences in his mind.

Ashley Easton.

As he turned onto the Freeway, he knew somehow they were destined to meet.

Providence was once again stirring the cauldron of fate.

NINE

Ashley idly watched the finals of the Green Hunter competition, reaffirming why she preferred open jumping. That handy American Saddlebred put in a near-perfect round and wasn't even called back. If the judges didn't know you, and it wasn't a Thoroughbred, how well you covered the course didn't matter.

But open jumping was judged solely by knock-downs, and no personal bias can color the results.

She sighed, shifting uneasily on the hard, backless bleacher. Time to start home, where an invective surely awaited her. Keith was furious she jumped Injun in the show. He had no interest in what's important to her. Why is he so intent on controlling everything?

Well, I'm finally doing my things, whether he likes it or not. It's not high school anymore.

Their lives were so interlocked at New Trier High School ... seemingly destined to be together. Would they have even dated if she hadn't been practicing cheers and got knocked down as he chased an errant pass during football practice?

But even from the first, everything always revolved around him ... his football and his relentless push for his own gratification.

He was so disconsolate after the Waukegan game, when O'Shay caught the winning pass.

Gee, you'd think he'd be happy we scored, but it wasn't his *touchdown.* Sue, ever optimistic, convinced her it was "just football."

A 3rd Time to Die

We were so much in love, but all that heavy necking and petting bothered me. What *was* acceptable for a "Good Girl?" He relentlessly cajoled her into more and more intimate contact. She slowed his insistent groping, despite getting really turned on by all the physical stimulation.

She'd descend into a glorious fantasy of uninhibited passion, sprawled on a lush carpet of grass in a shaded forest glade, surrounded by magnificent old trees. Mesmerized by that vision, her resolve weakened. She trusted Keith not to hurt her. After all, they were still just kids.

But trusting Keith had proved a mistake.

Ashley shrugged, casting away those memories. She was such an innocent. Nothing was served by rehashing *that.* She stood, tugging her riding vest in place, brushing wrinkles and specs of hay from her russet jodhpurs.

Time to go. The kids would be excited to hear of Mommy's adventures and see her trophies when they returned home from grandma's. Too bad Keith manufactured a reason not to bring them to cheer for her. She missed having family in the stands, rooting her on.

The face of that enigmatic stranger edged into her mind. A man she didn't even know, pulling for her. Next time she'll be more insistent. Her kids can see their grandparents anytime.

Why can't Keith just be happy for my success? Does he even love me anymore?

Was it any safer to trust her husband now than it was, fourteen years ago, when he selfishly shattered her innocence?

For the first time, she was seriously began to face newly hatched doubt.

TEN

"I can't believe you went back again, after I told you *not* to ride in that stupid show." Keith braced her as she joyfully burst through the double dark cherry paneled doors. The smile and warmth infusing her from her championship run wilted at the frigid blast of his invective.

Scowling, balled fists jammed against his hips, he blocked her way across the marble tiled foyer. Sidestepping, she hefted her silver trophy and three blue ribbons for him to see. He waved dismissively, snatching at her sleeve. She sighed.

"You did, but I did it anyhow." She shook off his hand and headed for the family room and the trophy case.

"*You* decided?" He trailed after her. "After I ordered you not to. What if ...."

"*Ordered* me?" She spun, her eyes aflame. "Who the Hell do you think you are, that you can *order* me to do anything?"

"I'm your husband. It was for your safety. I didn't want ...."

"Right. What a laugh." She threw her trophies on the sofa. "You should've come ... brought the kids ... saw how exciting it was. Be interested in *my* things, for a change."

Her skin prickled, the thrill of her strangely exciting weekend flushed away by the cold bath of his animus. No surprise. He hadn't shown concern for anybody but himself for the last five years. Tiny rivulets slid down her tanned cheeks.

"What's happened to us, Keith? What's happened to love?" her voice a bare whisper. She knuckled her eyes. He looked away, pulling on his right ear lobe.

"I was concerned for your safety. Yours and the baby's. Isn't that love?"

"The *baby's*? This *thing* you said you never wanted. That you *ordered* me to abort. You don't give a damn about the baby, Keith. I'm not sure you give a damn about me either."

"Stop. Sure I care." He jammed his hands into the pockets of his tan slacks, shrugging. "Just having a bad time at work. Things aren't goin' well, and the damned Board's still workin' off an outta date play book. Maybe I have been insensitive. I'm just preoccupied ... trying to devise a new game plan that'll get us a win. I'm sorry."

He nodded, avoiding her eyes, and headed for the den and his evening scotch. She was alone with her shiny platter and ribbons, the joy of the weekend drained away, rushing down a slick, black whirlpool of despair. It would be two hours before Ricky and Beth returned from their Sunday with his folks. Her parents never even met Beth. She'd been thinking of them a lot lately.

Mama would have loved seeing me win those events. But there was only one real fan there, that intriguing stranger who really seemed to appreciate what she did.

Sighing, trying to dispel the dark gremlins swarming through her head, she strode across Brazilian cherry wood planked floor toward their bedroom and master bath. The bubbling hot jets of their whirlpool tub beckoned her aching limbs.

Merde.

She blinked, shrugging. Even that lusty French voice, whispering to her, brought no thrill.

ELEVEN

Ashley sunk lower in the big tub until only her face showed above fragrant, foamy water. The spa jets, set on low now after ten minutes of high-speed pummeling, continued swirling warm water against her body, licking her aches. Three days of jumping large fences had taken its toll. She wasn't a teenager anymore. She relaxed, trying to let her muscles go loose, but it was hopeless while she was so agitated.

What *had* happened to them over the past eight years? They were so much in love in high school, so irresistibly drawn together, she the iron to his powerful magnet, clearly fated to marry.

Lots of girls had casual sex then, but she vowed to save herself for that magical first night as husband and wife. Fulfilling that fantasy was a bulwark against his impatient aggression ... his need for instant satisfaction. He almost destroyed their romance, when things were going so well.

They'd driven to their favorite little hideaway off Sheridan Road, after New Trier won the Suburban League football Championship, beating Evanston with Keith's last minute touchdown catch.

They'd barely parked his father's big Mercedes before he swarmed over her, and for the first time, his insistent hand made it inside her skirt, touching her *there*. She was in flames, drawn into the familiar fantasy she had constructed; a glorious, shaded forest glade, lush dew-damped grass, bordered by a bubbling brook, set deep in a mysterious oaken woods. It was the ultimate place of tenderness and love ... and sometimes, crouching in the deep shadows, a hint of terror.

Strange that while this delicious illusion only blossomed

during her passionate trysts with Keith, she somehow sensed he never quite fit comfortably in that fantasy. But that Indian Summer afternoon everything seemed perfect ... until she realized her panties were gone and he was looming over her, one leg wedged between her knees, his swollen penis magically freed from his trousers, hovering like a cobra, preparing to strike.

She twisted and squirmed, struggling to wriggle away, the leather armrest blocking her escape, as she tearfully begged him to stop. Finally, outrage supplanting panic, a sharp knee rammed forcefully into his groin, ended their evening ... and their romance.

I trusted him and he stripped me nearly naked. I actually allowed him to do it! Hell. He tried to rape me.

Ashley wallowed in the cavernous tub, hands fluttering, feet thrashing, as if drowning in a memory not revisited for twelve years. Pushing up, she sat with dripping hands covering her eyes, elbows wedged against her knees, struggling for air. Gaining control, calming the crescendo in her breast with two slow, deep breaths, she heaved herself from the tub, draped in a large towel, tears streaking her cheeks.

I was so naive, wanting to believe in love, but Keith was all about Keith, despite whatever else he claimed. I suppose I'm a typical woman, expecting her man to change, but I guess nothing really has, after all these years.

Jesus. How did things get so out of hand then? I knew it was wrong, even if we were in love. Was it my fault, teasing him out of control? She shook her head, barking a quiet laugh.

Just like me, finding excuses for everyone but myself. Truth is, he tried to rape me. No other word for it. I said "no" more than once, but he kept pressing.

So, why was she still so *consumed* with him after that? Swimming in hateful desire ... a burning *need* to be with him?

So, I thought I was in love. So what? How do you love someone who doesn't respect you? Who only thinks of himself? It should have been over.

Despite anger, her thoughts had remained crowded with all things Keith. Hot, sticky, needful thoughts. She'd been swept up by that idyllic vision of a pastoral clearing, a gurgling brook and sweet passion ... despite sensing something important was missing. It was a place she never expected to share again with Keith after that painful evening.

But things change and here they are. She finished drying, running a hand down her barely protruding abdomen.

Not bad for thirty-two and a mother of two. I look fit without even trying. Riding Injun's tightened everything that went soft, once I got over the early aches and pains. I was really stiff, those first few days. She opened her closet, looking for something to wear.

Can't understand why he's so angry about the horse? It's so petty. We can't even talk about the simplest things.

There's no connection anymore, despite the new baby ... a miracle child ... coming. Things are gonna have to change.

We can't live like this forever.

TWELVE

"Damn the wanton bitch," Craig Thornton grumbled, looking at his solar powered Casio.

"Midnight. She must be having one hell of a good time."

Toni was either sloshed into oblivion, or shacked up with some dilettante stud.

Or both.

A 3rd Time to Die

She was so damned cavalier about her affairs, and well on the way to becoming a full-fledged alcoholic. Why not? It seemed a family tradition.

He'd been so naive, thinking her upper class, high society parents were laid back and mellow. They were really *stewed* most of that time. Mellow was easy when you don't have to work for a living, and lubricate your lives with a pint or two of gin or scotch every day.

What really angered him was Toni's lack of guilt over her frequent sexual forays. That's just the way *they* did things. Very European ... if she bothered explaining at all.

What possessed him to marry her? What a fool. Who was it who said God gave man a penis and a brain, but only enough blood to fill one at a time? He let his cock rule his head. She was the sexy nymph, volcanic in bed, snaring him with the high-voltage energy of her passion, her amazing sexual appetite. He confused her insatiable lust with love. Easy to believe it was Nirvana.

She came from "old money." Real WASP robber barons. Indolent wealth, but nice people. She would never have given him a second look if he hadn't changed his persona. She chose him over a gaggle of suitors because he was different ... curly dark hair, with Mediterranean complexion and rugged good looks ... very non-WASP. He never challenged her parents' belief in his Norman ancestry. She didn't know how different he *really* was, but one of the things he had loved about her was her fierce independence, not realizing then it was really her need to prove she was in charge.

He gritted his teeth, his stomach roiling with molten lava. Or was that the frozen lasagna he'd eventually microwaved when he arrived home from the horse show and found both Toni and dinner missing? Heading for the bathroom and some antacid relief, he slipped, feet skidding out on the icy-slick floor.

"Goddamn it." He sat up, rubbing his right hip. "I keep telling the stupid maid *not* to wax the damned marble." Explosive venting, plus the medication he finally reached, helped calm him.

"Craig Thornton remains in total control." He laughed ruefully.

Craig Thornton. Hell, what a joke. He'd come a long way from Yonkers. Someday, if this marriage fell completely apart, he might just blurt out the truth. But, the real gag was on him.

He became Craig Thornton to hide his background and change his social position, but it was a hollow victory. Was this what he really wanted? There were no kids to play ball with or teach to ride. No *live* ones, anyhow. Marriage hadn't guaranteed family, leaving him more alone than he ever dreamed possible.

Her incandescent heat in the sack ... screaming orgasms, one after another, and gasped pledges of eternal love ... had deluded him. He never guessed how many other guys would share that pleasure. It reached a point over the past five years, when they did have sex ... an infrequent occurrence at best ... he used a condom.

He desperately wanted kids...three or four...but didn't want to die trying. Who knew what distasteful or even deadly things she might have acquired during her frequent nocturnal adventures.

Craig readied himself for bed, vaguely hoping Toni wouldn't return before he was asleep. His need for confrontation had slipped away, cascading down into the deep, dark secure vault where he locked away all his anger, refusing to let it fester when nothing could be gained. Anger wasn't practical, and if Craig Thornton were one thing, it was practical. That's how he had gotten ahead in life, if you considered *this* getting ahead.

Settling between flannel sheets, he took several deep breaths. In with the good air, out with the bad. Relaxing, slowly drifting toward dreamland, thoughts of the enchanting redheaded woman, jumping her big roan gelding, crept in.

Such beauty and grace, both rider and horse. He had been happily mesmerized, filled with a pleasant sense of familiarity.

Ashley Easton.

Why had the very sight of her set tenterhooks into his soul? He wasn't sure, but he knew he would certainly see her again. The Open Jumping scene was a closely knit society.

That thought brought a peaceful glow, as he finally slid into sleep, a single thought lingering in his head.

Ashley Easton.

THIRTEEN

What the Hell's wrong with everybody?

Keith hunkered over the mahogany bar, bisecting a corner of the dark cherry paneled family room, fixing his second scotch. He replaced the decanter on the mirrored shelf, his angry blue eyes glaring back at him. Snatching up his drink, spilling a few drops, he headed for the reclining, soft amber leather armchair where he could settle down and cool off.

No one listened to him. His damned wife ignored his orders; his father had his head in the sand, unaware a lion was chewing on his ass; and the stupid Board of Directors was afraid to make a move. His whole world was going to hell, and he was stymied everywhere he turned.

What did Ashley want from him? He's her husband. She's supposed to do what he says. But no ... that rarely happens, despite his demands. And what's wrong with giving orders? His father gave them, and everyone listened ... especially the women.

Not Ashley. She jumped that fool horse while pregnant, in spite of him. Pregnant. How in the hell did *that* happen? Anyone else, he'd think she were screwing around. But not prim and proper Ashley. The brat was his all right. A couple of drinks too many one night when Kristen was away visiting her parents in sunny Boca Raton. He'd been so damned horny.

Kristen. That's *real* sex, worth every penny he pays her. Not like Ashley, who starts out hot, then goes cold and stiff just when things should be getting good. What the Hell's wrong with her?

She's his wife, and should cater to him, like all the Easton women did with their men. But she's an only child and was pandered to as much as he. A fucking independent woman. Actually, a non-fucking, independent woman. He snickered, and then shrugged.

That's the least of his problems. His gutless father and their timid Board were running the company into ruin. They refuse to spend money developing new products, and fear exploring moving their factory to some favorable Southern labor market. They can't believe *their* company's big enough to build a new, modern factory with revenue bond financing, right in the midst of lots of cheap labor. They were rapidly falling behind their competitors, and if a move weren't made soon, there'd be nothing left to worry about.

Well, he could only do so much. No matter what happens, he'd still be safe. Ashley's parents were loaded, and saw that their only child would always live in style. That was one reason he married her. Sure, she was one the most beautiful girls at New Trier, and she seemed so hot. They were a magnet and iron, but even then he'd been clever enough to think about his future.

Her parents were discreet with their gifts, like paying for nursery school, and even buying their house. Plus a nice untaxable gift yearly, but nothing really *big*. Now that the old bastard and his biddy were gone, the family booty, including the deed to *their* house, was tied up in irrevocable trusts for Ashley and their brats.

He'd probably be gone by now, if it weren't for that safety net. A lot more erotic than the almost compulsive heat they had for each other, so long ago. Nothing but dead embers now.

He *had* loved her ... whatever that was. She was gorgeous and classy, and it felt good to be with her. Except in bed. That was a disaster, as if she expected a boogie man to jump them. She never said "no," but her obvious tension took all the excitement out of their sex. He just concentrated on enjoying himself, and the hell with her, if she couldn't respond.

Luckily, he found Kristen, and while strictly a pro, she made it *seem* romantic. He was The Hero, like in high school and college. That's how it *should* be.

But Ashley adored their two kids, not him. Not any more, anyhow. She treated him fine, usually respecting his needs ... despite this thing with the damned horse ... and having this new baby. The problem was, she expected to be treated the same way, not accepting a woman's natural subservient role.

It was her parents' fault. Probably her mother had scared her about sex. The bitch. That lucky auto accident got rid of those meddlers, but it didn't help. His damned wife thought she was just as important as he was. And their sex had long since perished.

Now with Kristen becoming harder to afford with things off track at work, he needed a real mistress. A hot babe who'd screw his brains out every chance they had. Probably less costly than the pro, but how to find a gal like that? A new challenge, one of many.

So his priorities were to pull the Board's heads out of their asses, save the company, and find the gal of his dreams, someone willing to share him. No way he's backing out of this marriage.

Ashley's family's wealth was too important to throw away, even without love. She was a high-class beauty, popular and socially involved on the North Shore, and her presence made him important and well liked.

And that was good.

He placed his empty glass on the polished walnut coffee table, disdaining the ring its wet bottom would etch into the wood, and stood, stretching. Time for dinner, and repairing the damage he'd done with his wife. He needed her happy and trusting, and he wasn't going to be too proud to make amends to achieve that.

Ride the stupid horse, for all I care. Maybe she'd fall off and abort the baby. Or hit her head and die. Hmm. That's something to consider. Sometimes luck needs a little help.

FOURTEEN

"I was out with friends," Toni said, pulling out a chair at their round, glass-top breakfast table. She carried a mug of black coffee, the rich smell of vanilla bean permeating the air.

"We had too much to drink, so I stayed over. Don't be so dramatic, darling." Smiling confidently, she settled, one bare leg tucked under her in that seductive feline manner she had perfected. She scooted her chair next to his. A gossamer black lace teddy did little to conceal her considerable assets.

"Poor Craig. So grouchy in the morning. We'll have to do something to cheer him up."

Tousling his hair, she drew his face into the warm, delicious prison of her copious breasts. Unbidden, his hands found the firm curves of her buttocks. She slid on to his lap, kissing him teasingly.

A 3rd Time to Die

Born on the soft, moist wind of her breath, her tongue tantalized his ear. His fingers developed a will of their own, stealing over the hills and swells of her lush flesh. A small, silver-chimed laugh escaped her. He was drowning in her pheromone fragrance, her narcotic taste, the silkiness of her skin.

Gritting his teeth, he struggled free from the drug of her sensuality, panting ... a deep-diver, fighting to the surface for a life-giving breath.

Goddamn it. She's doing it again.

The only time they had sex was when he challenged her about her increasingly blatant escapades. She would ply her sensuous wiles, seducing him, and he was powerless to resist.

She was a succubus, skillfully draining him of his energy, and finally, his resolve. But her erotic voodoo lacked magic today ... the carnal obsession waning. Had this last blatant infidelity been the proverbial "straw?" Whatever, he swelled with the strength to resist.

He had swum to the surface of his entrapping pool of lust, cherishing a carnally free breath for possibly the first times since they met. His addiction to her lascivious wiles fracturing, a tiny glimmer of a different future ignited in his mind.

Breathing a small growl, he pushed her away, disentangling himself from the enervating tentacles of her lust. Her sexual ardor, so easily ignited ... as myriad other men had discovered ... was suddenly lost on him. Coldly calm, he lurched to his feet, plunking her down and backing away.

"Stop this. It's not going to work this time."

Her hands ran over her trembling body, cobalt eyes, large as quarters, following him with amazement. So exquisite, but abruptly repellent to him. How was it he suddenly saw her as disgusting?

"Oh, Craig *darling.* I'm so worked up. You can't leave me

like *this*." She slipped out of her flimsy teddy, wantonly flaunting her sensual curves. She stalked after him, her perfect breasts thrust tantalizingly forward. He retreated, arms extended, palms up, as if holding back the waves of intense eroticism pouring out of her.

"Cut it out, Toni. You can't use sex to solve every problem. Not with me, at least. Not anymore."

But, why?

"Don't I excite you, baby?" Her lower lip protruded, a petulant little girl denied access to the cookie jar.

"We do such *glorious* fucking, and I want you so badly. Don't you *love* me?"

"I ... I don't know. It's hard to separate love and passion with you. Sex is what we do when you want something from me. Then it's not making love. It's just fucking."

"Whatever you call it, I need to *do* it, right now." She stamped her foot. No one denied Toni Rudolph Thornton whatever she demanded. Certainly never a man.

"Sorry, you'll have to manage it yourself. I'm outta here. And I expect you to be home when I get back from work. This late night catting around with 'friends' is gonna stop, or we're gonna have a serious problem. I mean it, Toni. A *serious* problem."

He hurried off, slamming the French glass-paneled front door almost hard enough to shatter the panes. Straightening his tie, he ran a hand through his disheveled, curly hair as he crossed the cobblestone drive, beeping the alarm on his maroon Jag convertible.

He was already late, and he'd scheduled a management meeting for first thing that morning.

FIFTEEN

Craig drummed his fingers on the leather-bound steering wheel of his Jaguar convertible, trapped in the slowly flowing river of steel called the Kennedy Expressway during the morning rush hour. The lazy current of traffic swept him along, requiring minimal attention, leaving his mind free to wander.

What a sorry state. Toni has cheated on him for years. Through his therapy, he realized she was fraught with insecurities. A loveless childhood had sent her on an endless, almost Quixotic quest for the passion her parents never supplied.

Where better to find "love," plastic though it may be, than in the arms of some desirable young man. The more men, the greater she saw her own worth, but it was never enough. There was always one more male windmill to conquer.

He chuckled mirthlessly. What would his highbrow wife think if she knew whom she actually married? Craig Tannenbaum became Craig Thornton, complete with a new, very non-Semitic nose, before he transferred to a new high school for his junior year.

He had a plan and needed a change, if he wanted an unbiased opportunity to succeed. Hard work and a sharp mind got the new Craig Thornton to Yale on scholarship, something more difficult to achieve for a Jew named Tannenbaum.

He pledged a top, WASP-only fraternity, paying his way doing dishes and waiting tables. His dark Gaelic face and mysterious, obsidian eyes, created a different sensuality Toni couldn't resist. The elite fraternity, top grades, and his father's "transportation" business, were high recommendations to her parents.

Wouldn't the Rudolphs be shocked to learn his father's

"business" was driving a hack in Manhattan? Craig grimaced, knowing these truths would be an odious ace up his sleeve, should he ever actually decide to fracture the invisible chains he ... and Toni ... had cast around himself, binding him in this strange marriage.

Despite Toni's excesses ... the men and the alcohol ... he stayed. But why? At first he thought he loved her, and was snared by her ardor and incredible sexuality, but there was nothing between them anymore. His highly successful upscale mail order business was his creation, straight out of college, elevating him beyond being just the Rudolphs' son-in-law.

Did he still love Toni? Had he *ever*, really, or was he blinded by her heat and beauty, and the lure of the different life he so fervently sought? He didn't know, but it seemed foolish to remain bound to a faithless lush. Didn't he deserve a real woman in a real relationship?

He thought of Ashley Easton, perched on her big roan gelding, soaring over the course, gobbling up fence after fence as if they were nothing more than cavallettes. As exhilarating as it was to watch, it also brought him a strange sense of comfort ... and strength.

Strength? Had watching her somehow shined a light on the realities of his fractured marriage? The two seemed totally unrelated, but, abruptly, he was no longer willing to sit idly by while Toni screwed her way through all the young men on the North Shore.

Did just watching Ashley Easton bring him to this resolve? He had no idea, but he was flooded with peace as he visualized her. She was apparently a new entry to the "horsey" set. He'd never seen her at any event before last week at Onwentsia.

Wonder if she's going to the horse-season's opening Gala? Maybe we'll meet ....

Jeez, don't become obsessed over a gal you don't even

[65]

know. But he *did* seem to know her ... somehow, somewhere ....

Too bad. Toni's the cheat ... not me. But there's something about that gal ....

Craig was jolted from his reverie by a blaring horn. There was a fifty-foot gap between his Jag and the next car. They'd finally crept past the confluence with the southbound river of vehicles from the Edens Expressway, and traffic opened up, heading for the Loop.

Driving required more attention, but in the back of his mind, he thought of the card in his wallet. A friend, a survivor of bitter divorce, had, over cocktails, pressed it into his reluctant hand when Craig unburdened himself about Toni's dalliances.

Mike McNeely, Private Investigations.

Honest and discreet, Jack said... and expensive. But the package he would amass would be unshakable in court, if it were needed. And if Craig decided on divorce, it *would* come to that. Toni bitterly disliked giving up things she thought of as hers.

Maybe he should put Mr. McNeely to work, just in case he finally had enough. It will be an easy job for a professional. Toni made no effort to be devious about her affairs.

It might be different if they ever had kids. Any that lived, anyhow. Clenching his jaws, tears welled up at the thought of their infant son, dead three days after his birth.

She murdered him, just as surely as if she used a gun. Fetal Alcohol Syndrome, the doctor said. Craig threw out all the booze when he found her totally sloshed during her second month, but she must have had a hidden stockpile. Poor little Andrew didn't have a chance. She never became pregnant again. If it happened now, it probably wouldn't even be his kid.

Yes. He just might give Mr. McNeely a call. Just in case.

SIXTEEN

Keith paused in front of the modern four-story building, its stainless steel and bronze glass walls set ablaze by the western sun.

A relentless stream of vehicles surged by on Michigan Avenue, filling the air with an incessant rumble. Peering through the double glass doors of the plush lobby, he spied an attractive blonde poised behind a large stained oak desk, checking in a steady flow of duffel bag toting men and women of all ages.

It looked inviting. Still he hesitated, considering the real reason he was there.

Nicole Phillips taught an aerobics class at the North Loop Health Center and Spa. She sounded like a goddess when he overheard two guys slobbering over her during lunch two days ago. He was intrigued as they speculated whether anyone was "getting any," impelled to come and see for himself, still hopeful of finding a full time mistress to replace the costly Kristen. The hooker was terrific, but he ached for a real lover whose life would revolve around him.

Maybe pissing in the wind, chasing some gal he didn't know, but it seemed the right thing when he left the office.

"What the Hell," he muttered, pushing through the doors into a marble-floored, wood-paneled lobby. The flaxen-haired angel, sensually displayed in black leotards, was seated behind the oak secretary. A real beauty, but clearly not Phillips, who supposedly had coal-black hair.

"May I help you?" Her warm smile lit up the room. God, she was exquisite. Could this Phillips dame be any more exciting?

"Hi. I understand you have a free, one month trial offer."

"That's right. If you apply now, you have until the end of

next month to buy membership. That actually gives you five free weeks."

"Swell. Where do I sign? If all the staff is as beautiful and friendly as you, why would anyone look elsewhere?"

"That's so sweet." She slid across an application and a pen, and then gathered up a small pile of brochures and rate sheets for him.

"I keep telling my husband we have the nicest members in the whole city." Still smiling, she handed him the small stack of papers.

"The locker room is the second door on your right. If you hurry, the next aerobics class is starting in ten minutes."

"Great. Who teaches that one?"

"Nicole Phillips, of course. That's why you're here, isn't it? That's why *all* the men are here every Monday, Tuesday and Thursday afternoons at two and again at four. It could give a girl a complex." Her chuckle was totally devoid of rancor.

"You're much too attractive to feel threatened by another woman," he said, smiling with her, and meaning every word.

"You *are* sweet, aren't you? You've made my day. But you haven't met Nicole yet, have you?"

"No, but I hear she runs a great class."

"Oh, she does. She does. I'm sure you'll work up a dandy sweat ... one way or another. If you hurry, she likes to meet new members before the class begins." She winked, grinning mischievously, before turning to a new arrival.

Keith grabbed his bag, heading for the locker room. Damn, his heart was doing a drum roll. How could Nicole Phillips be any more exciting than that little blue-eyed blonde ...? April Callahan, according to her name tag.

Too damned bad she was married. But so was Keith. If things didn't work out with Nicole, April might be a great second choice, husband or not. A married woman might even be preferable.

SEVENTEEN

Cantering out of the oak-shaded woods, Injun vaulted a small gurgling brook. Clutching his mane for support, Ashley squeezed with her knees as they bounded over two downed trees, with just two strides in between. Breathing hard, her heart pounding on pace with his flying hooves, they charged a moss-covered stone wall, looming thirty feet ahead. The powerful chestnut gelding took it cleanly, before heading out into an open meadow.

C'est bon.

Shaking her head like a dog fresh from the lake, Ashley blinked, twisting to look back. The practice ring slid into focus, the sweet pine-smell of the forest drifting away. Slowing Injun, she saw the training jumps ... the last a wall, and before that the white wooden rails of a two stride in-and-out, preceded by a four-foot oxer.

Those, and the six other jumps she set up had again been mystically transformed into this strange reoccurring vision, sweeping over her more and more frequently whenever she attacked a course. And there was French, cheering in her head.

This whole experience was terrifyingly insane, but as she began reluctantly releasing herself to it, also wonderfully exhilarating. She was usually conservative ... square, her friends would say ... but this bizarre illusion charged her with passionate recklessness. She was riding and jumping far better than she should expect, unable to harness a wild aggressiveness ... nor the gleeful French voice, chortling in her head. It was totally weird and almost sensually stimulating.

A 3rd Time to Die

She told no one because there wasn't a rational way of describing this apparently psychotic thing she called *The Metamorphoses*. Even more inexplicable, she always sensed another rider, following close behind her.

Exiting the ring, she dismounted on shaky legs, hugging the big horse, rubbing her face against his sweat-dampened neck. Tossing his head, he lifted her off the ground.

She giggled. They were becoming a formidable team. She glanced at the bleachers, then along the ring's white railing, but *he* wasn't there.

Who was that guy ... and why should she even care? Because he tossed out some good, last-minute advice? Or because he was so strangely alluring? Those bottomless dark eyes and quirky, thin-lipped smile peeked into her mind. She shrugged, shaking her head.

Quit it. You're a married woman. She turned to Injun, scratching behind his ears.

"I wonder if you see those fences as strangely as I do?" He nudged at the pocket of her vest, pulling at it with his teeth.

"Okay. Okay. You're as impatient as a little kid." She snickered, fishing out a carrot.

"You're a great guy, Injun, but what's life coming to when a horse is my best friend. I *do* love you, baby, but it just doesn't seem right."

Best friend? That slot should be reserved for a husband, but were they *ever* really friends? There should be more, with two children and another on the way. His family's company is facing a crisis, and that might be reason enough to be moody.

It's her job to comfort and support him, but he's never around and is withdrawn when he is. When was the last time they had sex? She patted her belly. Nearly four months ago, that's when.

She was isolated and alone, except for her two (and a third) children ... and Injun. Thank god for that horse. She hadn't been so lonely since their break-up in high school. Why did she ever let him back in her life after what he tried to do to her? Absently currying Injun's coat, thoughts again drifted to that turbid time.

Keith had beaten his head against the wall of silence she erected between them before moving on to greener pastures: Judy Winters, a girl of low morals. Keith was certainly not her first.

Ashley began dating Allen Clarke, a boy totally different from Keith. He *respected* her. They made out plenty, and she even allowed some light petting, but he always stopped whenever she made it plain he'd gone far enough.

She was doing more horseback riding, wanting to improve her jumping, and Papa hired a trainer.

She stepped back, dropping the currycomb, her fingers pressed against her lips.

Jeez, that's when this started. The sense of riding through woods, and whispered thoughts in French. Nothing as intense as now. Why did the fantasy only haunt her when jumping a horse?

Shrugging, she retrieved her brush, continuing to comb Injun's coat, a smile tickling her lips. She'd felt comfortable with Allen, a steady ship who'd stand firm against any waves of adversity. Was that part of her problem? Character, integrity, honesty ... things all girls sought, and *all* apparently missing in Keith ... had no magic for her.

How shallow. But, Allen lacked the aura of destiny that still cloaked that hateful bastard ... the guy who tried to *rape* her.

How could she long for him, after that?

EIGHTEEN

Keith slipped through the etched glass doors into the aerobics room, surprised at how many men, clad in shorts and tank tops, milled around the floor.

Working his way toward the mirrored front wall, he noticed only a few women, mostly young and fit looking. Probably not there for the same reasons as the guys. None among them fit Nicole's description.

"Aha. New blood to liven our afternoon."

The liquid melody of the voice fired delicious tremors down his spine. He turned, unconsciously holding his breath. It escaped in a quiet sigh as he saw her.

Nicole Phillips, an incredible 5'10" Amazon, blue-nailed fingers nestling on curvaceous hips, smiling mischievously. Despite the overheard ravings, he was totally unprepared for the beauty in front of him. Midnight black hair poured around an alabaster face, caressing the high cheekbones before tumbling over broad shoulders, ending a third of the way down her back.

Sheathed in a ruby, skin-tight leotard, décolleté and cut high at the thighs, the outfit emphasized a tiny waist and firm breasts, accenting two long, muscled, yet feminine legs. Almond-shaped emerald eyes, snuggled below lustrous arched eyebrows, regarded him merrily.

"Well, a new guy, here for my class." Her wide pink, full-lipped mouth was a siren's call. He struggled to reclaim his voice.

"Yeah. Your class. That's why I'm here." God, he sounded like an idiot.

"Good. Always room for one more. What's your name?"

"Easton. Keith Easton." He took a breath, back in control

except for the cacophony of his heart.

"You done this before, Keith? You look pretty fit, but I can take it easy today, if you're a first-timer."

"No, I'm used to a good workout." He was a jock and played racquet ball twice a week. How hard could it be?

"I was at another gym," he lied. "My favorite instructor moved to California, and no one else ran a good class. I heard North Loop was good, with more racquetball courts, so I decided to give it a try."

"Great. I play racquetball, too. Maybe we'll have a game sometime, but be warned, I'm pretty good."

He grinned, not knowing what to say. She spun on the ball of one foot, quickly surveying the room.

"Time to get going. Everyone find a spot. Here we go." She hit a button on her tape player, filling the room with the beat of a popular hit song.

"We'll begin by warming up and stretching." She faced the mirror, calling out cadence.

Keith watched, spellbound, as she moved from one routine to the next. She was a consummate professional, observing the class in the mirror, encouraging or correcting people as they progressed.

What did he expect, a dumb bimbo? She was the most exciting woman he'd ever seen, understanding April's resignation to second billing. Ashley, while striking, never looked like *this*, even at her best.

His eyes feasted on the lithe, athletic grace of the dark-haired beauty. He had to have her ... knew he was *destined* to have her.

NINETEEN

Ashley hugged the big red horse's smoothly muscled neck, laying her head against the silkiness of his flowing mane. He nickered, nuzzling her thigh. Sighing, still struggling to understand life. Had she done something to drive a wedge between them?

Memories of that last picnic with Allen reeled through her mind ...

She had discovered a secluded little meadow while horseback riding at the Skokie Lagoons. It was shaded by old oaks and maples, hidden, set well back from the path.

Irresistibly drawn to this out-of-the-way place, it reminded her of that magical glade she imagined when she made out with Keith.

Everything was perfectly arranged, just like before.

Before? She lifted her head. *I'd never picnicked in a place like that, so why was it so familiar? My favorite little fantasy? Maybe.*

She was so hyper, spreading the Navajo blanket just so, and arranging their sandwiches and iced-tea perfectly. She even smuggled out a bottle of white wine and two long-stemmed glasses. Everything had to be just right, this time.

This time? She hadn't really thought about it then, but it was as if she were on a mission. *This time?* But that was their first picnic.

It was also her first experience with *The Terror.*

Their bodies intertwined, kissing, slowly descending into delicious arousal, for the first time she allowed him to roam below the waist. He drew her to him, his hardness pressed against damp panties, her body resonating, opening like petals of a flower.

Wonderfully afire, Ashley didn't resist as he tentatively exposed one lovely breast, his tongue working a sensual little dance around her fully erect nipple. She moaned softly, searching for her vision—the place that always came to her in moments like this.

But this place *was* the fantasy. Had she known it all along? She was lost in the wonderful delirium of arousal.

TWENTY

Keith sagged against the wall, clutching a ballet bar, struggling for breath, his trembling legs barely supporting him. He managed to keep up for the entire hour, mostly through sheer willpower and an ego unwilling to let Nicole see him falter. He was no longer able to disguise his exhaustion at the end, but didn't care anymore.

He watched patiently, panting softly, waiting for his strength to return, while she talked to several male members from her group.

"You run a Hell of a class, lady," he wheezed, when she turned, raising one inky eyebrow at his haggard-looking condition.

"Thanks. Hope this wasn't too rough on you. I normally run a more rigorous routine, but usually ease up for new members until I see what they got. You sure you've done this before?" Her green eyes twinkled laughingly at him.

"Oh, yeah." *How could anything be any tougher than this?* "I've just laid off for a few weeks, looking for another gym. I heard you were good," he surveyed her slowly, "but they were wrong."

Obsidian eyebrows arched, wrinkling the smooth skin of her forehead, but he plunged on before she could speak. "You're better than good. You're terrific."

"Why thank you, kind sir." She laughed and made a little bow, openly displaying her considerable cleavage. Despite his exhaustion, he developed a terrific hard-on ... not something easily hidden in tight workout shorts. She probably noticed, but he didn't care. She was certainly used to being lusted over. He screwed up his courage, and charged on.

"Since you're done for the evening, can a new student be impudent enough to invite you for a cup of coffee or a drink?"

"Sorry. I'm busy tonight. I run two more classes tomorrow. Why don't you join us?" She smiled coyly. "I may be free afterwards."

I'll be lucky if I can walk tomorrow. He shouldn't seem too eager, and there was no actual promise she'd go out with him.

"Nope. Can't make it tomorrow. Busy. Maybe on Wednesday."

"No, that's my day off. My next class is Thursday, but Shelly Quintana runs a great class on Wednesday, if that's more convenient for you."

"Thursday is probably better for me." That would give him an extra day to recover, and he was going to need it.

"I really want to get back in shape after this little lay-off I've had."

While he was impatient to see her again, it would be a tactical error to come tomorrow, even if he were able. He was going to be very sore and stiff, and he wanted to play it slowly and keep her guessing.

This gal was used to men falling all over themselves around her. He would have to seem different, if he were to have any chance.

TWENTY-ONE

Ashley shivered, casting away the memory of that picnic, turning to Injun, caressing his neck. Gathering her currying tools, she returned them to the stall's pine tack box.

That was the first time. Allen got a lot farther with respect and tenderness than Keith ever had with arrogance and force. I was hovering on the very brink of ecstasy, and then there it was—the Terror.

She recalled gasping for breath, her eyes wide, head whipping to and fro, frantically searching the near-by woods. Something had changed. Slashed by a sudden sword of fear, her erotic rollercoaster evaporated. She had struggled to sit up.

Something was in the woods. A monstrous apparition swam in her head...a horned creature rushing from the trees, a fearsome beak and deadly weapon, hacking them to pieces with animal ferocity.

"*Mon dieu,*" she had wailed, leaping to her feet. "*Non! Pas encore.* Not *again.*"

A sudden noise in the near-by underbrush, a screech and loud thrashing catapulted her into action.

She chuckled mirthlessly, visualizing herself, shoes in hand, racing away as if her life depended on it.

Terrified, thinking in French again. I guess that was the beginning of The Terror. Why does it only come whenever I'm intimate? Because Keith tried to rape me?

No. It's something else. I can sense it. What's the matter with me, that I'm so petrified when making love?

Can't have been easy for Keith, especially as much as he craves sex, but I've never denied him. Somehow, I always managed to fight through The Terror.

"Life's not supposed to be so complicated," she muttered.

TWENTY-TWO

Ashley blinked, jerking reflexively at the gentle head-butt Injun delivered, snatching her away from memories.

Gotta stop obsessing. Rehashing the past won't help. Keith's going through a bad time at work. I've gotta be patient with him.

The sorrel nudged her, nipping at her pocket. She laughed.

"You sure know how to my change mood, Red." She stroked his snout. "Didn't you get a carrot?" He curled his lips, nickering.

"Okay, here's the last one." She produced the treat, and it was gone in seconds. He rubbed his muzzle against her cheek.

"I love you too, buddy, but I gotta go. The kids should be home from school, and maybe Keith will make it for dinner for a change." She wrapped her arms around the big red gelding's neck, lingering there, savoring his warmth while he nuzzled her.

Sighing, she wandered from the barn, visiting a horse here, glancing at a riding magazine there, and talking to a stable hand about Injun's feed schedule. Any delay for departure home, where she found love and comfort with her children ... and empty solitude from her more and more distant husband. She shrugged. Nothing gained by more procrastination. *There must be some way to reconnect with Keith. Maybe he'll go with me to the horse season's opening Gala next week. Get away from the kids and business. We haven't gone to a dance in years.*

She had to try something before the rift became uncrossable.

That familiar-looking smiling face seeped across her mind.

Wonder if he'll be there, too? She barked a short, humorless laugh, and strode toward the gravel parking lot.

TWENTY-THREE

Nicole chuckled as she watched Keith leave the aerobics gym for the locker room. The substantial bulge in his shorts confirmed that while he might not be in the best shape, little Dickey was certainly not having any trouble standing up.

Surprisingly, her heart was doing the hula, and there was a definite wet tingling between her legs. Keith Easton held a rare and mysterious attraction for her. He was athletic, sexy, and clearly hot for her, like every other guy. Might he be Mr. Right? Finally, a big bucks stud, ready for a long-term liaison with a sensuous gal who knew *exactly* how to make him happy?

She had searched for that perfect guy for years, discarding several candidates along the way, mostly older, who had only filled her financial needs. How special if the handsome Mr. Easton were *it*, someone who might actually excite *her* while she was driving him wild.

A strange premonition assaulted her. Something other than luck had brought them together. She was filled with eager anticipation.

That evening she looked at his membership application as she listened to April chatter happily about what a sweet gentleman Easton was. That the lovely blonde was taken with him, as apparently he was with her was no real surprise. Nicole was one of the few women on Earth who could out-shine April.

His come-on to the blonde verified what Nicole had guessed: Keith Easton was actively on the prowl. If she didn't snare him, April might, and he'd be damned lucky to have her.

Nicole knew April had been divorced for two years, continuing to wear the gold band to keep unwelcome suitors away. It sounded like Keith Easton had already graduated out of that group ... married or not.

Under the disapproving stare of the blue-eyed blonde, Nicole photocopied Easton's application before leaving for home. A quick call that evening to one of her admirers at a downtown P.R. firm, and she discovered he was Vice-president of Operations at his family business, a medium size manufacturer of small appliances.

He was married to the daughter of one of Chicago's wealthiest families, whose early and very violent deaths had left huge trusts for their only daughter and her children. Besides his own wealth, Keith had access to all the income from those trusts, reputed to be several hundred thousand dollars a year.

Finally, the brass ring she'd been patiently seeking. She wasn't about to let it slip away.

All the more exciting if she played him slowly, like a big bass on a very light line. Her pop had taught her to fish, and catching a man was very little different.

All you needed was the right bait, properly presented ... and patience.

TWENTY-FOUR

Ashley smiled as she pulled her silver Lexus SUV into the circular ocher brick drive of their sprawling ranch house, nestled on a prime half-acre lot in western Winnetka. She loved the warmth of the broken stone façade and black slate entry. The double, eight-foot paneled Brazilian cherry doors were the perfect accent.

Entering from the garage, she was met by a flurry of arms and legs, as her two children swarmed over her.

"Mommy, look what I made you in school." Four-year-old Beth pressed a crayon drawing into her hand. Ricky stood by, grinning.

"Let's see what you drew, sweetie. Oh, is that mommy?"

"Yes." She beamed, puffing out her chest. "That's you, riding Injun. See, you're gonna jump over that wall. Do you like it?"

"I *love* it, Beth. I'm going to hang it right on the fridge, where I can look at it every day."

"That's really pretty, sis," Ricky said. "When I was in pre-K, most kids could only draw stick figures." He hugged his little sister. Ashley took them in her arms, planting kisses on their heads.

This is love. Why is it so difficult for Keith? She ruffled Ricky's fiery red hair.

"And how was your day? Anything exciting in First Grade?"

"We got a new book," holding it up for her to see. These kids are doing so many things earlier than she did at their age.

"Can I read it to you?" he asked.

"Of course. Let's get comfortable in the den." Settling on the beige leather sofa, her arm around him, snuggling close, he opened his book. Beth stretched out, her blonde head in her mom's lap.

"I like Injun's smell on you, Mommy. When can I learn to ride?"

"Soon, sweetie. You can both come to the stable in the summer."

Why wasn't Keith there to share her pleasure in seeing their children grow and mature? She shook her head, banishing doubts and irritations. *It's her time to enjoy, even if she did it alone.*

A smile bloomed as Ricky began reading a Twenty-First Century version of *See Jane Run*. *He'd really gotten quite good.*

She checked her watch. Five-Ten.

Dinner is at Six-Thirty. Keith promised to be there.

That'd be a nice change.

TWENTY-FIVE

Another promise broken.

Ashley sat alone at the Gold granite-top bar in the den, nursing her second glass of Chilean Merlot. *What was so important at work to keep him so late, three or four nights a week? Was something else going on? That doesn't make sense. He has everything any guy should want right here. She never denied him anything. Could he ....*

She stirred at the sound of the garage door opening. *Home at last.* She rose to meet him at the door.

"Hi, babe." He pecked her on the cheek, setting his briefcase on the kitchen table.

"It's Nine-Thirty."

"You didn't wait dinner, did you?"

"Keith!"

"I know it's late, but I got tied up at the office."

"Oh, come on. What's going on? I can't believe ...."

"Listen, there's *nothing* going on but work. The team's in trouble and I'm trying to find a game plan to fix it. The evening is the only quiet time I get. It's already late in the fourth quarter.

I can't just let a three generation business go down without a fight, can I?"

"You and your sports jargon. Everything is not a football game, Keith. Are things really that bad?"

"Yeah, they are. We're playing in a tough league. Okay?"

"I'm sorry." She took his hands. "Just ... well, we expected you for dinner. Beth drew a lovely picture at school, and Ricky's reading a new book. They miss you ... miss you sharing their excitement. These years will fly by, and you're losing out as much as they are. They *need* a father, Keith."

"I know, but I can't just sit on the sidelines and let the company fall apart. Show me Beth's drawing, and you can fix me a little snack. I didn't have much time for dinner."

Keith munched on a cold turkey sandwich, while he examined Beth's crayon drawing.

Ashley, jumping that damned horse. Why should I be surprised? I aughta be around more, so they'd be interested in some of my things. Smooth things out around here.

But I gotta find a way to avoid that horsey party next week. A bunch of fucking dilettantes, I bet. She can go to that one alone, if it's so important to her.

Screw it. He was a stranger in this house, with little in common with his teammates. It was Kristen filling his needs that evening ... and Nicole feeding his fantasy.

What an angel. He was awash with a sense of destiny since he first saw that magnificent Amazon. She *was* going to be his ... be what Ashley never was. She'd have to understand about the trusts. No way would he leave his wife and all that money, especially with the family business looking so iffy. He'd have to make it worth her while to hang around until ... until what?

Eventually, he'd have to do something about Ashley and her trusts. Let her mess around with her damn horse while he seduced Nicole. That may take time, but he can pull it off, and that should be fun.

But Keith had no idea what really was in store for him.

TWENTY-SIX

Ashley rolled over, turning away from Keith's gentle snoring. She couldn't sleep, her musing stuck in an endless loop.

Why does Keith work so late, almost every night?

Why is he so distant, so emotionally uninvolved with his family?

Why don't they have sex (much less, make *love*) anymore. Is she so unappealing?

Why did he bother worming his way back into her life, after their bitter breakup?

Why, why, why? Seemed her life was filled with "whys."

And most importantly, why did she let him back in, when he had tried to *rape* her. Memories, etched as clearly as a HD projection, bloomed in her mind: Keith, fifteen years ago, sitting in the stands with her parents during the Onwentsia Spring Novice Open Jumper Class, her first competition of the year.

He smiled tentatively, looking very uncomfortable, and gave her the thumbs-up sign just as she began her round.

As she started for the first fence, strange thoughts had floated into her head ...

These are nothing. I've jumped worse with my eyes closed. Allez.

Thinking in French. Imagining what it might be like on a fox hunt. It seemed so effortless, as if she had done it all her life.

Like now. It tasted more like a memory than a fantasy, even

then.

She had handed Lady to a groom and climbed into the stands, knowing *he* would still be there ....

~~*~~*~~*~~

They sat together, all three smiling ... one big happy family.

What nerve, coming here, joining my folks, cheering my ride, as if nothing terrible happened.

Despite her righteous anger, her skin tingled and her heart was skipping.

Damn, you're still in love with that unprincipled bastard, regardless of everything. Like star-crossed lovers in a stupid romance novel.

He stood as she approached, grinning foolishly.

"That was a wonderful ride, sweetheart," Mama said. She had been an experienced rider in her youth and fully appreciated her daughter's skill. No one expected her to excel so quickly.

"There's only two more riders to go," her father said. "You might win a ribbon today."

"Ashley does well at whatever she tries," Keith said, trying to be part of the group. But he looked away and studiously avoided her eyes.

"It was fun, despite being pretty nervous at first. But, Lady did all the work, and I just tagged along for the ride. It seemed easy."

"It's sweet to be so modest, my dear," Mama said, "but I, at least, know that there is a lot more to jumping a horse than just sitting in the saddle. The two of you are developing the synergism of a good team. I'm proud of you."

"Me too," Keith braved her smoky eyes for the first time. "I think you're terrific, Ashley. Really terrific."

That's when the last nub of ice from her long-harbored anger melted. She'd give him another chance, if he showed her respect.

[85]

A 3rd Time to Die

~~*~~*~~*~~

Her restless turning interrupted the pattern of Keith's snoring, and the room was quiet. Maybe she could sleep now, if she can just shake those haunting memories. He'd hurt her terribly that bitter night, but she could never shake that strange sense of destiny fluttered around her. Despite all that happened, she was still drawn to him.

She made it clear they were starting over, like a first date. He agreed with an exuberance that made her feel special. Everything seemed back on a blissful path, and their love rebloomed like a delicate flower, nurtured into an growing, beautiful thing.

She sighed. That was the happiest time of her life.

They attended Northwestern to be together, despite her parents' plans for Vassar and his for Harvard. Keith played football, and she was, again, a cheerleader. Four years later, they graduated, he as an All-American wide receiver his final two years (despite the school's chronically pathetic football program) and she with suma cum laude honors in American History.

They married the next summer, the Crown Prince and Princess of two influential North Shore dynasties, the perfect couple.

But things weren't perfect, were they? Oughta be more to marriage than this. We have no partnership in anything anymore.

Oh, cut it out.

I've got two great kids and another little girl on the way, so I guess I've got nothing to complain about. Time to quit feeling sorry for myself and get on with life. This is just a rough spot, and we'll work through it.

But in her heart, as she finally drifted into a restless sleep, she wondered.

And with good reason.

TWENTY-SEVEN

"Keith?"

"I'm in the study."

Ashley's snakeskin high heel pumps rat-tat-tatted down the Travertine hallway. She carried a matching evening clutch and wore an ivory St. John sequined strapless sheath, ending just above the knees. She was surprised it still fit, but the growing infant hadn't made its presence visible yet.

Swinging open the already ajar door, she found Keith in khaki shorts and gray knit shirt, lounging at the desk.

"My god, you're not dressed yet. We're going to be late for the party."

"I'm not going. I gotta finish this budget for the new ball park. Maybe you shouldn't go, either. Weather Station says a big storm front's gonna blast through early this evening."

"Keith!"

"Look, if you're fixed on going, go, and have a good time. You look really beautiful. You know I got nothing in common with all those horse-lovers. I'd be in the way of all your fun. And I gotta get this done for the Board meeting on Monday."

"But ... but I hoped this would give us a chance ...."

"Sorry, I can't do it. Enjoy yourself. You won't even miss me, with all your new friends to talk horses with." His attempted smile was more a smirk.

Ashley glared at her husband, slouched in his black leather executive chair, twirling a wood pencil between his fingers, a picture of nonchalance.

The same old crap, she thought. *This could be a chance to reconnect, but no. Not even a meager attempt to seem interested in my things.*

"Okay, I damned well *will* go alone. Not so different from the rest of our lives, is it? No need to bother your head about anything. The kids' dinners are made, and I've given Maria instructions on bedtime tonight. There's a Disney movie on TV they want to watch, which I've agreed to, since tomorrow's Sunday."

"Yeah, whatever." His attention was on a stack of papers scattered across the home office's desk.

Jesus. He can't even feign interest in his own children. Spinning on a three-inch heel, she stalked off, gathering her matching St. John evening jacket, heading for the kitchen with last-minute instructions for Maria.

Keith followed her departure with hooded cobalt eyes, the corner of his wide mouth twitching up.

That worked out better than I hoped. Ashley and the goddamned horses are a pain, but this gives me a couple hours to zip down and see Kristen. Maybe the last time, if I can ever make it with Nicole.

His grin broadened at the reverberating thump of the garage door slamming.

TWENTY-EIGHT

Craig pulled his Jag into line, behind four cars from the entrance of the Renaissance Hotel, awaiting the valets to clear the cars in front. A tropical-style monsoon pummeled his convertible with watery fists, but nothing crept past the canvas top. Looked like a good turnout for the season's first Gala, despite rotten weather.

Finally under the protection of the portico, he retrieved his jacket from the passenger seat and handed the keys to the liveried young valet. Craig was wearing a midnight-blue tux over a white, collarless pleated shirt, avoiding the hassle of a bow tie. A robin-egg-blue cummerbund and onyx studs completed the outfit.

Every serious equestrian on the North Shore would be there ... including Ashley Easton? He intended to look the part of muted success, both in business and as a horseman. A position he was quite qualified to represent.

He followed two couples through the revolving doors and into the upscale hotel. Owning and training dressage horses or jumpers takes more resources than the average Joe can swing, but Craig was always pleasantly surprised at the general lack of snobbery from the horsy set. With few exceptions they were a friendly bunch of people, sharing a common love. He was not at all uncomfortable over being there alone. Crossing to the elevators, he joined six others for the ride to the fourth floor, and the Grand Ballroom, where the Gala was already underway.

He gritted his teeth and shrugged. No surprise Toni hadn't showed up for their departure. Probably better she didn't come. She'd get sloshed on vodka, and he'd probably have to pry her off some attractive single guy ... or maybe even a married one.

He didn't need the distraction. He was looking for new blood for his fox hunt later in the summer ... and he hoped to meet Ashley and learn from where he knew her. He just couldn't place it, but it was so damned unlikely not to remember running into someone so attractive ... and such a fearless rider.

Craig took a glass of merlot and three baby lamb chops from passing trays. He eased against a door jamb, and sipping and munching, cased the room.

[89]

No Ashley, but he saw four likely candidates for his hunt. Dropping the rib bones in a trash bin, he sauntered across the room, preparing his pitch. Still thirty-minutes to dinner, so maybe she'd still show.

Craig didn't know *why* meeting her was so consuming. Although she was a stunner, he wasn't seeking an illicit affair. Cheating was Toni's bailiwick, and he wasn't going to sink into that morass. There was some other connection he couldn't explain, but the need ... the absolute compulsion ... was there.

Well, if not tonight, maybe at another competition. She's certainly going to show that big sorrel gelding again soon. What a team.

"Hey, Timmy," he said dropping a hand on the shoulder of the thirty-something man.

"Oh, hi, Craig. Here alone?" He looked disappointed.

"What else?" Craig's dark eyebrow arched, taking a fresh look at the younger man as they shook hands.

"Listen, I want to invite you guys to my fox hunt this summer ...."

TWENTY-NINE

Ashley craned forward, squinting through the waterfall cascading across her windshield. This part of Old Willow Road was poorly lit and the tropical-style deluge made visibility almost nonexistent. Her headlights barely made out the blacktop road against the rain-darkened shoulder.

Damn. Gonna be late unless this cloudburst lets up pretty soon.

Once on the Reagan Tollway, with lots of lighting and modern drainage, she'd be okay, but she has to get there alive first, and ....

Whoa. A swale in the road had filled with water, creating a small, shallow lake. Her SUV blasted a shower of spray as she reflexively stomped on the brakes ... not the best where a thick sheet of water ensconced the pavement.

The Lexus's wheels, no longer contacting hard surfaces, locked, hydroplaning across the puddle, spinning, slewing crosswise across the shoulder. Shuddering to a final stop, the SUV rocked and teetered, one rear wheel suspended over the drainage ditch ... now filled with a two-foot deep rushing torrent. Luckily, there was no impact severe enough to deploy airbags.

"Crap, that was close," she muttered, swallowing her heart. She sat, knuckles white on the steering wheel, shaking and covered with a sheen of adrenaline-fueled sweat.

Nudging the accelerator, she found the engine dead. Shifting into Park, foot on the brake (and parking brake set for safety), she punched the Ignition button, eliciting a momentary clatter, then the strong whir of the starter and ... nothing. Three more protracted efforts to restart proved equally frustrating.

Ashley slumped against the wheel, unsure what to do next. Had the engine gotten wet in that fountain of spray? She wasn't about to drown out there, peeking under the hood, without the slightest idea what to look for.

Damn Keith. He knew cars and could undoubtedly fix this ... if he were only here. But he's never interested in doing any of *her* things.

She sighed, and then lit up the emergency flasher lights, in case someone came along to help. If it were wet plugs or something, maybe they'd dry out in a few minutes.

A 3rd Time to Die

I'm going to the party tonight, come hell or, literally, high water.

Ashley grinned despite her angst, and then shuddered as the car quivered. Water rushing along that drainage-ditch was buffeting her left rear tire, partially drooping into the culvert.

Girding up courage, she clambered ... the form-fitting St. John sheath hiking up to her waist ... over the center console and into the passenger seat, which was closer to the road. Despite the deluge, she would be out the door the instant she felt her Lexus being sucked into that rushing cascade. Wet was better than drowning in the ditch. She pawed through her purse for her cell phone. Flipping it open, she groaned.

Only one bar. Lousy reception out here.

Beep. Beep.

Damn. Low battery, too.

She dialed the Emergency number, but couldn't hear a ring.

"This is ... What is ... emergency." Contact, but the call was breaking up.

"My car's stalled on Old Willow Road, east of the Turnpike." She spoke slowly and loudly, hoping to overcome the bad connection. "I've slid off the shoulder and into the ditch, and it won't start. Can you send help?"

"What is ... name, and ...." Beep. She glanced at the display: *No service. Low battery.*

Shit. Hope they heard me. All I can do is wait it out.

She leaned against the door, eyes fluttering closed, trying to relax wire-taut nerves.

Mon dieu. Her head snapped up, smoky eyes flaring. *French? Now? What the hell is going on with that?*

She scanned the darkness, but saw nothing but pelting rain. She sagged back against the door, working her neck, rolling her shoulders, trying to loosen tension-cramped muscles.

What a mess. Give it a couple minutes and I'll try again.

Eyes flickered shut again. *Just relax, and stay calm.*
She sighed.

THIRTY

Craig circulated throughout the ballroom, munching baby lamb chops and coconut shrimp while sipping Merlot, as he worked the crowd. He renewed acquaintances not seen since last fall and added a half-dozen new names to his address book. He had hopefully convinced three new riders to join him on his fox hunts in September.

The one thing sorely lacking was that fascinating redheaded equestrian. He checked the attendance list, noting she'd reserved two places on the roster, but so far was a no-show. It was possible that the fierce downpour, assaulting the entire northern suburbs, had engineered her delay.

The overhead lights blinked the "dinner-bell" call, so he reluctantly headed for the dining room. He'd find a spot in easy view of the entrance, and try to hold two places at the table, in case she arrived late with whomever she was coming ... probably her husband.

Strangely, whenever he visualized her, his heart took on hummingbird wings, and his mouth went Sahara dry. She was a classic beauty, but it was the recklessness with which she and that great roan gelding soared over the course, gobbling up every fence in sight that snatched the breath from his lungs. The sense he knew her from somewhere must be fallacious. How could he forget such a magnificent dynamic pair?

Craig settled at a table near the entrance and surveyed the room. The Northern Illinois Horseman's Committee and the hotel's staff had done a superb job setting up the evening's theme.

Two full-size artificial Thoroughbreds, regaled in jumping paraphernalia, guarded the main doorway. The salad buffet was constructed from single-bar jumps, festooned with miniature English saddles, bridles and stirrups. Crops, blue and red ribbons, and riding caps adorned black-draped dining tables as center pieces, and a rainbow of banners spewed from the chandelier to all corners of the room.

A two-foot sterling silver urn ... the Horse Person of the Year trophy ... rested on a table at the very center of the room. All in all, a very "horsey" impression.

He eased back on the upholstered chair, glancing around the dance floor. Toni, unsurprisingly, never showed up. They used to tear up a dance floor in their early years, but she had little interest in anything horsey.

Several single gals might enjoy a dance, and two who might seek a more intimate kind of boogie in an upstairs suite ... an offer he'd politely turn down. Despite frequent temptations, he never descended to Toni's tawdry level.

Craig was jarred from his thoughts by a group circling the table.

"May we join you?"

A spare, straight-backed man, probably late sixties, rested a hand on the back of the next chair. His graying temples and aquiline nose were the picture of an aristocratic horseman.

"Sure," Craig said, rising. "I'm just saving two seats for friends who got waylaid by the storm."

"That should work. We're only five." He proffered a hand. "I'm Marlon Baines, and my wife, Buffy."

He turned, gesturing to a shorter, blonde, hard-muscled man, twenty years his junior.

"This is Avery DeMond, and his wife, Catherine. And their lovely daughter, Leslie."

"I'm Craig Thornton." He shook hands with the men. "You new to our Illinois horse scene? I thought I knew pretty much everyone."

Catherine bore a strong resemblance to the elder man ... surely his daughter. Ergo, the tall, slim, and very pretty blonde Leslie, probably early twenties, was the grand-daughter. Another family look-alike.

"Yes. We've purchased Leslie a new hunter, and we thought we'd experiment with some open classes, as well. He seems an eager jumper. This area appeared a likely spot to get her first taste of competition. Get our feet wet, you know."

"Well, today is a perfect day for that," Craig said. They chuckled, settling into the chairs to his left, with Leslie conveniently parked next to him. Her smile was saucy and inviting.

"Are you alone, Craig?" She leaned suggestively closer.

"Yeah. My wife had other plans tonight, and I wouldn't miss this bash." The up-turned corners of the girl's mouth twisted down. She shrugged, straightening in her chair. He grinned.

"At least I may have a dance partner. Gets pretty boring, sitting around while the rest of the crowd is cutting a rug, don't ya think." Her smile returned from a threatened sunset.

"Yes, that's sweet of you. I love to dance. It's just a different kind of ride." She winked.

Oh boy. I wonder what kinda ride she means. Not tonight, not with me, sweetheart.

He glanced at the entryway, wondering again, what happened to Ashley Easton.

THIRTY-ONE

Ashley jerked erect as the flare of headlights slashed across her closed eyelids.

"Finally," she muttered. Reaching over, she flashed her headlights three times and glanced at her watch.

Jesus, I actually slept for fifteen minutes. How do you do that in a situation like this? I guess my 911 call got through.

Through the deluge, now faded to a steady rain, she watched the vehicle slow, pulling alongside. A pick-up truck? Clearly not an emergency vehicle. A tall, bulky figure, swaddled in rain gear, exited the truck and stood, hands on hips, surveying her predicament.

Icy fingers tripped down Ashley's back, raising the fine auburn hairs on her neck.

Out here alone in the boonies, with a strange guy stopping. I need help, but what if ... I'm a sitting duck, if this guy is a psycho. Damn, I wish Keith were here.

Or maybe that strangely alluring guy who watched her competitions. Somehow she was sure *he'd* protect her.

Her hand scrabbled under the seat, coming out with the steering wheel anti-theft bar ... a good, hefty weapon, should she need one.

She flinched when the figure loomed suddenly outside her window.

"Ya got a problem, don't ya, lady?"

She squinted through rain-streaked glass at a chubby-cheeked, dark-haired woman, looking not at all threatening. Ashley couldn't see if her bulk were fat or muscle, but regardless, she shivered, with no one there to protect her. Psychos come in all shapes and sizes.

"Yeah, I hit a puddle and spun out, and now it won't start." She hadn't the courage yet to open the window or unlock the doors. Woman or not, the tingle of danger trickled across her spine. Something looked ominous, with her bulky shape, dreary sky and a lonely road.

"So I see," her Angel of Mercy (or minion of Death?) said. "Lemme see if I can get a chain on the front and pull ya away from that ditch. Then we'll try and get her started. You stay put fer now, 'cause any movin' around might tip her into the ditch."

Ashley hunkered against the door, with a firm grip on the heavy anti-theft bar resting in her lap. She was uncertain what to do next, but it seemed safest to stay in her seat for the moment, ready to bail should the car slip back into the still rushing sluiceway.

The woman reappeared, trudging across the roadway, dragging a heavy chain. She carried a large, ominous looking tool in her other hand. Ashley had a finger-numbing grip on her "weapon," her breath coming in short gasps.

Dreams, barely remembered, inched into her thoughts: a meadow, a winding brook, passion ... and deadly, unseen danger.

That place I'd envision in the beginning, when we were getting passionate? Why now?

Merde. French? Now, when she's in trouble? Was this all connected with ...?

Ashley flinched as piercing bright lights swept across her. She blinked, squinting through the glare. Another vehicle arriving.

Oh, thank God. A tow truck. Her 911 call must have gotten through. The driver, encased in a yellow slicker, clambered down and was soon in conversation with the other woman. After a moment, the latter gathered her chain and slogged back to her pick-up. A minute later she was gone.

[97]

A 3rd Time to Die

Pent up breath Ashley didn't know she'd been holding hissed out between unclenching teeth as the emergency vehicle driver arrived at her door. Ashley cracked her window open, quickly explaining what had occurred.

"I can give ya a tow back to town," said the beefy, middle-aged man. His heavily lined face sported a graying moustache below a thin-lipped mouth and dull brown eyes. "But why don't you see if she'll start now."

"Is it okay to move? The car could slip into the ditch if I..."

"It looks safe. I'll sit on the bumper to stabilize her ... give ya some support."

As he squatted on the front of the SUV, she felt the rear tilt up out of the culvert. Shrugging, she hiked up her form-fitting dress and again clambered over the center console, settling in the driver's seat. Planting a foot on the brake pedal, she pressed the keyless ignition button, lurching at the instant roar of the V-6 engine.

Oh, thank God. She released the parking brake and flipped the shifter into Drive, easing down on the accelerator.

"Hey, hang on there. I'm still out her, ya know." As the driver scrambled away from the front of the vehicle, the rear tires settled back into the culvert, drawing the SUV backward, toward the still racing, temporary torrent. She gunned the engine, setting the front wheels spinning, but the thing kept edging in the wrong direction.

"Shit." Wild-eyed, she saw the man jog alongside and drape himself across her hood.

"Ease off the gas and hit the brakes," he yelled. "Yer spinning out and losing traction."

Barely in control of her panic, she shifted into Neutral, and reset the parking brake. Their retreat into watery oblivion paused, but she could now sense water buffeting the rear wheels.

"This is getting kinda dicey," he shouted, "but I think yer stable now. You just hang onto those brakes, and I'm gonna get my rig back here and hook ya up."

You shoulda done that first, goddammit.

She shivered, her left leg shaking as it clamped down on the brake pedal, her hands white-knuckled on the wheel. The other foot kept light pressure on the accelerator, keeping the engine revving. She didn't want it quitting, now that she had it fired up again.

What a mess. Mascara stained rivulets trickled across the round hills of her cheeks. *Will I ever make it to the party?*

This compulsion to go was so unlike her, but somehow she knew she *needed* to be there. An image of a dark-eyed, curly-headed face flickered across her mind. She shook her head.

I don't even know who he is.

Glancing up, the man had arrived, dragging the tow cradle. He disappeared below the hood, and she sensed, more than felt, the rattle of metal to metal. A moment later, he popped up, the yellow slicker splattered with mud.

"Messy." He spit, and wiped the back of a hairy hand across his lips. "When the cable comes tight, ease offa those brakes and try a light acceleration." She nodded a he ran to his truck, activating the pick-up lever. The rain had moved off, but thick steel-wool clouds still hovered just above treetop.

The braided steel cable arced up from the muddy bank, causing the Lexus to tremble. Her left foot released the Parking Brake, then switching feet to maintain pressure on the foot brake, she shifted out of Park. The vehicle shuddered, inching forward as she fed gas to the engine.

"Easy on the gas, until you're clear of the soft mud," he yelled. She softened her strangle hold on the steering wheel, flexing fingers, trying to return circulation. Two minutes later she was on the gravel shoulder, moving under the SUV's own power.

Shivering, tiny faucets opened from her eyes, heaving and shaking with the uncontrolled release of tension. By the time her rescuer unhooked his cable and squared away his truck, Ashley was back in control, the tears having gone underground.

She shimmied her dress, bunched almost to her hips, back in place, dried her eyes, and fished in her purse for her repair kit. She must look a fright. The driver again materialized at her window.

"Okay, yer good to go. Don't look like ya did any damage. Ya need anything else?"

"No, thanks. I appreciate your help." She sighed, slipping her purse into her lap. "What do I owe you?"

"Fifty bucks'll do it. Crummy night, crawling 'round in the mud."

"I'll say. Here," she passed him a hundred dollars. "Keep the change. I'm just glad you came along. I didn't know if I could trust that woman."

"Who? Mattie? She owns a diner up the road a bit. A good soul. Thanks for this." He waved the bill, and then hurried back to his truck. It had started to drizzle again.

Ashley glanced at her watch. Golly, 7:30. They're probably sitting down for dinner. Only twenty-minutes away. If she hurried, she could still have an evening.

Ten-minutes later she was heading south on the Reagan Tollway. Traffic was light and she made good time, despite the very wet road.

Wonder if I'll see him there.

Finally get a chance to meet ... learn why he's so familiar.

THIRTY-TWO

Craig struggled to keep some separation from Leslie as they glided smoothly around the dance floor. With salads finished, she rose, offering him her hand. He followed her to the crowded floor, where she appeared eager to snuggle in his arm as they awaited the tenderloin and lobster tail main course.

Craig couldn't refuse her request to dance, but was determined to refute her every attempt at something more intimate. She was an appealing girl with a willowy, athletic body, but extra-marital sex was off the table. His marriage had to be rendered absolutely dead before he'd even consider an affair, no matter how tempting.

"Looks like they're serving the meal," he said, gladly breaking away and taking her hand. "Let's get it while it's hot." As he led the reluctant blonde toward their table, there was a clatter in the hallway, a thump, and one of the padded leather doors began opening. His heart jumped to a jungle beat, and the small hairs on his neck came to attention.

Had Ashley Easton finally arrived? And why was he so obsessed by a woman he didn't know, despite a strong sense of déjà vu? Shrugging, his eyes riveted the doorway. He sighed, sagging back into his seat when a hostess hurried through, but perked up again, since she was holding the door for someone.

The new arrival stormed into the hall, and eyes flaring wide, Craig almost bit his tongue. A black-haired beauty in an erotically décolleté white silk dress ... Toni, not Ashley.

"What the Hell is she doing here?" he muttered. He came out of his chair as her azure eyes found his, blood-red lips curling into a humorless smile. She glided to his side, planting herself in front of him, arms akimbo, head tilted back, her glance raking the table before centering on him.

"Ha. The big horseman. *My* stud. You making time while the cat's away? Who's the blonde cunt? Some new ride for you, baby?"

"Toni, watch your mouth." She reeked of gin. "Don't try to measure me by your standards. Not everyone's a trollop."

"Yeah, right." She wobbled unsteadily, her eyes glazed and unfocused. Totally drunk.

"What are you doing here?" Craig asked. "You never come to anything to do with horses."

"Yeah, well, my party pooped out, so I thought I'd find my sexy husband. Aren't ya glad to see me, baby?" She staggered, sagging into his arms. He caught her, resisting the temptation to let her drop flat on her face. As much as he was often tempted, it wasn't in him to be nasty to her, regardless of her excesses.

"You're totally sloshed."

"I know." She wriggled against him, her lush body, apparently sans undergarments, tantalizing his.

"Take me home, baby," she whispered. "Take me home, and take me to heaven, like old times. I *need you*, Craig."

"Yeah, well you don't give me much of a choice. Can't let you drive like this. No knowing who you might kill on the way." She moaned softly, going completely limp against him.

Craig scooped her up, turning to his table companions, who were inhaling the scene, looking a bit dumb-struck.

"Sorry about this. Please don't take anything she said personally. She occasionally can have a drinking problem. Wish we had more time to chat. Nice to meet you, and good luck with your new horse, Leslie. Maybe I'll see you at some events."

He headed for the door, Toni nestled against him, her head on one shoulder, arms circling his neck. Her soft, gin-laden breath caressed his neck, raising small goose bumps ... and unwillingly, something else.

Damn the succubus bitch. Something sent her on a bender, and then seeking me out. Ruined the evening.

It probably didn't matter now. The redheaded Mrs. Easton apparently was a no-show, and he had no other reason to linger ... except for that delicious looking meal, going cold on his plate.

THIRTY-THREE

Despite right-turn signals flashing for a quarter-mile, Ashley had to bull her way into the right lane, barely in time to exit at Spring Road. Traffic had been creep and park for over a mile, apparently due to an accident somewhere ahead. As if she hadn't had enough delays.

They're probably half-way through dinner by now. Finally slipping onto the turn-off, she raced ahead, happy her prepaid electronic toll pass would avoid further delay. Crossing Cermak Road, and spying the Renaissance Hotel ahead, she eased tense muscles, settling back into the comfortable leather bucket seat.

At last. She hoped she wasn't too late.

Too late for what? Dinner...or meeting that strangely alluring guy.

She couldn't grasp why he seemed to matter to her. It wasn't sexual...whatever *it* was. At least she didn't think so. Besides, she's a married woman and would never cheat on Keith. But that horseman was strangely magnetic, and she was sure she must know him from somewhere.

Maybe a jumping coach? Turning into the entrance drive for the hotel, she shook her head and sighed. Whatever it was, she hoped he was there tonight. She noticed the parking lot and the valet section were overflowing, so the storm had not dissuaded many guests from attending.

She coasted to a stop opposite the valet desk, behind a red Jaguar convertible pulling out. The bass-drum echo of thunder was soon followed by heavens bid for electrical pyrotechnics, igniting the sky with jagged streaks of fire, as heavy rain drops again bombarded the area. Luckily, the large covered portico provided plenty of shelter as she stepped out of her SUV, taking a claim slip from the attendant. Draping the matching sequined short jacket over her shoulders, she hurried inside, heading for the elevators. The Gala was on the fourth floor.

As the car began its stately rise, she plucked her compact mirror from her purse, rechecking earlier repairs to her makeup. Considerable engineering was required after she was safely retrieved from near-disaster, but other than a slight puffiness under gray eyes, all looked in perfect order. The elevator lurched to a soft stop, the doors swishing open to the upper lobby.

Ashley hesitated. The room seemed vacant, but the strains of a popular melody wafted out from behind double doors, bracketed by two large, artificial stallions, regaled in full jumping gear. She hurried across as quickly as the tight dress would allow.

"So damned late," she mumbled, approaching a table with several name cards still tented on top. Searching for hers, a tall, spare woman appeared from behind a screen. Her salt-and-pepper hair was pulled into a severe bun, behind a sharp angular face.

"May I help you?"

"Yes. I'm Ashley Easton. Reservation for two, but my husband didn't make it. Last minute business." *Why should I be making excuses for him?*

"Yes, of course, Mrs. Easton. Here you are. Held up by the storm, were you?"

"You've got no idea. Am I too late?"

"No, not really. You missed some great appetizers, but they're just serving the main course, so you've got time to get caught up. Then there will be the annual awards."

"Okay. Are there table assignments?" She gathered up her printed name tag and place card.

"It's open seating, but I believe Mr. Thornton was saving two places for you and your husband."

"Mr. Thornton?"

"Yes, Craig Thornton. Unfortunately, you just missed him."

"Craig Thornton? I missed him?" *Jeez, I sound like a dumb parrot.* The woman, Carla Smyth by her name-tag, nodded.

"Carried out his thoroughly sloshed wife. An infamous trollop, she is. Can't imagine why a nice man like Craig suffers her antics. I'm surprised you didn't see him on the way out."

The maroon Jag, pulling out as I arrived. The mysterious guy from the show. Craig Thornton? And he was looking for me, too. Damn that storm. At least now I've got his name.

"I think he was just driving off." She sighed. "Thanks. I'll go in and find a seat."

"There should still be two places waiting for you. Second table to your left as you enter."

Ashley nodded, turned, and pushed through the door. She found the open seats immediately, opposite two couples and a young blonde woman. Pulling out a chair, she nodded to them.

"Hi. I'm a very tardy Ashley Easton." The two men rose, the elder moving quickly to help seat her.

"We're the Baines...Marlon and Buffy...and the DeMonds. And my granddaughter, Leslie. Delayed up by the storm?"

"Yes. In a near-accident, actually, but survived without a bump or scratch. Really nasty out there, though."

"It certainly was," Marlon Baines said, as he settled back in his chair, "but I believe it's starting to let up."

A liveried waiter appeared with a shrimp cocktail and Caesar's salad, as a second was pouring a glass of red wine. "How would you like your filet done, ma'am?"

"Medium-rare, please, and no butter on top, if you serve it that way."

"Yes, ma'am. Please take your time with the shrimp and salad. There's plenty of time to finish before we start dessert.

"Thanks, and a cup of hot tea, if possible."

"Of course." He hurried toward the kitchen.

"You're Craig Thornton's friend?" The girl, Leslie, asked.

"Casual acquaintance, actually." *And that's stretching it. Maybe a future friend, though, as he seems as interested in meeting me as I am him.* "Do you know Craig?'

"Oh, we just met." She smiled. "I thought I'd like to know him better. He's a divine dancer. Then that horrible woman, his wife, showed up, drunk as a skunk. And so foul-mouthed. A shame, 'cause he seems so nice. A real gentleman."

Nice ... and a divine dancer ... and he apparently wanted to meet me. Maybe we'll finally meet ... soon, I hope. I think I'd like having someone interested in horses I can talk with.

She attacked her shrimp, first realizing how hungry she was.

But she was totally unaware of the winds of fate, infinitely stronger than the storm she'd just braved, swirling around her.

THIRTY-FOUR

Keith arrived at the North Loop Spa early Tuesday afternoon. He'd said good-bye to Kristine for the last time Saturday evening, while Ashley was hobnobbing with her new horsey friends. He wanted to find Nicole before the class began, but the dark-haired enchantress was nowhere around.

April sat pertly behind her desk, and they had a very pleasant chat. Her warmth and intelligence only amplified her considerable beauty. It was perversely amusing... a terrific lady like April, relegated to second fiddle by the incandescence of Nicole Phillips.

Nicole arrived in the aerobics room at 3:55, erotically draped in a brief purple, backless outfit that hid nothing and displayed everything. She immediately began preparing for her class, pointedly ignoring the small covey of drooling male admirers flocking around her.

She started fast with a rigorous, high-energy routine. By Five o'clock, the only ones with gas left in their tanks besides Nicole were two women fitness instructors on busmen's holidays.

Keith slid to the floor in a quivering heap, his breath coming in scorched gasps. And he was supposed to be a jock. A very out of shape jock.

He leaned against a wall, watching her, as his heart slowly quit trying to tunnel its way through his chest. She shut down the sound system, picked up a few hand weights left scattered on the floor, and was toweling off when he finally heaved himself up onto still shaky legs. If nothing else happened here, he certainly was going to get fit again.

"That's some brutal class. You almost killed most of us, those last few minutes."

"Oh? Sorry if you think I over did it. You did say you'd been doing this at your old club, so I thought I'd do something a little challenging for you."

"Well, you more than succeeded. At the end, I thought I was about to die and wished it would happen already. You know, put me outta my misery."

She chuckled. "But, you were still on your feet at the final bell, so you managed to survive."

"Yeah, well I never quit. Not on anything. There's something I want, I go get it. Which brings me to the question of you."

"Oh?" Her smile set him afire, her malachite eyes twinkling. "I didn't realize I was a puzzle to you. I thought you were interested in April."

"She's a great gal, but it's you I'd like to know better."

She shrugged, and bent, fishing in her gym bag, every sensual curve masterfully displayed. Slithering into a warm-up jacket, she left it unzipped for his unhindered view.

Damn. Fully aroused, he managed to hide the evidence behind a bunched up towel.

"How about that drink you promised me?"

"A drink? I don't remember promising you anything. When did I say that?"

"You didn't actually *say* it. You sorta smiled it last Monday."

"Did I? Smiled it, huh?"

"Yep."

"That's a new one. But, I always keep my word ... spoken or smiled. Meet me in the lobby in ten minutes. We'll go to O'Toole's. It's just down the street. All right with you?"

"Yeah. I'll be there."

So the seduction began, impelled by forces greater than either imagined. A few hours invested in research on Google and the phone revealed to Nicole exactly who her suitor was. That he was married was no obstacle, because he was "The Brass Ring."

Nicole teased and taunted him for five dates ... until he gave her the emerald that Thursday evening, while dining together at Mon Petit. That was their first night as lovers, fatefully bound.

During the nearly two-weeks of their courtship, Nicole's

erotic teasing built sexual tension in Keith no longer relieved by Kristen. Ashley happily found herself the subject of his passion ... wonderful love-making, descending into the vision of that idyllic meadow, always tempered by the onset of that damned Terror.

She'd fight through the fear, thrilled at again being loved by her husband. Where had this been for four months, when their last brief foray into passion had come and gone so quickly, leaving her pregnant with their third child? And they had been without the most intimate act of love for years before that. What had suddenly rekindled his ardor? And will it last, this time?

Ashley was hurt and confused when those sixteen days of wonderful love-making ended abruptly, and without comment, that Thursday night when he returned after midnight, smelling faintly of jasmine. Keith rarely touched her after that, as they again drifted apart. She had only two outlets to salve bitter loneliness and rejection: her children and Injun.

Jumping and training Injun filled her free time, creating a buffer, however hollow, against a growing solitude Ricky and Beth could hardly dent. Ashley ached for real friendship, more even than passion, to bring some fullness to her life.

Were Keith and she ever really buddies? She could only remember his lust. Had she confused that iron-to-magnet pull with love? It appeared that way now.

THIRTY-FIVE

It was a good practice.

Injun was a powerful jumper and very handy, so they could take shorter routes to the fences. That saves time on the course, and time determines a champion during a jump-off, if several horses make a clean round.

Weird how much better she rode a course when she descended into that eerie world of old, towering forest, mossy walls and real log fences. Never a knock-down, and she flew around the course with blazing speed, French, spilling joyously through her head, understanding the words as if it were English.

She hadn't spoken that tongue since Junior year in high school, and then pretty poorly. Languages in general were not her favorite subjects. It was a scary, yet exhilarating experience to which she had not yet become fully adjusted.

She gathered the curry-comb and brushes, depositing them in the storage box. Taking up a pick, she lifted one of the gelding's hooves, checking for stones or debris wedged against the iron shoe. Clean. Three others examined, with only one requiring a little work.

She smiled, stroking the big horse's still damp neck. He nickered softly, rubbing his cheek against her shoulder. Sighing, giving him a strong hug, she picked up a lead chain.

Grooming him, doing his hooves, walking him off after a workout ... these were things usually done by a groom. It's what she paid for, but she enjoyed personal contact with the animal, so did it herself. It cemented the bond between them, the only man in her life who actually loved her without question.

As she started for the corral she saw him, sauntering away from the viewing stands. He was apparently watching, but she got so entangled in that strange illusion of tearing through that magnificent, pine-scented forest, she hadn't noticed. She hurried into the barn, searching for a groom.

"Jimmy. Jimmy, will you cool down Injun and put him away. See he has some extra fresh oats."

"Yes, ma'am. I'll see to everything." Good. The gelding was in capable hands.

She ran back to the show area, her gaze sweeping the small crowd of horsy people, always around. Damn, he was just there, on the other side of the ring. She strode toward the parking lot, her scuffed English riding boots throwing small clots of dirt.

There he was, heading away. She broke loose from a small gaggle of student riders and hurried after him. When he saw her approach, he slowed, hands in his pockets like a six-year-old, a small smile (or was it a smirk?) on his lips. She walked slowly up to him. Now that she'd finally found him, she had no idea what to say.

"Uh ... hi," she said at last.

Terrific. What a witty opening. Injun could've done better.

"How are you, Mrs. Easton?" Of course he knew her name. He'd saved her seats at the Gala last week, hadn't he?

"I'm fine, thanks. Going champion at the last show was really special. I ... I wanted to thank you ... you know, for your tip. It was very helpful."

"My pleasure. You have a fine horse, there." His dark, wide-set eyes, under the arcs of chocolate-brown eyebrows, were friendly and warm, and the smile was clearly friendly ... not smug.

Why did she feel so connected to this man? Horses? Somehow, it seemed deeper than that. She nodded, giving a small smile.

"Yeah. He's my best friend. And my therapist. The problems of the world seem to disappear when I'm on his back." She wouldn't tell him how literally true that was.

"I know the feeling. You're a great team. Those three rides were a bit reckless though, weren't they? Looked like you almost lost your seat that first day."

"Yeah, well something ... different ... got into me last week. It's kind of hard to explain. But, I wanted to thank you. I'd hoped to meet you at the Gala last week, but got waylaid by that fierce storm. I think I arrived just after you left. You're Craig Thornton, aren't you?"

"Oh, sorry. I should've introduced myself. I was looking forward to possibly seeing you there, too, but got called away by a ... a family emergency."

Ho. A tactful way to describe carting off a drunken wife. Leslie said he was a gentleman.

They shook hands. His was smooth and strong, with just a hint of rider's calluses. His six-foot tall body was thin waisted and leanly muscled, typical of many horsemen.

"Well, we finally met." Her grin widened. "Do you teach jumping, Mr. Thornton?"

"It's Craig. And no, not professionally, but I've been involved with open horses most of my adult life. I have my business to earn a living, but horses are my avocation.

"Aha. A real live entrepreneur." Ashley shifted from foot to foot. That didn't come out as she meant it to sound.

"I'm not a trust baby, if that's what you mean. That's my wife's family, but I built this business from scratch."

"Sorry, I didn't mean to sound judgmental. Actually, it's good to meet someone who has succeeded on his own." Her gentle grin somehow brightened the air around them.

"Thanks. I like my independence, and the horse helps me get away from that world. I also run a pseudo-fox hunt twice a month out of Barrington, during the season."

"A fox hunt? How strange."

"Why strange? It's just a dragged scent for the dogs and some fun jumping over more natural obstacles."

"Oh, I didn't mean it that way. It's just last week, every time I went into the ring, after the first jump, it would feel like I was riding through a beautiful old forest, jumping trees and walls, exactly like I've always pictured a real hunt. It was weird."

Why had she blurted *that* out? She had vowed to keep it to

herself.

"That *is* strange. What was it like?" He seemed acutely interested.

"Kinda scary, actually. I'd rather not talk about it." He would think her a nutcase if she told him everything. She wasn't even fully convinced of her sanity, since those haunting visions swam through her head. They seemed so *real.*

"Sorry. I didn't mean to pry. Say, we're having our annual show in Barrington in two weeks. Are you coming?"

"You keep your horse there? I hear it's really nice."

He nodded. "It's a convenient base for the hunts. So, will you come?"

"I was thinking about it, especially after how well I did here. Just gotten back into jumping, and I need some work on my technique." She blushed at her utter lack of subtlety.

"Really?" He chuckled. "From what I saw, that's like saying Ted Williams needed someone to teach him how to hit a baseball.

"I guess we could refine a few things ... maybe teach you a little patience on the course. So, you can enter our show and send your horse up in the middle of the week. I'll arrange a stall. You've got an unusual animal ... so big, yet so fluid. I'm sure I can find time to work with you, if you'd like."

"I thought you didn't teach." Was that an offer to help? He seemed to know horses and jumping, and god knows, she needed the help... somehow to control the ride when she was in the vision.

"Not for hire" he said. "Just for the satisfaction of aiding a horse and his rider reach their potential. Maybe I'm being too forward."

"Oh, no. It's not that. In fact, it's kind of exciting. I haven't found anyone here that inspires much confidence."

"Swell. Look, here's my card, Ashley. Okay if I call you

Ashley?"

"Sure, since we'll be working together ...."

"Right. So, call me early in the week and we'll set things up. Arrange for a hauler to bring Injun up mid-week. I'll fix my schedule so we'll have some time together. I'm looking forward to it. That horse of yours has so much promise. You both do."

How nice. No double intent, no sexual innuendo ... just honest friendliness. He was not 'Hollywood handsome,' but his rugged, tanned face, with strong cheekbones, a square jaw and squint-lines at the corners of obsidian eyes, were more than just attractive. A wide, bow-shaped mouth may be his best feature. But his looks were not what made him special.

Craig was a man she instinctively knew she could trust... and one whose very nearness orchestrated thunder in her breast.

Easy girl. We're just two people who share a love for a sport.

He's only a friend in the making ... someone she could relax with. She shifted from foot to foot, struggling for a calm façade.

"Sounds good," she said. "I'll have to see what's going on with my kids, but I think it shouldn't be a problem. My housekeeper takes care of them when I'm out." *I'm rambling.*

"Fine. I gotta run, now. My wife'll be wondering what's keeping me. But she knows how crazy I am about jumpers. See you next week."

They shook hands again, and he hurried off.

She followed his departure, her tumbling heart settling into a more normal rhythm, before turning back toward the stables to check on Injun. What would Mr. Craig Thornton think of her jumping big open fences, nearly four months pregnant? She hadn't begun to show yet.

That was news she'd keep to herself for now. She shivered slightly at the idea of working with a real expert, someone who actually seemed to care.

He was natural and easy to be with. Then there was the flutter of butterfly wings in her breast and a slight trembling of knees when she looked into those eyes, leaving her slightly breathless.

Once again, an ancient legacy was stirring its pot.

THIRTY-SIX

"Don't check him so hard," he shouted, as Injun started collecting himself for the jump. "Let him stand off and take it in stride. It's not a big fence."

She eased the pressure on the reins and the big red horse surged ahead, flowing easily over the three-foot high pseudo-red brick wall. That cleared, they cantered to where he was leaning against the white railing of the show ring. Interesting that training sessions with Craig were rarely intruded upon by The Metamorphoses.

"Well done," he said, patting the gelding on the neck, looking up at her. "He's a great athlete, and at 17 hands, there's nothing in any competition he can't clear. Just let him do the work, and try to stay with him when he takes off."

"That's the hard part." She was laughing, patting her distended belly. "This little gal's throwing off my balance, and I'm getting left occasionally. Just can't get forward enough with this kid in the way."

She was nearly in her eighth month, and it was about time to stop jumping. Just riding would be okay, but the baby was a problem when going over fences. No need to take an unnecessary fall.

"You can grab his mane for extra support, but I think it's

time to quit the fences until after you have the baby. No sense in being reckless."

Jesus. It's almost like we read each other's minds.

"I was just thinking the same thing," she said. "I can still ride, though. Both Injun and I need to keep fit, but I'll take it easy for the next three months."

He fetched a step to help her dismount, supporting her at the elbow as she came down. Craig took the reins. As they sauntered back toward the stables, Ashley absorbed the moment ... the smells of freshly raked earth, hay, and even the manure. The sun, a huge orange ball, was sneaking below a white, cottony fabric of scattered cumulus clouds, spilled just above the distant red and orange leafed tree line.

He draped an arm casually around her waist, triggering a ridge of goose bumps scurrying down her spine. A fleeting picture of a cool, shaded meadow and lush grass tripped across her mind. Shivering slightly, she disengaged his hand, giving a gentle squeeze to his arm as she stepped away.

Why, suddenly that passionate fantasy? They were just friends. Very good friends, but that's it. They were both married, so there could never be anything more. Still, busy bird wings were fluttering in her breast. Glancing at him from the corners of her eyes, she saw his eyebrows raised and his lips tensed, before turning away, giving a small head shake.

"I think you're smart to start winding down," he said, after a moment. "You've had a great season."

"Going champion in all four shows is good, huh?" She grinned, punching him lightly on the arm. He smiled, gently patting her back. She relaxed, gazing covertly at his chiseled profile. She breathed a nearly imperceptible sigh.

Amazing. We've known each other less than seven months, but we're as close as if we've been friends for life. Almost daily contact and he's never made an improper gesture ... not even a little one. What just happened was just camaraderie. We're buddies, sharing a love of horses and jumping.

If it were any another couple, she'd be certain romance was involved. She pursed her lips, shrugging, somehow embarrassed by the disappointment of that truth. A momentary picture of that resurgent forested fantasy tickled her thoughts.

Friends. Just friends. Why did she need to constantly reassure herself of that?

"I guess you'll be busy for a while with the infant," Craig continued. "God knows how well you'll do, once you get back in the saddle."

"I've breast fed all my babies, and this little girl won't be any different." She took his hands, turning him toward her.

"But I'll want to get back as quickly as I can. I was thinking about some Grand Prix events next season. What do you think?"

Her gray eyes studied him for a reaction. His weathered, slightly craggy face was more honest ... more appealing ... than Keith's classic handsomeness. Her heart was skipping rope as she awaited his reply. Craig would never lie to her. He was someone she could trust with her life.

"It'll take some serious work, but you've got all the tools. He's a great horse, and you're so instinctive ... really aggressive ... when you're jumping show fences, which isn't like you."

"You think so?" They continued their stroll, her fingers lightly brushing his.

"Yeah. You're normally kind of quiet and reserved, usually even during practice sessions like today's. But you seem to blossom in the ring, sorta morphing into a wild daredevil. You're a totally different person when you're competing. It's pretty exciting."

"Yeah, and kinda spooky." *He should only know.* "How d'ya think I'd do on a fox hunt?" She grinned, elbowing him lightly in the ribs.

"Sorry, ma'am, but they can get pretty hairy, and even a good horse can go down. No place for a very pregnant lady. They'll still be there next season."

"I know. But I like to needle you. They do sound like fun, though."

"They are, and we get a pretty good crowd. Jumping natural obstacles in fields and woods is really quite different than this."

Not to me. I've seen a lot of them these last few months. Wonder who's on the horse that always seems right behind me? Weird.

Ashley blinked as they entered the dimly lit stables. She tasted the strange combination of sweet and acrid odors, shivering imperceptibly at the kaleidoscopic sensations these sent roiling through her. Her past came rushing back at her at times like this ... her callow and uncomplicated youth with never a dream of an unhappy marriage.

She shook her head briskly. She was here now, with two wonderful children and a third on the way, in the company of a really good friend who shared more of her life and interests than her husband ever had.

Though it was strictly friendship ... totally platonic, she reassured herself again ... she couldn't help but think how much better a husband and father he would be than Keith.

Stop. This'll take me nowhere.

Even if there were something there, Craig's interest was strictly as a friend. A groom came to take Injun back to his stall. She would check later to see he had been properly cooled and fed.

They sauntered back into the failing late fall sunlight. The leaves, glistening reds, yellows and oranges, had begun their swirling descent, skimming in mindless patterns, like her troubled thoughts, across the dry, trampled ground. Long fingered shadows from the near-gaunt trees stitched the land in crazy-quilt patterns.

They settled at a little weathered knotty pine picnic table under a huge elm, in no hurry to end the day. Being with him calmed her soul.

He reached over, massaging her neck and shoulders, his strong thumbs expertly working down her upper spine. It was therapeutic, totally devoid of sensuality.

"Oh, that feels so good. This kid is murder on my back."

"I bet. You got a name for her yet?"

"Janine. Janine Elizabeth Bradford Easton. Some mouthful, huh?"

"Sounds good to me," he said. "And after you've had her, you've got a new goal: Grand Prix events. It gives *me* something to think about, too, and I need that right now." She sensed his mood change, seeing the sadness in his eyes.

Ashley recognized the signs. Craig's wife, Toni, was an *upper* upper class society gal, and a heavy drinker. He never put a label on it, but Ashley guessed she was a full-fledged alcoholic. They had no children, a great disappointment to him.

"More trouble at home?" she asked.

"The usual. She parties with her friends until Four A.M. Gets home just in time to puke all over the foyer floor. She keeps promising to get help, but never goes. It's pretty depressing."

"I can imagine. If you need to talk, you know where I am. Any time, Craig. I mean it."

"I know, and I appreciate that. But, enough. We're so into your jumping, we hardly get to just sit and chat. How's it going with you?"

She sighed. "I don't know. Keith works late several nights a week. He's so preoccupied with problems at work that I don't see him much."

"That's rotten. Gotta be lousy for your kids, especially Ricky. Boys need a dad."

"Yeah. Well, we've drifted so far apart, it doesn't even seem to matter anymore. They barely know they have a father."

"That's too bad ... for *all* of you. You need a relationship with a husband, especially now with the baby coming and, while I know you're a great mom, your other kids need some male influence. Why don't you bring 'em around to the horse? We can teach 'em to ride, and go on picnics. Oughta be fun."

"No picnics," she blurted. Strange that so many years later, the memory of that scary afternoon with Allen Clarke still haunted her.

"But I think I *will* bring them, even before I have Janine. It's time to get them started riding, especially if I'm not jumping now."

"Good idea." He pulled her to her feet. "Well, m'lady, 'tis time we sally forth. 'Tis a cold wind, venturing out of the North, and darkness is upon us." He chuckled, bowing grandly before her.

Her spine trembled to a ghostly chill, unrelated to the cooling evening air. His play-acting sent goose bumps down her arms and neck. She glanced at the lengthening shadows, her tongue darting across her lips, sensing some hidden danger.

"Walk me to my car, will you Craig?"

"With pleasure." He offered his arm.

She shivered. Something was out there. Something lurking. Something dangerous, waiting for her. Was it related to The Metamorphoses? Whatever, it *was* there. She felt it.

Mon dieu. Not again.

Now, where the Hell did that *come from?*

~~*~~*~~*~~

Craig watched her drive off, an unfamiliar tightening cinching across his chest. She was a friend ... probably his best friend ... but when he unthinkingly draped an arm around her, his whole world tilted. He was suddenly flushed, his heart thumping, a brief image of a shady meadow flitting across his mind.

Ashley gently rejected his touch, clearly uneasy at anything suggesting intimacy, and he understood. They were *friends*, each married. While those unions were clearly unhappy, and maybe even in jeopardy, that didn't condone anything else between them.

As he entered his convertible, he wondered what would happen if both their marriages dissolved? He could easily picture a life with her, but would she reciprocate? Spurning his touch created considerable doubt on that front.

That's it. We'll just stay buddies, with no complications.

Why did that sadden him?

THIRTY-SEVEN

Ashley parked the SUV three spots away from Craig's Red convertible. The Onwentsia lot was less full than usual for a weekend. Ricky and Beth unbuckled in the rear seats, jumping down and closing the back door.

"Hands," she said, taking one from each child. Too many crazy drivers, even here, to leave the kids unattended until they were clear of the pavement.

"Is Mr. Thornton here?" Rick asked, pointing to the red Jaguar.

"Looks like he beat us. He's going to help teach you about riding."

"He's a good rider, huh?" Beth said.

"Yes, he is. He's helped mommy become better, too. He's ... oh, there he is." Craig materialized, coming around the corner of the office. Ashley's russet eyebrows arched, and she grinned.

"Well, look at you, all decked out in riding paraphernalia."
He was sporting jodhpurs, a riding shirt and vest, and helmet.

"Yeah. Since I'm the official instructor today, I thought I'd
look the part."

They'd discussed the coming lessons for her two children,
and agreed they may better take instruction from someone other
than their mother. Children tend to act out less and listen better
to a "teacher" than a parent.

"Okay. You rascals ready to learn how to be real
equestrians?"

"You bet," Ricky said, reaching up to deliver a high-five.
Beth nodded and giggled. They were comfortable with Craig, as
they'd sat with him in the bleachers many times, watching their
mom compete. They already had a concept of good riding, as
Craig had grasped those opportunities to point out the skills and
faults of riders in those competitions.

Craig had often related to Ashley how much he enjoyed his
time with her kids. And the side benefits were Keith, realizing he
might be supplanted by another man, began throwing a football
with Rick and teaching him a few wide-out's moves. And on the
few evenings he was home early enough, he would read to Beth,
and work with her on her phonics.

While happy with his effort, Ashley suspected it was more a
'competition' by Keith than any real effort to be a father to their
children.

"Aww, where's Injun?" Ricky asked when a groom led out a
pony.

"Aren't we gonna ride your horse, mommy?" Beth asked.

"He's a little big for you guys," she said, patting the little girl
on her riding helmet.

"Get good at riding on Bobby, here, and you'll move up to
Injun. Besides, I think he'd be so scared of you guys falling off, I
probably couldn't get him to even walk. Bobby's a good little

horse who's used to children. I guarantee you're going to have fun with him."

"I bet he doesn't jump like Injun," the boy said, the corners of his mouth drooping.

"No, he certainly doesn't," Craig said, winking at Ashley. "Most horses can't jump like Injun. That's why mommy and he win all the time. But Bobby *does* jump little fences we call 'cavallettes.' "

"Yeah," Ashley said, grinning and shaking her head, "but that's not going to happen for a very long time. First learn to ride. Then we'll talk about jumping."

"Okay," Craig took the reins from the groom. "Rick, how about 'ladies first?' "

"Sure, let Beth go. I'm bettin' she's gonna be a better rider than me, anyhow." He patted his little sister on the back, smiling.

Ashley beamed, pressed her palm against her breast, trying to still her fluttering heart. Somehow, she'd raised two terrific kids ... without much help from Keith. It took tons of self-control to stand back while Craig got her daughter's left foot in the stirrup. With very little help, she stepped up into the saddle. Unable to restrain herself, Ashley helped her best friend adjust the stirrups. They grinned at each other across the neck of the small horse, and Craig winked again.

"Okay, little girl, here's how to hold the reins," he said, positioning her fingers, while Ashley held the lead line.

"Good, now push your feet out ... oh, you've got it already, it seems. Okay, now we're gonna go for a nice slow walk around the corral, while mommy stands over there and wrings her hands." Ashley chuckled, drying her perspired hands on her jeans, and taking a couple of deep breaths to relax.

Beth was with a man who would take as good and careful care of her as she would. No need for tension, and besides, her daughter already looked like she was born in a saddle. She thought about The Metamorphosis, and her first experiences in learning to ride. Ashley was a 'natural' then. Why should she expect Beth to be any different?

Two hours later, the four of them sat at a picnic table in the shade of a giant elm, drinking pink lemonade.

"Have fun, guys?" Ashley asked, ruffling Ricky's brick-red hair.

"Yep, it was great," he said, "but like I thought, little sis is gonna be the pro someday." He grinned, nudging the little girl softly with an elbow.

"How about it, Beth? You gonna be a rider, like mom?" Craig said.

"Yes. And jump big fences and win contests, too. Will you keep helping me, Mr. Thornton? Like you do with mommy?"

"Sure. Your mom's not going to do much serious riding for the next few months, at least not until after your baby sister arrives and gets settled in. So, if she keeps bringing you guys out ...."

"... you're going to get to be real riders," Ashley finished for him. "As quickly as both of you picked things up today .... "

"... you'll probably be putting us to shame in no time," Craig said. They burst out laughing. Ashley wrapped arms around both her children, drawing them in for a snug hug.

She beamed a brilliant smile at her friend, and mouthed, "Thank you." He grinned and shrugged, mouthing back, "Anything for you."

She was awash with contentment, only slightly dampened by the thought, *Why couldn't this be Keith, instead of another man?*

THIRTY-EIGHT

Ashley slumped at the kitchen table, nursing a cold cup of strong coffee. What had she done to turn Keith away again?

He's unhappy about her riding, though she's no longer jumping, but he'd felt that way for months. Still, they became lovers again for a short time, despite her ungainly shape...and then suddenly... nothing. Is it because the baby was so near...or was there something else?

She was alone in a house full of people. Thank god for Ricky and Beth. Even Craig's warmth and support could not assuage the trickle of tears, streaking her cheeks each night as she searched vainly for the solace of sleep. She concentrated her thoughts on the baby, soon to arrive, bringing some measure of fullness back to her life.

The time was near.

Janine had made her entrance right on schedule, like all her kids, but the only ones there during delivery were her in-laws...and Craig.

It was six hours of exhausting, hard work, and no surprise, Keith was away on one of his mysterious business trips when he should have been with her. At the least he could have called, but even that was too much to expect. His limited forays into interacting with their children was waning, too ... not that it was ever very committed to start with. His late evenings at work erased any real chances of them spending time together.

But Craig was there, a friend who always seemed available when she needed one. He was a better buddy than Keith ever was. Her in-laws came, too, eager to hold their new grand-daughter. How proud her parents would have been. Maybe they were watching from Heaven.

There was no real reason to be surprised at her husband's lack of interest. Nothing she had tried seemed to bring them any closer together.

It was Craig and her in-laws who watched over her during and after the delivery. Janine's grandma stayed with her until she got back on her feet.

Keith's trip was something about the new factory he wanted to build. It surely could have been scheduled for another time, knowing she was about to deliver, but it would have made little difference. When he finally returned home, he was out late again, nearly every night. She was either asleep, or faking it, by the time he showed up.

Can't be burdened by self-doubt. Keep moving forward.

She immersed herself in her new infant and the love of her other children. They'd made several repeat trips to the stables, with the baby in a carry trundle, and Beth and Ricky taking riding lessons from Craig. She watched, sitting restlessly in the bleachers. Beth really took to the horse, while Rick seemed along mostly to be with the family. Whatever, it was good bonding for all of them, including ... magically ... Craig.

And only seven weeks after delivering Janine, Ashley was back at the stables, working Injun and herself back into shape. Craig was there, full of support, a rock for her continued sanity.

Keith seemed more distant than ever.

THIRTY-NINE

Another month passed before pain of cold rejection eventually fermented into heated anger, inciting her to finally question her husband about his late night whereabouts.

"I told you, I'm working at the office," he said, when she finally braced him.

"Until Eleven or Twelve? C'mon, Keith. Nobody works that late."

"Well, I am. I've finally convinced the Board to consider a new factory in the South. I'm working on that, three or four nights a week."

"And Saturdays, too?" Russet eyebrows arched.

He shrugged. "Yeah, Saturdays, too. It's quiet, just like at night. I get more work done 'cause there's no one to disturb me."

"What, exactly, are you doing that's so time consuming?" The whole thing was really hard to believe.

"Evaluating the opportunities. We've gotten industrial inducement packages from over twenty communities throughout the South. I've developed a weighted rating program to evaluate them. It's very time consuming."

"There's no one to help you with this? You shouldn't have to do it alone, and at the expense of your family." Was she being selfish, wrong to have mistrusted him? He was obviously doing the best he could.

"You know no one supported me on this. They think I'm nuts. I gotta do all the work myself."

It ended there, leaving Ashley uneasy and filled with a full-blown case of burning curiosity. After stewing for a week over the injustice that kept her husband from his family and too exhausted to make even occasional love to his wife, she called her father-in-law to complain.

"Hi, dad. It's Ashley."

"Ah, what a pleasant surprise. How are you, my dear? And my lovely grand-children?"

"Fine, I suppose. Janine's growing fast and is eager to see her grand-parents again."

"Wonderful. I'm glad you're such a happy, growing family."

A 3rd Time to Die

She trapped her lower her lip between her teeth, fighting for courage, then forged ahead. "That's why I'm calling. You're working Keith too hard. Can't you give him some help on the new factory proposals?"

"More help?" He sounded amused. "He's already got half Industrial Engineering on it, and committees from Sales, Purchasing and Production, each developing plans for their departments. Everything's going ahead faster than I ever expected."

"Oh?" Bands of steel ratcheted tightly around her, squeezing the breath from her lungs. It took a moment before she mustered enough air to speak.

"I ... I didn't think the Board was behind Keith on this."

"We weren't at first, but that husband of yours is very persuasive. He's got our full backing now. We've even finalized a site: Crowley, Louisiana. Everything seems even better than Keith predicted. Construction on the building will begin in less than two months, and it's all being paid for by the community floating Revenue Bonds."

"Oh, that's wonderful," she mumbled. "Keith never tells me anything. He's just so busy. Anyway, it was good talking with you, Dad. Give my love to Muffin." Keith's mother preferred her nickname, rather than 'Mom.'

Ashley sat by the phone, staring vacantly into the back yard.

This doesn't make any sense. If this means he's not working late, then where the Hell has he been every night? There must be a logical explanation. She shivered, suddenly chilled. Did she really want to know the truth? She could call Cynthia. Her husband, Howard Higgins, was Vice-president of Manufacturing, and one of Keith's closest friends.

I'd seem such a fool if there's nothing to worry about. I... I don't want to sound like a ditsy wife, but it's time to get some answers.

George A Bernstein

After several false starts, she saddled up her courage and placed the call to her friend.

There was a long pause, thick with indecision, after Ashley asked Cynthia if she knew anything about Keith's late hours.

"I can't really say, Ashley," she finally said.

"C'mon, Cyn. Keith and Howard are buddies. I'm sure you've heard things. Am I paranoid, or is there something going on? I've got to know."

"Oh, Ashley. It's not my place..."

"*Please*, Cyn. We're friends. You'd want to know, if you were me, wouldn't you?" That's what friends were for, and she wasn't going to let her wriggle free.

"I ... I suppose," Cynthia said. "Would you really tell me, if it were ... not good?"

"Of course I would." Ashley hoped she sounded more positive than she felt. It wasn't good, Cyn said. She trembled, despite the warmth of the room.

"Well ... I heard Howard talking with Keith several months ago. It seems Keith was seeing a ... a professional woman."

"A *hooker?*" Ashley shivered, suddenly glacially cold.

"Yes. A very high-priced one, I understand. Kristen, I think. I asked him about it, and Howard says he's heard men actually fall in *love* with her, if you can believe *that*."

"Keith's in love with a *hooker?*" Her brain stalled. Nothing made sense.

"Uhh ... not any more. I understand he's...uhh...stopped seeing her." Some gentle throat clearing punctuated another chilly pause.

Was there more to this debacle? Ashley gritted her teeth, her voice a bare whisper.

"So, he's not fooling around anymore? Is that right?" There was a soft moan before her friend finally answered, her words flowing like cold molasses.

[129]

"Not exactly. I believe he's taken a...a mistress."

"Oh, *shit*. The bastard. The fucking bastard." Cold no longer, her hand shook, face flushed.

"Ashley. I'm so sorry. Maybe I shouldn't have...."

"No, Cyn, no. You did the right thing. Who else would tell me? No one will ever learn where I heard it, don't worry."

"I promised Howard. He'd be very angry if he knew."

"Cyn, no one will ever know. I'll say I hired a detective, if I ever face him with this."

"You mean you aren't going to say anything to him?" Cynthia sounded surprised.

"I don't know. I just don't know. I've gotta sort things out. Gotta think of our kids. Some of it must be my fault, somehow."

"*Your* fault? Don't be ridiculous. He's *cheating* on you, for God's sake. How can that be your fault?"

"There's got to be a reason. If I were all he wanted, he'd have no cause to stray. Maybe I ...."

"Bullshit." Her friend was no longer reticent, now that truth was in the open. "Is *he* everything you ever wanted? Was he *ever*? Be honest. No man is."

"I don't know. We always seemed to have something special ... something pulling us together. He was never perfect, I guess." She thought, fleetingly, of Craig Thornton. *He* seemed a lot more perfect than Keith, especially now.

They said their good-byes, with Ashley again pledging to keep her friend out of it. She needed time to think. Some of this *had* to be her fault. The horse, all the attention she gave the children, the new baby he never wanted. He felt left out, not the focus of their attention anymore. He was used to being the main attraction, but she had allowed other things to compete.

Yes, she was at least partly to blame. She could see that now. She wouldn't say anything for the moment, and would try to fix the marriage, try to make him happier at home, the center of their world again.

She would get professional help, if necessary. Make this marriage work. But underneath this bravado she sensed the hollowness of her determination.

Did she *want* it to work anymore? Did she even care? Can something this broken ever be fixed? She recognized in her heart that his absence the day Janine arrived was a harbinger of their future.

Her thoughts again drifted to Craig Thornton, wondering what marriage to a man like him would be like? She shivered, goose bumps ridging her spine, casting the thought away.

Infidelity? Not something in her nature ... however alluring ... despite Keith's apparent adventures in that realm.

Yet Craig's face lingered in her mind.

FORTY

For two months Ashley battled growing uncertainty, laboring in a concentrated but futile effort to make things right. She struggled to draw Keith into family events and involve him in their children's activities, but little changed. Keith made an occasional effort to get involved with his family.

On the few nights he made it home early enough, he might help Ricky with homework or read to Beth at bed time. Both those were rarities. He studiously avoided caring for Janine at all. Mostly he remained distant, as cold as Chicagoland's frozen, snow-covered tundra, coming home late and smelling of jasmine. He insisted everything was work related.

Who the Hell smelled of jasmine at work? She could no longer repress her burgeoning anger.

A 3rd Time to Die

Innocent sounding phone calls to wives of several of his associates verified there were no weekly dinner meetings. The two "all male" continuing education workshops he attended, one in New York City and the other in Denver, proved well represented by wives. Calls to hotels to those cities verified his attendance with a very memorable, raven-haired 'Mrs. Easton.'

Bulldog tenacity uncovered Nicole's identity, and Ashley was curious enough to attend one of her afternoon classes. What a brutal workout. She was frankly unprepared for how magnificent Ms. Phillips was, but after staggering through her class, she gained understanding of where that gorgeous body came from.

Ashley stayed to shower after the class, observing Nicole nude in the next stall. Her naturally busty, narrow waiste, long-legged young body was depressing. Ashley had never looked that good, even at twenty.

Nobody did. It couldn't *all* be from exercise.

Ashley suspected Nicole knew exactly who she was, since Keith dutifully carried a family photo in his wallet. The raven-haired Amazon purposely paraded herself, clearly wanting Ashley to understand what she was up against.

Not wanting to create a scene, Ashley dressed and left quickly. Driving home, her head was mired in a swamp of troubling ruminations.

Their marriage *was* a failure. How much of that was her fault? Had she driven him to other women because of the numbing fear blanketing her whenever they had sex?

Why was she looking for something dangerous to leap from the shadows? It was crazy.

Well, for whatever reasons, any positives left in their marriage were being sucked into a morass of disillusionment. Maybe they *should* separate ... take some time alone to sort things out.

Time alone. Shit. All I've had is time alone. Maybe my panic attacks during sex are part of the problem. That certainly could be a turn-off.

Once things settled down with the baby, she would see a therapist. Maybe some of her friends at the country club could recommend a good man. Not a Freudian. She didn't have three or four years to figure things out.

One final stab at fixing things before finally seeking an ending to this apparent charade called a marriage.

FORTY-ONE

"What?"

She cantered up to the white wooden railing, a devilish grin splitting her face, her palms held up in an ageless gesture.

"Don't give me that." He couldn't restrain a laugh. "Just stay away from those big fences. Your legs aren't ready for that yet."

"Not my fault. Injun wants to jump them."

"Of *course* he does. Just take it easy for now. It won't be long before your strong enough again."

"Jeez, I've been back a month already. This seems such a long way from a Grand Prix. How'll I ever be ready if I can't work over the big jumps?"

"Patience, madam. Good things come to those who wait. Seriously, we want to work on getting back your timing, and you're just beginning to regain your leg strength. But we can think about technique now."

"Like what, boss?" This friendly banter had never existed

with Keith. But then, her husband never liked horses, and didn't discuss family matters. He always told her to do whatever she thought was best, never making a decision affecting anyone other than himself. Why had it taken so many years to realize that?

"For one thing," Craig said, pulling her back to the moment, "you need more control of your route to the fences."

"I don't understand."

"Injun is so fast and eager, he can get to jumps before you're ready. I've noticed when you circle into a fence, you often end up taking it at an angle. That effectively makes the jump bigger, especially the wide ones, like walls and oxers."

"Yeah." She had dismounted and was rubbing the horse's velvety muzzle. "I see what you're driving at. The damn things are big enough."

If he only knew what they really looked like to me.

"Right. So you have to make a slightly bigger circle to get squared up to the bars. A little thing to make life easier."

They strolled toward the stately old stable, Injun following like a well-trained dog. So easy to talk about things they *both* loved. How he had grown on her. She watched him from the corner of her eye, bathed in the gentle glow of their familiarity.

It was the gentle, sensitive, compassionate man inside, not his looks that made Craig such a special friend. She never felt so much trust in anyone. Certainly never Keith, even in the beginning. In the less than a year she'd known him, Craig had become the most important person in her life, next to her children. Time spent was always easy and comfortable with him.

A groom took Injun to cool him down before putting him away. She sighed softly. Even the sweet-acrid smells of damp hay and manure were a pleasant familiarity. They stood together, watching the big red horse disappear around the corner.

A covert glance at Craig brought a strange stirring, a trembling of her heart. She was momentarily suspended in a surreal world, grasping for images she couldn't quite see, something she didn't understand.

Something different.

Something special.

Something that made this *more* than just friendship.

C'est bon.

She blinked. *Quit it.*

French again. Seemed it pops up mostly around Craig.

Dwelling there will only make life more difficult. Things were confusing enough at the moment. Like Scarlett, she would think more about it tomorrow. She turned to her new best friend, her confident smile belying the turmoil within.

"Wanna grab a bite?" he asked.

"Read my mind. I'm starving. The grub any good in the grill room here?"

"Not bad. They make a really tasty grilled chicken Caesar salad, if you're in the mood for something light."

"Sounds good. Lead the way."

FORTY-TWO

Craig pushed the large, bowel-shaped plate away and sighed.

"Yum. Just right after a hard morning's work on the jumps."

"We didn't work *that* hard. I need some time on bigger fences, if I'm ever going to try Grand Prix."

"We've been over this. You *need* some easier competition over smaller courses, until you get your legs and timing back. There's a show in Elgin next week-end. Let's enter that and see how things go. We've gotta work up to this slowly. Don't be so impatient."

"I know. I know. I'm just antsy. How about a fox hunt. You got one scheduled soon? I really want to ride a fox hunt."

"Yeah. In two weeks, if the dogs get back from Wisconsin in time."

"Wisconsin?"

"My cousin's running a hunt out of Menomonee early that week. Should be plenty of time to get the hounds back to Barrington."

"Good. Count me in. I can hardly wait." She fidgeted restlessly in her chair.

"Jeez, Ashley. I've never seen you look so wired. What's bugging you?"

"Nothing's *bugging* me. Anyhow, I don't want to talk about it."

"So that's it? You don't want to talk about what's *not* bugging you?"

Her laugh had a nervous edge.

"Trapped myself, huh?"

"Look, it's okay. But if you need to unburden yourself, I'm here."

"Oh, shit, I don't know. My life's not working out like I expected. I never planned on a cheat."

"Keith?"

"Yeah. The bastard was seeing a *hooker*. Very exclusive and very expensive. But it seems he's dumped her for a full-time mistress. He's never home, either out with his bimbo, or in Louisiana, building the new factory. He didn't even *call* for two days after Janine was born.

"What's scary is, I don't even miss him, but the *kids* need a father. I'm not ready to give up, but he's gonna have to toe the line from now on."

"And if he doesn't? What then?"

"I ... I don't know. I can't picture myself divorced. Just not in my nature to quit. But I can only take so much crap. It's gonna be up to him."

She didn't tell him she had an appointment with a highly regarded psychiatrist to try to work things out. She needed to understand her role in their failing marriage, sure a lot of it must be her fault. Especially that strange fear ... The Terror ... swamping her those infrequent times last year when they did make love.

That hadn't happened since those happy few days in her fourth month carrying Janine. Freezing up in panic certainly didn't help. If she can figure out why she's searching the shadows for monsters, maybe they could become lovers again. That might even bring them back together. Provided the mistress was just a diversion, and not something serious.

Either way, she'd have to figure it out. She hoped this doctor was as good as his reputation.

FORTY-THREE

Heading home down Skokie Highway, Craig's mind was centered on things other than his driving. Luckily, traffic was light.

Ashley was in a tough spot, not so different than his. Strange that he and this great gal, now his closest friend, were both facing decisions about cheating spouses.

Her biggest concern was getting Keith to become a good father, and providing a sound family life for her children. That seemed more important than her happiness.

He wished *he* were a father in a happy family. Why had Toni never gotten pregnant again while they were still having unprotected sex? She was young and healthy, if she had only cut out the drinking. Was there something physically wrong with her?

He should check it out. Could the loss of their child and an inability to have another be the root of this self-destructive behavior? Maybe. When, exactly, did all this catting around with other men actually begin?

She could probably use some psychiatric help. He grunted. Little chance of that happening. Would he even want to try again, if it were something fixable? A baby, adding new chains to an otherwise fractured union.

Ashley Easton's face wormed into his thoughts. *She* was the kind of woman he wanted to father his child.

Looking up, he braked sharply, almost missing his street. Maybe he'd talk to Toni's doctor. See if were something medical. He was still giving his wife the benefit of the doubt.

FORTY-FOUR

"Have a seat, Mrs. Easton." Dr. Feldman ran a hand through thinning salt-and-pepper hair and motioned her toward a large, comfortable-looking burgundy leather armchair. He reclined in a duplicate, facing hers, dressed in aqua wool slacks and a long-sleeved paisley shirt, open at the collar.

He was fiftyish, a short, dapper man, with a pencil-thin mustache under a large Semitic nose. It was a compassionate, trustworthy face. Leather loafers adorned his feet, crossed at the ankles in front of him. Informality, it seemed, had penetrated everywhere.

"Shouldn't I be on the couch?" Perched on the edge of the seat, Ashley was uneasy. Her legs quivered, hands gripping the chair arms, like an edgy doe in a field, ready to bound away at the slightest provocation.

The psychiatrist chuckled. "A couch is the stereotype for psycho-therapy, but it's not usually necessary. Let's first see what's troubling you.

"I see I was recommended by Shirley Baxter."

"Yes. And others." She blushed. "You seem very highly regarded. I ... I sorta checked you out. I even read your book."

"Nothing wrong with that, and I appreciate another sale. I'd do the same. Now, how can I help you?"

Ashley paused, screwing up her courage. She sucked her lower lip between her teeth, and then sighed.

"I don't know how to begin. It's so complicated."

"Just sit back, relax, and say whatever comes to mind. It's my job to sort it out. I'm pretty good at that. There's usually one final thing that pushes people to seek help. What was that?"

"My marriage, I guess, but there other things, as well."

"Okay. So, why don't we start with what is bothering you about your marriage. The rest will come at its own pace."

Ashley looked up, a tear sliding slowly down her cheek. "It's in dog doodie. The marriage, I mean. Keith, my husband, and I haven't been in sync for several years. I know it's my fault, but now he has a mistress, and he's never home."

"He has a mistress?"

She nodded, dabbing at her eyes.

"Why do you feel that's your fault?"

"Somehow I've driven him away. I'm so involved with our children. We just had our third, a total accident. He never wanted her. And I ride my horse every day. I compete in jumping tournaments."

"When do you ride the horse?" he asked.

"Usually in the early afternoon. A friend is helping me train him for a Grand Prix event. That's like the World Series of jumping."

"Is your husband home at those hours?"

"Well, no," she said. "He didn't get home from work... you know, even before the mistress ... until 6:30 or so."

"So, now what time does he get home?"

"Eleven, twelve. Sometimes never. He's out of town a lot, building a new factory in Louisiana."

"And the children. What about them?"

"The baby mostly sleeps and eats. She's no trouble. The older ones dine with us ... me, actually, since he's rarely there for dinner. Afterward we read a story, or maybe a little television, and then they're off to bed. Their homework is always done before we eat."

The doctor leaned forward, hands on his knees. "So what you're saying is, neither your riding nor most of your care for your children interfere in any real way with your being with your husband. Right?"

"I ... I guess so," she answered slowly.

"Then I ask again, why is it your fault he's found another woman?"

"Because, he's not the center of my world anymore." She spit it out, the words bitter acid on her tongue. "And there was always the damned sex."

"So, it's *your* fault because your life doesn't revolve solely around him and his needs? Do you think *your* needs are important, too?"

"I suppose, but ... but he was the star athlete. He's *used* to people adoring him. I love him, or thought I did, but I also want things for myself."

"That's perfectly natural. He's not a star athlete now, is he?"

"No-o-o." She settled back into the folds of the chair,

moistening her crimson lips.

"That was then, and not now. Marriage is about growing together and sharing. You're entitled to attention and consideration, too. If he's not giving that to you, that's his problem, and certainly not your responsibility. We may need to do some joint counseling, if he'll agree."

Ashley shook her head, evoking a tiny groan. "I doubt it. He doesn't even know I'm here. He's in Louisiana, probably with *her*, building that new factory."

"Okay. We'll worry about that later. You mentioned sex. What's the problem there?"

"That *is* my fault. I get scared and freeze up."

"Scared? How do you mean?"

"Well, at first, I get all aroused. My heart's pumping, and I get really wet, you know, down there. But after we actually start intercourse, I start getting ... actually terrified. I keep looking around, expecting someone to jump out and kill us, or something. Maybe it has to do with an incident that happened when I was a teen-ager."

She recounted the long-ago picnic with Allen Clarke, finishing by telling him, "The strange thing was that I found myself thinking in French. And I don't *know* French."

"French? Is that the only time that happened?"

"No." She paused, studying him through slitted eyes, and then shrugged. After all, he *was* a psychiatrist. "When I'm jumping the horse, too. Mostly during competitions."

"You think in French when you're show jumping?" He raised thin dark eyebrows.

"Yes. I studied it in school for two years, but I really don't remember much of it. But it seems so natural ... so fluent ... when I'm riding. It just bubbles happily around my head then."

She hesitated, fidgeting in her seat, her hands in a death grip on the chair's arms. Leaning forward, auburn hair falling across one eye, she pushed doggedly ahead.

"It seems as if I'm on a fox hunt."

"I don't understand." He cocked his head, one eyebrow raised.

"It happens mostly when I'm jumping in a competition. It's kinda spooky. Suddenly, the show ring seems transmuted into a beautiful forest, and I'm jumping trees, streams and big fieldstone walls, 'Tallyho' ringing in my head with a definite French lilt. I sense someone else riding, just behind me, and the ring doesn't come back in focus until I've finished the course. "

"Does this frighten you?" He sat upright, very alert. She paused before answering.

"The first time I was terrified. Almost fell off the horse. I've gotten used to it now, and it's actually pretty exhilarating. I seem like … like someone else … a carefree horsewoman, totally in charge, thrilled with the ride and the countryside. I'm not normally so audacious. And, everything racing through my head is in French.

"I'm a good rider, but my friend says that in competition, it's as if I become someone else. A more fearless, natural horsewoman than I ever was. You're only the second person I've ever told about this. Am I crazy, or what?"

"What you are describing is very unusual," he was smiling reassuringly, "but not in any way 'crazy,' as you put it. Something deeper is manifesting itself in this manner. It may very well be related with all the things we've discussed today: you're willingness to accept the blame for your husband's transgressions; your fear of something bad happening during sex; and these illusions while jumping. Tell me, have you ever actually ridden on a fox hunt?"

She laughed. "No, that's the strangest part. But, my friend runs them monthly. He's hunted real fox in England and Spain. From what he's said, my visions are more like a European hunt than anything I might see here. I plan on joining him on one next week. Then I'll be able to make a comparison."

"That's interesting," Doctor Feldman said, rising. "I'm afraid we're out of time, but we'll want to get into this more next session."

She stood and stretched, feeling unusually calm, somehow relieved that she had gotten so much off her chest.

"Do you think you can save my marriage, Doctor?"

"That's not up to me. What I *can* do is help you sort out your feelings and a sense of who you really are, and who you want to be. Not who your husband wants, but your own person. I may help you understand your marriage better, but in the end, it will be up to you to save it, or not.

"We may try hypnotic regression to find a point, probably in your childhood, where these anxieties first took root. It's something you apparently have buried in your subconscious, and that's the quickest and least painful way to get at it. We'll see what happens during the next few sessions first."

"Okay," she said. "So, I'll see you on Monday."

Feldman sat at his desk, studying his notes from Ashley Easton's session, vaguely uneasy. Her strange visions smacked strongly of what some would insist were past life memories, especially since she experienced it in a foreign language.

Bull. There's no such thing as past lives, much less memories about them. She studied French in school. It was a subconscious vehicle to express other repressions ... memories from *this* life.

Still, how could he explain her sudden superior riding skills and her increased fluency in French, while living this hallucination? He shook his head, taking a slow breath.

Well, the next few sessions would shake all of that out, and it would prove perfectly logical. Probably a stifled trauma from her childhood.

So, why did he feel so edgy?

FORTY-FIVE

"So, Mr. Thornton, what can I do for you? Not PMS, I hope."

"No thanks, Doc." Craig chuckled. "I'll leave that for your patients. Just wanted to talk about Toni for a minute. I promise to be quick."

"That's quite all right," Dr. Green said. "A gynecologist doesn't get many opportunities to talk to a man. Is there a problem?" He adjusted his white smock, repositioning the stethoscope. Thin, manicured fingers brushed at his small, graying moustache. Very professional.

"I'm not sure. Uh, when was the last time Toni had a check-up."

"I looked when I heard you asked to see me. It's been ten months."

"So she's due again soon."

"Yes, but your wife seems a reluctant patient. She often stretches her annual physical to eighteen months. The best we can do is sending a reminder. So, I ask again, is there a problem I should be aware of?"

"Same answer. I don't know. She *does* seem a little lethargic lately. Not full of her usual energy and bounce." Craig had decided on this small lie to get to the question he really wanted answered.

"I can't imagine a reason for that without examining her. If you think there's something wrong, you should see that she comes in ASAP. How's her appetite?"

"Good, I guess." *Especially for other men.*

"Has she gained or lost any significant amount of weight?"

"No. Just as trim and gorgeous as ever. But, she ... she doesn't seem as interested in ... ah ... sex anymore." Another white lie. He was speaking for himself, not the rest of the male population of the North Shore. He needed to approach this subject with extreme care if he expected to get a straight answer.

"Well, I can't tell you much else without an examination. Get her in here, and we'll see what's going on."

"I'll try, but the last time you saw her, she seemed in good health?"

"Perfect. A magnificent ... uh, I mean excellent health. Couldn't be better." Dr. Green's tongue flicked nervously across his lips.

Craig suddenly saw him with new eyes: about fifty, fit looking, and a pleasant face with distinguished graying temples to go with the lip hair. Another of Toni's conquests, he realized. Probably how she paid her bill. He wondered if they did it right there. Even a doctor was human.

"Could she be depressed," Craig asked.

"Depressed? Toni? I seriously doubt it. What would a beautiful, vibrant, wealthy young woman in her prime have to be depressed about? It could be hormonal, I suppose."

"I thought, maybe the baby ..."

"The baby?"

"Why not? We lost our son right after birth. Maybe she's depressed over not getting pregnant again."

"Not likely." He made a depreciating gesture with his hand.

"I don't understand."

"Women rarely get pregnant after having their tubes." He stopped abruptly, staring at Craig, face aflame, and then dropped his gaze.

"Sorry. Patient confidentiality. I've said more than I should."

[145]

He started to turn away, but Craig sprang forward, grabbing his shoulder, spinning him around.

"What about her tubes, Doc?"

"You'll have to ask your wife. I'm sorry. I should..."

Craig snatched a handful of white smock at his throat, twisting it tightly, pulling the taller man's face down level with his. His narrowed eyes bore into the other man's.

"What about her tubes?" The words hissed through tightly clenched teeth.

"I—I can't—" Green's topaz eyes were large and round, as the angry man twisted his grip tighter.

"The *tubes,* Doc?" A tightly fisted hand appeared in front of his face. He struggled for breath.

"Tied. Had them...tied. After the baby." He sucked in a grateful breath as the pressure on his neck went slack. He stumbled backwards, away from those burning eyes, so filled with fury. And hate?

"The bitch. The fucking *whore.*"

"She never told you?" The older man struggled for breath, as his fear eased. Thornton's anger was no longer directed at him.

"No. She kept up the future family charade to keep me around."

"Surely you wouldn't seek a divorce over ..."

"I don't know *what* I'm going to do. Why should you care? When you fuck her again on her next visit, you won't feel so guilty."

"*Mr.* Thornton! I never ..."

"Cut the crap, Doc. You're just one of dozens. I suggest you wear a rubber. And when you next do her blood work, you might want to look at something other than cholesterol and hormone levels. For your own safety, if not for hers."

Doctor Green's face told Craig he wasn't going to await Toni's next visit before doing some blood work...his own.

FORTY-SIX

Craig slouched at his office desk, thoughts racing as he scrolled aimless circles on a blank piece of paper. His head throbbed, a three aspirin headache.

The cunning bitch. She'd been fucking him for the past five years without ever climbing in his bed.

Tied her tubes.

The *bitch*. The dog's would be the only patter of little feet in their house. She knew how badly he wanted kids. The promised family to keep them together. She knew exactly what buttons to push. Manipulation was her forte.

How different she was from Ashley.

Ashley.

Knowing her gave him reason to hope for something better. His perfect plan of love along with position and money has really blown up in his face. He gained nothing from his efforts, tied to a conscienceless trollop who wouldn't let him go without a bloody fight. He never needed her wealth or family connection, having succeeded in business strictly on his own.

What to do? What to do? Had he and Toni *ever* really been in love? Certainly lust. Lots of lust. But love? He didn't know anymore. He was so damned confused.

Maybe he should try some more therapy. Bruce was a no-nonsense psychiatrist, moving things right along. He might help sort things out. It never paid to make rash decisions. He'd already learned that lesson. He couldn't let thoughts of Ashley (so warm and wonderful) interfere with doing what was right.

They were, after all, just *friends*.

Okay. I'll call Bruce tomorrow and arrange an appointment. At least he'd be doing something. Things couldn't stay as they were.

But, he had no idea how much they were about to change.

FORTY-SEVEN

Ashley looked up from her *Cosmo* as the raised-panel cherry door opened.

A heavyset, middle-aged woman emerged, dabbing at tear-reddened eyes, hurrying out of the waiting room. As the outer door closed, Dr. Feldman appeared in the doorway of the inner office.

"Come in, Mrs. Easton." he said, holding the door for her.

She thought of their past three sessions as she slipped into the office, settling in the familiar leather chair. Over the past several weeks, she'd come to realize her behavior during their marriage wasn't so unusual, and certainly not unfair to Keith. In fact, she *had* treated him with consideration and affection.

Finding a lover was *his* need, and had nothing to do with any inadequacies in her. Blaming herself was just a rationale to stay in the marriage. She was no longer sure that was a very good idea. Divorce, if it came to that, would be because of what he did, not her.

She made so much progress in understanding her relationship with Keith, but nothing explained the unreasoned fear that would grip her while making love ... the terror that something or someone was about to attack her from the shadows. Then there was the strange world surrounding her whenever she jumped Injun.

Dr. Feldman told her last week he felt the two things were somehow intertwined. The quick, practical way to unravel it was through hypnotic regression ... their agenda today.

"I think we should begin the regression immediately," he said. "Are you nervous?"

"Yes. And scared."

"I assure you, there's nothing to fear. You'll see everything as if watching a movie, not as an actual participant. There'll be no need to relive any pain or anxiety we might uncover, and when we're done, you may find yourself much more at ease. You can either sit in the chair, or use the couch, as you prefer. Some are more comfortable if they are lying down."

"I think I'll sit right here."

"Fine. Ready to begin?"

She nodded and sat back, folding her hands in her lap.

"Good. Now, close your eyes and relax. Let your mind go blank. Your facial muscles are going slack. Your neck is free of all tension. The energy is flowing out of your arms, out of your body, draining down, down, down."

Five minutes later, Ashley was in a deep trance, visualizing herself descending a long staircase, as the doctor's soft voice continued to direct her.

"Now you are in a beautiful garden, filled with flowers of all colors. Reds, blues, greens, pinks. Do you see it?"

"Yes. It's so peaceful." Her usually musical voice was hollow and mechanical.

"Good. There is a gazebo there, and a bench inside."

"Yes, I see it."

"Go to the gazebo and lay down on the bench. It is very comfortable. You feel very relaxed and at peace. Are you there?"

"Yes." She sounded drowsy, responding to his standard suggested "images" that he found a most successful platform from which to launch a regression.

"Fine. Now, your body is relaxed, and can release your higher self to rise above it. A bubble of safety protects you. It surrounds you as you rise up - up - up. Your higher self is free of all Earthly constraints, as you rise up - up - up."

Good. She was responding perfectly.

"Now, I'm going to count down, and when I reach "one," you will enter a tunnel.

"Three, two, one. Are you there?"

"It's dark, but very peaceful."

"Good. Now you are being drawn back ... back ... back. Back to a time in your youth. Back to when you began horseback riding. Three, two, one. Are you there?"

"Yes. Mommy rented a pony." It was the high voice of a small child.

"How old are you?"

"Six. I am so happy." She giggles. "I have the reins. I kick the pony and we run away from the man leading us. Everyone is yelling, but I ride around and around the ring. It's easy."

Feldman rubs his chin. She was an instinctive rider from the very beginning. He paused for a moment, allowing her to enjoy the memory.

He said, "Okay. We are going to leave that time and go forward to when you were ten, when I count down to 'One.' "

A moment later she was there, describing what was happening.

"I am in our apartment. Papa is reading to me."

"This is a happy time for you?"

"Yes. I'm cuddled against my dad, with his arm around me. He's reading me about a dog; Buff, a Collie."

"Has anything happened, either at home or in school, with a boy, or a man? Has anyone touched you in your private place?"

"No. I take my own bath. Not even Mama touches me anymore."

"And your papa?"

"No. He never comes in when I might be naked."

"Okay. When I count down to 'one,' go forward to the time when you first experience this fear of intimacy ... the fear someone is going to attack you." Quickly, she "traveled" seven years.

"I am on a picnic at the Skokie Lagoons with Allen Clarke. We've driven to a hidden spot. It seems so familiar. I'm partly undressed and so excited. He's touching me everywhere, and it feels so wonderful. Oh! There is a noise in the woods. *Mon dieu! Not again.*"

She was clearly agitated, her voice taking on a distinct French accent. "I grab my clothes and run away. Allen, he follows." Feldman's brow wrinkles. *What's with that Gaelic inflection?*

"All right. Nothing can harm you here. That bubble of safety protects you. Look back at what happened on the picnic. Is this the beginning of your fear of some lurking danger?"

"No. It was already there." Her voice calm and without accent again.

Feldman was frustrated. This was not what he expected. No sign she was ever molested as a child, so these fears must have manifested themselves as a teenager, first discovering her sexuality. He kept trying.

"Go back to an earlier time, when you first were serious with Keith. How did you feel when he attempts to force you? Three, two, one." She had related that incident to him in their last session.

"I'm angry ... and ashamed at what he had me do to him. But I sense the fear there, stalking me, even before we became so physical." Her voice was quizzical, as if she were also confused.

"Can you bring it to the surface? Face it. See where it came from?" Such a direct move could be dangerous, but he didn't

A 3rd Time to Die

know what else to do. They had to get to the origin of her terror, or she would never lead a sexually fulfilling life.

"'Tis old. I feel 'tis very old." The timber of her voice had changed, and the inflections were definitely French again. In utter frustration, he made one final, fateful, stab.

"Okay. I'm going to count backward again, and I want you to go to that time, whenever it was. Go back to the very incident that first created this deep fear. Three, two, one."

Feldman paused as a coquettish grin transformed her face.

"Are you there?" He was unaccountably tense.

"*Oui. Oh, c'est beau. La forest, est magnifique.*" She rattled on in elegant French, her voice youthful, full of music. His skin erupted in goose bumps, the hair prickling on his neck.

He knew enough of the language to recognize the woman speaking to him now *was* French. No one, other than possibly a long time resident, could speak it so beautifully. He was having difficulty understanding the rapid stream of her comments.

He said, "Please, speak in English."

"*Oui.* It is just that I am so aroused." She was breathless.

"Where are you?"

"In Devonshire, of course. Armand, that sniveling dandy, and I are the guests of the handsome Lord Wallace."

"Devonshire? Devonshire, England?"

"'Tis there another?"

When was she in England? And who is Armand? Or Lord Wallace? She never mentioned any of this before. This had to be fairly recent.

"What is the year?"

"The year of our Lord, 1695."

"1695? You're in Seventeenth Century England?"

What the Hell's going on? Past Life regression was crap. He struggled to stay calm. This fantasy should be the key to her fears.

"Who are you?"

"Victoria Chevalier, Countess du Beaujolais." She laughed, vivacious and enchanting.

"My husband, Armand, we are in England for a month. The Earl of Devonshire is our final, and definitely most wonderful host." Her chuckle was soft, seductive. Quiet, reserved Ashley's demeanor was transformed into a sensual flirt.

Feldman took several slow, deep breaths, fighting some strange inner turmoil. "Tell me what's happening."

She settled back, her eyes rolling up under their lids, as she remembered....

FORTY-EIGHT

"Sir Charles Wallace, Earl of Devonshire, he stands in his stirrups, waving his hat.

"Sound the assembly. The Sun's up, and time's awasting," he calls.

"'Tis a *magnifique* day, full of glorious promise." She smiled wickedly.

"*Oui*. A promise between only us. *Quel homme*. His sensuality, it sweeps over me like a storm. I drown in a desire beyond my ken. The hunger in his eyes, it tells me he feels the same. Clarice, his bitter, cold wife, she clearly ignites nothing in his heart...or his loins."

The copper-haired seraph, 'Victoria,' speaking to him is as different from Ashley Easton as pork is from trout. The corner of her mouth turns down, a frown wrinkling her forehead.

"How is it that my father wed me to this foppish clown?" she said. "Armand, Count du Beaujolais, who prefers *les jeunes hommes.*"

"Young men?" The doctor asks.

"*Oui.* Boys, actually. My loins ache for the love of a real man ... for a man like Charles."

Jesus. Could her subconscious really have invented this?

"Arranged marriages. Bah. Neither Chevalier, nor the earl's icy wife will offer any real obstacle. This very day, Charles and I, we will find our true destiny."

"Ah, the hunt begins. The trumpet sounds, and 'tis a melee." She explodes with laughter, slapping a hand on her knee.

And the story of the race through a lush forest of mighty oaks and towering fir gleefully unfolds with vivid imagery, narrated in a sensual Gaelic voice.

"Tallyho! Tallyho!" the two-legged vixen howled, leaning forward, striking the side of her chair with an imagined crop.

Dr. Feldman studies her, fidgeting uneasily in his chair.

Where has this come from? Didn't she say she's never been on a fox hunt?

Soon she's alone with Charles in a picturesque glade, shaded with giant oaks, and bordered by a tumbling brook.

"I am in Charles arms," her voice husky with passion. "Ah, *dieu*, I have the weak knees and mountains of the goose bumps. His dark eyes, they consume me. We kiss."

"He is my destiny, this Charles Wallace, handsome Earl of Devonshire. We make the love. The smell of wild flowers, the song of a little brook ... it all makes a heaven on earth. *C'est magnifique*. I am lost." The radiance of her smile ignited the air in the dimly lit room.

Feldman crouches forward, transfixed. She had sex without fear, finding it wonderful. He, on the other hand, was becoming very agitated, his breath coming in short, shallow gasps, as if he were running. He closes his eyes, immersed in the vividness of her descriptions, visualizing them lying naked in the grass, her russet hair spread like a coppery halo around her head.

He *sees* them so clearly, coupling on the ground. In his mind's eye, everything seems familiar *(how is that possible?)* but leaves and twigs obstruct a clear view. He is unaccountably breathing hard, his face flushed.

How can the Earl do this? Cheating his noble lady. He has known this French harlot but a week, damn the witch. Already they seem to share a love, a harmony of souls. 'Tis a sin before God. They are married to others, but that has not tempered their immoral lust.

Feldman shakes his head, blinking his eyes. *What the Hell is this? Why am I so angry? And why do I feel I'm in the middle of her story, seeing everything so clearly?*

"*Ayy.*" Ashley pants softly. "Twice we make the love, and now lay again in each other's arms. This thing, 'tis a miracle we cannot fathom."

Feldman was quivering, squirming in his chair, fists tightly balled.

The bastards. Might they even consider divorce?

They are tangled together on the lush green carpet, streaked with ribbons of sunlight creeping through the mighty canopy of leaves and branches. The sight of them, even with brush cluttering the view, fuels his anger.

He lurches back in his chair, suddenly chilled.

The sight of them?

I'm not just seeing it through her eyes. It's as if I'm there. And, he first realizes, he has an unseen companion.

Suddenly they are both charging out of the woods, and he's consumed by rage.

A lesson must be taught.

Lesson? What Lesson? Why am I so ...?

"*Ayy,* Charles, I am yours. I...*qui est-ce?*...Who's there? Charles! Look out...."

[155]

A 3rd Time to Die

Feldman senses the two of them rushing upon the naked lovers. There is a whirring beat in the air. Something heavy strikes the unsuspecting man. His head is stove in.

"No! *Mon dieu*, don't...."

Her pleas are snuffed out, her face dissolving into a bloody pulp, as deadly blow after blow smash down upon them. They are not just killed, they are torn asunder. Somehow, he's watching the slaughter, mesmerized and seething with hate.

Feldman blinks, blinks again, shaking his head, his ears still echoing with her anguished screams. He's suddenly aware his patient is scrunched back in her chair, screeching in terror.

"We are dead. Oh, *mon dieu*, we are dead."

What the Hell is going on? Struggling to recover his composure, somehow drenched with sweat, he speaks to her as reassuringly as he can manage, through his ragged breathing.

"Mrs. Easton. Try to control yourself." His voice is a hoarse croak. "There's nothing to fear. You're only seeing this from a distance. It's like a movie. You feel nothing. Please, try to calm down. It's okay. It's not real. Nothing can hurt you in your protective bubble of safety."

Ashley wept, her cheeks stained by the lava-flow of mascara, face gone slack, her body a pile of old rags, almost without shape or definition.

"We are dead. We are both dead." She's racked by sob, body convulsing, her arms wrapped around her in useless defense.

Strangely, Feldman's own vision lingers. Even with his eyes open, he saw them (he sensed his companion there) standing over the bodies as blow after blow is delivered with maniacal intensity, mutilating the two lovers beyond recognition.

Still the flush of great anger filled his breast. Then the images began to fade, sucking all his emotion after it, leaving him numbly empty.

Fighting to grasp control of the present, he saw Ashley,

huddled in the depths of the large chair, moaning softly.

"We are dead. Dead."

"Mrs. Easton, you're safe," his voice a choked rasp. "Safe in your protective bubble. Nothing you're seeing can hurt you. It isn't real." *Time to end this.* His tongue darts across parched lips.

"Now, you're being pulled back ... back to the sunny garden... back to your peacefully sleeping body ... back to the present. Nothing can hurt you. You flow quietly back ... back ...."

He brings her down, hurrying her into wakefulness. He was badly shaken, and his shirt was soaked. Her eyes opened, cautious slits, sweeping the room for danger.

"That was terrible," her voice barely audible. "You said this would be painless and restful, but it was *awful*." Tears continued coursing down her muddied cheeks.

"I'm so sorry. Things just got out of hand. I've never experienced anything like that from a patient before. I should have handled it better."

"But, what *was* that? Was I actually someone else, in another life? 1695? My god."

She dabbed at her tears and blew her nose, shaken, looking at him for answers he wasn't sure he could give.

"Many people believe in Past Life regression, but it is all just the work of a powerful subconscious mind, inventing fairy tales to explain things they can't consciously understand. It's like a dream. A nightmare, in this case. But, it *is* a useful tool in uncovering hidden anxieties and fears, as it has today with you."

"But why French? I barely know the language, and I was rattling it off like a native. I can understand the horses. You know I love to ride and jump. But this Victoria was a reckless, carefree rider, so much more skilled than I. A French Countess? And that magnificent forest ... on a *fox* hunt? I've never seen or done those things, except during what I call The Metamorphosis in the show ring. It must be she who takes over when I'm jumping Injun. How could I make that up?"

"You did study French in school?"

"Yes, two years at New Trier, but I ..."

"Ah, yes. A fine school. And I'm sure you've read novels. Romances, possibly?"

"Not so much now, but when I was younger ..." She was finally unwound, sitting more easily in the big chair.

"But, you're subconscious remembers all. Even though you may remember very little French consciously, everything you learned is stored in your memory. The romantic descriptions of the hunt, the woods, the language...even the perfect lover. It's all stored in here," pointing to his head, "awaiting the right retrieval codes."

"And this regression? That supplied these codes?"

"Exactly."

"But why? Why suddenly now, after so many years?"

"We don't know that yet. It may reflect the current condition of your marriage. We need more time to explore this more fully, but it's been a great start. As terrifying as this was, I suspect you will be far less fearful of sex after today. This should be a catharsis for you. We still need to find where this illusion was born, if you're to get complete relief from so many years of anxiety."

"But it seemed so *real*." Her voice choked.

"Of course it did. So do many dreams. Tell me, if you can, exactly how you saw your lives end in this fantasy."

"The man, Charles, and I were making love when something struck him down. I couldn't really see our attacker. I ... I had an impression of some hideous creature with horns and a beak, and then everything went blank. It *killed* me, too."

"Remember, this is something made up by your subconscious. It never really happened."

"But it seemed so *real*," she repeated, sounding tired, drained and forlorn. They talked for another ten minutes as he slowly and expertly placated her.

When she finally left his office, Ashley Easton was again calm, convinced now everything would be all right.

FORTY-NINE

Feldman sat motionless, unable to summon the strength to rise, long after Ashley departed. Although he succeeded in hiding it from her, he was still quite shaken by the session.

There were no such things as past lives. He was certain of it. Or at least, he used to be. He supposed one could try to explain everything away ... the suddenly fluent French; the total change in voice and speech patterns; her innate facility for riding and jumping; the terror. Too many things, too perfectly described to succumb to the simple explanation he fed her.

And most troubling, *he* saw it all, too. As if he were *there*. The face of Victoria *was* Ashley's, only different. Younger, commanding, so vibrant.

If it were only a concoction of his mind, fed by the vivid colors of her description, then why was he filled with such a terrible rage? Most disturbing was *her* memories ended with her death, while he continued witnessing their total annihilation as he stood over them, seething with anger.

This was absurd. Or was it? Could those two people have actually existed over 300 years ago? If so, and he were wrong about past lives, then he may have been a murderer ... three-hundred years ago.

Preposterous.

There was a way he might check it out. Maybe he would call tomorrow. Did he really *want* to know if it were fantasy ... or truth?

He wasn't sure.

FIFTY

"Woo-eee!" Ashley whooped, leaning forward, urging the gelding on. She tore around the outside of the white-fenced corral, clods of soft earth hurling from Injun's hoofs. Craig, astride his big gray, his face splattered with mud, sped after her. Pulling her well-lathered horse to a skidding stop in front of the stable's huge double doors, she swiveled in the saddle, her face split by an incandescent smile as Craig cantered up. He dismounted, tossing his reins to a waiting groom and hurried to help her down.

"Your servant awaits your pleasure, m'lady." He bowed.

Ashley chuckled, tucking a stray wisp of coppery hair behind her right ear. "And a good thing, too, with me in such a weakened condition, so soon after having a baby."

"Weakened condition?" His eyebrows arched, a sly grin splitting his face. "You led the wildest, most reckless hunt I've ever ridden. I could barely keep up with you. I can't believe this was your first time."

Her slate-gray eyes, still twinkling merrily, searched his before she spoke. "Actually ..." she hesitated, brow slightly knit, then hurried on. "... it seems I may be a lot more experienced than I thought."

His grin widened. "Oh?"

She shrugged gracefully, a small smile tugging at the corners of her mouth.

"I'll tell you later. We having lunch?"

"You bet. The club grill here does a tasty soup and sandwich."

"Okay. I'll get Injun straightened away so the hauler can take him home." She glanced around. "Where're the locker rooms? Gotta change. That was sweaty work today."

Craig laughed. "The way you rode, it certainly was."

Ashley grinned. It *had* been fun. No longer apprehensive at *The Metamorphosis*, she understood she was just seeing through the eyes of Victoria Chevalier. Her French persona was bold and confident, more carefree and reckless than Ashley ever was. How could *that* be, if there were no such thing as past lives. She had taken two books on the subject from the library but had yet to read them. Maybe she better find time to do that.

She really didn't know *what* to think, but as Victoria, she spoke French and rode horses far better than she did either as herself. Just machinations of her subconscious mind? That's pretty hard to believe.

A groom untacked Injun, putting the gear into the back of her SUV, and was cooling the big red horse down prior to loading him in the commercial eight-horse van. He'd be home long before she.

Carrying her duffel bag and following Craig's directions, she headed for the ladies locker room. Craig had already disappeared, intending to take a quick shower before coming up for lunch.

That sounded like a good idea to her.

FIFTY-ONE

Craig sat back from the epoxy-covered knotty pine table, dabbing at his mouth with a napkin.

"Sure do make a juicy turkey burger."

"Mmmm. Delicious." She sighed, stretching languorously, immensely comfortable, clad in a long, tan leather skirt and a sunflower-yellow, long-sleeve cotton shirt, loose at the throat.

It was easy to relax around Craig. She gazed out the huge glass wall. Spread before her was the main show ring—fences and mock walls arranged in an orderly procession. A children's class was schooling their mounts over cavellettis and low jumps. Beyond the ring were endless rolling meadows and geometrically tilled farm land with new stands of corn pushing up. To the North were the open woods of the Forest Preserve, where they had just completed the morning's fox hunt. What a panorama. Unconsciously, she reached out, placing her hand atop his.

"Another glass of wine?" he asked.

She grinned, shaking her head, copper tresses swirling around her face.

"I'm already a little buzzed. The proverbial 'social drinker.' One drink and I'm very social." Her smile was a dazzling sunrise.

He chuckled. "All right, then. Don't want to get you into any trouble at home." The sunrise plunged into a dour sunset, the corners of her mouth turning down.

"No chance of that. No one home to disapprove."

Thick, dark eyebrows arched. "Oh? Where's Keith off to?"

"Back to Louisiana. Supervising the building of their new factory, he says. No calls. No letters. His mistress is undoubtedly down there with him. Having a gay old time, I suppose, if that's *possible* in rural Louisiana."

Craig shook his head. "Boy, he's got balls, being so open about an affair. What're you gonna do?"

"I don't know, damn it." A forlorn sigh. "We haven't had

much of a marriage for years. I always blamed myself. You know, the kids, the horse ... things that didn't seem to involve him."

"That's a crock of crap. Your world doesn't have to turn around his every whim. You're *both* entitled to some time to do your own things."

"Yeah, my therapist has helped me see that. For the first time, I'm actually considering divorce, or at least a separation. Thing is, I don't want him coming after the trusts Papa left for the kids and myself. Be just like him, especially now."

"Look, if he's cheating on you, you can divorce him for cause. I doubt he'd like all that publicity."

She smiled sadly. "But how do I prove it? It'll be his word against mine, and Keith can be a very convincing liar. He's been fooling me for years."

"I can give you the name of a detective. Honest and very discreet."

"A detective? Why on Earth would you know anything about a detective?"

"I've had it with Toni. She's a complete lush, and she'll hop in the sack with anything that has two legs ... male or female. I told you we've never had a child, but that wasn't completely true. There was a little boy, five years ago. He ... he was born badly underdeveloped." Small tears bloomed in the corners of his soft brown eyes.

"He only lived a few days. Fetal Alcohol Syndrome. I just couldn't get her to stop. She drank so heavily, it was like she were *trying* to kill him." He massaged the bridge of his nose, wiping away the tears.

"Oh, Craig, I'm so sorry. I know how much you want kids. You'd be a really great dad, too."

"Yeah, well it might be time for me to move on, too. I ... I don't think I could do it, if I hadn't met you."

[163]

He studied her, and then smiled. "There *are* real women out there, after all, and I'm still young enough to find one and start a family. Twelve years of marriage to Toni has been eight years of torture. So, the P.I.'s documenting all her transgressions. It's absolutely encyclopedic."

"Do you *need* that? Won't she give you a divorce, if you ask her? There can't be any value left in your marriage for her either, at this point."

"You don't know Toni. She craves possessions. That's what I am to her. She just can't let go. Got nothing to do with money. Her family's loaded. I'll need lots of hard proof to pry her loose, and he's getting it for me. He can do the same for you, if you think you'll need it."

He was very still, watching her.

Ashley sat quietly for a moment, her head nodding occasionally to an inner voice.

"Yes," she said, finally, "I guess it may come to that. I don't think Keith would go quietly, either." She placed her long, elegant fingers on his hand, giving a gentle squeeze.

"You're the first real friend I've had in years, Craig. Knowing you has made getting to this point a lot easier."

He took her hand in both of his. "Me, too. We've both learned there's sanity in the world, after all. You mentioned that you're seeing a therapist. That should be immensely helpful."

"I guess. I'm coming to accept that our problems aren't entirely my fault. Keith's responsible for his actions. But my last session was really kind of weird."

"How so?"

She hesitated, searching his eyes. He wouldn't laugh at her, but still she was reticent. Past lives, imagined or not, weren't an easy topic. His face was so filled with real concern that it made her decision easy.

"My therapist regressed me through hypnotism, trying to

darkness of her despair.

They eased apart, eyes flared wide. She had *never* felt this way with Keith. Her whole body resonated, and she was lighter than air.

"My *god*." he murmured, as she drew him back into a fierce embrace, their tongues dancing sensually together. Her heart crashed against her ribs, flooding her with electric heat. Finally they drew apart, struggling for breath. He looked furtively over his shoulder.

She was swamped with the smell of grass and trees, a gurgling brook, the passionate rasp of their breath. A ridge of goose-flesh erupted down her back. Suddenly she was on the edge of panic, frantically searching for danger in the shadows.

Mon dieu. Not again.

Nothing there. No monsters, no whirring instrument of death. But, still the paralyzing fear. Dr. Feldman was wrong. She *wasn't* cured. Not yet.

Holding her at arm's length, his voice was laced with pain ... and something else.

"Ashley, we can't. Not now."

She blinked. "I know. I know." Dark red tresses cascaded around her face as she shook her head. This was so perfect, yet impossible. What really just happened? She sighed.

"We have to resolve our marriages before ... well, just *before*." And why was she still plagued by this paralytic terror?

"You're right." He said. "This thing ... how we feel toward each other ... we gotta put it aside ... locked away 'til we figure out what needs to be done at home."

"How *do* we feel about each other, Craig?" She clung to him, rubbery legs offering no support, filled simultaneously with passion and the remnants of panic, her heart an air-hammer against her ribs. She sensed she was at a moment she had awaited all her life.

[167]

"I... I love you." he stammered, eyes wide with surprise. "I guess I've loved you from the first moment I saw you. I just blinded myself to it. It's as if I've loved you *forever*."

"Yes. There's something ... a connection I've never felt with anyone before. Not Keith. Not anyone. I guess that's why it was so easy to be your friend. I ... I never allowed myself to think about love, until now. How could I have been so blind?"

She laughed ruefully as anxiety fell away, like water spinning down a drain. She was calm again. Calm, but strangely empty. There was more to be faced than just their love.

"We have to ignore what happened here, if we can." She spoke slowly, sifting her thoughts. "Try to solve our problems at home. If either of us decides on divorce, it *must* be because our marriage can't be saved. Not because we've suddenly found someone else." She searched his eyes, her heart at full gallop again at what she saw in those inky orbs.

He nodded.

"I guess." He pushed back a russet lock of hair, planting a tender kiss on her forehead.

"Anything else would be a permanent burr under the saddle. I may go back to my therapist, too." No way could he *ever* ignore the utter bliss that had happened here.

"You've been in therapy?" she asked.

"Yeah. For a while, years ago. Marriage to Toni isn't easy on my self-esteem. I've got a good man who helps me get my head straight."

"Good. I'm going back to my guy, too. I've got more things to work out than I thought."

They continued to talk, holding hands, friendship tenuously reestablished over passion. He walked her to her silver Lexus as they discussed future riding plans.

Craig had mapped out a training schedule, aimed toward entering some Grand Prix events in the next year. Their bond of horses and jumping drew them painlessly back to a comfortable sense of companionship.

Thoughts ... at least conscious ones ... of love and arousal were carefully relegated to hidden chambers in their minds, places where, hopefully, they might be controlled.

But, in their hearts they knew things were changed forever. And for once, change promised to be a happy event.

As she drove off, the detective's card in her pocket, heading for a home empty of love and passion, except for her children, her mind lingered on the one thing she could not hide from.

I was still swamped by The Terror. We were kissing, and I was looking for demons.

Why, damn it? Why?

She'd have to see Doctor Feldman again soon.

That prospect made her very uneasy.

FIFTY-TWO

Craig was parked at his mahogany desk, the new quarterly financial report for his mail order company spread in front of him, but unread. Continued attempts at lassoing his concentration, dragging it back to the affairs of his business, were repeatedly fractured by visions tumbling through his head of that glorious week-end.

What a hunt. What a totally unbelievable day. I've never seen anyone chase the hounds with such recklessly glee, as if she'd been doing it her entire life.

She's amazing.

Then a blissful lunch, filled with easy camaraderie. And the story she told. A past life as a French horsewoman. That could explain so many things, if you believed in those things.

A 3rd Time to Die

Could there really be past lives? Was he there, too? That might account for their easy camaraderie ... the feeling he'd known her forever. That seemed a bit far-fetched.

The surprising culmination of the day though, was The Kiss. Kisses, actually.

God, he'd never felt like that. Toni's lips spoke of raw sensuality. Ashley's filled him with such ... what? Jeez, there *was* no word for it. Thrill, excitement, passion, happiness, blended together into something unimaginable.

Then a sudden chill, looking over his shoulder, searching for danger in the shadows. Strangely, he sensed something similar in her, as if they *both* were expecting something evil to occur. Goosebumps ridged his back at the memory.

Time to sort things out: Toni, Ashley, this sudden anxiety when he held her close. When had their friendship turned to love? No doubt that's what it is.

Glorious love, making his heart sing ancient psalms.

Love igniting his very soul.

Love for a lifetime.

Love for *eternity*.

And she loved him, too. It was there from the first, he realized, resisted because they each had spouses. Unpleasant, cheating spouses, but spouses none the less.

These were things to be separately dealt with. They can't allow this newly discovered wonder to shatter their marriages. Those had to founder on their own set of rocks, despite every effort to save them. Better never to fulfill this wondrous thing than taint it with a less than honest attempt to rescue his crippled marriage.

So, he would go back into therapy. Bruce knew everything about him. He'd help him work it out and lead him to the right decision. No more delays making the appointment. Next week for sure. He was eager to begin, already confident of the outcome.

Ashley!

It *would* be Ashley. No way would Toni ever make the necessary long-term commitment to put their fractured marriage back on sound footing.

Ashley.

It *would* be Ashley.

He could hardly wait.

FIFTY-THREE

"So Mrs. Easton, have a seat and tell me how things are progressing?"

She perched uneasily on the edge of the cavernous chair, rigidly upright, her fingers tensely interlocked in her lap.

"Not as well as I had hoped, Doctor."

"Oh? You seem tense. Try to relax, and tell me about it."

She settled tentatively into the folds of the soft leather.

"This thing ... The Terror ... it isn't over."

"Your fear during sex?"

"Yes. It happened again, a few days ago, just as strongly as ever."

"You were making love with Keith and you became afraid again?"

"Yes and no. My horsy friend and I suddenly discovered we were more than just pals. It was only a kiss ... a wonderful kiss ... but the same panic was there, stronger than ever. I thought that terrifying regression was supposed to cure everything."

"When dealing with the mind, there's never any guarantees." He fidgeted, knowing where this was going, uneasy with that knowledge, but there seemed little choice.

"Sometimes we have to do several regressions to find all the incidents conspiring to interfere with a normal life. Are you willing to try again?"

"God, that was so horrible. I couldn't bear going through it again."

"You won't have to. We won't go back to that time. We'll see if there is something else contributing to these anxieties."

"Anxieties sound a little mild. According to you, I invented my own murder. That's pretty bizarre, don't you think?"

"What I think isn't important, but the mind *does* do some pretty strange things to cover its tracks. Another regression may be the only way to unscramble this mystery."

"Is that necessary? The last one was so ... so terrifying."

"It's your choice, of course, but if you want to resolve things ...."

"Yeah, but it still makes me nervous. We going to do this now?"

"If you're ready. No time like the present."

"Oh, all right. Let's get it over with." She sighed, leaning back, resigning herself. "This spookiness has gotta stop."

"Close your eyes then, relax, and empty your mind."

FIFTY-FOUR

She slid into a deep trance, descending those stairs, lying peacefully on the now familiar bench, her Higher Self hovering above her body.

"You are going back, back, back in time. Back to the time of your fear. Not all the way back to 1695, but to the next time you became afraid of making love.

"Three, two, one. Are you there?"

"Yes." She frowned, a look of sadness clouding her face.

"Albert, stop the carriage. I will walk from here."

Carriage? Warning bells went off in his head.

"What are you doing now?"

"I am walking home. I worry about father. He is ill. I am overwhelmed by unpleasant thoughts."

Feldman knew her father had died six years before, but wasn't it an auto accident? Was she doing it again? He began to hyper-ventilate.

"Where are you and what is the year?" His voice tense, knowing he wasn't going to like the answer.

"Philadelphia. 'Tis the Summer of 1845."

Oh, boy. Here she goes again.

But he had to see this through, for himself as much as his patient.

"What is your name?"

"Morgana. Morgana Quincy."

"Tell me what's happening." He unconsciously clenches his jaw.

"I am lost in thought ..." she begins, spreading before Feldman a narrative of torment over her father's illness and eventual death, disillusionment at her husband's blatant affair, and the blooming but somehow familiar love for Robert Isaac. That tale, drawn over nearly a year, segues into a surrey ride to a picnic in a picturesque forest glade.

As she unfurled the details of that last afternoon, Feldman is drawn back with her. Her descriptions are so happily crafted, it's as if he is there. He actually *sees* them making love languorously beneath the shade of a huge old tree.

Anger boils up, surging through him like flowing lava.

That bastard Jew, fucking the selfish bitch, right in the open, cheating us of our right.

[173]

He reels back into his chair.

Oh, God, not again. I can't be doing this again.

Feldman struggles for breath. *Oh the cheating bitch. She'll pay for her infidelity.*

He's uncontrollably burning with rage again. Somehow, he *sees* them, locked together in a tangle of arms and legs, moaning in wicked ecstasy.

He senses someone rising from the ground beside him. A hand grasps his shoulder, pulling him to his feet, pushing him forward.

He rushes out of the woods, joined by a shadowy other.

The whirring and thumping of some mighty tool of destruction swamps his head, as the slaughter of two newly-found lovers is repeated ... 150 years later ... reducing them to unrecognizable chunks of flesh and bone, scattered across the meadow. Slippery gore covers everything.

You bitch. Feldman's thoughts rage. *How could you do it? You bitch.*

Morgana's cries ring in his head.

She is dead, turned to bloody pulp, but still her sobbing screams resound around him. He is paralyzed by his seething anger.

Punishment. The goddammed bitch needs to be punished.

Strangely, her calls continue, impinging on his brain. *But she's dead.*

"No. Oh, god, no!"

He blinks, and sees Ashley, curled in a fetal ball, a coppery veil of hair spilling over her face. Choking sobs rack her body, her arms crossed rigidly in front of her face, her hands curled stiffly, claw-like.

"Mrs. Easton?" His throat parched, the words a rasping caricature of his normally soothing voice.

"Mrs. Easton." A dry squawk but stronger, as he regains

some control of his own senses.

"Oh, god. It killed us. It killed us again." She rocked back and forth in the chair, her body still twisted and stiff.

Feldman takes a deep breath, struggling for control.

"You're still safe in your protective bubble." The therapist forced calm quiet into his voice, but his tongue burned with a terrible ache.

"Nothing can harm you there. Relax. You are just seeing these things, not feeling them. It's all over now. It's time to come back. Back to your body, lying peacefully on the bench.

"Back to the present ...."

FIFTY-FIVE

"...3,2,1. You're awake now." He reaches over, touching her forehead. "Safe, here in my office."

Ashley remained scrunched into a tight, quivering ball, wedged into the corner of the big leather chair, keening softly. He had to regain control.

"It was only a fantasy," his voice gravely. "It wasn't real."

But he was no longer so sure. What's going on here? He blinked several times and wiped his brow. He was drenched with perspiration.

"But if *felt* so real." She was still panting, slowly catching her breath. Though the tears were drying up, she was crumpled and disheveled, dark bands of mascara streaking her cheeks.

Something was very wrong. He was the therapist and should be in control. Instead, he sat helplessly and allowed his patient to wallow in absolute terror.

Inexcusable. But it felt so *real* to him, too. Why was he

drawn into these horrifying visions, seeing them as if he, too, were there?

Ashley was still crammed in the corner of the big chair, knees drawn up, her arms crushing them tightly against the chest. She rocked back and forth, moaning softly, her eyes jammed tightly shut, contorting her classically lovely face into a ghastly mask.

God, what have I done to her? He shuddered, a cold spear lacing his spine.

"Mrs. Easton." Time to take control. "I want you to take two deep breaths and open your eyes. That's it. Slowly. Slowly. Now, try to relax, a little at a time. Unclench your jaw and wiggle in back and forth."

She began to respond as he forced his voice to be soothing again. Her gray eyes peeked open as the fear slowly seeped away. "Good. Now, release your arms. Let them go slack. Drop your legs back to the floor, or tuck them under you if that's more comfortable." She glanced warily over her shoulder, and then tentatively complied.

"Fine. Now we're getting back to normal, and can discuss what happened."

"What *did* happen, doctor? Another fantasy?" Her voice hoarse and strained.

"Exactly. An invention of your subconscious." Did his face reflect his growing doubt?

"Jesus, why? Why would I want to kill myself so brutally ... *twice*? It makes no sense."

"Whoever said the subconscious is logical? It acts out for reasons of its own, often to hide or disguise other feelings we're unable to face directly."

"I've done nothing to warrant my murder." She shook her head vigorously.

"Even falling for another man and thoughts of divorce?"

"That's no reason to kill myself. Anyway, it doesn't add up."

"How so?"

"Well, I was unhappy in my marriage long before I met *him*. And, how does that explain my speaking and thinking in fluent French? I don't care what you say, I never knew enough of that language to speak it so perfectly.

"And why do I ride and jump so much better when I'm Victoria?" She paused, dabbing red eyes with a tissue and taking a deep breath.

"And why would I pick places like Devonshire and Philadelphia, places I've never even been? Places I never even remember dreaming of. Why would any of those last three things have anything to do with punishing myself with a vision of my own savage murder?"

"Frankly, I don't know."

And he had to put a good face on this until he *did*. There was a lot more going on here than he could possible tell her.

"What I *do* know, however, is that going through this, however terrifying, will be another catharsis for you. Despite the reasons for these unpleasant fantasies, they're out in the open now." He saw her eyebrows arch, eyes filled with doubt.

"I know it seems strange, but this should be a strong step toward quelling the fears you've had. Not an automatic cure, mind you, but a huge step in the right direction. Knowing the source of fear is a major step in conquering it."

He rubbed the bridge of his nose, fighting a splitting headache. Thank God this was the last session of the day.

"I hope you're right. What a draining experience. Don't want to go through *that* again." She lurched unsteadily to her feet, holding the chair back for balance.

"I don't blame you. It was difficult for me, as well. I'm mortified that I let it get so out of hand. There'll be no charge for today's session, and I hope you'll accept my apology."

"Certainly. All you did was help me go to these places. I apparently manufactured the terror. It still makes no sense, but actually, I *do* seem to feel more ... confident, I guess, now that everything's out in the open.

"Do you think it likely that I may have still another of these so-called lives?"

"I doubt it, but see how you do with what we've accomplished so far. I suspect you'll see a marked change in your emotions. Give it a little time. I'll be here if you need me again."

"Thank you, Doctor. I'm not sure I could take very much more of this."

She paused at the door, turning back to him.

"You know, it's interesting. In both these lives, I was saddled with unhappy marriages, just as I am today. I wonder if that has any particular significance?"

"An excellent question. Perhaps we'll find the answer during your next visit."

"Okay, but no regressions for a while. I've had all I can take."

"Right. No more regressions for now. I promise."

She nodded, straightening her skirt and blouse, again a woman of the Twenty-First Century, back in control.

FIFTY-SIX

Twenty minutes later, Doctor Feldman was sprawled on his couch, massaging his temples, awaiting the magic effect of three aspirins. He was worried. Actually, he was terrified ... more afraid than he'd ever been during his adult life.

Nothing in his professional experience remotely explained

what happened to him during Ashley Easton's two regressions. Despite all his calming words, he could *not* rationalize what she went through.

There was no such thing as past lives, despite what many of his colleagues said.

Or were there? He was no longer so certain. *She* seemed convinced, as she described them both in perfect detail ... and once in such elegant French.

Victoria du Chevalier, Countess of Beaujolais, in love with Charles Wallace, the Earl of Devonshire, in 1695. Then, Morgana Quincy, daughter of Jonathan Denton, shipping magnet, enamored with Robert Isaac in 19th Century Philadelphia. Had such people really existed? Certainly, an experienced historian could find records of their lives ... and deaths ... if it were *not* fantasy.

He shivered, and sat up. The damned aspirin weren't working. Hurrying to the bathroom, he made the toilet just in time to catch the remains of his lovely Italian lunch. It tasted bitter now, on the way back up. He flopped back, sitting on the cool tile, panting, covered with perspiration.

Good god. He'd been so smugly certain of himself. But what if those romantic colleagues weren't so foolish, after all. How was it possible *he* saw everything she saw ... and more? And why had it caused him so much anger?

It *felt* as if he were there, meeting out punishment. Each time, he had been furious with her, as the death blows fell.

He trembled, still sprawled on the chilly tiles. If he were wrong, and we *did* live past lives, it seemed pretty obvious that he'd been a murderer ... *twice.*

Gut knotting and churning, he crawled back to the toilet to finish purging his stomach. He slumped to the floor, too weakened to move, grimacing at the acrid smell of bile permeating the air. His lunch was gone, but the fear of his guilt still shrouded him, a heavy quilt of doubt, smothering his breath.

He needed to know the truth. They can't punish him now for something he may have done hundreds of years before as someone else. Retribution would be left to himself, if he were guilty. He had to know the answer, if he were to survive in this life.

And, he knew just the person who could check it out for him, if he would only ask.

He shouldn't delay it any longer.

FIFTY-SEVEN

The Green Monster ran rampant around them.

Walking arm in arm through the bustling concourse, Keith couldn't restrain a small smirk. Men and women, owl-like, swiveled their heads to follow their progress.

Nicole drew their envious attention, and no wonder. A nearly translucent robin egg blue silk blouse, unbuttoned well into her cleavage, did little to hide the firm arch of her magnificent breasts, which bobbed and jiggled enticingly as they headed for baggage claim.

A wide leather Gucci belt girded the narrow isthmus dividing those from the wonder below … rounded hips and curved "bubble-butt" buttocks, encased in a tight silk skirt of the same color, ending well above her knees. Long, shapely legs were fully displayed for the frequent gawker.

Keith slipped an arm around her waist, relishing her movement against him. She grinned, pinching him surreptitiously on the butt, while a fall of fine, inky hair brushed his face. His heart pounded at the wonder of this incredible creature.

He never openly risked so much before, but his need for her in his arms, the raging passion, the pure physicality of their every encounter, was more addicting than the most powerful drugs. How could he live without her? She smiled at his continued stare, fine eyebrows arching above emerald eyes on a perfect, heart-shaped face.

"What?"

"God, I love you."

She chuckled. "Love, huh? Sure it's not lust?"

"Nothing wrong with lust, but this more than that. Lots more. Where have you been all those wasted years?"

"Right where you found me. But, let's not dwell on the past. What about our future?"

They reached the escalators to baggage claim at Houston International Airport. He pulled her against him, nuzzling her ear as they descended.

"Are you really interested in spending your life with me, Nicole, or is this just a fling with a hot stud who knows how to get you off?"

"I'm insulted you'd even ask that. Studs are a dime a dozen, and I can have my pick of the best."

His turn to chuckle. "I bet."

"Damned tootin'. I chose you because you're different. There's a kinda of magic between us. Sorta spooky, too. There's been plenty of guys. You're the only one I've ever wanted to spend the rest of my life with."

He glanced at her from the corner of his eyes.

"Yeah, that's terrific. But, you didn't say anything about love."

"And you didn't say anything about the rest of our lives."

"Okay, you get the bags while I get started at Hertz. We got a two hour drive to Crowley, so we'll have plenty of time to talk."

She caught him by the arm, spinning him into her grasp. Eyes locked for a moment, and then they kissed, tongues fencing a passionate duel.

Fireworks exploded in his head. They slid apart, and she said, "Just remember *that* when we're in the car."

He laughed and headed for the rental counter.

FIFTY-EIGHT

Despite Keith's promise, they talked very little during their drive East on Interstate 10, neither ready to broach the subject of their future. The scenery was unexceptional ... flat bayous rimmed by southern pine, cypress and small stands of live oak.

He set the cruise control at 70 once they past Beaumont and Lake Charles, and punched buttons on the radio until he found a station playing Country ballads. The white Jaguar four-door sedan he reserved was a terrific road car.

He leaned back, trying to relax, an impossible task because Nicole had managed to snuggle against him, despite bucket seats. The heat of her body and her busily prowling fingers agitated and aroused him almost beyond bearing.

Two hours later Keith pulled in front of a white ranch house on the corner of Magnolia and Acadia streets, in the heart of Crowley. Variegated ginger hedges bracketed the fieldstone walkway leading to two nine-paned French doors.

"What's this?" she asked.

"I asked the mayor to rent a house for us. We're gonna spend a lot of time down here, and this is more private."

"Cajun country isn't exactly the High Life, buddy."

"Yeah, but nobody'll bother us here. We can be as open as

we want. Layfayette's only forty minutes, and New Orleans an hour and a half, so there'll be plenty to do."

"Okay, but how are you explaining me to the local brass?"

"Told 'em you're my wife. You're Nicole Easton here."

"Now, that's more like it."

One arm snaked around his neck, she attacked him with her mouth, hands and body, sending him up in flames. Jumping from the car he dragged her up the walkway, fumbling for keys.

"We'll get the bags later. I need you right now."

Her throaty laugh said he wasn't the only one thoroughly aroused.

FIFTY-NINE

Dr. Feldman plopped into the wooden chair, dropping the pile of thick books he had collected onto the long table. A young woman, probably a student, glanced at him, and then returned to her reading. The Research Department at the Northwestern University Library was usually busier than this, but it was a Saturday, and the kids were probably all at the football game.

Feldman sighed, glaring at the books, then shrugged and withdrew his notebook from his briefcase. He found Jack Wexler's note and list of suggested reading. Wexler offered to dig into the French history side, but left anything happening in England and America up to Feldman. The best he could do was suggest where the doctor might look.

Feldman crosschecked the volumes he'd pulled against Wexler's list. He had all but one, but it was enough to get started.

He drew a thick one out of the pile, studying its name;

A 3rd Time to Die

"English & Scottish Royalty Lineage: 1200 AD – 2000 AD." He flipped it open to the Index. Unsure how to begin, research never being one of his shining skills, he started with names.

Wallace seemed pretty common, and the most frequent reference was to the Scottish noble, William Wallace, depicted in the movie, *Braveheart*.

Working down the list was arduous, filled with references and cross references for a surprising number of Dukes and Earls. It took forty minutes to scrape his way down to the Wallace clan of Devonshire.

Goosebumps tripped down his spine at the discovery: the Earls of Devonshire. Ominously, the line expired in the year 1695, with the apparent death of Charles. He was without scions, so his holdings were returned to the monarchy after his death and that of his surviving widow, Clarice.

Feldman shook as he read, his brow beaded with perspiration. The names and dates jived with Ashley's "memories," but the cause of Charles death was not mentioned.

He slammed the heavy book shut, sagging back in his chair, trying to gather his thoughts. Was the lovely Ms. Easton perpetuating some sort of hoax? He shook his head, groaning softly. That was snatching at twigs while being swept away by a torrent of guilt. The story he was so eager to disparage was based on facts, and he, it seemed, knew more about the history of Charles, Earl of Devonshire, than this book.

Well, he had two more to dig through on English aristocracy, plus a "Who's Who" for Nineteenth Century America. He glanced at his Rolex. Less than an hour left before he had to scurry home. They were expecting company for dinner. He may relish the distraction.

Fifty minutes later, he returned the books and replaced in his briefcase a yellow, lined note pad, filed with his scrawling. He'd made some other discoveries, none of which salved his fractured conscience, but he was on his way.

Departing the library, he formulated a plan. Time to visit with Anton Krause, and with his help, maybe begin his personal search of the past.

He was no detective, but he was eager to learn more ... however damning it may be.

SIXTY

Ashley's high heels clickity-clacked along the light gray tiled hallway. They cypress wainscoted wall ended at a stained, wood-paneled doorway. She paused, glancing at the card in her hand, then the gold leaf lettering on an onyx plaque on the door.

Mike McNeely
Private Investigations

Still she hesitated. Should she really do this? Were things so irretrievable that she should hire a detective to spy on Keith? She shrugged and sighed. This might be the only way she *would* know for sure. She had no hard proof he was seeing Nicole Phillips. Did it even matter anymore? Whatever drew them together (was it ever love?) had long since evaporated.

An image of Craig flitted into her head. She flushed, her heart skipping faster.

God. How did I confuse those shallow emotions for Keith with love, when Craig makes me feel like this?

Well, it was past time to learn the truth. Rumors of Keith's infidelities weren't enough. The facts, ma'am. Just the facts. Nothing meaningful could ever happen with Craig, if it came to that, unless she could put Keith entirely behind her. She'd stay locked in this loveless marriage if these accusations proved false. Fight through any other problems they might have, for their children, if for no other reason. Besides, she isn't a quitter.

Better unrequited love for Craig than a future built on perfidy. They can still be friends, but that would be it. Wonderfully, Craig felt the same. She looked at the door again, and smiling wryly, squared her shoulders. Did she really doubt the detective would find any surprises?

Entering quickly, before she could change her mind, she found herself in a small paneled reception area. Two large painting ... original, well-done oils, not prints ... hung on adjoining walls: one a snowy mountain scene, and the other of a doe and a buck whitetail deer, grazing in a small meadow, surrounded by majestic oaks.

Goose bumps trilled across her neck at the memory of a similar place, recently discovered. A pretty thirty-something, dark-haired woman perched behind the desk dressed in a business-like but feminine suit: *Lauren Thomas,* according to the plaque in front.

"May I help you?"

"I'd like to see Mr. McNeely."

"Do you have an appointment?"

"Uh, no. I never thought ... Craig Thornton recommended me."

She'd been so ambivalent about coming, it never occurred to her the man might have a busy schedule.

"That's all right." Her smile was friendly. "Have a seat for a moment. I think Mike'll have time to see you if you're a friend of Craig's."

SIXTY-ONE

Five minutes later, she was shaking hands with a trim, redheaded man with hawkish nose, bracketed by two nuggets of coal for eyes. Flame-colored hair like that could only be natural ... pure Irish. The room was reminiscent of her father's offices, paneled with dark wood ... cherry, she thought ... with an imposing desk in the same material, neatly ordered. Two buff-colored leather chairs and a sofa clustered around a small granite inlaid coffee table.

The detective, about five-foot ten, dressed in a smart, light tan wool suit and a preppy Yale tie, was a long jump from what Ashley had expected. A Mike McNeely should be a large, beefy red-faced man, chomping on a stale cigar, in a wrinkled, ill-kept suit, the desk littered with papers and empty beer cans. So much for Hollywood stereotypes.

"Thanks for seeing me without an appointment. I didn't think...."

"Not a problem, Mrs. Easton. Luckily, I happened to have some free time. What can I do for you?" He gestured her into one of the comfortable chairs and settled in the other.

"I'm...I'm not sure. It's probably foolish."

"I understand. You're uncomfortable about this, whatever it is. That's why people come to me ... to prove to themselves that they have nothing to worry about. Many times, they're right. Sometimes, though, their concerns *are* real. So, why don't you tell me about it, and we'll see if I can help."

"It's...it's my husband."

The detective made no response, so she hurried on before her resolve deserted her.

"He's out late most every night. We don't have sex any more...he didn't even call until several days after I had our last child." It was all strung together and spewed out at a machine-gun clip. She blushed and studied her shoes.

"Was he away?" The voice was gentle and understanding.

She looked up, nodding.

"His company is building a factory in Louisiana. He was there."

"Anything else?"

"I think he has a mistress."

"Oh? Why do you think that?"

"A friend … the wife of one of his business associates … told me. Her husband knows the woman. Has seen them together."

"Okay. What else?"

"*I've* seen her. She's gorgeous."

"Do you know her name?"

"Nicole Phillips. She's an aerobics instructor at the North Loop Fitness Center." He jotted notes on a yellow lined pad as she talked.

"I know the place. Is that where you saw her?"

"Yes. I wanted to see the competition. She *flaunted* herself at me."

"Hmmm, interesting. You think she knew who you were?"

"Looked that way."

He leaned back, steepling his fingers under his chin. "So, what do you want me to do?"

"I don't *know*. I guess I want proof. Documented proof, with photos, maybe. So I'll have what I need if I decide to file for divorce. If he's really cheating on me."

"Shouldn't be a problem. Maybe a week or two, if he's in town."

"But he's in Louisiana. Been there all week."

"So, it may take a day or two longer. I get $750.00 a day,

plus expenses. Probably First Class tickets to New Orleans and a rental car. One or two nights in a motel."

She paused. Should she really do this? It seemed so tawdry, but she *had* to know. Things had already dragged on too long. She sighed.

"Okay. That sounds reasonable."

"Good. I'll need a $2,500.00 retainer. I'll bill you for the rest when the job's completed. I'll need any details you can give me, including an address in Louisiana."

"Fine. A check okay?"

He nodded. She withdrew her check book from her purse. It was an account she started two years before, one Keith didn't know about. No need for him to see something that might make him suspicious, in case she was only being paranoid. Otherwise, it wouldn't matter.

Fifteen minutes later, she was heading for home, feeling as if Injun had just been lifted off her back. She'd made the first move and would soon know the facts. Either way, she could get on with her life.

She was flooded with warm stirrings, visualizing a future with Craig Thornton, pretty certain of the results of McNeely's investigation. If she were right, her conscience would be clear. She would be leaving Keith because of *his* actions, not her love for Craig.

She shook her head and grimaced.

How tawdry, happy my husband is giving me a solid reason to divorce him.

She couldn't contain her grin.

Finally, something positive to look forward to.

SIXTY-TWO

Keith finally unloaded the car two hours after they charged into the house, their passions twice slaked, first on the carpet just inside the front door, tearing at each other's clothing, two wild creatures in heat. That barely completed, he scooped Nicole up, staggering into the master suite, tumbling together onto the bed.

Over the next forty minutes, she teased and aroused him almost beyond bearing, then straddling him for a raucous gallop to an explosive finish. They collapsed together, unable or unwilling to move for the next quarter-hour.

Eventually recovered, they showered, and were dressing for dinner. They'd been together for months, but Keith still couldn't take his eyes off this raven-haired Amazon. She was totally sensual, whether naked, in lingerie, or dressed. She'd slipped into a short, backless, flowered dress, accented by the wide belts she favored, setting off her delicious curves. She twirled slowly in front of him, arms held high.

"How do I look?"

"Stupid question. You *know* how you look."

"Yeah, but a girl likes to hear it."

"You're gonna have all the guys drooling in the plates, and you know it."

"Well, a girl's gotta keep her options open."

He drew her to him, his tongue caressing her neck. "I'm your only option."

She purred. "Ooo, that's nice. Problem is, I'm only Mrs. Easton when we're out of town. What about that talk we're supposed to have?"

"What talk?"

She pulled her ear from his lips and pushed away.

"The future. *Our* future."

"Look, you know I can't stand being without you. I'm never home until Ashley's asleep. There's a lot of things I gotta work out. We've got three kids, ya know."

He wasn't going anywhere without those trust funds, or at least without control over the kids' assets. Ashley wasn't likely to give any of that willingly, especially if she learned about Nicole, so he was stymied. Be perfect if she'd fall off that damned horse and kill herself.

Nicole studied him, hands on hips, lips pursed.

"Don't pretend you care much about those kids, Keith. That's, pretty obvious. So what's the deal?"

He studied his shoe tops. "It's not that easy. I just need some time to work it out. Meantime, I'm keeping you happy, aren't I?'

She shrugged. "Yeah, delirious."

"Okay. Let's eat." He didn't know what else to say.

After dining on a huge plate of shucked Gulf oysters, followed by a heaping bowl of fried crawfish tails, they found a bar with a Juke Box. Three hours past, drinking wine and dancing to the mellow refrains of "The Look of Love," played repeatedly.

Retired for the evening, Nicole lolled in bed, unable to sleep. Keith's steady breathing told he wasn't having the same problem.

Something was going on with the hot-blooded Mr. Easton. Something he wasn't telling her, and she couldn't figure it out. He'd been with her long enough to be totally hooked, and in turn, so was she.

Keith was the first guy she ever wanted to marry. God, what a stud. And all that money, both his and his wife's. This was the culmination of all her dreams. So why won't he ditch his redheaded bitch? Was there something else holding him there?

Time to do some research when they got back to Chicago. She could be patient, but would only wait so long. Keith had to shuck Ashley, one way or another. She fully intended to see that happen soon. He was only a man, and she'd never met one she couldn't get to do her bidding, if she were determined enough.

And by god, she was getting *very* determined.

The winds of Fate swirled around her as she finally drifted off to sleep.

SIXTY-THREE

Craig Thornton teetered on the edge of the big leather chair, sun-darkened hands clutching his knees, curled like the claws of some great bird of prey, ready to swoop down on an unsuspecting quarry. He glared at some invisible target above the other man's head. The psychiatrist's smile was filled with compassion.

"Sit back Craig, and try to relax. What's got you so wired?"

"Ah, shit. She was out again all night, Bruce. No explanation. No excuse. Just acted as if nothing happened. The bitch."

"You're angry about that?"

"Damned right. And why shouldn't I? My wife's openly cheating on me."

"That would appear to be true, but that's been going on for years. There's nothing new in her behavior, something that you've been calmly resigned to in the past. What's changed, to make you so angry now?"

"I ... I don't know. Maybe I've just had my fill." He slumped back into the soft folds of the chair, limp as a deflated balloon.

"You really think so? You've always accepted her infidelity as a price you paid for what you felt was marrying above your social position, especially since Toni doesn't know you're Jewish. This anger is something new. Stop dancing in the shadows. We can't deal with it if we can't see it."

"You don't think I have a right to be mad at my wife fucking anything with two legs and a dick?"

"You know I don't judge those things. You've accepted her behavior all this time. What's changed?"

Craig sighed, looked the man in the eyes, and shrugged.

"My new friend, I guess."

"Ahh. The horsewoman?"

"Yeah. The wonderful, compassionate, warm-hearted, exciting Ashley. The wholesome girl-next-door beauty of every man's dreams."

"Those are a lot of adjectives, Craig. You have strong feelings for her?"

"Yeah, I guess so. We've just been good friends for months, enjoying the horses together. I've had this strange feeling, as if I've known her forever. She says the same thing. Then suddenly, everything changed after the fox hunt."

"She rode in a hunt with you?"

"Yeah. We were talking afterwards, and next thing I knew, we were kissing. It was so ... so scary."

"Because you were cheating?"

"No. I don't give a damn about that. Fuck Toni. It was something else. I ... I felt ... nervous, I guess. Scared, maybe. Like something bad was going to happen."

"Like what? That someone might see you?"

"More like someone might *kill* me."

"What?"

"Yeah. I kept looking around, expecting someone to come

out of the shadows and attack us. I wouldn't put it past Toni to put a contract on me if she saw us together. Ashley seemed just as nervous. It's weird."

"Do you think Toni hired someone to spy on you?"

"I doubt it. Just being paranoid." He waved a dismissive hand.

"Okay, so you were nervous. What's developed since then?"

"We're not rushing into anything physical, if that's what you mean. We're both married to cheaters, but we don't feel that licenses us to do it, too. We've kissed a few more times, and it's wonderful. But, it also *terrifies* me."

"You feel physically threatened?"

"Yeah. It's frustrating. I'm flooded with this fear ... terror, actually ... of mortal danger, when I should be reveling in the bliss of loving such a terrific gal."

"So, you've fallen in love with her, and that terrifies you?"

"No. Loving her is amazing. It's just *being* there that feels so threatening. I can't explain it any better than that."

"You've never experienced this fear before?"

"Never."

The doctor rubbed his temples, trying to short-circuit a growing headache. This was going nowhere. He had treated Craig for several years and could think of no basis for this sudden new anxiety. Time to try something else.

"This is probably the results of something buried deep inside your subconscious. The aftermath of some trauma from long ago, possibly as a child. It's the first time it's come up in all the time we've worked together. Maybe finding what you perceive as real love triggered it.

"We can dig for this in conventional fashion, which could take months, or we can try to speed things up through hypno-regression."

"Hypnotism? I don't know ...."

"It's perfectly safe. Once under, we'll regress you to your youth, or wherever the incident occurred. You'll view it from the outside, like watching TV, never actually re-experiencing whatever it was causing the problem now. Most people find it very rewarding."

"All right. I'm game, if it can really help. When do we start?"

"Not today." The psychiatrist rose. "We're about out of time. Next session. We'll get right to it, so we have plenty of time."

"Okay," Craig said, heaving himself out of the chair. "Now, I can hardly wait."

"I'll set an appointment for you in two days. AM or PM?"

"After lunch. I've got a catalog meeting in the morning."

"Done. See you then."

SIXTY-FOUR

"You are being pulled *back, back, back* in time."

Craig lay on the couch, eyes closed, hands loosely clasped across his stomach, locked in the peaceful depths of hypnotic trance. They had already explored his teenage years in the last session, finding no basis for his new fears.

"You are flowing back, all the way back to the time, whenever it was, that this anxiety first arose. Can you see yourself there?"

"Aye. Careful, there. Take the tree to your right. 'Tis better footing."

"What do you see?"

"We're riding to the hounds, hot after that furry bugger."

Ah, good. So the trauma was far more recent, if he's on a fox hunt. Strangely, his voice took on a different tone. Some sort of accent. The doctor edged forward in his chair.

"Good. Where are you?"

"In the woods of Devonshire. Where else?"

Devonshire? England? Bruce Feldman hitched around in his chair, his hands suddenly sweaty. This had a familiar ring. Oh, shit. Didn't he say the woman's name was Ashley?

"What is the year?"

"'Tis 1695, of course." Feldman flinched, lurching back. What the hell was *this?* As Craig spoke, the doctor realized the change in inflection and accent were British.

This couldn't be happening *again.* He gritted his teeth.

"Tell me what's going on. Who are you with?"

"We've split the party. The French angel and I lead the chase. Gore. She rides like a bloody demon. No obstacle gives her fright."

"Who is this woman?" He bit his lip, already sure of the answer.

"A goddess. She's set an inferno in my heart, and methinks, I in hers. T'will be a task, finding a way around our vows, but I must have her. Never before 'ave I felt like this."

"Who are *you?* Your name?" The therapist was strangling the arms of his chair.

"Charles Wallace, Earl of Devonshire."

Ooofff. Dr. Bruce Feldman slumped back in his seat as if taking a bolo punch to the midriff, though the statement was no real surprise. Struggling for breath, he asked the question he didn't think he really wanted answered.

"And the woman? Her name?"

"Ahhh. The exquisite Victoria. Victoria du Chevalier, Countess du Beaujolais. A woman like none other."

The doctor slouched, head down, both hands pressed against his temple, quivering with epileptic intensity, slowly filling with a blinding rage, as the familiar story again begins to unfold.

He sees them through his eyes, lying naked in the secluded glen, coupling with an intensity he's never known. He and his companion are moving through the trees, stalking the unsuspecting pair. Through the blinding red miasma of his rage, his Twenty-First Century professional mind calls out to him. *Stop this before it's too late.*

"Stop." It's a barely audible croak.

"Stop." Louder this time.

"We've seen enough in this life, Craig. You *must* stop. It's time to move on." His head was about to split open. No amount of aspirin would kill this thumper. His patient sighed softly.

"She was so beautiful. So vibrant."

"That's all right, but it's time to move ahead." He was fighting to keep himself together. He *had* to know everything.

"Now, you are moving toward the present, safe in your protective bubble. Moving to another time you may have felt danger. Can you see yourself there?"

"Yes. I'm in Philadelphia."

Damn. It wasn't possible.

"Who are you here, and what is the year?"

"'Tis 1845. I am Robert Isaac, a Jew. 'Tis a miracle of God that this doesn't matter to her. We are so in love."

"Who is the woman? Her name?"

Feldman's stomach roiled, knotting. Sour bile rose in his throat. He was going to be sick again, but he had to stick this out. This was more important.

"She is Morgana Quincy, a goddess of wonder. I am her deceased father's barrister. We're about to picnic in a peaceful little meadow I've discovered just outside the city."

God, will this never end? This can't be. And how in the hell did I end up with both of them on my couch? Stop this now, before losing control again. Fighting through the excruciating pain trampling his head and gouging his eyes, he spoke.

[197]

"All right. It's time to come back to the present. Back to your peacefully resting body. Back, back, back...

SIXTY-FIVE

"... Three, two, one, and you are awake. How do you feel?"

"Confused. What *was* that, Bruce? Were those really Past Lives?"

"You know I don't believe in Past Lives, Craig. Those were just dreams, fantasies of your subconscious." His voice was barely a raspy whisper.

"Jesus. Whatever, they were so wonderful. Why did you pull me away so quickly?"

"We were running out of time, and I could see they weren't taking us anywhere helpful." The lie was a bone lodged in his throat. He swallowed hard to hold down his rising gorge.

"Too bad. My love for these two women was indescribable. Like with Ashley. Gee, it was almost as if they *were* Ashley. It felt so familiar. Strange, she's found past lives in therapy, too."

Feldman shuddered, rubbing his temples. Demons were in there with picks and hammers, pounding their way through his skull. And now his lunch was looking for a way out, but he had to hang on for a few more minutes.

"I have to cut today's session a little short, Craig. I'm not feeling well."

"Okay. You do look a little peaked. But tell me, these fantasies, how does seeing them help with this new anxiety when I'm with Ashley?"

"I ... I don't know yet. We'll have to explore that next time." He moaned, expecting his head to detonate any minute. One more thing to confirm before ending the session.

"Have you talked to anyone about this type of regression recently? Anything that might have put the idea in your head."

"Uh, yeah. I guess I did. Ashley told me about hers, but few details. Funny, she was riding on a fox hunt, too. Her guy agrees with you, that they're not real."

"She didn't give you names, places, things like that?"

"Just that she was on a hunt. Oh, and she was French. Gee, *that's* a coincidence."

Feldman doubted that. Chance seemed less and less likely.

"Okay. That'll be all for today. See you next week." He rose on new colt legs, a thunderstorm raging between his ears, and said a hurried good-bye. As Craig opened the door, the doctor threw him one final question.

"This woman, Ashley, what is her full name?"

"Easton. Ashley Easton."

No surprise there.

SIXTY-SIX

Bruce Feldman lay on his couch, trying to think ... not an easy task with kettle drums still doing a crescendo in his head. Two problems needed attention. The first ... and easiest ... was passing off one of his patients to another therapist. He would never treat two people separately who were intimately involved with each other. And it appeared that Craig Thornton and Ashley Easton were much more deeply connected than even they suspected.

Since he had a long-standing relationship with Craig, he'd refer Ashley. Rachel Caslow was a perfect choice, if she had room in her schedule. She was an experienced hypno-therapist, more open to the possibilities of Past Lives. They'd had many heated debates on the subject. He'd be in for a lot of teasing, once she learned the main reasons for the referral.

Good-natured teasing from Rachel was the least of his worries. Despite previous doubts, it appeared these two knew each other... intimately... in some previous incarnations. *Twice.*

Or they were pulling an elaborate prank, and that seemed very unlikely, especially since he saw *himself* there both times, through *his* eyes, not theirs, and he saw more than they did. Not only did he *see* their murders, he may have *committed* them.

Feldman was afraid ... the most afraid he'd ever been during his usually well-ordered life. If he were to figure this out, he had to do some comprehensive research. See if these things really did happen 150 and 300 years ago (did he really retain any doubt?).

He needed to return to therapy, the first time since beginning private practice. It may be the only way to discover how he was actually involved. He'd call Anton Krause first thing in the morning. There was one other call he couldn't put off, if he were going to learn the truth. He'd do that tomorrow, too.

Then back to the library for more research, now that he had more to work with.

SIXTY-SEVEN

Ashley scanned the park, scattered with jungle-gyms, a sand box and slides. Stately elms and a few oaks shaded the walks. She located him sitting on a bench, reading some papers.

"Mr. McNeely?"

He looked up and smiled.

"Mrs. Easton. Have any trouble finding me?"

"No. But why are we meeting here?"

"I'm avoiding someone I don't want to see today. Please, have a seat."

She perched next to him on the wooden slats. Staring out over the grassy glade, her gaze found young mothers with small children playing on climbing bars and in the artificial beach. It was so peaceful in this cool oasis of a shaded meadow.

She had a fleeting vision of a similar glade in the woods of Devonshire, splattered with crimson stains. She shuddered.

"Cold?" he asked.

"No. Just an unpleasant memory of a pleasant place." She glanced at him, sitting patiently beside her.

"It's only been four days. Surely you're not finished."

"Finished enough for your purposes. Here's my report."

She stared at the small folder, probably fifteen pages thick, and was suddenly loath to touch it.

"Why don't you summarize it for me?"

"Sure. Well, your suspicions were correct, as far as they went. It's a lot more complicated than I think you guessed."

"What do you mean?"

"He's had a long term affair going with Ms. Phillips. They have an apartment together on the Near North Side, and she travels with him to Louisiana, where they've rented a small house. Folks down there think she's his wife."

"The bastard. Well, she may get the chance."

Ashley shook her head, amazed at his arrogance. The detective's eyebrows arched at her quiet acceptance of the news.

"I took the liberty of checking her out, as well. As you've seen for yourself, she's incredibly gorgeous, and very conniving. She'd already used those assets to work herself into quite a comfortable position before she met your husband. Mostly through illicit relationships with wealthy, older men. She would let things mature for a while, and then pushes them to divorce their wives. Acquired several very generous 'gifts' to move on."

"She's trying to find a wealthy husband?"

"I doubt she intended to marry any of her lovers ... until now. Just an erotic form of extortion. Your husband's the first guy she's hooked up with that's anywhere near her age.

"They've been having a very ... uh ... hot time together, if you catch my drift. I'm guessing she really wants to destroy your marriage and marry him herself. It's a strong lure ... hot sex and lots of money."

"Ha. The dumb bitch is in for a rude surprise."

"What d'ya mean?"

"Got the proof I need? Photos? Everything?"

"Yeah. Videos, audio tapes, copies of hotel registrations and leases. Everything you'll need to chop him off at the knees in a divorce. But that's what Nicole Phillips wants. You to cut him free for her."

"Until she learns he doesn't have much of his own."

"What?"

"Never bothered to check out *his* finances, huh?"

"No. I just presumed...."

"I understand. Well, he doesn't have any. Not much, at least."

"How's that possible? His family business, the house?"

"Their company's in serious trouble. Leveraged to the hilt to build and equip this new factory. They're pinning everything on its success. I've been busy, too. My accountant says one small glitch anywhere will probably push them into bankruptcy. One modest, unexpected expense. Murphy's Law will see to that, don't you think?"

"Probably. Nothing ever goes smoothly. Especially a new factory in a rural, non-industrial area like Crowley, Louisiana. Jesus, that *is* the heart of Cajun-land."

"See what I mean? Even his BMW is leased. The house is a gift from my father, but it's held in trust. Never understood why ... until now. Dad was apparently a better judge of character than I."

She rose, walking in slow circles as she talked. She stopped in front of him, hands jammed in her slacks pockets, grinning, clearly enjoying herself.

"What about joint property. All *your* wealth. I know who Michael Bradford was."

"Oh, there's plenty of money. More than enough to satisfy Nicole Phillips, I'm sure. But she isn't going to see much of that, either. The unlucky bitch."

"In trusts, huh?"

She gave a wicked laugh, and danced a little jig.

"Yes. Beautiful, impenetrable trusts. He won't see a penny from them. Good old dad to the rescue."

He looked at her happily beaming face and smiled.

"It's tough, seeing you so broken up like this."

She laughed almost hysterically, doing a quick spin and a curtsey. Emotional floodgates burst, sweeping away months, even years of damned up tension and anxiety. She was relieved to finally have it out in the open.

~~*~~*~~*~~

There may already be another man in the picture. Might it be Craig Thornton? She couldn't do better than him, if he ever got around to divorcing his tramp. What a terror *she* was. He stood and withdrew a large manila envelope from his briefcase.

"Here's all the evidence. More than enough to do the job. And my invoice. Four days is $3,000.00, and $1,500.00 expenses. That a balance of two thousand. I'm guessing you're happy with the service."

"Ecstatic." She plucked a check, already written, from her purse. "There's something a little extra in there for such fast, thorough work."

He peeked at the check, whistling softly to himself. Five Grand. A very sweet bonus, indeed.

"It's been a real pleasure doing business with you, Mrs. Easton. If there's anything else—?"

"One more job, if you don't mind."

"Of course. What is it?"

"When I'm ready, I'll want you to serve the divorce papers. You can do that, can't you?"

"Certainly. It'll be my pleasure."

"He may still be in Louisiana."

"No problem. Plenty enough here," he waived her check, "to pay for that. Just a one day trip."

"Good. When you do, emphasize how unpleasant I can make his life, should I release all this evidence to, say, the newspapers. I'll smear him across the whole city, if he contests this divorce."

"Sure. I can do that."

He liked this lady more and more every minute.

He'd be sure Keith Easton got her message.

SIXTY-EIGHT

Two-Twenty. Craig couldn't remember the last time he took off work in the middle of the afternoon. Lucky (*Smart. No luck involved, and you know it.*) he had such competent people running the business. No sense in hanging around today, because he was getting nothing done.

His earlier session with Bruce left him edgy and filled with the memory of those strange visions. What *were* those two things ... fantasies, he called them ... that swam through his head like an endless ribbon of film?

They sure seemed real enough ... and incomplete. Why had he stopped them just at the best parts? He was making love to that glorious French angel, and he could *feel* the wonder of it. Then Bruce pulled him away, as if snatching him from the jaws of danger.

Then he was with Morgana, 150 years later. Such gentle beauty. A warm peace filled him as he pictured her ... them ... on a big blanket in that shadowy meadow. His heart fluttered happily at the memory.

Two such incredible women. Three now, with Ashley. Nothing at all like the immoral succubus he married. Meanwhile, these regressions haven't seemed to provide any real progress toward solving these new anxieties.

They hadn't helped him resolve what to do about Toni, either. No confrontation yet over her tying her tubes. Leading him on about having a family. Why was the wanton bitch so determined to hang onto him, when there was nothing left to save?

Possessions. Toni related everything to ownership, and men are her most prized trinkets. Why has he delayed making the break? Was he actually afraid of her? She'd go absolutely ballistic. He had no doubts Toni could be dangerous ... *physically* dangerous ... if she were crossed. Then there was big brother Brad, who would do anything she asked of him.

This was nuts ... obsessing over his wife's reaction to a move he hadn't even made. About time to do something now, though. McNeely had provided all the physical evidence he needed to shove a divorce down her throat. Toni would have to agree. Her father wouldn't stand for public disgrace.

God have pity on the first guy to get in her way after *that*. Or woman, for that matter. Got to keep Ashley totally out of things

A 3ʳᵈ Time to Die

until it was all over. She had enough problems.

Thoughts of his new love had him smiling as he turned onto his street. Swinging into his drive, he had to brake abruptly to avoid clipping a shiny white Lexus sports coupe, sitting squarely in front of the garage.

Damn it. Toni must have guests.

Entering the house, fuming, he looked for someone on whom to vent his anger, preferably his wife. Finding no one in the family room or study, he headed for the patio. The French doors were open, two empty wine glasses sitting on the round glass table, but no one was in sight. Typical Toni. Well, the Hell with her. He was going for a swim.

He was half way up the stairs to the bedroom when he heard them. Grunts, moans, a high pitch, giggling little shriek.

Thump--thump--thump. And another shriek ... Toni's familiar sounds of the coming orgasm.

Craig hesitated for an instant, then continued quietly climbing, stopping for only a moment in the upstairs den to find something in the closet. Moving quickly to the master bedroom, he threw open the door and strode in.

Toni was straddling a young hunk whose face was buried in her considerable bosom. She continued to rise and fall, sucking the juices out of him. As Craig watched, a wave of relief flooded him, his anger gone. He chuckled softly.

She'd done it. Made things easy for him. There was only one small thing left to do.

"Ahh hum." She froze in mid-stroke. The guy's face peeked out from between two luscious mounds of flesh, eyes popping with obvious fright.

"Say cheese." The flash popped, followed by a whine as the Polaroid camera ejected a photo.

Pop ... whine. Pop ... whine. Pop ... whine. Craig calmly ran off all the film remaining in the camera, catching them in various stages of uncoupling and scrambling.

"You bastard," she screamed. "What the fuck are you doing here?"

"It's my house, darling. Even paid for it myself."

"Who the Hell is *he*?" the man asked as he was struggling into his pants. "Your husband? You said you were divorced."

"Won't be long now. Be patient, son, and she'll be all yours." Craig was enjoying himself more than he should.

"You son-of-a-bitch. I'll *never* give you a divorce." Her face was contorted by rage, no longer lovely. Certainly not sensual.

He smiled, strangely relaxed. He held up six photos, fanned in his hand like playing cards. Now fully developed, the figures were plainly recognizable.

"Good likeness, don't you think, darling. I'll send you a set for your album. I'll bet papa would love such cute shots of his daughter at play. Of course, the society columns are always interested in what the Rudolph's are doing."

Toni hurled herself at him, a screeching banshee, long red claws seeking blood. Left hand filled with the snapshots, he could only catch one wrist with the other. Yanking her to him, he quickly spun, turning his back to her, doing a neat shoulder throw. He hadn't forgotten the judo training of his youth. Still, two nails caught him on the left cheek as she sailed by, landing hard on the thick carpet.

She sat there, massaging her wrist, perfect teeth bared like a cornered cat, cobalt eyes spitting cold fire.

"I'll *kill* you, you bastard. You'll never get away with this."

"I already have. These pics are only the coup d'gras. I've had a detective on you for a month. File's five inches thick. Lots of photos, and even some video and audio tapes. And of course, there's the tied fallopian tubes you never bothered to mention to me."

She blanched, drawing back, hissing at him.

"Funny thing is, I was still trying to find some way to save things, right up 'til just now. But, you've made it easy for me. It's over for good."

He glanced at the other man, dressed now, edging for the door. Blonde, muscular, middle twenties, and very scared.

"Look, man. I'm sorry. I didn't know. She said—"

"It's okay. She's hard to resist. Just go. And, you might want to get a blood test."

He turned gray and looked at Toni, tongue darting between her lips like a cornered snake.

"Uhh, the photos?" He fidgeted for a moment. "I wouldn't want...."

"Not to worry. Her daddy's got more sense than she does. I suspect everything will wind up very quietly."

The younger man nodded and hurried out of the room. A moment later, the front door slammed.

Craig turned back to his wife, still crouched on the floor, watching him. How exquisite. How dangerous. He shook his head in disgust at himself.

"I'm going to pack some things and move to a hotel. Understand, I'm *not* giving up the house. I don't know why I was clever enough to title it solely in my name, but this is just simpler until we finalize things. My attorney will be in touch with you. I think, after you've discussed it with Daddy, you'll be quite amenable to a No Fault Divorce, don't you?"

He went for a suitcase. When he returned, she was wearing her sexiest teddy, and smelling of fresh perfume, sidling up to him as he began packing.

"Craig, darling." A hand stroked his neck, her warm breath caressing his ear. The smell of jasmine and spice, combined with her musky odor, was intensely erotic.

"Don't, Toni." He moved away slightly, but she followed.

"Darling, it was all a mistake. I love only you."

"It won't work, Toni."

"Oh, baby, I *need* you. If you weren't off with the horses so much, I'd *never* be naughty. I just need to be loved."

He sighed. "It's no good, Toni." Her warm body was pressing against him. Her touch, her smell. In spite of his resolve, he was becoming aroused. She was a goddammed succubus. Slamming the suitcase shut, he pulled away roughly.

"Not this time. You're a fucking witch, but the spell's broken. I'm outta here, and there's *nothing* you can do about it."

Screaming, she leaped at him again. He snagged both wrists this time, but she managed a knee kick that barely missed its mark. It would still leave a sizable bruise on the inside of his upper thigh.

Shoving her away, she bounced off the bed, slipping to the floor with a soft thump. Grabbing the suitcase, he started for the door. She glared at him.

"You'll be sorry. No one walks out on Toni Rudolph. No one."

"There's always a first time. 'Bye, darling. See you in court."

Her screamed profanities followed him down the stairs and out the door. He smiled, dabbing the still oozing scratches on his cheek.

It was finally over, with no room for regrets. He eagerly anticipated a new future, hopefully including Ashley.

But, he had no idea how dangerously things were actually progressing.

SIXTY-NINE

The big, dark-red horse nickered, tossing his head. He reached back, nuzzling his mistress, nipping at the sleeve of her shirt.

"Hey. Cut it out. You'll get your apple when I'm done and not before." She giggled as he nudged her again while she continued currying his mane. Satisfied, she began brushing his long, powerful neck and shoulders. Another determined nudge almost sent her sprawling.

"Hey." She laughed, wrapping her arms affectionately around Injun's neck.

"Delightful to see you in such a good mood, even when being shoved around by a pushy guy."

She spun around, russet eyebrows arched, one hand to her throat. Craig was leaning against the gate of the stall, grinning, his dark eyes devouring her.

Hummingbird wings fluttered in her breast, a delicious heat filling her. Auburn locks swirling, she sucked in a ragged breath, trying to calm her galloping heart, but the sight of him turned her long legs wobbly, like a new-born filly.

"Hi, buddy," her voice hoarse and softly breathy. "What're you doing here in the middle of the week?"

"Thought *you* might be here this afternoon. Getting him all fancied up for something?"

"Yeah. We're having a tenants-only show this weekend. The fox hunt was great, but I thought it was time to ease back into competition, now that Janine's a little bigger."

"Getting ready for the quest for a Grand Prix title, huh?

"I hope so. You got some free time to work with me? I ... I really need the help." The look in his soft dark eyes sent goose bumps trilling down her spine.

"There's *nothing* I'd rather do. To spend as much time with you as you can stand."

"What about your work?"

"I've got the best general manager in the business. He could run that place for months without me. And I'm only a cell phone away." He sidled forward, taking her long, slim fingers in his.

"Handy little gadgets, aren't they?" She drew him closer. "But, won't Toni be upset if you're spending so much time with me?"

"That's not a worry anymore." One corner of his mouth tilted up, his gaze holding hers.

"Oh?" She trembled, her hands suddenly damp. She seemed unable to draw a breath.

"I caught the brazen bitch bare-assed in the sack with some young stud. I'm getting a divorce."

Ashley exploded, laughing almost hysterically, gripping her sides as if to keep them from bursting. Craig's face bloomed red, a quizzical frown crinkling his eyes at such unexpected merriment.

"What's so damned funny? It was no real surprise."

"Ohhh." She struggled for breath. "Not ... funny. Just ... can't ... Ohhh."

She flopped down on a pile of hay, still holding her sides, rolling back and forth, cackling uncontrollably. He began to chuckle, her levity infectious. This beautiful woman was really having a great time, apparently at his expense. The expression on his face clearly said he didn't really care. He settled on the ground beside her, gently picking straw from her hair as she rocked from side to side.

Two minutes passed before she gained sufficient control, struggling to a sitting position, catching her breath.

"Now I know what it means to be rolling with laughter," he said, grinning.

"Pffft. Ohh, no!" She erupted, off again in gales of unrestrained glee.

Craig wrapped one arm around her shoulders, nestling his nose in her russet locks. Happy tears streamed down her cheeks as she snuggled close, still out of control.

Even after she finally stopped, they sat quietly, savoring their nearness.

"Now tell me what so hilarious about my pending divorce?"

"Only that it's a happy coincidence." She sighed, scrunching tightly in his arms. Her smell was an intoxicating blend of lilies, mingled with the musk-scent of fresh perspiration.

"What d'ya mean?" he asked. What could be happier than this?

"I've finally kicked Keith out. I'm filing for divorce, too."

"You're kidding."

"Nope. I hired McNeely. Did a great job. Photos, tapes, videos. The whole shebang. My darling husband's been living with that gorgeous bitch in Louisiana, telling everyone she's his wife. Well, now she'll have a chance to really make that happen."

"Wow. So, we'll both be free." He took her chin in his hand, her gray eyes consuming him. She raised her lips slowly toward his.

"No." Her voice was husky. "I'll *never* be free. I'm happily trapped by my love for you."

The kiss was tender, yet filled with a blinding heat. Her heart was galloping around inside her breast, her whole body quivering, every nerve alive with delicious fire.

Mon amour. She sighed. Musing in French seemed somehow so appropriate.

How remarkable to find love with your best friend.

SEVENTY

As their lips lingered together, singed with a delicious heat, a momentary image of the French Countess flashed into Craig's head. This aura of tranquility and excitement, this sense of *completeness* with his newly discovered love for Ashley, was *identical* to how he felt toward Victoria in that wonderful, imaginary incarnation. It must have been his sub-conscious mind's way of telling him how he felt toward this angel now in his arms, just as Bruce said.

So, why was he still so uneasy, the braced arching of his back, the prickly skin on his scalp? How could he feel so charged with joy while also plagued by senseless panic?

Her fingers were in his hair, and he could feel her trembling, molded tightly against him. Slowly, they parted, his world coming back into focus. Eyes wide, he devoured her. Everything was okay. More than okay.

"My *god*. How was it that for all this time, I never realized I loved you?" he asked.

"It's the same with me. But wasn't this best? Good friends first. Love has a better chance this way, don't you think?"

"I suppose. But, I've *never* felt like this, even in the beginning with Toni. Everything's so much more intense ... so much more concentrated. I can't bear the thought of going home without you tonight."

"Me, too, but we must be careful. Feeling like this ... it's ... it's a wonder beyond my wildest dreams. But we're still married. How would it look?"

"Oh, my darling." He pulled her close again, nuzzling her hair. "Wishful thinking. Just wishful thinking. You're right, of course. We've both gotta establish legal separations. Let the world know we're getting out of our rotten marriages."

"Right. People will wonder why the split, even though I bet Toni's and Keith's reputations are widely known. Our ... our relationship will certainly look suspect, regardless of how cautious we are."

"Yeah," he nodded thoughtfully. "Toni's already trying to

blame you. Her family thinks she can do no wrong."

"Will she give you any trouble?"

He snorted. "Trouble's her middle name. It's her father who'll speed things along, once he sees what I've got on her. He won't want stuff like that to come out in court. A blemish on the Rudolph name.

"What about Keith?" he asked. "How did he react?"

"I don't know." She stood, brushing hay from her jodhpurs and started pacing with short, nervous little bursts.

"What d'ya mean? You didn't tell him you're filing?"

"No. He's still in Louisiana. Mr. McNeely was supposed to fly down with the papers yesterday to serve him. He thinks he can convince Keith to go along quietly. I've hired someone to come in and pack all his stuff. Once he's served, I'll move everything to his mother's. No need for him to ever come back to the house."

"You think he'll fight a divorce, if he's so hot for this other woman? You're making it easy for him."

He took her hands to corral her nervous meandering. She glanced up, producing a bitter-sweet smile and a helpless shrug.

"It's money. It's *always* about money."

"Jesus, Ashley, he's an Easton. They got oodles of dough. Why would he need yours?"

"I ... I shouldn't say. It's confidential things. I owe them that much." She studiously examined the tips of her brown leather riding boots, polishing one, then the other on the back of her pants.

"Is it their business?" He cupped her chin, raising her eyes to his. "I shoulda guessed. Their stock has slipped twenty per cent in the last month."

She held his gaze, but said nothing. Her eyes glistened with unshed tears.

He said, "That's why they rushed into that new factory in

Louisiana, isn't it? To cut costs, before it was too late?"

Her nod was barely perceptible. "My accountant says it's probably *already* too late." It was barely a whisper. "They're such nice people. His parents, I mean. I feel so badly for them. I'm having trouble mustering any sympathy for Keith, but I hate to see his folks in so much misfortune."

"So, with his financial future bleak, you figure Keith was counting on you keeping his bed filled with roses? But, isn't virtually everything in trusts?"

"Yeah. He won't get much from me, especially with what McNeely's got on him. It'll really piss him off, and I bet his girlfriend goes bonkers."

"You think she's only in it for the green?"

"You bet. Oh, she may love the louse, but McNeely found she has a history of doing very well for herself with her affairs. She's surely expecting a lot more from Keith than he'll be able to provide now, or ever."

"Wow. D'ya think he'll try anything funny?"

They were outside the stall now, the gate closed. She stood quietly, feeding Injun his promised apple.

Holding her closely, Craig felt her shiver slightly. The horse plucked the crisp, white remains from her palm, and she turned to him. He wrapped her gently in his arms, his face in her silky hair. How could she still smell so delectable after a day at the stables? She slowly relaxed against him.

"What he can do? He'll rant and posture and act macho. But in the end, it'll mean nothing. My attorney says he couldn't get much without my consent, even *without* all the things I have on him. The trusts are impenetrable. If I had any respect for him at all, I wouldn't be getting a divorce, despite how I feel about you. I'd stick it out, and you and I would just have to stay friends.

"Lucky for me ... for us ... he's an utter louse," she said, "and I have absolutely no compunction about leaving him."

A 3rd Time to Die

She leaned against Craig, warm and safe in the circle of his arms. Turning her head, she reached up, delivering a tender kiss to his cheek, and then stood back and sighed. Taking his hand, they began walking slowly down the dimly lit aisle between the stalls toward the sunlit doors.

She kicked aimlessly at small piles of hay as they ambled toward the entrance, the sunlight shining as if at the end of a long tunnel. Was there happiness there, or ...? An unaccountable chill laced her, raising fine auburn hairs on her neck.

Where'd that come from? She shivered, glancing at Craig.

"What about you?" she asked, finally. "Any doubts about leaving Toni? Think you'll miss her at all?"

He grunted, giving a short, derisive laugh. "Not for a minute. The last few years have been an erotic Hell. She's a damned witch, taunting me with great sex whenever it suited her. When she needed to placate me, mostly. But, it doesn't work anymore. Not since I met you. Even *before* I realized I was in love with you. If there were never anything else between us, that woulda been enough. Dayenu."

"What?"

"Dayenu. It's Hebrew. It means, 'That would be enough.' It's part of one of the Passover prayers."

"Interesting. How did you ever learn that?"

He paused, pulling her to a halt, just inside the big double doors of the barn. He studied her face for a moment, and squeezed her hands gently, before answering.

"Because I'm Jewish."

"You're kidding. With a name like Thornton?"

"It started out Tannenbaum. I changed it, and this nose, in high school. Does this bother you?"

"Not a bit." She smiled, leaning over and planting another soft kiss on his cheek. Life takes funny turns. Robert Isaac was Jewish. Had she somehow known this about Craig and invented that existence to make it acceptable to her WASP upbringing? The mind's a powerful thing.

He squeezed her hand again, as they started for the parking lot, both floating on a pleasant aura of happiness. After so many rotten years, their lives were surging down an unexpected but very wonderful path.

But there were bricks in their road.

Very large bricks.

SEVENTY-ONE

Bruce Feldman slouched next to the same table he'd visited the week before, at the Northwestern Library. A smaller pile of different books were stacked before him, awaiting his interest.

"I hope Wexler can find something," he muttered softly. The French History Department's historian had agreed to research their version of the "French Connection," and had also given Feldman some new venues to follow.

He sighed, opening the top book, wondering why he was so compelled to find the facts ... if they even existed ... to something to which he was already pretty sure he knew the answers. Craig Thornton's amazing memories, almost exactly duplicating Ashley's, verified their reality.

The only thing still obscure was *his* involvement. Who was he in both those lives, and what was his real culpability in the murders? That was the question most nagging him.

Well, time to play detective again. *Hi ho, hi ho, into the books we go.* The small smile was more a grimace.

Twenty minutes later he was reading what amounted to a 17th Century obituary: the brutal death of Charles Wallace, Earl of Devonshire, apparently at the behest of some wild creature, thought to be a rogue bear. No mention of visiting French countess also as a victim.

Pretty taciturn, with few added details, but it was something. He turned to another book, seeking confirmation of the gristly event in 19th Century Philadelphia, when his cell phone began vibrating.

Glancing at the screen, he grunted, and after an indecisive pause, punched the 'talk' switch.

"Jack," he whispered, drawing an irritated stare from the girl sitting across from him. "I'm in the library. Wait 'til I get out in the hall."

He rose, almost knocking over his chair in his haste, and scurried for the exit.

"Okay," he said, as the door swished quietly closed behind him. "What's up?"

"Bruce, I found it!"

Feldman gritted his teeth, knowing what "it" was.

"Yeah? What?" he said.

"Wait 'til you hear this. Unbelievable." His enthusiastic recount of what he's learned was no real surprise to the doctor.

Looks like he *was* a murderer ... at least once before.

SEVENTY-TWO

"C'mon Nicole, we gotta boogie."

"What's the sudden rush to get back, Keith?" She posed, framed in the open doorway to the bedroom, hands on her hips. She looked amazingly sensual, simply garbed in a short black skirt and a lightweight charcoal cotton blouse, open, as usual, well into her cleavage.

"I gotta get back to Chicago. See if I can talk sense into that bitch. If we don't go now, we'll miss the last flight outta Houston." He was enroute to the front door, towing a wheeled carry-on, and shouldering a small duffel bag.

"Jesus. Do you think you can actually talk her out of the divorce, after seeing all the stuff that detective has on us? Even Miss Goody-Two-Shoes is gonna move on, especially now that she's found 'true love.' This is perfect. Now we can be together openly."

"You're kidding, right? You got any idea what the fuck you're talking about?"

"Hey." She strode up to him, delivering a solid slap across his left cheek. He staggered back, almost tripping over the small suitcase.

"No one talks to *me* like that." Malachite eyes threw lightning bolts at him. "Who the Hell do you think you are?"

"Jeez, I'm sorry, babe. I didn't mean to sound like I was putting you down. But I gotta stop Ashley somehow, before it's too late."

Anger diffused, she moved in, planting a wet kiss on the growing red welt on his cheek.

"I don't understand, Keith. Why can't we just move on to a glorious time together? No more need to sneak around. After the divorce, I can become the *real* Mrs. Easton. Isn't that the goal here?"

"Yeah, it's all I dream about, but there's a problem."

"What problem?" Her hand was in his hair, her skilled tongue wreaking havoc on his ear.

"Money. That's the problem." She arched back, hands on his shoulders, inky eyebrows raised.

"Money? Christ, Keith, you're an Easton, COE of Easton Industries. You got plenty of money ... don't you?"

"Actually ... no." He rubbed the corners of his eyes, sighing. "The company's not doing well, and I've taken a 50% cut in salary. This move to Louisiana is our last chance to save it."

"Terrific. And if this factory fails ... " She stood back, arms akimbo.

"... the business fails. That's why this thing with Ashley ...."

"Jesus. All this time, you've ... *we've* ... been living off Ashley's money?"

"Yeah." He dropped onto a sofa, his face buried in his hands, groaning softly.

"It's all in trusts, too," he muttered. "Hers and the kids. No way for me to get at it if we're divorced."

"Look." Nicole settled next to him, one arm around his shoulder, a hand under his chin, raising his face to hers. "You're not that redhead's patsy, buster. You're better'n that. We just gotta come up with a plan."

"You're not gonna bug out on me, Nicky? I know you expect the good life, and if I can't ...."

"Hey, I admit your good looks and all that money were the magnet at first, but there's some kind of innate attraction here that goes way beyond the obvious. I'm actually in love, and I expect my honey to suck it up and do whatever it takes to fix this.

"Going back to that bitch isn't gonna cut it, so were gonna have to devise another way to get our hands on that money. We're both clever, so let's hatch something that'll work, but keep us safe."

"Yeah, okay, we'll think of something. Wish she'd fall off that damned horse and break her neck." Nicole slithered onto his lap, strong arms around his neck drawing his face into the luscious prison of her bosom.

"Nice idea. Maybe we'll have to work on that." Unbidden, his hands found their way under her skirt, as his shirt disappeared, followed by her blouse. Heat blossomed full-bloomed in him, rushing blood from his brain to his groin, as their clothes fell away. Tumbling to the thick carpeting, they grappled in unrestrained ecstasy.

"The plane," his voice a hoarse whisper.

"Screw the plane. Fuck me *now* ... and then we got a plan to make. That bitch's got no chance against the both of us." She inhaled his iron rod, switching around so he could taste her, two tongues slathering with erotic bliss. As he finally entered her, locked in the steel of her arms and legs, gripped by the muscles of that incredible moist, velvet glove, a thought wedged into his brain.

The horse. That's the answer. That's always been the answer. He shuddered, gasping as they orgasmed together, the thought slipping away for the moment. But the seed was planted.

The horse.

Somehow, that *was* the answer.

SEVENTY-THREE

The haggling had droned on for nearly an hour.

Craig slouched in the comfortable leather chair, doodling aimlessly on a lined yellow pad, totally bored. Not disinterested ... just bored.

He glanced at the six people sitting across the polished rosewood conference table, all listening with varying intensities to Max Leverstein's fifth attempt to clarify his clients' position.

They just refused to understand. Craig placed a placating hand on Max's sleeve, giving a little squeeze.

"This is getting us nowhere," he said. "You people just aren't listening."

"I'm very good at listening, Mr. Thornton," said Archie Smithson. "I just haven't heard any ...."

"Let's cut the crap. It's really very simple. I don't want anything from the Rudolphs, and Toni isn't getting a dime from me." He looked at her parents, sitting at the end of the table.

"You people have more money than even she can spend. You've shielded her all her life, and you're not about to quit now. If you want a nice, quiet No-fault divorce, that's the way it's gonna be."

"You *bastard*." Toni exploded, leaping to her feet, hands braced on the table, leaning across at him, cobalt lasers flashing from her eyes. "I'll *never* let you go. I'll never ...."

"Fine." Craig stood, despite Max's attempt to restrain him. "Then I guess I'll see you in court, with all the messy pictures, videos, recordings ... the whole shooting match. There'll be plenty of local press there, too. Count on it."

"I don't give ...."

"Toni. Sit down and shut up."

She froze, mouth open, in the middle of forming another invective. Her father never talked to her like that. She turned, a plaintive little girl now. Craig marveled at her skill.

"But, Papa, I only ...."

"Just sit down and be quiet." Harrington Rudolph had not raised his voice, but the steel in it was quiet thunder. She sank back into her chair, tears in the corners of her eyes.

Rudolph turned to Craig, who had slowly lowered himself back to the edge of his seat.

"Why are you doing this, Craig? To Toni, to all of us? Haven't we treated you like another son?"

"I got no real complaints with you, sir, except you're permissiveness has allowed your daughter to become an amoral tramp."

His wife snarled at him, but her father's upraised hand cut her off.

"Those are pretty strong words, considering you have been with your own lover for many months now. The sword cuts both ways."

"Ashley's been a friend, and *only* a friend, up 'til now. Toni, on the other hand, will sleep with anything with two legs and a dick. And, without a dick, for that matter. I sat back and watched for longer than I shoulda, but no more.

"My friendship with Ashley has no bearing on this, except for showing me what a *real* woman is like. This was coming, with or without my knowing her. I want nothing more to do with your daughter. I'm really afraid of catching something deadly from her now."

"That's preposterous." It was the first time Craig ever heard her father raise his voice. "You can't talk about her like that."

"I have no desire to talk about her at all, unless required to do so in court. There's only two options. Either we do it my way, which hurts no one, or I'll see you in court. It's up to you."

"Hey, wait a fucking minute. This is *my* marriage. You can't...."

"Toni, will you be *quiet!*" Face beet red, the elder Rudolph, turned back to Craig.

"You refuse to overlook a few modest indiscretions? I guarantee it will not happen again." He shot his daughter a menacing glance, as she barked an abrupt, disdainful little laugh.

Craig shook his head, exasperated. "No. *You* refuse to see things for what they really are. I'll not back down again. We're getting a divorce ... neat and quiet, or noisy and messy. Your choice. But, I'm getting out. Now."

"You're a sanctimonious bastard, Craig," Toni's brother growled.

"Stay out of this, Brad," his father said, suddenly sounding old and uncertain. "Hot heads won't help matters."

"I don't give a damn. He's fucking around with his bitch, and he expects my little sister to get the short, dirty end of the stick. Who the Hell do ya think you are, Thornton?"

"Look, this is getting us nowhere. If you guys wanna view this little tramp with rose colored glasses, that's your problem. Fools will believe whatever they want. I was one once, too. But no more.

"The fact remains, Ashley Easton had nothing to do with this. Her behavior's been exemplary, despite whatever wild tales Toni might have invented. Toni's the problem, not Ashley. One's a trollop and the other's a lady. You figure out who's who. I'm outta here." He turned to his attorney.

"Work it out, Max. Either they agree to a No-fault on my terms, or we go to court. That's it. No compromise." Craig closed his briefcase and, shoving back his chair, headed for the door.

Toni leaped to her feet, fists balled, slamming them on the dark stained tabletop with a resounding bang.

"You can't do this to me. I'll never let you go. I'll fight you in every court in the land."

"Toni ...."

"Shut *up*, Daddy."

Harrington Rudolph's jaw dangled comically as he visibly shrunk back from the scorching heat of his daughter's anger.

"You're *mine*, Craig. I *never* give up what's mine. I'll kill you first. You *and* your fucking Ashley Easton. You'll be sorry. You'll see."

"You're a petulant little girl, Toni. Used to be kinda cute when we were dating, but it's worn thin. Very unattractive." He opened the conference room door and paused.

"So, I guess I'll see you in court, unless good old Daddy can talk some sense into you." He waved off-handedly as he slipped through the doorway.

"I'll get you for this, Thornton," her brother hollered after him. "You can't do this to my sister. You'll pay, big time."

Max Leverstein looked at their attorney, eye-brows raised. Archie Smithson shrugged, the picture of elegance, and mouthed, "We'll work it out."

Max sighed, and nodded. He hoped so.

Things certainly had gotten way out of hand.

Divorces were seldom easy.

SEVENTY-FOUR

"So, Bruce, it's been a long time, eh."

Dr. Krause, settling on the edge of his 18th Century French mahogany desk, raised one bushy eyebrow, smiling at his friend and ex-student. Feldman marveled at the full head of wavy white hair still crowning his mentor's thin, angular face.

"About three years, I guess, Anton. How have you been?"

"Can't complain. Getting a little creaky, but that's to be expected at 72, I suppose."

"You look great," Dr. Feldman said, grinning. "Still working out?"

"Yeah. The stair-climber, the machines, sit-ups. All the usual crap. But, I suspect you're not here to discuss my health? What's up, my young friend? You look harried"

"I ... I've run into something really strange. I need some advice. Maybe *more* than just advice."

"Tell me about it." The older man moved behind the huge old polished desk, sinking into his dark leather executive chair.

Feldman said, "First, tell me, how you feel nowadays about Past Life Regression? Any new ideas?"

"Hmm. Well, it's certainly been getting a lot of attention lately. Many interesting stories that sound convincing, but are hard to prove. I still feel the experience is a self-induced fantasy, orchestrated by the subconscious to assign reason and understanding to events we can't handle in any other manner. We've discussed this before. I've not seen anything new to dissuade me from my position. You've been exposed to an incident in your practice, I take it?"

"Yes. But more than that."

"Tell me about it. I'm not expecting my next patient for an hour."

"Good. Well, hold onto your hat. You may be about to revise your thinking."

"Oh?" Eyebrows raised, the older man sat forward with rapt attention.

"I acquired a new patient several months ago," Feldman said. "She came to me harboring an irrational fear of sex. Not just reluctance, but real terror. Almost a fear for her life. After several sessions, we decided to try regression. All the symptoms pointed to childhood abuse, though that seemed unlikely, knowing her family background."

"And—?"

"Nothing, not even in her earliest years. Finally, I told her to go back to whenever the reason for this anxiety first occurred. Next thing I knew, she was speaking French. Not school French, either. Elegant, perfect French. I asked her to speak English, and she did, but with a French accent. She saw herself as a French Countess in the late 17th Century. The Countess Victoria du Chevalier." He paused, rubbing the bridge of his nose, sighing softly.

"Go on. This is getting interesting."

"You can't imagine. Cutting to the heart of things, she was having an affair with an English nobleman, Charles Wallace, Earl of Devonshire. They were brutally murdered while making love in the forest."

"Ahh. The reason for her terror, I take it." Dr. Krause had steepled his fingers under his chin, eyes half closed as he listened.

"That's what I thought. I explained the fantasy to her and sent her off. Case closed, right?"

"Apparently, there was more."

"Obviously. The panic was still there. So, we tried again. This time we ended up in mid-19th Century Philadelphia. Now, she was Morgana Quincy. Without going into tedious details, it was a somewhat similar situation. And it ended in the same manner ... the brutal murder of her and her lover, while picnicking in the woods. Again, they were making love when the act occurred."

"A double whammy, huh. Murdered twice. Certainly enough to make her afraid, fantasy or not."

"Yes, but that's just the beginning."

"Really?" Dr. Krause leaned forward, jotting some notes.

"Shortly afterwards, I began seeing an established patient again; Craig Thornton. He was having problems with his marriage to a promiscuous vixen. Those details aren't important. We did a regression, searching for something that had begun bothering him."

Feldman held his older friends eyes for a moment, then sighed, settling back in his chair, rubbing the bridge of his nose.

"We apparently found it ... in 17th Century England."

"You're kidding?" Krause was alert, sitting very straight, hands flat on the desk in front of him. "Don't tell me he was—"

A 3rd Time to Die

"The Earl, Charles Wallace."

"My God. Do they know each other now?"

"Their good friends, actually. Through horseback riding. But, none of this past life stuff had ever been discussed between them."

"His memories. Were they the same ...?"

"*Identical.* I stopped him short of seeing his murder. I was really shaken, I can tell you that."

"And the 19th Century. Was that him again?"

"Absolutely. And again identical memories. I didn't let him see his death there, either."

"Are you still seeing them both?"

"Of course not. I referred Mrs. Easton to Rachel Caslow."

"Good choice. She may be more comfortable with a woman, and Rachel has a lot of experience with regression."

"I know. That's why I chose her. But there's more, Anton. Something extremely disturbing."

"Good god, man. What you've already told me has shaken everything I believe in. What more can there be?" He sat back and grimaced, as if bracing for a blow to the head.

"Would you believe, during their regressions, I found myself there, too?"

"Where?"

"The 17th and 19th Centuries, *that's* where."

"*What?*"

"I don't understand it, either. But, as Mrs. Easton, now the French countess, saw her last hours, I began to actually *see* them making love in that forest glade. It was as if I were with someone, spying on them through the thickets. I saw myself ... us, actually ... sneak up on them. We rushed out of the woods. I saw them *die*."

"My God, man ...."

"It was horrible. Even after *her* memory ceased, I continued

[228]

seeing the blows obliterating them. They were bludgeoned into an unrecognizable pulp. She sat in my office, screaming in panic, and I could do nothing but watch."

"Horrifying."

"That's not the worst of it."

"Jesus, what could be ...?"

"I was filled with anger. Deadly anger. It's possible I may have been their killer. I *hated* them."

"Unbelievable. Utterly ridiculous. You don't have a violent bone in your body." Krause stood, beginning to pace.

"Not now, maybe. But what about during the 17th and 19th Centuries?"

"You were there ...?"

"Both times. The same hate, the same fury, the same involvement. Again, I saw their total annihilation, even after her memories ended. I was part of it, both times."

"And you believe this?" The older man stood, shaking his head in wonder.

"What *else* am I to believe?" Feldman rubbed his eyes, trying to head off a headache.

"A coincidence? A synergistic fantasy?"

Feldman's laugh was a derisive bark.

"C'mon, doctor. That's pushing the envelope, even for us. Besides, I have more proof."

"Proof? How could you have any real *proof?*"

"You know Jack Wexler?"

"Professor of History at Northwestern?"

"Right. More specifically, French history. He researched this for me. So did I, in fact. Jack called me yesterday. In the year 1695 Charles Wallace, Earl of Devonshire, and Victoria du Chevalier, Countess of Beaujolais, were found torn to shreds in the woods of Devonshire."

"I found what amounted to the obit, but Jack found the

details. They had come up missing during the first fox hunt of the year. They were naked, their clothes found in a neat pile at the edge of the glade. All *exactly* as Mrs. Easton ... and I ... remember it."

"Could she have read the story?"

"Never. It was so obscure, it took Jack a week to find it. A bear was blamed for their deaths."

"And the 19th Century?"

"I've been working on it. I found a Jonathan Denton then, in shipping, with a daughter named Morgana. There was an attorney, Robert Isaac, registered in Philadelphia. I've learned that much, but I've got to do more digging to discover what happened to them."

"Jesus, Bruce. Apparently, you already know."

"It certainly seems that way, doesn't it?"

"Well, if you believe in past lives ...."

"I'm converted," Feldman smiled wanly. Krause nodded.

"I'm not surprised. But as I was saying, as I understand the theory, small groups of souls tend to travel from life to life together, sometimes changing relative roles, sometimes not."

"I know, and that's what worries me."

"That these two lovers are together again...?"

"And so is their killer."

"It can't be *you*, Bruce. Not in this lifetime."

"How do I know that? We all have the beast harnessed within us. Who knows what ancient hate might set it free?"

"So, there may be only one way for us to settle the real facts."

"I know. Do my own regressions, and face the consequences. That's why I'm here. You're the only one I can trust with this."

"Thank you ... I think. But, there's no time left today. I can clear two hours on Thursday, at 2:00 p.m. Is that good for you?"

"Of course. We can't dilly-dally. Time may now be short."

SEVENTY-FIVE

Craig swung out of the saddle and stepped over to take her bridle, steadying the horse as she dismounted.

"That was fun," Ashley said. "I love cantering through the woods. It's so invigorating."

"Yeah, me too. It was great to get off by ourselves a little." He stood close to her, savoring the odor of lilies coming to him from her hair. A hard morning's ride and she still smelled like fresh flowers.

"People pestering you about the divorce?" she asked. Injun nuzzled her jacket, in search of a treat.

"Sure. The Rudolphs are running a full-fledged smear campaign. But, it's all bark and no bite. Everybody who knows Toni *knows* Toni. They take it for what it's worth, but they still want all the nasty lowdown."

"Did she really threaten to kill you?"

"Yeah, both she and her brother. Just bags of wind. Despite her ravings, the attorneys will settle quietly, and out of court. Harrington Rudolph isn't about to let his spoiled brat sully their name in public.

"How about you?" he asked. "Keith giving you any trouble?"

She nodded as she finished feeding the big red horse a carrot.

"Jeez. He didn't even need a phone for me to hear his screaming from Louisiana after McNeely delivered the divorce petition. Lots of blustering, then begging, and all kinds of promises he'd never keep. Under everything, I could tell he doesn't really give a shit about me. He just wants to keep his hands on the trust money. That may be all he *ever* wanted."

"So, what's the outcome?"

"Same as you, my darling. I've got all the dirty deeds recorded. He can't afford for it to become public. An out of court settlement."

"Will he get anything?"

"Not a penny from me or the trusts, but he won't have to pay child support. He can drown his misery in his green-eyed mistress. You ought to see her. What a cold, arrogant beauty."

"So, he's not giving you any real problems. That's good."

A groom had come from the stables and gathered the bridles of both horses, leading them back toward the stalls.

"Actually, I'm getting more flak from his brother, Larry. Keeps calling me, asking me to be 'reasonable,' whatever that is."

"Ha." Craig shook his head. "Regular brother acts."

"Huh?" They watched the two horses disappear into the shadowed maw of the big white barn.

"Oh, nothing. Just that Toni's brother, Brad, has been really threatening. Just a big brother, little sister thing, I guess."

"Think it's serious?"

"Nah. Just macho posturing for Toni's benefit. He's always struck me as a loudmouthed bag of wind." No need for her to know how really dangerous Brad had sounded.

"What a mess," she said.

"All worthwhile, knowing you're here."

"Me, too."

She slipped her arms around his waist, her gray eyes shining. Cupping her chin, he pulled her face gently to him. They kissed with a soft intensity, tongues languorously fencing, an act of pure love much more that passion. Parting slightly, he stroked back a few loose strands of her coppery hair.

"Want some lunch?" he asked.

"You bet. I'm starved."

Arm in arm, they strolled toward the clubhouse. Only their stomachs were empty.

Their hearts were surfeit to the point of bursting.

They sat in the third floor, glass-walled restaurant. Their table provided full view of the entire facility, and the woods beyond.

Absently she stirred her coffee. Craig grinned at her.

"A quarter for your thoughts. I'm paying inflation wages."

She chuckled, glancing up, her face glowing.

"Just how happy I am. Like I've finally found what I've searched for all my life. You fill me with joy."

"Me, too. It's like I've loved you forever. It's just so *comfortable*."

She shivered slightly. How strange for him to say that.

"But, enough of this gushy talk," he said, laughing. "You still plan on shopping for a new saddle this afternoon."

"Yep, but I think I'll shower and change. I brought fresh clothing."

"Sounds good. I need one, too, but I didn't plan as well as you. How about we go up to my new apartment? We can shower and dress there, and there're a couple of tack stores near-by."

"Sounds good." She leaned back, stretching. Watching her, his heart did back flips. He signed the check, adding a 20% tip.

"Great. I'm ready whenever you are."

SEVENTY-SIX

"That bastard. Who the Hell does he think he is?" Toni prowled around Brad's family room, a caged leopard looking for fresh meat.

A 3rd Time to Die

"No one walks away from Toni Rudolph. No one." Her sapphire eyes shone with an intensity Brad had never seen.

"How'r ya gonna stop him, sis? That dick's got a book two-inches thick on you. Photos, video, audio tapes...he musta planted mics and cameras somehow. You shoulda been more careful."

"Fuck that." She whirled on him, her balled fists jammed against her sides, arms akimbo. He perched on the edge of a large overstuffed chair, enthralled by her intensity.

"You'd just let that bastard screw me over like this?"

"What d'ya want me to do." He shrugged, arms out, palms raised. "Kill the son-of-a-bitch?"

"That'd be a start. And his redheaded whore, while you're at it."

"You're kidding, right?" Brad stood, taking her hands to calm her. She pulled away and started circling again.

"I don't know, but I've gotta do *something*. How'll it look if the most desirable girl on the North Shore gets dumped by that piece of trash?" She studied her linebacker-built brother. He'd do anything she wanted, but would he draw the line at murder?

"You know, he's been playing me for the fool all these years." She pushed Brad onto the sofa, settling next to him.

"What? How? I don't think he ever cheated...."

"He lied to me, sweetie." She inched closer, one thigh against his, her hand on his neck, the thumb stroking his cheek.

"He lied to all of us. I got my own detective. D'ya know he's a fucking *Jew*?"

"What?" He gathered her hands. "How is that possible? He ...."

"It's true. Changed his name. Had his nose done. Lied to us, lied to his fraternity. Lied to everyone. Just so he could get close to me and our money. His dad's a fucking New York cab driver. Transportation business, my ass."

Brad sat, stunned, not grasping the reality that everything Craig did happened well before he met Toni.

"That fucking kike, sticking that unclean thing in you. I aughta...."

"What, baby?" Toni crawled into his lap, both arms around his neck, faces inches apart.

"Would you do it?" She kissed his ear, her lips grazing his cheek, then his eye.

"Would you kill him for defiling your little, defenseless sister?" Her lips found his, her serpent's tongue fencing lightly with his, her bosom teasing his chest.

"I'd never let anyone hurt you, baby." His voice a hoarse whisper. "I love you too much." His arms tightened around her as the kiss heated up, and a hardness grew in his groin.

"Yes, my hero, yes. Love me Brad. Love me and protect me. My handsome hero."

Somehow they were stretched out on the sofa, clothes coming off, as he lavished years of pent up passion on the most beautiful, desirable woman he'd ever known, not seeing her smug smile as he entered her.

He'll do anything I want, now. Anything. Even murder.

She released herself to her own raging passion, finally slaking years of lust for this one man always denied to her ... the perfect lover.

Now all she had to do was think of a plan. Craig and his lover didn't stand a chance.

SEVENTY-SEVEN

Craig dropped on the edge of his new queen-size bed, flipping through the last month's sales report. Shipments were up at record levels, as were profits. Upscale mail order was doing very well, even in a less than booming economy.

He glanced at the bathroom door as the shower turned off. She'd be dressed soon, and it would be his turn. It was cool during their ride, and he hadn't worked up much of a sweat, but he was looking forward to the shower. He didn't feel fresh, but mostly, it was the thought of being exactly where she had just been that fired a warm glow in him.

His newly discovered love for Ashley filled him to the point of bursting, a dizzying experience he couldn't begin to put to words. He was awash with peace and contentment, as if a long, frustrating search was finally completed. So different from life with Toni which *had* been a long and frustrating journey ... to misery.

"Damn." he heard Ashley mutter to herself.

"Got a problem?" He stood, adjusting his robe.

"I left the duffel with my clean clothes in the car. Do you have a dressing gown I can use?"

"How about a big shirt?" He only had one robe. Many of his things were still at the house. He had moved out in a hurry, eager to be away.

"That'd be great. Then you can shower while I'm getting my stuff to dress."

Rummaging in the antique oak dresser he'd purchased, he found an old flannel long-sleeved shirt. His heart tap-danced, visualizing her in it. Knocking softly, he opened the door wide enough to pass the shirt through. Her fingers caressed his arm from elbow to wrist. A gentle kiss brushed the back of his hand as it was relieved of the shirt. Goosebumps ran in an avalanche down his back, his heart soaring on hawk's wings.

God, I love her.

Two minutes passed before the door opened, emitting an

angel on invisible wings. Damp auburn hair hung in gentle waves to her shoulders, framing her face, free of cosmetics, and all the more lovely for it. She had rolled up the sleeves of the beige shirt, which dangled half way to her knees. It was the first time, he realized, he'd ever seen her bare legs. The strong yet feminine calf, the luscious, curving thigh. No ancient sculptor ever chiseled marble from a lovelier model.

A mischievous smile, smoky eyes twinkling, opened the door to the banked embers of his love, flooding him with warmth. She executed a slow pirouette, the hem of the shirt ballooning to reveal most of her legs. His heart skipped to his throat, choking off for the moment any ability to comment.

"Okay for a thirty-three year old mother of three?"

"Don't exaggerate." His voice a hoarse whisper. "You're still only thirty-two."

She giggled, stepping forward, taking his hands. "Close enough. Let's not split hairs."

"It's not splitting hairs when I tell you how you fill my heart. There's no words for it."

Her smile was a Key West sunrise.

"I know." She sighed. "I never imagined I could be so happy. We're both *free*, Craig. Free to be together, where we belong."

"So many wasted years finding each other." He folded her into his arms, burying his face in the soft dampness of her hair. Pulling back slightly, she looked up into his gentle brown eyes.

"Yes. So many wasted years. But no more." A slender finger traced his cheek, then his lips.

"Not one day longer."

He bent her face to his, their lips fusing, molten flesh on flesh, lightning bolts igniting wild fires in them. Their bodies fused together, the wonder of her soft curves pulsing against the hard contours of his. Venturesome hands left trails of fire, kindling volcanic passions, new, yet somehow very familiar.

A 3rd Time to Die

In a moment they found the bed, his robe slipping to the floor, her shirt cast aside. His ravenous mouth consumed her, voyaging slowly across her face, her ears, her neck. It lingered at the swell of each breast, nipping and suckling, before descending the ridged hills of her ribs, pausing to lap at the pool of her belly.

His moist tongue wended its way through a small curly red forest, descending finally into the throbbing, slippery valley. He tasted of the freely flowing spring, nestled there, before climbing slowly to the small, quivering nodule.

She gasped, arching herself to him, as his lips and tongue enfolded the tiny mound, gently sucking and tweaking. Hands, tangled in his curly hair, guided and encouraged the moist adventurer as it continued its exploration. She shuddered as wave after crashing wave inundated her senses, turning her whole body into an exploding mass of nerve endings. Drawing his questing mouth more tightly to her, she moaned softly.

"Mon dieu. Mon dieu."

His tongue was everywhere, darting, caressing, licking, consuming the flowing wellspring of her juices. Her body, taut and quivering, pulsed desperately against his ravenous lips, her whispers choked by ardor.

"Oh. Oui. Oui. Mon Amour. C'est magnifique!"

His lips ventured leisurely along a downy, passion-dampened body to her mouth. His kisses engulfed her, drowning her hold on reality. Magically, they lay in a lush meadow, shaded by giant oaks, reveling in the first consummation of their love. Her ears rang with thunder as he entered her, body tensed against the rapid onrush of quivering ecstasy, and then there was something ... a movement in the shadows.

Somebody ... or something ... there. She blinked, struggling to make it out.

It's coming. Ca vient.

She writhed, striving to see, a flood of terror thrusting at the relentless tide of ecstasy, turning her helpless.

There. *Mon dieu*. A fierce mask, filled with hate, materialized from the gloom. Two horrible creatures burst out of the dark, rushing at them.

"*Non! Non!*" Lost in his passions, he didn't see them, and she couldn't make them out, but they were almost upon her, some fearful weapon whirling in the sky above their heads.

The weight of her lover and her forlorn panic froze her ability to resist. Clutching Craig tightly, she wept, knowing it was the end.

"*Non! Mon dieu, non.* Not again."

Her body racked and shuddered as she entangled herself with him, trying to hide from the blows, about to annihilate them.

"Not again." she whimpered.

Everything went black.

SEVENTY-EIGHT

"You're drifting back now. Back, back, back to another time."

Bruce Feldman reclined in the large, soft leather chair, eyes closed, breathing at a slow, steady pace. Dr. Krause sat to his right in the dimly lit room, speaking softly, his soothing voice continued to deepen the hypnotic trance. A recording of gentle waves, washing against a sandy beach, murmured softly in the background.

"Voyage back to the time that you first saw yourself, in 17th Century England. Are you there?"

"Aye. The hunt 'tis well begun." Feldman's voice has taken on a Cockney lilt.

"What's happening? Tell me what you see."

"I'm ahorse, hot after the Earl and the French harlot. 'Tis me charge to keep 'em well in hand fer m'lady. She suspects 'im o' diddling the Frog wench." Krause hunched forward, studying his younger disciple, chilled at the deepened, rough timbre of his voice.

"Good. Move ahead now, to when you observe them making love."

"Aye, I spy 'em, though the view ain't clear. I'm afoot now. There be two o' us, sneaking through thick bresh. See there. The cad's atop the whore. How can the bastard treat his lady such?" He twists and fidgets in the chair, his body drawing taut.

"How do you feel about this?"

"Flamin' mad. M'lady Clarice deserves better. We creep up fer a better look. Out o' the brush now. We rush on 'em. I'm filled with fury."

"Who is your companion? Can you tell?"

"Nay. I see 'im, but 'tis dim, fer all the shadowy bresh. Must be an angel, glitterin' so in the broken light."

"What happens?"

"The Earl's affronted Lady Clarice, in the sight o' God 'n man. He must pay the cuckolds price. Ahh, he hears us, turnin' from her milky flesh." Feldman winces, jerking back in the chair.

"Ah, God. He's dead. Struck down, 'n she's quick ta follow, her head poppin' like a ripe gourd."

"Did you strike the blows?" Dr. Krause leaned forward, perched on the edge of his chair, eyes intent. He caught himself holding his breath.

"I ... I know not. I be so filled with hate ... hate, 'n now fear fer what we done. God, it should never 'ave come ta *this*."

"Look hard. Rise above yourself. See who is striking the blows."

"I cannot. I cannot. Me shame blinds me. Dear god, I never

figured it ta come to this. What 'ave I done?"

Bruce Feldman slunk back in the chair, eyes squeezed tight against the vision in his head. He moans, his voice a choked whisper.

"What 'ave we done? What 'ave we done?"

With any other patient, the psychiatrist would have insulated him from the remembered terror and pain. But his younger friend needed to see all, if he could, to sort things out. The problem was, the trauma and guilt were so intense that he was suffering from panic-induced myopia, a frequent syndrome of one unwilling to face past guilt.

"Look around you. Is your companion still there? Describe him to me now."

"Vanished. There, I see his shining glow, disappearin' through the bresh. An angel, mayhaps. An angel o' death."

"What else do you see?" he asked, easing back in his chair, disappointed. They had learned very little new.

"The Earl 'n his harlot are dead, torn beyond ken. The glade be ripped 'n covered with gore, as if gamed by the frenzy o' some huge, wild beast."

"Look at yourself ... your hands, your clothing."

"Ah, God. Blood, 'n tatters o' flesh. I'm awash with it. God forgive me. What 'ave I done?" He wept, body heaving in agony.

"All right, lift above this. Free yourself of these memories. Lift up. Up. You are insulated from the pain and guilt, safe in your protective bubble." He could see the man slowly loosen up in the chair, a tightly wound spring hesitantly uncoiling.

"You are free to move forward to another time and place. Breathe slowly, deeply. Relax your body, your mind. Relax."

Feldman's ragged breathing slowed and steadied. Five minutes of gentle cajoling passed before Anton Krause felt it safe to journey on. One more try that day for illumination. He spoke tentatively, unsure if this were really wise.

"Move ahead to that time in the 19th Century, where you again saw these two together. Three, two, one. Are you there?"

"Yes." His voice was again calm and strong.

"Find yourself in that last hour. Although you will see everything from your eyes there, you are insulated from all feelings, all emotions. Tell me what you see."

"They be in a one-horse carriage, disappearin' inta a woods. We be following on horseback." A different voice now, no longer Cockney, but again of the working class of the time.

"You are with someone again? Do you know who it is?"

"I canna tell. I be in front and canna see the other rider. We've rid inta the woods and are dismountin'. We creep through the forest ta the little meadow, where they stopped ta picnic."

"Do you know why you pursue them?"

"Nay, but I be bitter angry at the woman. She's cheating her husband of all that should be his. 'Tis time fer revenge."

Dr. Krause paused, rubbing his temples, uncertain if he should continue. Did they really want to hear the bloody details of what was about to occur? He sighed softly, running his hands up through his bushy gray hair and down to the back of his neck.

They had to go on. It was the only way to unravel this mystery. He knew Bruce, at least in this life. There was no way he could have committed these crimes. He hoped he was right.

"Tell me what happened next ...."

SEVENTY-NINE

"Three, two, one ... and you're awake."

The past ten minutes were spent reliving a terrifying, blood-soaked memory. Despite his mentor's directions to remain emotionally uninvolved, Bruce Feldman was inexorably drawn into the anger, the fury and the gory destruction of the two young lovers, ultimately dissolving into a tearful, panic-filled lament that racked his soul.

Awake finally from his hypnotic voyage, he sat, head in his hands, body still shuddering from the remnants of these devastating memories.

"Christ, Bruce. That was pretty intense."

"Tell me about it." Feldman took several deep breaths, trying to calm himself.

"And you can't say who your companion was, not in either instance?"

"No. It was never clear. Like watching a film through a wet lens ... all a little blurry. God, I feel like I've been run through a shredder."

"You didn't learn anything new?"

"Yes. One thing."

"Which was—?"

"That it was the same person, I think."

"Who?"

"My companion. The same soul in both lives."

"Ahh, I see. Makes sense, though, if you believe in the theory of Past Lives."

"And you still don't, Anton? After this?"

The older man removed his glasses, rubbing the bridge of his nose, a gesture Feldman knew indicated strong feelings of uncertainty.

"I ... I don't know *what* to think, my friend. This all *seems* very real."

"Well, *I* don't know any other way to explain it. Three people seeing the same things ... *identical* memories ... of the same occurrences. Things a historian verifies really happened three hundred years ago. Even without the intense reality of my own memories, I'd be a convert. So should you."

"I suppose so. As I said, it fits into the theory that souls tend to travel from life to life together, finding ways to continue interacting."

"They're supposed to be resolving problems from past lives, aren't they?

"Yes. Or paying penance for previous bad behavior."

"Well, that makes sense for Craig and Ashley. They've had very little time to revel in their love, so they keep trying. But what explanation is there for me? And my companion, for that matter?"

"The theory isn't that clear cut. There's a reoccurring motive of revenge for one of you. I'm putting my money on the other guy."

"Maybe not. In this life, trying to help people. Maybe that's my penance for being a ... a murder." The word stuck in his throat.

"Or are you here to protect them?" Krause stood. "Whatever, if this *is* the repeat of past lives, those two may be in grave danger."

"Yes," Feldman said. "That's what worries me."

He'd go back, face those horrors again if necessary, until he had all the answers. Look for things he missed the first time.

The truth was there. He just had to find it. It was a trip he would have to make alone. Not something to look forward to.

EIGHTY

"*Non. Mon dieu, non.*" She wailed, her body racking convulsively.

"Ashley! Ashley!" Slowly emerging from their erotic whirlpool, Craig was lying over her, his arms hooked protectively over their heads, a cold chill lacing his spine. His teeth were clenched, his body braced as if expecting an attack, all super-imposed over the glorious wonder of their first love-making.

Another panic attack. Where the Hell does it come from, and why now, when I've finally found real love?

"*Non! Non!*" Clenching him against her, Ashley whimpered, still awash in her terror.

Craig gaped at her as she continued moaning in both French and English, her eyes screwed tightly shut, her face distorted. Something terrified her.

"What is it, darling?" Spent from the intensity of their mutual orgasms and his weird panic, he struggled futilely to free himself, but the steel cables of her arms and legs shackled him.

"Ashley, what's *wrong*? There's nothing to fear." He needed to believe that as much as she. Her beautiful face was horribly contorted by an inner agony only she saw.

Slowly, she relaxed, the planes of her cheeks and brow sliding back to normal. The clenched chin and knife-slit mouth eased. The elegant arched lips reappeared, lightly stained by her own blood. She gasped two quick breaths, as wary, slate gray slits regarded him with surprise now, as fear slipped away.

"Craig?"

"Yes, my love." He too had wound down, left only with the glory of their love-making.

"We're alive?"

"Of course we are. Making love is rarely deadly." What a thing to say. He chuckled softly, despite his just ended bout with panic, brushing hair from her face, kissing her gently on the forehead, then each eye.

She groaned, a muted final release from The Terror. Rigid muscles went slowly limp, her arms and legs sliding away from him. She began to cry, the tears rolling down her cheeks, pooling at the notch of her throat.

"What's wrong, my love? What terrified you so?" His own fright dissipated, icy steel came into his voice. "Did Keith hurt you...?"

"No, no, nothing like that." She smiled weakly, blinking away the salty remnants of tears.

"It was just sort of ... a reoccurring dream I've had lately. A horrible nightmare. I'd swear I saw them coming."

"Who?"

"The ... the beast. Coming after us. It was so *real*. I was shuddering as it struck me."

He grinned, lightly licking at the alkaline trails on her cheeks. He lay on his side, one hand gently tracing the wonderful curves, hollows and hills of her incredible body.

"That, my love, was the Mount Vesuvius of orgasms."

"An orgasm? *My* orgasm?"

"You bet. And mine was right on its heels. I've never experienced anything like that before." And *that* was more true than she would ever know. Wondrous joy and unbridled terror, all in the same instant.

"Me either." She sucked in a deep breath, rolling to one side, coming up on her right elbow.

"I don't think I've ever even had one before. Certainly nothing like that."

"You're kidding."

"No." She sat up, serene now that visions of danger had evaporated. "Our sex really dwindled off after Ricky was born, and it was almost non-existent after Beth. Janine was just a lucky accident. Sex was seldom very special for me ... until today. He never did any of those wonderful things you do. Just a few kisses, a little touching, and then the whole thing was over in a flash."

"What a bastard. He had no interest in your pleasure at all, did he?"

"I don't know. I guess not." She shrugged bare shoulders.

He feasted on the alabaster smoothness of her, needing to cradle her in his arms, feeling her cool fire, nestled against him. No strange panic, searching the shadows for something unknown and deadly, would ever keep him away.

"Maybe he didn't know any better," Craig said.

"Whatever. Just another reason to be glad he's out of my life. You're who I want to be with."

Long fingers stroked the side of his face, and then trailed gently across his lips. She kissed him softly on the mouth and sighed. He slipped an arm around her, pulling her to him. She snuggled close, resting her head on his shoulder, utterly at peace.

"So, what's with this scary dream? Got anything to do with those visions you have when you're jumping Injun?"

"How did you know that?" She trembled at the memory.

"Because you were babbling in French, like when you're jumping a course."

"God, I love a clever guy. But, they're not dreams, really."

"What, then?"

"Sort of memories. I've always had this strange fear of sex, like something bad was going to happen. With Keith, or anybody else, whenever I got close to making love. As far back as high school."

"Like afraid of getting pregnant?"

"No. More like afraid of getting *killed*. I ... I felt it with you, when I first realized we were becoming more than just good friends."

"Wow." How interesting. His new anxiety started at the same time.

"Yeah. Anyway, that's why I decided to see a therapist. See if we could figure out the problem."

He chuckled, shaking his head in wonder.

She pulled abruptly away, slipping off the bed.

"I don't see anything funny about it." She was obviously hurt.

"Hey. I didn't mean it that way. I've been in analysis, off and on, for years. It's just a funny coincidence that I've gone back to my guy, trying to resolve a few of my own new, and very strange emotions."

"Having any luck?" Grinning now, she began dressing.

"Can't you tell?" They laughed. "But it's been kinda weird."

"Hmmm. Mine too. I told you we did some regression under hypnotism. I know what scares me now. We just don't know where it came from. I've been reluctant to discuss it with anybody, it's so eerie."

"Jeez. Me, too. Hypno-regression and everything. Mine was kinda wonderful."

"How interesting. We'll have to trade stories. Can't do it now, though. It's too late to shop for a new saddle. The kids are already home from school. Gotta run, lover."

She was tucking her silk blouse into her designer jeans while slipping into her loafers. Looking up from stuffing her horsy duds into the canvas duffle, a delicious little pout pursed her lips.

"Can't see you tomorrow, darling. Got too many errands to run. Wednesday?"

"Afraid not. Got appointments all day. I've gotta show my face at the office occasionally."

"Thursday, then? I've got to get some practice in before the Bolingbrook show."

"Right. We'll shop for your new saddle first. We can break it in that afternoon, if we find something you like, then send the horses up that evening."

"Swell. Call tomorrow evening, once you know your schedule." She dropped her bag at the front door, turning to him.

Taking her in his arms, he nuzzled her hair.

"Ashley, it's a three-day show. Should we get a hotel room?"

"One room? Together?"

"Yeah. A mini-suite, with a king-size bed. What d'ya think?"

"I can hardly wait." She squeezed him possessively.

"Me, too. Might be hard to keep our minds on show jumping."

She looked up, chuckling softly, and found his lips. Their kiss was slow and gentle, yet filled with wondrous passion.

He stared at the door long after she'd left, already missing her.

~~*~~*~~*~~

Ashley threw her bag into the passenger seat of her Lexus SUV. She had followed Craig in her car from the stables, never noticing the white Jeep Cherokee that trailed her there, now parked fifty feet down the street. Hooded eyes of its solitary occupant followed her departure.

The bitch. He blames his failed marriage on his wife, but that whore's the real problem. She's put two marriages on the rocks and she's fucking everybody, one way or another. Something needs to be done before it's too late.

Well, it'll probably be up to me. No one else has the guts.

If I can't get help from the one person I should be able to count on, I may have to manage it alone.

Something I'll enjoy all the more.

EIGHTY-ONE

His heart still racing, the soft, hypnotic music filled Bruce Feldman's head as he steered his course back to consciousness, eyes opening warily when his mental count reaches "one." Awake, he lies very still, searching the shadows of his office.

Nothing threatening lurking there.

He punched the "Off" button on the tape player resting on the small table beside his chair, bringing silence into the shadow shrouded room.

He'd used self-hypnosis tapes to achieve relaxation, but today was different. This one, provided by an associate of Anton Krause, was designed to aid in self-hypnotic regression, especially Past Life regression.

That it worked exceedingly well was no longer any surprise. He's done a 180 on the subject, now believing people *are* reborn, time after time. He's living proof.

Sighing, Feldman stretches, easing tension born from three hundred years of time travel, trying to fathom his role in two heinous double murders. Did he really learn anything new ... *who* he was with, and *why* these two lovers died ... twice?

Finding those answers might be paramount in saving them in this life ... unless it *was* he who had killed them.

What an exhausting journey. He had intended to separate himself from the action this time, floating above, free from the heat and anger inundating him during those terrible, deadly minutes in each lifetime.

It didn't work.

Each time he was sucked down a vortex of maniacal fury. His struggle to see his mysterious companion more clearly was thwarted by a fuzzy picture of the events unfolding around him.

Apparently each subject glimpses these regressions with different levels of clarity. To Ashley Easton, it was like watching a big screen movie in a darkened theater, with full surround sound. Craig Thornton saw things nearly as clearly. For him, it was like looking through turbid water ... plainly visible, but lacking sharp detail.

Nevertheless, he managed to learn his companion was hideously ugly. A shiny, grotesque face, with a huge, snarling mouth and fathomless, black eyes.

A *mask*. Of course. A mask, or possibly an armored helmet. An ancient battle mask, perhaps? Like the suit of 16th Century chain mail armor, standing in his Loop office, with its horned and beaked helmet and weapons ... a broad sword, a long knife and a chained mace. He'd been virtually compelled to bid at that auction, four years before. Now maybe he understood why.

How had the same or similar thing come into their hands in Philadelphia, 150 years later? Another mystery.

What else? He tried to free himself enough from his swirling emotions to evaluate his own physical activities. It wasn't easy, but he had no sense of expending the necessary effort to wield the heavy weapon, whatever it was, that dealt such horrific death. Maybe that was good.

But, why then was he covered with so much blood and tatters of flesh each time? Was it just spatter from being close by? He didn't know.

Rubbing his temples, Bruce Feldman stood, looking for pain-killers. Visiting the past gave him a terrible headache. His stomach heaved and roiled, bringing the taste of bile to the base of his throat. Seeing and smelling such butchery.

God. That's right. He *smelled* it, too. The thick, cloying odor of blood, then vile putrid stench of innards, torn asunder. He retched at that memory, rushing to his bathroom, slipping, and falling to his knees as he reached the toilet just in time to safely discharge his very expensive lunch. Several more contractions emptied whatever was left. He wriggled to a sitting position on the floor, slumped over, back to the sink, face flushed and damp, trying to catch his breath.

Head in his hands, tears gushed unabated, sobbing and struggling for breath. He hadn't done that in ... well, not for a very long time. He couldn't remember when. He didn't care. A good bawling was often an excellent catharsis.

Ten minutes later, he had managed to pull himself together. Straightening his tie, he turned to the sink to wash his face. The visage staring back from the mirror was almost unrecognizable. Dark, haunting rings surrounded the soft brown eyes. His face, red and blotchy, was cratered and seamed from strain.

Five minutes of cold compresses and a comb through his hair wrought reasonable repair. Thankfully, there was only one more patient that day. He would finish his docket for tomorrow, but maybe he should cancel appointments for next week. Even the next two weeks.

Gotta tough it out. Uncover what really happened, so long ago. All the facts, however painful. His only punishment now for atrocities inflicted 300 years ago would be self-imposed.

And who was his companion? Was it he, rather than Feldman, who did the actual killing? He was sure it was the same person in both "lives." It seemed imperative to discover that identity, in case he was here, again ready to commit mayhem.

There were several likely candidates: Ashley's husband, Keith, probably bitter at being cut off from her wealth; Craig's vixen wife, whose ego probably wouldn't stand for rejection; and brothers from both families who had investments in the marriages. And other persons unknown at this time? And maybe Feldman, himself, who had been party to both past atrocities.

But, he was a different person in this century, not only in body but in mind. Bruce Feldman could never have committed those crimes. Still, he wondered at the anger ... the frightening, intense fury that flooded him.

It was madness. A killer's madness.

What was his stake in such maniacal savagery?

Could that virulence still lurk deep inside his subconscious, waiting for the moment to strike out?

He was scared...of himself, and of what it seemed he may have once (or twice) been.

A murderer.

This will require more research.

He trembled, vaguely aware of a need to hurry.

EIGHTY-TWO

"It's time to journey back. Back to the garden. Back to this time. Flowing back ... back ... back. Back to the beautiful garden, where you see yourself lying peacefully on that bench."

Dr. Caslow moved her slowly, giving her patient time to gather herself before returning to this world. And then she was awake.

"So, Ashley, how do you feel, having revisited these two events?"

Ashley Easton sat surrounded by the folds of the huge, soft easy chair, dabbing the remnants of tears in her gray eyes.

She shuddered slightly and sighed, unconsciously shaking her head, her swirling hair giving the momentary impression of a burnished copper halo.

"I ... I don't know. I can't get used to seeing my *murder* ... twice."

"I can certainly understand that. But this time, we insulated you from the actual terror and pain, didn't we? You were more of an observer."

"Yes, I guess so. But I still felt so sad. I cry at the movies, you know. Sometimes even a good commercial. You can imagine how this hits me." A small, self-deprecating smile crept across her face.

"Me, too," Rachel grinned. "That's a woman's job ... to feel things the men are afraid of. It's okay. You're a sensitive, intelligent lady."

"Craig's not afraid."

"Craig? Oh, the new love in your life."

"Yes, but he feels more like an old, comfortable love."

No surprise. You may have known him for 300 years.

"What about him?" she asked.

"He cries at a sad movie, too."

"Sounds like a very special guy."

"Oh, he is. He definitely is." The luminous smile told all.

"That's wonderful. But, now let's talk about today's session."

"Okay." Happiness melted from her face, the tissue in her fingers twisted into a ball.

"I know this isn't pleasant, but it *is* important. It's important because you faced these two visions more dispassionately. Not without pain or sadness, but at a greater emotional distance. Isn't that true?"

"I guess. It wasn't so ... so devastating this time."

"Wonderful. That's exactly why we went there again. To build some separation. You see, it's not important if these so-called memories are real or imagined. There are many theories, but nothing anyone can prove, one way or the other."

Until now. The doctor hitched around in her chair, folding her hand in front of her.

"Real or imagined, the fear ... *understandable* fear... from these vignettes is what has crippled you sexually. Who *could* make love while subconsciously worrying they were about to be slaughtered?"

"It seems so *real*. That ugly war mask, horned and a blood-red beak. Even that seems familiar." She shudders. The tissue is in tatters in her hands.

"I see things coming out of the shadows ... terrible things, when I should be in ecstasy. It's like I'm Victoria, talking French and everything."

"Exactly. Having sex ... making love, actually... triggers these visions of violent death. But, that's all they are ... visions ... memories or not, despite how vivid they seem. You understand this now, and that truth will help defuse the terror."

"So, I won't have these hallucinations anymore?"

"It's not that easy. They may still pop up, but you'll know what's *really* happening. You'll be more able to control your fear."

"You really think so?"

"Yes, but it may take some time. You may have to pause in the middle of things ... take a breath or two, before starting again. That may not be easy at first, but you can learn to do it."

"Jesus, you're kidding. How do you do *that?*"

"I said it wouldn't be easy. It'll be sort of like getting anesthetized. You'll have to be patient, but it'll get better. You'll see."

"God, I hope so. This has been so ... so *paralyzing*. I want to move on with my life. My life with Craig, I hope. How could I do it, this way?"

"Well, now you can. It'll take some work on both your parts, but you *can* do it."

Ashley sighed, smiling doubtfully. She was staring at the tiny white bits of paper scattered on her lap. Gathering the scraps and rolling them into a small ball, she looked up.

"I sure hope so. I suspect we'll get a real test this week-end."

Dr. Caslow nodded. "You're planning a week-end together?"

"Yeah. A big three-day horse show. You think that's okay?"

"Of course. It should give you a real chance to prove to yourself you *can* handle this." Glancing at her watch, she continued.

"Our time is up for today. I'm sure you'll be fine, but I'll be interested in hearing how things went." They stood.

"Me, too," Ashley said, turning to leave.

EIGHTY-THREE

"She's unbelievable," Craig said, as he pulled the magnetic keycard from the slot and pushed open the door, holding it for her.

"It's been two, sometimes three calls a day ... either Toni or her lunatic brother. Ranting, raving, even threats. Screaming that I can't do this to her. That she's an innocent victim. Can you imagine that? Toni, innocent about *anything*?" His laugh was without humor. Picking up their bags, he entered behind her.

"How can you stand it? Can't you monitor the calls, somehow?" Ashley's coppery tresses swirled in a way that made his heart beat faster.

"Yeah. Well, my secretary recognizes their voices. Tells 'em I'm busy, or out of the office. They started giving her an earful, so I've told her to just cut 'em off. I use the answering machine to monitor the phone at home, and I have caller I.D. So, I'll know if it's you, you won't have to wait for the machine."

He placed her overnight bag on the king-sized bed and dropped his atop the dresser. He glanced around at their suite.

"I think I'd better get that, too." She perched on the edge of the bed, bouncing slightly to get a feel of the mattress. Craig opened the suitcase stand, moving his small leather case onto it, and then settled next to her.

"Keith giving you trouble?"

"Yeah. Same as you … angry phone calls from both him and his brother. They act as if I did something to *him*, conveniently forgetting it was *he* having the affair."

"Sure, they're accusing us of already being lovers before we caught 'em in the act."

"It's so ridiculous. We didn't even discover we were in love until after our marriages were already in the toilet." Her chuckle was humorless.

"Marvelous, isn't it?" His hand traced the line of her cheekbone, sliding across her mouth, cruising over her chin and down her neck. She smiled, her eyes finding his.

"What? Being in love? Yeah. Loving you is a wonder beyond my wildest fantasies."

"Me, too." He drew her to him. They kissed, softly at first, but with a quickly growing ardor. Her hands were entwined in his hair as she pulled him down across the bed.

Nestling close, she felt his heat. Wooded glades danced in her head, and the air filled with the smell of the forest.

No. This is reality now. Not that dream. The vision faded.

She glanced furtively around the darkened room.

There are no monsters here. It's only a dream, and …

Oh, shit. It's coming again.

A dark figure moved quickly across the room. She sucked in a frightened gulp of air, her back going stiff. The apparition evaporated, only to be followed by another, and another.

Oh, God. There's more than two this time, coming from nowhere. Coming to kill us. Why can't they leave us alone? Why can't they …?

Oh, you ninny. She swallowed her heart back where it belonged, and took several slow breaths. Her attackers were only shadows on the ceiling, caused by the headlights of passing cars.

Nothing threatening. Nothing dangerous. Relax. Listen to the doctor's advice. Stop and regroup.

Her rigid body slowly went soft and pliable again.

Easy. There's no danger here. Only love. Glorious love.

Craig was there, touching her, kissing her, igniting blazing embers in her very soul.

This is where she belonged. Safe in his arms.

EIGHTY-FOUR

She lay, cuddled closely against his damp nakedness, wonderfully spent.

My first orgasm. I don't count that one at his apartment. This is the first I'm actually aware of, and I had it as Ashley Bradford, not Victoria du Chevalier.

She grinned, realizing she had just used her maiden name. She no longer thought of herself as an Easton. She would shed that name as quickly as she would the man. Didn't know how she would handle that with the children, but she'd figure it out.

Right now, she didn't give a damn. Maybe she'd be Mrs. Thornton so soon it wouldn't matter anyway. Craig could even adopt the kids. Keith might like not being responsible for child support.

They lay together, hands gently venturing over the other, not erotically, but full of wonder at the reality of their nearness. This was no dream, no hopeful fantasy. They were here together, openly and without shame, right where they belonged.

Ashley wiggled around, blissful that he seemed unwilling to release her. Her fingers outlined his eyes and nose, followed by gentle kisses.

"Happy?" he asked.

"Deliriously. You?"

"Like a dream. Makes all those years with Toni seem so hollow. Even the relatively good, early ones."

"Know what you mean. First time I felt like my real self."

"I noticed. No French today, huh?" He grinned mischievously.

"Nope. Just me. At least I now know where the French things come from. Want to hear about it?"

"Sure. I want to know everything about you."

"Okay. But promise not to laugh. It's kinda strange."

"Scouts honor." He made the usual two-finger salute. She sighed, taking his hands, her thumbs gently stroking his palms.

"Well, I told you I've been seeing a therapist. These visions ... riding on a real fox hunt, the French, and especially this weird terror when making love. It scared me. I needed to understand it, or it could cripple our future. Was that foolish?"

"Oh, no, darling. I told you I've been in and out of therapy for years. Mostly about dealing with Toni. You know I've gone back again too, for that very reason."

"Right. Well, remember I said we tried some hypnotic regression, to see if there were some traumatic incident from my childhood... and I landed in a past life? Two lives, actually." She paused, searching his face.

"Past lives? Wow." His eyebrow arched.

"You're not laughing at this, are you?"

"I promised I wouldn't, didn't I?" He grinned. "You can't imagine how well I understand this."

"Why? You don't think that's *strange*?"

"Not when you hear what happened to me. But you tell me your story, and then I'll tell you mine."

"Okay. Anyhow, the doctor says past lives are only a mechanism of the subconscious to help explain other fears, or something like that. Actually, I've seen two therapists who both say the same thing."

She curled into him, legs tucked under her, the sheet pulled like a cloak around her against the air conditioning.

"Two? Why?" he asked.

"The first referred me to the second. Maybe he felt I'd be more at ease with a woman. She's really very good. And these apparent memories, or whatever, they seem so *real*. They start so wonderfully, and end so terribly. It's ... it's really scary."

She searched his eyes, perplexed, as he shook his head in apparent denial. He'd think she was a flake.

"Really stupid, huh?"

"Oh no. I'm not doubting you. Not a bit. It's just a strange coincidence. In fact, I was looking for reasons for something bugging me, so my therapist regressed *me*, and I dropped into some past lives, too. Really weird, isn't it?

"Gave me the same story about it not being real, but now I know why I love fox hunting so much. I was doing it in one of these supposed past lives."

"How funny. Me, too." She caressed the side of his face, a wondrous smile splitting hers. "See how much alike we are. Tell me about yours."

"I will, but I want to hear who you were first."

"Okay, but remember, you promised not to laugh."

"Cross my heart," he said, drawing his finger across his chest.

She beamed, much more relaxed. Why had she ever doubted he would understand? This was Craig, not Keith.

"I *do* love you." She grinned, planting a swift, tender kiss on his nose.

"Anyway, I've already told you that in this so-called memory I was riding through the woods. It was a fox hunt. I'm French, a fearless rider, totally into the chase. That's where my French thoughts and the hallucination of riding in the forest seem to come from.

"It's sort of amazing, though, 'cause, while I did study French for two years in high school, I was never very fluent. In these dreams, I'm rattling it off like a native."

"Funny. I thought fox hunting was much more an English thing than French."

"You're probably right, and I *was* in England, riding my britches off after the furry little buggers. My husband and I were apparently visiting, spending time with various noblemen throughout southern and central England."

"Noblemen? How interesting." One eyebrow rose. "And were you royalty, as well?"

"My husband was a Count in that first memory, and I, of course, was a Countess, but our marriage was just political. There was no passion in it. I'd fallen secretly in love with my handsome host, a wonderful, masculine man. All things my husband was not."

"Your host?" A strange look was slowly transforming Craig's face. "Was he also a nobleman?"

"Of course, silly. I already said that. Don't be jealous." She laughed, reaching out, tenderly touching his cheek again.

"Anyway, a countess would never fall in love with just anybody. He was Charles Wallace, Earl of Devonshire, also in an arranged marriage to an icy bitch named Clarice."

She watched with rising concern as Craig's jaw dropped open, and his eyes took on a wild cast. He drew back slightly, as if to see her better. An Arctic chill flooded her, raising mountainous goose bumps. Something was wrong.

"And you? Your name?" His voice was a choked whisper.

"Craig! You're scaring me. Are you all right?"

"Yes." His voice broke. "Your name, Ashley? What was it?"

"I was the Countess of Beaujolais—"

[261]

"Victoria du Chevalier," he interrupted, his face sliding from shocked wonder to an almost silly happiness. It was her turn to drop a jaw. She had told no one but her therapists.

"How in the *Hell* did you know that?"

They were sitting upright on the bed, each staring at the other with quizzical grins, the sheet she had been wearing like a cape now discarded.

"You'll never believe me." His eyes were drinking her in with a new ardor, a look she had not seen before.

"Try me. I could surprise you."

"Okay." He was still grinning foolishly. "I told you I also found past lives. Two, actually. In the first, I was also on a fox hunt ... in England. I was in love with someone other than my wife, a passionless harpy from an arranged marriage. This new object of my dreams was a beautiful, exciting young woman ... a French countess."

He took her face gently in his two hands.

"Her name was Victoria, and *mine* was Charles Wallace, Earl of Devonshire."

Ashley, who had risen slowly to her knees as Craig unfolded his tale, sat down hard, clamping a hand over her mouth, her smoky gray eyes as big as half-dollars.

EIGHTY-FIVE

Bruce Feldman paused, battling last minute indecision. Shrugging resolutely, he slid the key into the lock, listening for the click as the deadbolt slid home. He studied the polished brass plate on the stained oak door:

Dr. Bruce Feldman, M.D.

And murderer?

Slipping his glasses into a leather case, he sighed, rubbing the bridge of his nose, trying to massage away the aching imprints. The aspirin were just starting to kick in, and none too soon. His struggle with himself over the last hour had yielded little more than a splitting headache.

Finally, realizing that there was really nothing else he could do, he left a message for his secretary to cancel and reschedule all his appointments for the rest of the week, and leave the next week as open as possible.

He was taking a week, possibly two, as a sabbatical. He'd some important research to do.

He would go home, take a stiff brandy ... or three ... and try to relax. He needed a good night sleep ... something missing over the last several days ... with no alarm set.

He'd work for a few hours in the morning with his stamp collection. Nothing else absorbed his total concentration as sorting and examining his new acquisitions. He must be totally at ease when he again faced his ancient deadly past.

He intended to learn what really happened in those final, gory minutes, so many centuries ago. All previous doubts were jettisoned. He was totally convinced these *were* actual memories.

Rachel Caslow joined his camp as another convert after her recent sessions with Ashley. And old archive had verified the redheaded woman's memories, as well as Craig Thornton's.

Feldman visited the library again the previous day. A lot of digging into the Who's Who of 19th Century Philadelphia had uncovered that shipping magnate, Jonathan Denton, had died in the Spring of 1845. In another book of recorded legal filings, Feldman discovered shortly after Denton's death, his daughter, Morgana Quincy, filed for divorce from her husband, William, alleging physical abuse.

He was becoming a regular detective. It took searching two other volumes to discover that in the spring of 1847, while on picnic with attorney, Robert Isaac, Morgana and Isaac were savagely attacked, apparently by a rogue bear. Their bodies were horribly mutilated.

Back to the legal records, he learned since she was childless, and with the divorce not consummated, all of Denton's fortune fell into the hands of Morgana's soon to be ex-husband, William.

It was all exactly as Ashley "remembered."

In the elevator, swooping toward the parking garage, he shivered at the thought.

Exactly as Ashley remembered.

That final piece of the puzzle, combined with Rachel's call that afternoon, and his terrifying visions, had scrapped any last vestiges of doubt.

People *are* reborn, again and again. He could only assume these two kept finding each other in a heretofore futile effort to live full lives together. Why he, along with his mysterious companion, kept showing up to perpetrate these horrible acts of death and destruction, was still beyond him. Could it again be a struggle for wealth denied?

He started at the swoosh of the elevator doors sliding open to the underground parking lot. He blinked as he stepped onto the concrete floor, waiting for his eyes to adjust to the gloomy surroundings. It was well after office hours, and only night safety lights were still burning.

He peered carefully into the shadows, suddenly uneasy. Victoria du Chevalier and Charles Wallace were here, 300 years after they were first murdered. They had found love together for the third time, and he had found *them.*

It was reasonable to suspect his accomplice in their deaths may be nearby, too. The who-where-why of that person were still a mystery to him. A mystery he was intent on resolving. He doubted the library would tell him much about that. It was up to him and his own regressions to sift through the potential culprits. Unfortunately, there were many to choose from.

Reaching his car, he fumbled with the keys, fingers numbed by sudden fear. An intuitive panic of the prey. Strange for one who had seemed the predator in those terrible times. Somehow, he knew there was more to it ... a lot more.

Those details were exactly what he needed time to discover more fully.

EIGHTY-SIX

Ashley crouched, legs tucked under her, the sheet draped across her lap, one hand clasped across her mouth. She was still as an alabaster sculpture. A wood nymph caught by surprise, hanging motionless for what seemed an eternity. Her eyes flared wide, starring at a whimsically smiling Craig.

He shrugged.

"You?" She finally found her voice, a bare whisper. "Charles Wallace? But how ...?"

"Don't have the foggiest. Bruce regressed me to that life three-hundred years ago, totally by accident. Told me it was all just a figment of my mind."

"Bruce? Dr. Bruce Feldman?"

"Yeah. D'ya know ...? *Wait* a minute. Was he *your* therapist, too?"

"Yes. No wonder he referred me to Dr. Caslow."

"You gotta be kidding. He regressed us both to the same life, to the same *incident*, and was still feeding us the 'it's all in your mind' crap. Jesus."

"Wow. It may have been traumatic for him, too."

He shook his head, lips curled in a thin snarl. "I can't imagine why?"

"Because he doesn't believe in past lives, and here we are, shoving it down his throat. He couldn't ethically tell us about the other's experience, could he?

"So he passed me off to Dr. Caslow, which has worked out fine. She's easier for me to talk with. Dr. Feldman seemed very disturbed by all of this."

"I can imagine. We musta knocked the foundation right out of something he apparently was very sure of. No wonder he seemed so stressed."

He took her in his arms and she scrunched up tightly against him, resting her head against his chest.

"There were two lives, weren't there?" he asked. "The second time, were you Morgana Quincy, in Philadelphia? About 1845?"

"Yes, and of course, you had to be Robert."

"Ahh, so that's why my being Jewish wasn't an unpleasant surprise for a dyed-in-the-wool WASP like you." His chuckle was soft and teasing.

"Maybe so." Smiling, she laid her hand gently on his cheek. He drew it to his lips, absorbing her delicate odor as his tongue traced her fingers.

"But, what was there for you to fear from those lives? Loving you then seemed so glorious."

"You don't know?"

"Only that we were perfect together. Making love was delirious Nirvana. Just like now." He grinned impishly, but she frowned.

"Didn't ... didn't you see the end of our lives?"

"No, did you? Was it wonderful, all those lovely years together?"

"Hardly." She shivered, steadfastly avoiding his eyes.

"You saw us both times, making love in the woods?"

"Yeah. In little meadows, surrounded by tall trees. We were just beginning to make love a second time when he brought me back. Very disappointing, too, 'cause I was having such a wonderful time."

"It didn't last." She shuddered, wrapping her arms around herself, unable to dispel a sudden chill. Goosebumps flowered on her neck and back as she visualized those final minutes.

"I don't understand." He was no longer smiling. "Did we have a falling out?"

Trapping her face between palms, he turned it toward his.

"More like a falling down. Down and out."

"I still don't get it. You're talking in riddles. I remember that we had some outside conflicts in our lives, other spouses and my being Jewish, but the way we loved each other, what coulda possibly gone wrong?"

"How about ... our *murder*?" She choked out the words, a muted hiss.

"Murder?"

"We were brutally murdered, twice, while we were making love in those idyllic little meadows."

"Murdered?" His face screwed up, somewhere between doubt and anger. "But why didn't I see that?"

"Dr. Feldman knew what would happen. It probably shocked him, and he brought you back before you had a chance to see it all. Believe me, he did you a favor."

"And in the second life?"

"I guess he wanted to double check that the whole thing was real. That we really were Victoria and Morgana and Charles and Robert. He must have been stunned, having his beliefs scrapped like that."

"Son-of-a-bitch. He coulda told me. Murdered together twice, and here we are again, and I never knew.

"Maybe that was the basis for my recent anxiety, when we were ... together. Feldman knew and never told me. He supposed to be helping me, not hiding the truth."

"Ethical restraints again, I suppose," she said. "All he could do was let you experience it yourself. And for some reason, he seemed almost as distraught as me."

She hadn't really thought about that until now. He had seemed so shaken, especially after her first regression. He had no reason to believe these were actually past lives at that point.

He didn't hypnotize Craig until much later, yet he seemed almost ... what? Frightened? Yes, terrified. But why?

"Hey," Craig said, taking her head between his hands. "What's going on inside that gorgeous dome of yours? You look like you're mile away."

"Sorry. I was just visualizing that first lifetime. I wonder why he was so upset?"

"Yeah. And why he didn't let me finish mine, murdered or not? Maybe those lives have some influence on my problems, too."

"I think we should ask him."

"What?"

"We should go to his office together and ask him. What does he think of all this, and why does he feel so ... so involved?"

"Y'know, you're right. Ask him point blank. I think there may be more going on here than we know."

"Yeah," she said, shivering again, despite the warmth of their room. "That's what's beginning to worry me."

"What d'ya mean?" He wrapped his arms back around her, pulling her close.

"Well, I've been reading books on Past Life theories. Imaginary or not, it was having a profound effect on me, and I wanted to understand it better. Those authors make a strong case for it to be real."

"And—?"

"Well, the mantra is groups of souls tend to travel together through time, not always in the same rolls. Be a bad guy in one and a good guy in another. You can even change sexes in different lives. But souls tend to do it as a group ... sort of a team."

"But we've been the same ... two people in love."

"Yes. The belief is that you come back to fix things that didn't work out the last time. Or sometimes pay penance for things you did wrong. And some souls are forever linked by love."

"Like us." He kissed her nose. "So, you think we're together now to try to make up for ...."

"... having our love and lives cut so short. Twice," she finished for him.

"That sounds great. So what's the problem?"

"Maybe I'm being paranoid, but there *were* other souls involved with us in those past lives, weren't there? Very *dangerous* souls."

"Our killer. Or killers, if it were a plot. You mean they might be coming after us again?"

"Exactly." She was trembling. "And there *were* two of them. I saw it when I went back again with Dr. Caslow. I think they were the same souls both times, too. One wore a horrible battle mask of some sort. It seemed so familiar."

She burrowed closer to him ... lean, hard and strong ... as if seeking protection from some nearby danger. He stroked her coppery tresses and caressed her back, offering security.

"Jesus. But, won't they have to be regressed, too, to know us. How likely is that?"

"Who knows? They may not have to know about their past lives to find a reason to hate us now."

"Hate *us?* Who would possibly ...?"

[269]

"Try Keith and Toni, for starters," she said, turning to study his face.

"Shit, you're right. And her brother, Bradley, who said he'd 'get' me. She could manipulate him into anything, maybe even murder."

"And Keith's brother, Larry, who blames us for everything. Keith's been supporting him from my trusts."

"So, it's one or more of them ...."

"Or maybe someone else we haven't even thought of." She shivered again, despite his warmth. He pulled the blanket up around their necks.

"Or no one at all," Craig said. "Maybe the murdering bastards missed this life all together. That's possible, isn't it?"

"I suppose, but I guess we oughta be careful for a while. Still, we can't let the past, however frightening, dictate to us now. Can't live our lives looking over our shoulders, can we?"

"No way. Loving you is ... well, this is the happiest I've been since ... since I don't know when."

"How about 1845?" Her soft smile brought a happy chuckle.

"Right. And I don't want to waste another moment now." He kissed her neck and ears, his hand trailing sensuously down her back.

"Oh, Craig." She was already breathless, as she turned to offer herself to his tantalizing touch. Her hands slid through his hair and around his ears, while his lips and tongue ventured in a sinuous, erotic path over her neck, across her flaming breasts, moving lower, ever lower. Quivering with restrained tension, hovering already on the verge of delicious eruption, she tasted the sweet smell of uncut grass, the moist earth pressing against her back.

"Oh, Charles. *Mon cheri.*" She slit her eyes cautiously, on the edge of panic, searching the dark corners of the room for danger. Nothing moved, no threatening monsters there, no terrible death lurking. Held breath escaped in a soft sigh, only to be sucked in again as he entered her.

This was a different kind of tension, a wondrous flood of heat, snatching her to the brink of ecstasy.

"*Ayy*, Charles. Ahh, Robert. Oh, Craig … my darling Craig." She spun away in the wonders of orgasm, knowing she was safe.

Safe at last. At least for one glorious moment.

EIGHTY-SEVEN

Bruce Feldman lay on the chaise in his den, the soft background music and the gentle tones of his own voice drawing him back to the Twenty-First Century. He'd reentered that chilling past, resolutely determined to make at least one more stab at finding the truth, no matter how condemning.

He had been a part of two gristly murders, either as perpetrator or witness. He needed to learn which, and discover, if possible, the identity of his companion, then and now.

He reluctantly revisited that vision, the two of them crouched behind willow thickets, watching the Countess and the Earl, tangled together in the meadow. He seemed *eager* to challenge them. A mailed glove dropped on his shoulder, squeezing softly.

"Reggie, stay yourself. We must see the fullness of their infidelity before we act. To have the whole memory to feast upon."

His companion hunkered next to him on the fringe of the thicket, streaks of sunlight shimmering on chain-mail armor and fierce, horned battle mask.

"Now we make them pay, Reggie. Now." The glittering

apparition darted into the meadow, fast closing on the two immoral cheats, still writhing with ecstasy on the ground.

What's that ... swinging? A chain, and ... Oh my god. No! No!

Too late.

Burnished metal flashed in the sun. There was a scream and a thud. The shiny armor was splattered with red. He looked down, aghast. He too was showered with gore.

"*Mon Dieu.* No. No." That rich voice snuffed out by another shattering blow.

"Stop. For god sakes, stop," the man he had been 300 years before cried out. He sensed his shame and anger.

"I never bargained fer this," he shouted.

"Then step aside and let me do a man's work."

The echo of crunching bones and the splat of rendered flesh continued, until finally there was silence. He had fought ... then and now ... to hold down his gorge.

"'Tis done, no thanks to ye."

Filled with rage, Feldman, the observer from another time, fought to retain a separation, hoping to discover that which he sought.

That voice. He lay on the couch, eyes blinking. *Do I know that voice?*

"How could ye do this?" he had blurted. "See 'im punished fer adultery. Bring charges agin 'im. But not *this.*"

"Shut thy mouth, my frail varlet, or I'll have thy tongue. 'Tis what needed doing. That craven bastard'll never cuckold his lady again."

Feldman had finally seen the other clearly through Reggie's eyes.

Could that be ...? I never would have thought ...

The face was subtly different, the physique unrecognizable under the armor. But the voice. Didn't he know that voice, despite the old English accent? If only he could be sure.

The memory wavered, fading, and his higher self was sucked into a shadowy tunnel, hurtling back to the present. A few moments later, he mentally stumbled into wakefulness. His eyes slit open, warily scanning the room for danger. He was sprawled on the couch in his den, exactly where he'd begun this voyage.

He struggled up, sitting with his face in his hands, elbows braced against knees.

We *are* reborn, time and again. Somehow chance, or the workings of higher souls (Masters, they were called in what he had read) had brought him to the two people with whom he'd shared two long-ago lives ... and deaths.

And today he may have recognized a third. He visited his own memories now, no longer shackled to Ashley's or Craig's. What had brought them to that terrible moment in time? Reluctantly, he would go back, time and again if necessary, to discover all that had happened, before and after those brutal moments. And unmask the real perpetrator.

He stretched, flexing cramped shoulders, and groaned softly. At least it wasn't he committing these atrocities. The anger filling him with a raging blindness was not aimed at these two lovers, but at their murderer for this unwarranted act of savagery.

And what about 1845 and Morgana Quincy and Robert Isaac? Was it the four of them again? Probably so, but he had to know for sure.

He would visit there tomorrow. He was actually looking forward to it, expecting again to find he wasn't the one delivering those murderous blows.

But, he knew one thing now, without doubt.

Ashley and Craig were in danger.

Deadly, brutal danger.

EIGHTY-EIGHT

Easy, buddy." Ashley shortened her lead on Injun, as he pranced with mincing little steps at her side. The big roan butted her playfully with his head and nipped at her pocket, searching for the apple.

"Hey, you don't get that until you're loaded." Two horses were still in front of them, awaiting their turn to enter the big, blue commercial van. The specially designed semi-trailer was built with an eight-foot wide door in the center of one side that lowered as a cleated ramp. The inside was divided into narrow mini-stalls just wide enough to comfortably accept a horse, cross-tethered to hold him in place.

The confined space gave the animals support and balance while on the road, and the wood floor was heavily strewn with new straw. Eager as she was to leave, she wasn't going anywhere until Injun was properly secured for the trip home. Then he would get his apple.

He deserved it.

They had destroyed the field at this show, which had included two Olympic hopefuls, winning the Open Divisions on Friday, Saturday and Sunday, and going Champion of the Show. The three of them were certainly ready for Grand Prix competition; she, Injun ... and Victoria du Chevalier.

The French countess filled her head at every competition, taking control, managing the course with a fearless expertise. What a rider Ashley had been, 300 years ago. She embraced what had at first caused such fear and panic, followed by confusion, then wonder...and now a joyous transformation.

Understanding the reality of those past lives ... the abandon of Victoria; the intense passion of Morgana ... had largely freed Ashley of the stifling terror plaguing her for so long.

Small flashes of panic, bred by those ancient histories, lingered in the shadows, but with Rachel Caslow's guiding angel metaphorically on her shoulder, she was learning to manage it. It was easier each time Craig and she made love, and that was happening with wondrous frequency these last three nights. A thirst, hundreds of years old, is not easily slaked.

"Aren't they ready for him yet?" Craig's arm fell lightly across her shoulders, drawing her close with a tender possessiveness. She trembled, catching her breath, as moist petals of her newly discovered flower opened eagerly. Luckily, her clothes, and especially her pants, were drenched and stained with sweat. No one would notice the new, damp circle growing there.

"Cold?" he asked.

"Hardly." She turned to him, stroking his cheek, her gray eyes fastened on his.

"Oh, I see. luckily, I've arranged a late check-out at the hotel."

"How wonderful. We can hardly wait."

"We?"

"Victoria and Morgana will be there, too. How can I deny them your love after so many centuries of longing?"

"Sounds exciting. Most every guy dreams of making it with two gorgeous women at once, and I'm getting three."

"You can always invite Charles and Robert to join you."

"Can't seem to summon them up like you do. But, that's okay. I think I can handle it myself."

He chuckled, holding her tightly and kissing her forehead, inhaling the delightfully combined smell of hay, fresh perspiration and her perfume.

"Lilies." He buried his face in her hair.

[275]

"What?"

"Your fragrance. Lilies. It's how you smelled ... before."

"Oh ... yes. I think it was Victoria's favorite."

"And Morgana's?"

"I think so." She smiled softly.

"And mine. Definitely mine." He kissed her eyes.

"Ah-hum." They looked at the trailer.

"We're ready fer yer horse, missy." A large black man in a worn leather vest and scuffed boot stood on the ramp, picking his teeth with a straw.

"Okay, Charlie, he's all yours. I'll come in and check he's all right once he's hooked up. I still owe him an apple, and he knows it."

"Not a problem," he said, taking the halter rope and leading the red gelding up the hay covered wooden ramp.

EIGHTY-NINE

Ashley slid onto the wooden bench, taking Craig's hand, and resting her head on his shoulder. She had never been more at peace, even during her happiest moments with Keith. This was her destiny ... a 300 year old promise ... and the third time was going to be the charm.

They sat silently, gazing over the pastoral setting, the sweeping canvas of the world's greatest artist. The ordered pattern of white fences, artificial walls and broad jumps in the show ring. Several horses and two new-born colts capered in the cross-fenced field behind.

The sinking afternoon sun glittered off the brightly painted barn, casting broad, intricate shadows across the landscape. Two huge maples shielded them from the unseasonable heat of the late spring day. They lolled together, absorbing the miracle of the other's presence.

"This is weird," he said. "Wonderful, but weird."

"What is?"

"Being with you. All three of you, actually. You know, with all the memories from before. It's so ... I don't know. I can't really explain it."

"But good, huh?"

"No, not good. Fantastic, unbelievable, indescribable." He caught her chin in his hand, tilting her face, kissing her gently.

"I love you beyond words. All these years of searching, not even knowing what I was looking for. How did I ever end up with Toni?"

"And me with Keith. I can't imagine why I was so drawn to him."

"Think maybe they're from the past, too?"

She nodded. "I guess it's possible."

"Hmm. Bad marriages. I wonder if we're somehow fated to have bad marriages before we're allowed to find each other."

"I don't know. Maybe we *are* required to overcome some obstacles first. But, if you can accept the stuff I've read, we may be destined to come back together, but what we do here is not controlled by some greater power."

"Like God?" he asked.

"Whatever. They call them Masters. But the point is, they don't control us down here. Even finding each other is up to us. We could spend a lifetime looking with no success.

"Yeah? Well, thank god ... or the Masters ... that didn't happen this time. Finally, we'll get everything we've been cheated of in the past."

"Yes. Finally. I just hope ...."

"What?"

"Nothing."

"C'mon," he said. "You were going to say something. What?"

"What if...?"

"Yes? What if...?"

"... he's here now, too."

"Who?"

"Whoever killed us ... before." She searched his eyes, hers welling with tears.

"Oh, Ashley." He pulled her close, kissing the wet gray pools.

"This is a different time. Even if he were here, he still may not know us. Anyway, we won't get surprised this time. Nothing's going to get in the way of our happiness. Nothing."

"I know." She snuggled closer to him, feeling safe. "I'll probably still worry ... but not when we're together. I promise."

"Okay. And by the way, our late check-out room is waiting."

"Yay." She stood, pulling him up into her arms. Their kiss was intense. Her legs wobbled, her head filled with French exclamations.

"We have a better place to do this," nuzzling her ear.

"I can hardly wait." She took his hand as they started toward his parked Jaguar.

"Should we stay the night? Maria can care for my children. I can call her, if it's okay with you."

"Better than okay. It's never easy to tear myself away from you."

"Me too." She grinned, her arm circling his waist, holding him close. They'll be together for many nights, once their divorces were final ... hundreds of nights, thousands of them. Hell, they were still young. *Tens* of thousands.

Every night, once they were finally free from their cheating spouses. And surely there was no danger. How foolish to worry.

Still, those other two times... but this was now, with no real reason for concern. Still...?

Look at them. So cocky, so brazen, kissing and pawing, out in the open.

Narrowed eyes, hidden behind amber-lens sunglasses, watched the lovers stroll toward the parking lot. They looked so damned *happy.*

Happy over the ruins of others' lives.

They think they have everything. Things rightfully mine. But, aim will set it straight. And I've got the perfect thing for that.

How lucky.

NINETY

"No answer?" she asked.

"Nope. Just the service. Says he's away for a week, maybe two."

"Damn. I wanted to know why he was screwing us around." She flopped on the leather sofa, and patted the spot next to her.

"Oh, c'mon Ashley. You said yourself that he had ethical considerations over what he could say. I've known Bruce Feldman a long time. He wouldn't do anything to intentionally hurt us." He perched beside her.

"I guess. But, I still wonder why he seemed so shook up after my regressions. There seemed more to it than just surprise."

"That is strange. You said he looked ... what was the word?"

"Apprehensive. Scared, maybe. I was too terrorized to notice, but thinking back, he was in a real sweat, his eyes kind of glazed. He looked numb."

"You think he saw what you saw?"

"I don't know how. It was my regression, how could he see it?"

"Maybe he was shocked by you regressing into a past life."

"Why? He had no reason to believe it until later. It makes no sense."

"Nothing does in this whole thing?" He pulled her close to him, almost protectively. Her baby was napping and the house was unusually still.

"I called Dr. Caslow." She laid her head on his shoulder. "She didn't have much to say."

"Did you tell her about us ... the 'old' us?"

"Yeah. She thought it was very interesting."

"That's all? Just very interesting? What about all the crap she fed you about no such thing as past lives. Feldman must have told her why he was kicking you to her."

"I asked. No comment. Just wanted to know how I was doing."

"Great. No clue on Feldman's whereabouts, huh?" he asked.

"Didn't ask. Didn't know he was incommunicado at the time."

"More likely hiding out."

"That's ridiculous, Craig. Why would he hide? He did nothing wrong. There must be something else. Maybe a vacation?"

"The service said he canceled a whole week of appointments. That eliminates a planned vacation, wouldn't you say?"

"I suppose. Well, we'll just have to wait until he gets back. Meanwhile, you promised me a whole day tomorrow."

"Right. I was thinking about a picnic ... "

"A little cool for the beach, isn't it?"

"I was thinking more of the Preserves. I found a great spot we can ride the horses to. There's even a little pond for atmosphere."

She shivered slightly and snuggled more tightly into his body. A mental video of a shaded meadow, towering oaks and a tumbling stream reeled briefly through her head.

"Something wrong with that?"

"No, it's okay. Sounds like fun." Was it also déjà vu?

It was sixteen years since she and Allen Clarke were spooked while picnicking in the Skokie Lagoons. Not surprising, considering what happened to her twice before. Could this little venture be tempting fate?

A third time to die?

She shook her head, gritting her teeth. That was then, hundreds of years ago. She refused to let foolish memories of ancient times get in the way of her happiness now.

Nothing really to worry about. So, why was she so tense?

NINETY-ONE

"Still no word from Dr. Feldman?" Ashley had just finished packing their picnic. Craig hovered behind, his hands lightly on her shoulders. They had remained circumspect in her house.

"Nothing" he replied. "His service hasn't heard from him all week. The girl actually sounded concerned. Said that even when he's away, he never goes more than two days without calling in for messages."

"You think he's all right?"

"Don't know, but it'd sure be a lousy trick for him to disappear, or maybe die, before we had a chance to learn what's going on."

"Oh, Craig." She shoved him playfully. "What a terrible thing to say."

"Yeah, I know. I'm just frustrated. I really like the guy."

Hefting the pair of wicker saddlebags, bulging at the seams, the necks of wine bottles protruding from each corner, he grinned.

"Looks like enough there for an army," he said, chuckling

"I just wanted to be sure we had everything."

She was incredibly sexy when she did her "little girl" pout. He pulled her into his arms, tilting her face up, her warm gray eyes igniting a fire in him.

"You *are* everything. I don't know how I've lived so long without you."

"Yeah." She smiled at him. "A hundred and fifty years *is* a very long time."

"Damned tootin'." They shared a soft, lingering kiss, filled more with delicious warmth than flaming heat. She sighed.

"Not now, lover."

He nodded, stepping away, one hand trailing along her arm.

"You're right," he said. "We start this and we'll miss our picnic. It's a beautiful day."

She gathered a light denim jacket and a large canteen filled with cold water. Dressed in faded jeans and a light-green plaid flannel shirt, she looked nothing like a French countess, or even the daughter of a Philadelphia shipping tycoon. She was Ashley Bradford now (he'd already dropped the name Easton from his thoughts) and that was fine with him.

"So, do we ride the horses to this place?" she asked.

"Gotta drive first. I borrowed my trainer's Explorer and trailer. It's about a 45 minute drive, then maybe a thirty minute ride. But there's no hurry. We got all day."

"Right. The kids won't be home from school 'til after three, and Maria's here with the baby. She'll have dinner ready, even if we run late."

"Good. It's no fun if we're rushed."

"You're eating with us tonight, aren't you?"

"If I'm invited."

"You're *always* invited. I want ... I *need* my life filled with you. Day *and* night."

"Me, too, but isn't that a little premature. The night thing, I mean. We're both still married, and what about the kids?"

"We've had legal separations for months. We'd already be free if it weren't for all the haggling. I'm getting my final decree the end of next week, thank God."

"About time, isn't it? Rudolph's dragging Toni in, screaming and yelling, but mine should be over in a few weeks, too."

"She's still threatening you? You think she could be ....?"

"I don't know. She's a lot of things, but I don't know if she could stomach murder. Her brother, Brad, maybe ...."

"Jeez, that's scary." She shook her head, arching russet eyebrows. "These people have no grasp of reality, do they?"

"Nope. They seem to feel they're exempt. But I'm not gonna let them dictate our lives for us. They've done that for too many years already."

"Yes, too many bad times, treading water, watching the years slide by. But, we have each other now, and that's why I want you here every chance I get. Ricky and Beth need to get to know you better, and Janine can grow up with you. I've waited all these years... hundreds of years... and I'm not going to let them make me wait any longer."

"Okay. Together day and night. But let's not flaunt it. No need to give 'em any new ammunition in these last days of the war."

"Frankly my dear, I don't give a damn."

He marveled at the look of fierce independence that filled her face. She turned at the door, looking back into the house.

"Maria, we're going. Should be home by four. Mr. Thornton is staying for dinner."

"*Si, señora. Buena suerte.*"

"What?" Craig asked.

"Good luck. Strange thing to say."

They hurried through the door to the waiting SUV and trailer.

NINETY-TWO

The monstrosity of it.

His face covered with perspiration, he lay shivering on his sofa for a moment before opening his eyes. He blinked several times, searching the familiar surroundings of his den. No danger here. Not yet, at least.

Bruce Feldman's hand touched his neck tentatively. He swallowed. Everything was working. Only memories, but he shuddered at their reality.

Such cold-blooded calculation, right to the end. And when it was over, others shouldered the guilt, freeing this maniac to continue life unfettered by conscience or punishment.

Got to get up, shake it off, and get a hold of myself.

This final trip had drained Bruce Feldman's reserves, sucking away his energy.

Five agonizing ventures back to the 17th and 19th Centuries in search of the truth ... a full accounting of what really happened to two young people brutally denied their lives together, and how *he* had been involved.

He gingerly turned his head side to side, stretching the cramped muscles of his neck, thinking again of his own complicity, and how that bastard had let no one stand in the way.

He'd finally reconstructed most of the story from both lives ... and deaths ... each trip becoming easier, clearer, more detailed ... and more frightening. He'd see things through *his* eyes, both before and after the horrible deaths of Ashley and Craig in those lives.

He was now certain of his companion there, and the psychotic logic spawning such ghastly deeds. The two lovers weren't the only ones who had suffered.

And, one more thing he learned. Ashley's and Craig's murderer was here again, living in Chicago, and certainly knew them. He doubted the motive to kill had changed very much over the past 300 years.

Feldman struggled to sit up and rubbed his arms across his body. His throat was dry and raw, his head pounding. Once again, the two young people were in danger. After what he'd just learned, that might be sooner than later.

The private line on his phone was winking a message. Patients were looking for him through his service, but he had no time to retrieve complaints from a bunch of neurotics. There was a much more important task at hand.

The clock was running.

He massaged the back of his neck, trying to ease the tension cramps. He waggled his tongue back and forth between his cheeks and then over his teeth. The ache at the back of his mouth slowly dissipated.

Damn, those visions were vivid ... *painfully* vivid. He needed to revise those self-hypnotism tapes and how he handled this with patients. There wasn't enough insulation from regressed sensations, especially now that he understood their reality.

He lurched to his feet and lumbered somewhat unsteadily into the bathroom, looking for pain-killers. The thunder in his head was keeping an agonizing beat with his heart.

After washing down three pills with a large glass of water, he returned to his study, slumping into his desk chair, propping his head up in his hands, elbows on the desk, fingers gently massaging his temples. He'd give the medication a few minutes to begin working before he tried to reach Craig Thornton.

Thirty minutes later, feeling more relaxed, the throbbing in his head relegated to distant drums, he dialed Craig's office.

"Sorry, Doctor," Melissa, Craig's personal assistant, said. "Mr. Thornton has been out most of the week."

"He hasn't been there at all?"

"Well, yeah. A half-day on Tuesday and a few hours yesterday morning. But he told me he'd be gone all day today, and maybe tomorrow. We might not see him before Monday."

"Can he afford to be gone that much, Melissa?" He was just treading water, wondering what to do next, trying to cordon off the rising tide of irrational anger, swirling out of the depths of his subconscious.

"Oh, sure. If there's no new sales promos on tap, this joint pretty well runs itself."

"Okay. Well, leave word I called, but I'm going to try to track him down."

"Is it that important?"

"Yes, I think so."

"Then try Mrs. Easton. He's probably over there."

"Just what I had in mind, Melissa. Thanks."

Fucking that immoral bitch, ruining their marriages.

He blinked. *Stop it. For God's sake, stop it.* None of this was their fault. He's no avenging angel. Not in this lifetime, anyhow.

At least he hoped not.

He sat, struggling to relax every particle of his being, his headache under the control of the pain-killers. Time to act professionally. He flipped open his book, searching for Ashley's phone number. A moment later, the phone was answered.

"*Bueno?*"

"Hello?" *Who was this, the nanny?*

"*Sí?*"

"Is this Mrs. Easton's residence?"

"*Sí.*"

"Is she there?"

"No. No *es* here."

"Do you know where she is?" He spoke slowly and clearly.

"*No. No es* here. Go out."

"Was she alone?"

"No. With *Señor* Thornton."

"You don't know where they went?"

"*No, señor.*"

This was getting frustrating. He'd better go there to await their return, and speak to them today. Time may be running out.

He slammed the lid hard on the pulsing thread of fury trying to sneak out of the iron vault to which he had banished it.

NINETY-THREE

Bruce Feldman paced restlessly in front of the unlit fireplace of the sitting room. Despite his preoccupation, he couldn't help but appreciate the classic elegance Ashley had produced in the modern ranch house. The walls, dark raised-panel cherry, were accented with intricate moldings, the furnishings 17th Century French ... antiques or reproductions? He wasn't expert enough to know. Was all this a subconscious reflection of her life as Victoria du Chevalier? It seemed likely.

"Sorry, *señor*. *La bambina*, the wet diaper."

"No problem," he said, "but I must find Mrs. Easton. She didn't tell you when she was expected home?"

"No, *señor*. Only that *Señor* Thornton, he will take the dinner with us."

"But no specific time?"

"Si, after four, I think. Maybe later."

"Oh? Why is that?"

"They take *mucho* food and *vino*. No have the hunger for many *horas* after."

"They packed a lunch, you mean?"

"*Sí*. For the ... *como se dice*? Picnic? *Sí, una* picnic."

"They went on a *picnic?*" He started to shake, his voice cracking. This was terrible.

Fucking everybody else while they're fucking each other. They don't give a damn for—"

No. Shut up, he ordered the restrained anger, hammering on the door of its cell. He beat it back with a wavering determination. He was there to help, not kill ... he hoped.

"Where, Maria? For God's sake, you must know where."

"*No se, señor*. They go on *los caballos,* I think. Me see the trailer."

"On the horses? A picnic by horseback?"

"*Sí, es possible.*"

Damn. Just like twice before. Won't they ever learn?

But, how would they really know? Probably jumping the gun, but it didn't *feel* like paranoid delusions. It felt dangerous. He had to find them. But to do *what*? That was what worried him.

"Think, woman. It's very important. Didn't you hear anything that might tell me where to look."

"Maybe," eyes cast down, stroking her chin. "a drive—*Sí*, she says *quarento-cinco*—forty-five *minutes* they drive. Me remember. Forty-five *minutes* they drive, then on *los caballos una media hora.*" She looked at him, shrugging.

"This helps?" she asked.

"It's a start. Thanks. May I use the phone?"

She nodded, pointing to the small table near a large stuffed chair.

NINETY-FOUR

They arrived at Craig's secret glade just after Noon. In no hurry, they had enjoyed the countryside as they cruised leisurely up Highway 60 toward their destination.

It always amazed her how rural this area remained, so close to the bustling city. At first there were scattered residential enclaves, mostly modern cookie-cutter homes, pandering to young executives and professionals looking for secure neighborhoods. Even these were separated by fields and surprisingly thick woods. Farther out, everything was farm land and trees, the houses rustic and widely spaced.

The entrance to the state park was so densely forested it could have been northern Wisconsin. Once inside, they found wide fields dotted with barbecues, picnic tables, volleyball nets and a softball diamond near the parking lot. A few canoes and kayaks were beached along the shore of a small lake, sparkling like a sapphire in the late morning sun.

Paved bike and unpaved hiking trails split off into various directions into a lush woods of tall firs, oaks and maples. Horse paths, lightly used or regularly maintained, trailed into the woods. They were smooth and uncluttered by droppings.

They unloaded Injun and Bellwether, Craig's horse, at the back of the lot and saddled up. Both animals accepted the bulky wicker baskets without fuss, and they were off for a leisurely ride through the trees, pausing frequently to observe two cardinals and other colorful birds, flittering among the branches. Small animals, busy with unknown tasks, darted along the path.

After about fifteen minutes, Craig turned off the trail and into the woods. Ashley followed along a scarce track she would never have noticed on her own. They arrived, a half mile later, to an idyllic clearing. Wild flowers perfumed the air, a thick cushion of grass carpeting the ground, a serenade performed by the gentle burbling of a tiny creek wending its way sinuously along the shaded border of the little meadow. They dismounted, standing in silent awe for several minutes, absorbing the peaceful glory of the spot.

"How did you ever find this place?" she asked. "It's so beautiful."

"Yeah, isn't it? I like to explore. Found some survey maps and kinda suspected this might be here. It's better'n I expected."

"It's marvelous. And it feels so comfortable, almost like I've been here before."

"Funny, me too." He took her free hand in his.

"You know what I think?" she asked, still gazing at the surrounding woods.

"What?"

"This is a lot like the place where we were first together."

"When? We've never been in a place like this that I can remember."

"You're not thinking back far enough."

"I don't understand." He turned her to him.

"Close your eyes and visualize it." Hers closed as she spoke. "Remember that spot... not now, but 300 years ago. Don't you see it?"

"Oh, yeah, I see what you mean. It did look like this, didn't it? You were so beautiful, my Victoria."

"As you were handsome, my dashing Earl."

He pulled her into his arms, trembling at the feel of her, molded against him, her head resting on his shoulder. The horses, reins dropped to ground hitch, were quietly munching grass.

"I don't need memories to love you, Ashley. No French countess had anything on you. You're the most beautiful woman I've ever known in this life, and that's good enough for me."

"Ah. You love me only for my beauty?" She nuzzled his earlobe.

"Yes, if real beauty is measured by *who* you are as much as by how you look. I know you a lot better than I knew Victoria, and there's never been anyone I've loved more, then or now."

"Boy, you sure know how to turn a girl's head." She chuckled, pulling his face down for a tender kiss.

"It's easy when you're in love," he said when they finally parted.

"Yeah, I know what you mean. C'mon, let's get the horses unpacked. I'm getting hungry."

NINETY-FIVE

The white Jeep cruised slowly through the big lot. A Ford Explorer and horse trailer were parked in a cul-de-sac at the end, not easily noticed at first.

So, this is it. Took their horses down that trail for a little party. Time to join the fun, playing the same old game.

How interesting to learn we did this little dance twice before. It really makes it so much easier this time.

The Jeep, in 4-wheel drive, started down the horse path,

easily following the clear sets of hoof prints on the recently swept trail. A bulky duffel bag sat on the other seat.

How fitting for it to end like this.

Again.

NINETY-SIX

Bruce Feldman's gunmetal gray Acura SUV sped up the highway, heading for Lake Forest and the stables where Ashley boarded her horse.

A phone conversation with Al Crown, the stable manager verified that Mrs. Easton and Mr. Thornton had loaded Injun into a two-horse trailer and drove off. He thought Billy, the groom who helped them, might have some idea of where they were going. Mrs. Easton usually left that information, in case of an emergency.

But Billy went home for lunch, so Feldman decided to go to the stables. Wherever they went, that would be the starting point. Once he knew that destination, he had just one ... no, two more phone call to make, but he could use his cell phone for that.

An instinctive tightening in his gut told him no more time should be wasted.

A picnic. How stupid.

How perfect, an inner voice whispered.

They were probably headed for one of the forest preserves, dotting northern Lake County.

Hadn't they learned *anything* from all those regressions?

Jesus, he hoped he wouldn't be too late. He punched his accelerator a little harder and scanned his rear-view for any sights of police.

He couldn't afford to be detained, even for a minute.

Of all the foolish and rash things to do.

A picnic, for God's sake.

For a moment he wondered again whether he was hurrying to save them...or *kill* them? He sensed this was the time. Another may be there, planning their death for the third time. The timing was just too perfect.

He intended to help them, but would his anger transform him, like the Incredible Hulk, into an abettor to a murdering monster instead? Just like before?

He couldn't be sure of the answer, and that scared him.

~~*~~*~~*~~

Feldman's SUV hurried West on State Road 60 toward Mundelein and the state park that lay beyond. His phone calls were made, and now he concentrated on making time on the narrow, two-lane highway. Thank God traffic was light.

He was really worried. The first call, filled with sinister news, verified his concerns. A nemesis was stalking for a third time those whose new-found love threatened a position not easily relinquished.

And the two young fools have offered a perfect opportunity if that one were still homicidally psychotic. No reason to expect anything had changed.

The second call was made in a panic, searching for help. But there was no guarantee any would arrive in time. Was that what he was subconsciously hoping for ... leaving it just to the four of them?

He glanced at his watch: 12:45. Still lingering over their picnic, he hoped. Probably safe for the moment. Maybe today wasn't the day, after all. If so, they would be okay, fully forewarned for the future.

But Feldman wasn't optimistic. Too much was aligned for

things to go wrong. He might be all the help they could count on, so no timid lingering allowed.

He grimaced. With only him to rely on for their lives, they were in serious trouble. He was no macho man, no action hero. But, if they *were* in danger, it was largely his fault. He had to try to make it right.

He would handle this alone, if he had to. He wedged his conscious mind against the inner vault, bubbling with blinding heat.

Hate.

How had he come to harbor so much hate, especially after what he had learned about his companion in previous mayhem?

He snapped on the radio to a local station, seeking distraction. The first thing he heard was a breaking news story that set his heart hammering against his ribs. How strange for *that* to have happened just now. Was there a connection to his current mission?

He hoped not.

Things were complicated enough.

NINETY-SEVEN

She refilled his glass with the red wine, a Beaujolais. It was her favorite. No surprise there. They polished off most of a roasted chicken and a tasty Caesar's salad she had prepared herself. A loaf of French garlic bread was the perfect complement to the meal.

"Time for dessert," she said, bringing a small plastic container out of the seemingly bottomless basket. He was stretched languorously on a brightly colored wool Navajo blanket. Struggling comically into a sitting position, he rubbed his belly and groaned.

"You're kidding. I don't think I could squeeze down another mouthful."

"French pastries." She opened the container and passed it back and forth under his nose.

"Umm, smells good. French Pastries, huh?"

"Yep. Filled with an amaretto cream."

"Oh, you're so wicked. That's my favorite."

"I know. That's why I baked them."

"*You* baked 'em?"

"Sure. I'm a damned good cook. Always especially loved to whip up something French. I guess that shouldn't be a surprise."

"I guess not. Keep this up, though, and you're gonna turn me into a blimp." He reached for one of the sweets.

"Wait. I've got hot coffee to go with that."

"You amaze me."

Chuckling, he held the powdered sugar-covered confection where he could savor the odor while she poured steaming black coffee from a thermos into a wide bottomed mug. Empty plates and plastic containers were neatly stacked on one corner of the huge blanket.

"Yum," he said, taking a bite. "You're gonna spoil me."

"I hope so." She settled next to him, snuggling closely. He laid his head against her silky copper tresses and sighed.

They hung together for several minutes, each happily filled by the other's presence. He set down his empty coffee mug, and she wiggled deeper into his arms. The fresh scent of lilies ... always his favorite ... was in her hair, while he smelled of leather and saddle soap, wonderful, happy odors to her. She chuckled softly.

"Something funny?"

"Not really. I was just remembering something from high

school."

"Tell me about it."

"Oh, it was nothing really. I went on a picnic like this ... but no horses ... with this guy I was dating, Allen Clarke."

"I thought you dated Keith in high school." His fingers gently caressed her hair as he planted a soft kiss on her forehead.

"Allen was between Keith ... and Keith.

"I liked him. We'd had our picnic and were getting, well, kind of physical—"

"Like this?" Now Craig's tongue was gliding along the side of her neck and into and around her ear while his other hand was working its way lightly along her thigh.

"Oh, nowhere nearly this good." Her lips sought his, a hand sliding up the back of his neck and into his hair, tangling her fingers in his thick, dark curls.

"What happened then?" His voice was muted as his mouth ventured teasingly over the sweet curves of her throat. She sucked in a quick breath, already overcome by raging passion.

Mon Dieu. Thank you Victoria, for opening me to such wonder.

"I'll...tell you...later." She shuddered, racing toward the glory of total arousal, the likes of which she had not known before this man.

At least, not in this life-time.

Her hands were inside his shirt, running over his warm, moist skin, his slick muscles trembling with tension. Her flannel shirt slipped to the ground as she tugged at his pants. The muted sounds of opening zippers and the rustle of discarded clothing, and they were tangled in each other's arms.

Shrouded by foggy bliss, she barely sensed their nakedness, plunging through gate after gate of pulsating rapture, hot-wired nerve endings aflame. He was in her now, her legs and arms cables, binding him close, as they soared on ethereal wings, engulfed by a volcano of almost unbearable ecstasy.

And then the red miasma of eruption, hurtling her into oblivion, momentarily lost in a nether-world of angels.

"*Ah, mon amour. Mon amour. Très bien. C'est perfait.*" Still throbbing, she clutched him tightly, legs and arms fusing him to her.

NINETY-EIGHT

They sprawled together, motionless for several moments, slowly winding down, fluttering back to the world they lived in. Reluctantly, they relaxed, lying in each other's arms, catching their breath, bathed in the sweet scent of their bodies and the perfume of the meadow.

"You went back again," he whispered. "To England, I mean. To Victoria."

"No, I was right here with you, every glorious minute. But, Victoria ... I don't know ... I guess she just fills my head when we make love. She was so much more freely passionate than me. She just seems to take over. Do you mind?"

"Not a bit. I loved her then just as I love you now. Anyhow, it's wonderful, making it with two hot-blooded beauties at the same time."

"Oh, you nut."

"But, it's true. I'm just lucky that neither of my lovers will ever mind. Will they?"

"Nope. Never." They chuckled softly together. Keeping her close, he groped around, finding his shirt and draped it over their shoulders like a small blanket.

They lay quietly, snuggled together, savoring the moment. Finally, he broke the silence.

"So, what were you telling me, before we got so distracted?"

"Huh?"

"About a picnic while in high school ...."

"Oh, yes. Allen Clarke."

"Right."

"It was sort of strange, thinking about it now."

"How d'ya mean?"

"Well, we went on this picnic at Skokie Lagoons ... a place a lot like this, actually, well off the regular paths. I'd found it accidentally once, when I rode off the main trail."

"Did you guys go on horseback?"

"On the picnic? No. He didn't ride, so we walked. Took maybe twenty, thirty minutes, but it was a pretty summer day, and everything was so green and fresh.

"We ate the food, then started making out. I'd ... uh ... never done *it* before. Not all the way."

"So that was your first time? A lot of gals weren't virgins by that age."

"True, but I was still a virgin right up to my wedding night."

"Yeah, you told me. So, what happened to stop you? It sounds like you were ready to make the move."

"Maybe I was. Things were getting pretty hot. I'd never been so worked up before. I think that was the first time it ever happened."

"What? An orgasm?"

"No, darling. I told you. I've never had one of those until you."

"Oh, yeah. It's just so hard to believe."

"Well, Keith was only into his needs, and I didn't know any better. But, what I meant was, suddenly my head was filled with French words."

"Victoria?"

"Who else? She was the passionate one. Getting so turned on must have dredged up some of those old memories. I got scared."

"I can understand that." He caressed her face, planting a gentle kiss on the end of her nose.

"I don't think you do," she said. "I was afraid of *being* there. I should have been enjoying all those wonderful sensations, but I was staring in the shadows, looking for monsters."

"So you were remembering more than just Victoria's passion."

"I suppose so." She sighed and wiggled around for a new position. Her right arm had fallen asleep.

"Then it happened. Something was moving in the brush."

"Oh, boy."

"Yes. I remember yelling something in French, and I was up and running, like some half-naked wood nymph, trying to get into my clothes as I went."

"Wow. The guy musta freaked out."

"You got that right. He grabbed up a few things and came after me. He was scared and didn't even know why."

"You think somebody was after you then?" He kissed her eyes and neck, his hand slowly working down her back.

"No. Just a raccoon. Allen went back for the rest of our stuff ... oohhh, that feels so good ... and found an abandoned nest.

"Ahhhh." She shivered, turning to him, bringing her lush breasts close to his face. His mouth was a busy adventurer.

"Never could go to a place like ... Oh *god*... that again 'til now. Never felt safe—oh, yes. My darling—before. Oh, Craig, I love you so." She clutched his head tightly as his mouth and hands began rekindling one wild fire after another. Snatching his wrists, halting his amorous advance, her head tilted back.

"Craig?"

"What, my love?" He kissed her nose.

"What's— what's going to happen?"

"When, Ashley?"

"Now. After our divorces. They're almost final. Do you ... have plans?"

He grinned, kissing her eyes. "I was going to wait for a romantic moment to ask you to marry me."

"Something more romantic than this?" Her smile lit up the air.

"I guess not. Thought maybe we should wait a few months ...."

She shook her head.

"... but I guess there's no need. Will you marry me, darling?"

"Oh, yes. Yes. As quickly as possible." She planted a short, heated kiss on his lips.

"I ... I haven't even bought a ring." He was grinning. "We gotta make plans ... find a place for the ceremony ... send invitations ...."

"No. No big wedding. We'll have a minister...or a rabbi...or maybe both. Something quick and private, with just my children, your family, and maybe a few close friends."

"Okay, if that's what you want. But don't you think we should wait a while before—?"

"No, we have nothing to prove. I want to be your wife as quickly as possible. I've waited three hundred years for this, you know." They burst into laughter, and she snuggled close, resting her head on his chest, still giggling. Her eyes found his.

"And there's another reason." She smiled softly, gray eyes twinkling. His hand caught her chin, dark bushy eyebrows arched.

"I missed my period." She searched his face, his eyes wide.

Ashley nodded. "And the little stick turned blue. You're going to be a daddy."

"My god."

"Happy?"

"You bet. To have a child with you is beyond ...."

"Shhh." The kiss was the embodiment of their love, as they melded with ardor new for even them. Soon she was soaring again in the haze of ecstasy, consumed by the raging fires he so expertly ignited. She entangled herself with him, legs and arms, clutching him fiercely, welding them into one.

Ah, dieu. Mon amour, mon amour.

NINETY-NINE

She was close, hanging on the brink of release, poised for that delirious plunge that would rock her to the very core of her soul. She had learned to do this without fear. She had never—

What was that?

Something impinged on the edge of her consciousness.

Oh, shit. A cold tentacle of fear snaked out, wrapping her heart in its icy clutch. The old fear. Her flaming ardor plunged into a chilly bath. How foolish to think she had dispensed with it.

She squirmed, fighting for control. Pull back a little, Dr. Caslow had said. Gain control. She was safe here, with Craig. Nothing to worry—

There *was* a sound, something at the edge of the woods. Her heart was fluttering, her breath coming in little hyperventilating gasps, she erupted in a cold sweat, all unrelated to her passion of just a moment before.

Control. Gain control. It was just her imagination again ... those terrible memories.

A 3rd Time to Die

She blinked her eyes, trying to see, but there was only Craig's shoulder and neck, slick with perspiration. Stay focused. Don't slide away from such rapture, giving in to the old terrors, so shallowly buried.

She took several calming breaths, slowly reclaiming the heat of the moment. She was with the man she had loved for centuries—carrying his child. Nothing could ....

There it was again. A twig cracking, the rustle of branches. Were those footsteps?

Oh, God, heavy footsteps. Just like those she'd heard, twice before. Her stomach heaved, bile burning the base of her throat. Don't be *sick*, now.

Don't panic. Just my imagination. The wind in the trees, maybe. Still ....

She craned her neck, all passion long gone, fully alert, straining to push Craig to one side.

"Ashley, what's wrong?" His voice still thick with his unreleased ardor. "What's ...?"

"*Oh, mon dieu*. Not again."

She thought she could hear it coming now, shaking the ground. She visualized the gruesome face leering at her, spinning some terrible weapon of destruction.

Imagination. Fight it off. Just bad memories. But it felt so *real* this time.

No use. She was losing to it now, her heart thumping painfully against her ribs. Her eyes grew big as half-dollars, her face twisting with fear. Could she ever liberate herself from this irrational panic?

Craig struggled to free himself, but her adrenaline-fueled arms and legs locked him against her, frozen by the terror mushrooming inside her.

The ground resonated to the unmistakable thud of a heavy tread, and a piercing shriek echoed across the glade.

Oh, God. It *wasn't* imagination this time. Was it happening again? How *could* it be happening again?

Then she saw it.

A thing ... a fierce apparition ... the horrible ugly head, the body shimmering in the broken sunlight, lumbering toward them across the meadow, bellowing fearsomely.

Whump! Whump! Whump!

Reverberations beat upon the still air.

She lay rigid with panic, a squirming Craig immobilized by the steel bands of her grip.

"Oh, God, not again." Her voice a broken whimper.

"Please, not again."

The creature came on, whirling something on a long chain over its head.

Something glittering in the light.

Something deadly.

Whump! Whump! Whump!

Ashley screamed and screamed, while Craig struggled futilely, trying to escape the chains of her panic-stricken grasp.

It was almost upon them, still bellowing some sort of war chant, when it paused and cocked its head to one side.

"Look at you," the voice, muffled echoing hollowly from the helmet, "helpless and insignificant. How easily you will die again." A soft chuckle resonated inside the mask.

The weapon had come to rest ... a short steel handle, three feet of heavy chain, and a spike-studded iron ball.

Very sharp spikes.

Ashley numbly realized where she had seen this before. The weapon, the armor, the mask, all of it displayed in Dr. Feldman's downtown office.

"Dr. Feldman?" Her voice was a hysterical shriek. "Why are you doing this?"

"Because it needs doing." The words muffled by the helmet.

"You're ruining too many lives, like always. Don't you ever learn? It's your time to die again."

The engine of death bobbed up and down on its chain, then chuckling softly, the thing hefted it overhead, whirling in the air, singing its deadly song.

Whump! Whump! Whump!

Ashley wailed, burying her face in Craig's neck.

"Ashley, for God's sake, let me go."

"Too late. You're mine now." Two quick steps, the ancient mace spinning faster in the air.

Whump! Whump! Whump!

She cringed into a fetal ball, moaning softly, Craig clutched against her, still unable to shake loose.

Grunting with the effort, their attacker spun the weapon high into the air, preparing to strike, when a figure exploded from the woods, racing across the meadow. Howling, it drove head first into the creature, spilling them both onto the ground.

Finally rolling free of the chains of Ashley's arms, Craig fell beside her, gaping at the two bodies, thrashing on the grass, a mere ten feet away.

Their attacker rose ponderously to one knee, the ancient armor shining dully, gruesome battle helmet askew. A mailed fist backhanded its attacker, sending Bruce Feldman sprawling across the field, panting for breath. A jagged gash bloomed across his forehead and left side of his face, bleeding heavily.

"You." the thing shouted, the voice echoing hollowly inside the mask. "You turn against me again?"

"You know?" Feldman was panting, fighting for breath.

"Yes. I've had the dreams ... gone back with the help of a *real* friend. What a wonderful surprise to find myself just where I've been, twice before." The chain rattled, the sharply studded steel ball suspended, waiving back and forth.

"You can't get away with this," Feldman said.

"Why not? The third time won't be any luckier for you." It cackled with wicked delight, rising.

"There's a bear loose in these woods again."

Ashley cowered, numb and confused. If this monster weren't Feldman, who was it? No matter. She was going to die. They were *all* going to die.

The steel ball swung out on an arc, whirling in a deadly circle over its head as the creature started toward them.

Whump! Whump! Whump!

It was the time for action ... for heroics. If not bravery, then flight. Couldn't they outrun their attacker, burdened by armor? But she was immobilized by fear and ancient memories of death. She saw Craig from the corner of her eye, gathering himself for a charge, but she knew it would be futile.

"Run, Ashley, run." Voice hoarse, thick with anger, he was about to sacrifice himself for her.

But she could not move.

Could not think.

Could not leave without him.

She flung her arms over her face and groaned.

Please, not again.

English. A numb realization that she was about to die, and her thoughts were in English.

"Oh, Craig." She huddled close to him, tearful eyes closed. He hovered over her, covering her body with his as best he could. His hand groped on the ground, searching for some weapon, anything that might give him a chance.

A hollow chortle reverberated from the mask.

"It's time to die. Nothing can save you. All good things come in three's."

Whump! Whump! Whump!

The engine of death was whistling through the air, so close she felt the breeze it stirred, but Ashley was rooted to the ground, covered by her lover's body. His hands, close to her face, balled into fists, one holding a small filet knife. He would wait for the thing to get even closer, trying to get under the sweep of the twirling mace, but it wouldn't matter.

Nothing would help them.

They were all going to die again.

Oh, God. Won't this ever end?

Rearing back to strike, the monster hesitated, stepping backward at a cracking sound, like a distant branch snapping. There was another, and then a third.

The arc of the mace faltered, losing speed. The armor-clad figure lurched forward two wobbly steps and dropped its fearsome weapon harmlessly to the ground. Three tiny red circles bloomed on its breast. The thing slumped to its knees with a moan, tottered for a moment, expelling a soft, final gasp before slumping backward, legs tucked under as it sagged to the ground.

Then there was silence.

They stared, frozen in place, at the motionless incarnation of death, its burnished armor glistening in the sunlight. A crashing in the undergrowth yanked them from a surreal nightmare. A beefy, red-faced man burst into the clearing brandishing a pistol.

"Police. Don't nobody move." He paused, gasping for breath, his eyes fixed warily on the figure on the ground.

Apparently satisfied, he started forward, galvanizing Ashley and Craig, who scrambled to cover their nakedness.

"Jesus. I ain't used to running through the damned woods. Looks like I got here just in time, though.

"Bruce, is that you there, all covered with blood?"

"Yeah, Marty. Thank God you made it.

"Help me up. I want these two lucky people to meet my brother, the only Jewish detective on the North Shore."

ONE HUNDRED

With their blanket tented around her, Ashley struggled into her pants and shirt, while a less modest Craig dressed in the open.

Marty Feldman was examining his brother's head wound, making clucking sounds under his breath.

"A nasty flesh wound, but nothing serious once we stop this bloody geyser."

"Craig," Ashley's voice still choked, a hoarse whisper, "there's a small First-Aid kit in the leather pouch on Injun. If you get it, I'll see what I can do for the doctor."

She stared at her trembling hands, wondering if she could manage it. It was a struggle just to button her shirt.

We're alive.

She shuddered, tears running in tiny rivulets across tanned cheeks.

Thank God, we're still alive.

Craig hurried, barefooted, to the two horses tethered to trees near the edge of the clearing, while she finished dressing. Panties and bra remained discarded for the moment in her haste to cover herself.

She scampered on wobbly legs to where the two other men knelt on the ground, as Craig arrived with a small plastic box emblazoned with a large red cross. A minute ago they were terrified for their lives, and here she was, tending to others.

Flipping back the lid, she selected a small bottle of alcohol and a cotton pad. Numb fingers spilled some of the clear liquid on the cotton.

"This may hurt, but we've got to clean that out." Steeling her nerves, she began gently dabbing around the edge of the wound.

"Umpff," he grunted, gritting his teeth.

Once the matted gore was cleaned away, the ragged nature of the wound revealed itself. Sharpened studs on the back of the armored fist had done most of the damage. There was a brief glitter of white behind the torn flesh. Cut clear to the bone. He would need stitches. Lots of them. Ashley shuddered and swallowed, fighting the bitter taste and the rising tide in her stomach.

She glanced furtively at the weapon, the spiked metal ball partly buried in the soft earth, and shivered again. How easily and completely that would have destroyed them.

Turning back to her patient, she squeezed his shoulder. "You're going to need a bunch of stitches. Got the bleeding pretty well stopped now with a couple of butterfly bandage. Should hold together 'til you get to the hospital. I'll cover it with some gauze to keep it clean."

"You're pretty good at this," Feldman said, wincing as she applied the bandages.

"Two rambunctious kids can make you an expert."

Drained of adrenaline, her words came slowly, partly slurred.

"Thank you, my dear," Feldman said. "Lucky for me you're so well equipped."

"Not nearly so lucky as it was for us," Craig said, "that you happened by, Bruce. What the Hell are you doing here, anyhow?"

"Give me a minute to gather myself, and I'll explain everything. Marty, help me to that stump so I can sit with some kind of back rest."

"Jeez, big brothers are always pushing us little guys around." The smiling detective, who stood five inches taller and forty pounds heavier, guided his shaky sibling to a more comfortable perch.

"Ahh, that's better," Bruce said.

"Here." Ashley's still shaky hand held out a small bottle of water and three pain-killers. "You're going to need these."

"Yes, I believe I will." He tossed the pills down, wincing, and took a large swig from the bottle. Leaning back, he closed his eyes.

"What's this all about, Brucie?" his brother asked.

"It's the regressions, isn't it, doctor?" she said. "The other lives."

"Yes."

"Other lives?" Marty said, eyes wide. "What other lives?"

"Mine. Mine and Craig's."

"And mine," Bruce said.

"Yours? Oh, I *see*. You *were* there, too. That's why you looked so shaken?"

The doctor nodded, grimaced, pressing fingers to his temples, and then sighed.

"That one, too." Feldman tilted his head toward their fallen attacker.

"All four of us?" Craig looked bewildered. "All of us, both times?"

"Seems like it," Feldman said, gently prodding at his bandage.

"Would someone mind telling poor stupid me what the hell this is all about?"

The detective was kneeling next to the corpse, but still watching them, he pulled off a gauntlet and felt for a pulse. He shook his head, turning back to them, his face the picture of comical confusion.

"I was hypnotically regressing Mrs. Easton, trying to get to the root of an unexplained fear she was struggling with, and suddenly she was a French countess in the 17th Century."

"A countess? In the 17th Century? You're kidding, right?"

"No. Of course, I didn't believe it at first, either. But, there she was, having a romantic tryst with an English Lord in a meadow much like this. They were stalked and brutally murdered by two people."

"This one?" Marty prodded the body on the ground with his foot.

"Yes. And me."

"*You.*" The cop's jaw dropped, his eyes wide.

"That's why you were so upset," Ashley said, clapping a hand over her mouth.

"Yes, I was there. Somehow, Ashley's memories sparked mine. I could see everything happening as she was describing it, but through my eyes, not hers. I was seething with anger at her for seducing my master's husband."

"Reggie?" Craig grunted, shaking his head. "You were Clarice's Head of Household?"

"Right. And her occasional lover, when she wanted something special from me. I've been back many times to gather all the facts."

"You helped with our murders?" Craig's brow wrinkled, the corners of his mouth dipping into a scowl.

"I thought I had, at first. I was so filled with animosity. Lady Clarice hated being forced to marry Charles, so she was rarely a wife to him. That didn't make her any less bitter at his many affairs, not caring that it was her frigidity pushing him into softer, warmer arms.

"She knew of the flirting between these two and insisted that we follow them on the hunt."

"The hunt? Now I'm really confused."

"Riding to the hounds, Marty. A fox hunt."

"Oh, yeah."

"When we dismounted and she donned her ancestors armor

and mask in the woods, I thought it was just to frighten and embarrass the lovers. I never saw the mace in the bag she was carrying. A fearsome weapon."

"You're tellin' me," Marty said, nudging the studded ball with a toe. He began tugging at the helmet of the dead attacker, trying to work it loose.

"Anyway, I learned the anger filling me then was at her, for what she'd done to you. You saw yourself die, Ashley. I saw your bodies mutilated beyond recognition."

"Oh, god, how horrible." Craig wrapped his arms around her, cradling her like a baby. She cried softly, her cheek against his chest.

"When I regressed myself," Feldman continued, "I learned that I told Clarice I intended to report her to the sheriff, so when we returned to the mansion-house, she accused me of slandering the Earl, and summarily had my tongue cut out."

"Jesus. You *saw* that?" Craig averted his eyes.

"Yeah. Not very pleasant, despite how insulated you're supposed to be during a regression."

"I bet." Ashley's words were choked, barely audible.

"Anyhow, trying to make this long story shorter, things were pretty similar in 1845."

"Who was she then?" Ashley asked.

"Maggie Germaine, your husband's mistress. I suspect Keith was William in that life."

"So that's why we were so drawn together ... by fate."

"Possibly. You sensed a connection, not realizing it was an unhappy union."

"Yeah. It's same story now as in 1845, isn't it?"

"Right. When Morgana filed for divorce, he was cut off from her wealth, which Robert," gesturing toward Craig, "had tied up in trusts. William Quincy's family fortune was in serious decline. Maggie thought she'd finally hooked Mr. Big Bucks, and now he

[311]

would be broke."

"Sounds familiar, doesn't it?" She gave a wry laugh.

"I guess. Anyway, I managed the club where she sang and had been her lover, before Quincy. I went along that day, hoping to win her back. Didn't know she'd gone completely over the hill. Didn't know she'd somehow stolen the armor and an ancient mace from the Philadelphia Museum, muttering how she'd end it once and for all. Maybe in her lunacy, she had seen the past. I don't really know. But she killed you both, again mutilating the bodies."

"Couldn't you do anything?" Tears streamed down Ashley's cheeks.

"I was stunned. It was over so quickly. Before I gained the courage to say something, she seduced a seaman, cut his throat in her bed, and framed me as the jealous lover. No one believed me after that.

"She visited me an hour before my hanging, babbling this was the second time she'd killed that bitch for trying to cheat her. Somehow, I knew I'd been there before."

"How horrible." Ashley shivered in Craig's arms. "And you saw yourself hung?

"Yeah, everything right up until the drop broke my neck. Not something I'd recommend. I'm only sorry I didn't discover everything in time to warn you. All of this might have been avoided."

"So, who is this?" Marty asked. He had finally removed the stubborn helmet.

"Toni, I suppose, or maybe Brad," Craig said, his eyes averted.

"No," Bruce said. "But, you won't have to worry about Toni anymore."

"What d'ya mean?" Craig stared at the corpse.

"I heard a news bulletin while driving here. The elder

Rudolph found Toni in bed with her brother. He nearly killed the young man with a fireplace poker, and badly beat your wife. Both are in critical condition."

"Jesus." Craig's brow knit. "So, if this isn't Toni ...?"

"Actually, that's Nicole Phillips."

"Who? But I thought—"

"How the Hell does *she* fit into his?" Marty asked. "My head's spinning with these twists and turns."

"Wow," Ashley said, "Keith's mistress?"

ONE HUNDRED-ONE

Ashley freed herself from Craig's protective grasp and walked cautiously to the body. The exquisite chalky face lay in a pool of midnight black hair, crimson mouth trickling blood, frozen in a surprised pout, emerald-green eyes, dull now, open but vacant in death. A thin gold chain circled her neck, disappearing into her covered cleavage. Curious, Ashley tugged at it, but whatever hung there was trapped in her shirt and the armored collar.

"Right," Bruce continued. "A real conniving beauty. I dated her about three years ago. It didn't take long before I realized she was only looking for the Brass Ring, but she was like a seductive drug. Now I realize why.

"Strange. When I finally screwed up the resolve to break it off, she made some comment about how I had always been a weak-kneed wimp. I wonder how much she knew, even then? It made no sense to me at the time."

Ashley morbidly kept worrying the chain, slowly working it loose.

"So then she found Keith," Craig said.

"Or more likely, Keith found her." Ashley said. "He was looking to replace his hooker." She almost had the chain free. A locket or pendant, she thought.

"When she saw all the money, she latched on, not realizing it was mostly mine. That Keith's family business was near bankruptcy. Eighteen-Forty-Five all over again."

"That's my guess," Feldman said. "Your husband was handsome, apparently wealthy, and looking for action. The perfect mark. She probably encouraged their open relationship, planning on taking him away from you, not knowing that he'd be leaving most of the money behind."

"He wouldn't have gone willingly. The trust funds are too important to him. Luckily, his fooling around brought Craig and me together. Otherwise we may never have discovered our love. Keith forced things into the open."

She continued fussing with the gold chain, doggedly slipping a finger under Nicole's metal collar. The cloying odor of blood and an emptied bowel, voided in death, didn't diminish her curiosity about whatever hung at the end of that chain. Somehow, she knew it was important.

"And my meeting Ashley, and Toni's blatant cheating made it easy for me to finally end my tortured marriage," Craig said.

"Yes. It was them, and their infidelity bringing us together." She looked up from her task, a strained smile forcing its way onto her tear-ravaged face. A final tug popped the chain free, causing her to flinch.

"Oh, shit. That *bastard*. Look at this."

"What?" Craig knelt at her side.

"My emerald pendant, the one Papa gave me the year before he died. The son-of-a-bitch put it around her stinking neck. I'd thought I'd lost it, somehow." Anger fueled the next tug, breaking the chain.

Marty rolled his eyes but kept his mouth shut.

"It still doesn't make sense," she said, turning the pendant over in her hands, rubbing away a trace of blood.

"Keith knew where the money was."

"But Nicole didn't," Bruce said, "and her sexuality was narcotic. I doubt he ever told her. She probably discovered the truth and decided it was up to her to get what she deserved."

"Looks like that's exactly what she *did* get." Marty helped his brother to stand on unsteady legs.

"But why kill me ... us? What would *she* gain?"

"All the money," Craig said, cradling her in his arms. "You haven't thought to change your will, have you? If you died before the divorce were final, everything would go to Keith and the children. He'd certainly be their guardian, with total control of their trusts."

"Hmm," the detective said, "I wonder what kinda alibi Mr. Easton has today?"

"My guess is, a pretty good one," his brother said. "I bet he has no idea what Nicole was up to. She'd kill Ashley and Craig out here where they may never even be found and not say a word to him. He's probably at work, with a solid alibi."

"Okay, that's possible. But how'd ya figure this was the day, Brucie? You tryin' to put me outta a job?"

Bruce Feldman winced at the shooting pain his laughter caused.

"I thought I recognized Nicole from my regressions. The relationship in each life felt so familiar, so dominating. I ran into her at the City Club a few weeks ago, and she told me she finally found Mister Right, a rich guy with an even richer wife. Said she was going to get it all. Later, I heard her voice on these trips back in time, and eventually I figured it out."

"But why did you follow us here today? And how on earth did you even find us?" Ashley asked.

"I called your house to warn you of the danger. When Maria

said you went on a picnic with the horses, warning bells went off in my head."

"Of course. The same scenario as the other two times." Ashley shivered.

"Exactly. I called my service to see if you or Craig had left a message and learned that my downtown office had been burglarized and the armor and mace were stolen.

"It never dawned on me until that very minute why I had been so compelled to buy that whole display at an auction. That was two years before I started dating Nicole."

"It ... it looks exactly like the same one from my memories."

"I believe it may be, my dear. Nicole saw it in my office and was totally taken by it. Even asked me to sell it to her. More than just a coincidence, I think.

"Anyway, once I learned what was happening today, I rushed over to your stable, and the groom told me you were coming to this park. I found what I presumed was your car and trailer in the lot and saw what looked like fresh tire marks on the horse trail. Those led me to Nicole's Jeep, and the horse tracks were easy enough to follow back here."

"Good thing ya called me from the car, Brucie. I don't get here when I did, things mighta turned out a lot different."

"I was counting on you, Marty. Didn't think we'd have much of a chance without you. Nicole was strong. I've seen that girl bench 140 pounds."

"Wow. Well, you got lucky. Why didn't ya call the local Sheriff, though? They were a lot closer than me."

"Right. They'd be real quick to respond to some lunatic babbling about a murderer from a past life." Bruce chuckled, and then groaned, bringing a hand to his bandaged head.

"Ya got a point there. I'd better call 'em now, though. We'll need the local cops and the meat wagon, and there's gonna be a lot of questions. Just routine, but it's gotta happen."

"C'mon," Bruce Feldman said. "Let's give these kids a chance to finish dressing."

"Okay. I'll call the sheriff from my car radio while they get organized."

In a moment, Ashley and Craig were alone. She sagged into his arms, tears filling her gray eyes, soft sobs shaking her. Adrenaline fueled tension had devoured the last of her reserves.

"It's okay baby. Let it all out. It's over, and we're safe."

He stroked her russet tresses, enfolding with protective arms this woman whom he had loved for ... three hundred years.

Finally, they'd have a lifetime together. Their new family was already started. Nothing Toni or Keith could do would stop them.

The circle of death was finally broken. For now.

EPILOGUE

"Is it finished, Master?" The neophyte soul asked.

"Yes. They will have a full life to explore their love. Something long overdue."

"And when they return to us, when this lifetime is completed?"

"They are destined to join the Fourth Level, as Masters."

"Never to return? Will this one lifetime together suffice them?"

"They will be joined for sixty years, creating two new souls. There are many tasks for them as Masters, guiding younger souls. Their unique synergism will be a great benefit."

"They will continue to work together, once they return to us?"

"Yes, always together. A rare thing indeed."

"And the other ... the one just sent back?"

"It must return for at least three lifetimes of goodness and aid to others before even being considered for the Fourth Level. It will be many of their centuries before that time will come."

"But, with the progeny of these two still on Earth, will that soul give up its quest for their destruction? We have rarely seen one so unwilling to mend its ways."

"True. It may never join us, and that may be best."

"Yes. That may be a soul never to be trusted."

"Possibly. Time and new lives will be determine that."

THE END

If you enjoyed this novel, please leave a review at Amazon, Goodreads, or any blog service you may use.

Feel free to contact the author at: suspenseguy@aol.com with any comments or questions

George A Bernstein